Praise for
Book Two in

"Prepare for adventure, romance, and intrigue in nineteenth-century South Africa. Linda Lee Chaikin has done her homework, exploring the world of diamonds and gold mines in the land that would become Victorian Rhodesia. A page-turner of a story told by a veteran novelist."
—LIZ CURTIS HIGGS, best-selling author
of *Thorn in My Heart*

"Linda Lee Chaikin never fails to deliver a dynamite story! In *Yesterday's Promise* she weaves the complications of love and history into a storyline that is a sheer joy to read. I can't wait for book three of the East of the Sun series!"
—DIANE NOBLE, award-winning author of *Phoebe*

"I love, love, *love* this series by Linda Lee Chaikin! It has everything I'm looking for right now in a good read—memorable characters, intrigue, believable romance, fascinating history. If the third in the series were out, I wouldn't be writing this… I'd be squirreled away, reading!"
—LISA TAWN BERGREN, best-selling author
of *Christmas Every Morning*

Praise for *Tomorrow's Treasure*,
Book One in the East of the Sun Series

"*Tomorrow's Treasure* invites the reader to look closely at God's fatherly care for his orphans and widows, particularly those whose families were martyred on the mission field. An engaging historical novel!"
—C. HOPE FLINCHBAUGH, author of *Daughter of China*

"Absorbing human drama, intriguing mystery, heart-pounding love interests, a dramatic setting—this novel has it all, including a good message expertly woven into the greater story. I can't wait for book two!"

—LISA TAWN BERGREN, bestselling author
of *The Captain's Bride*

"Adventure. Intrigue. Romance. Settle back for an enjoyable read. *Tomorrow's Treasure* is as old-world as the setting yet as contemporary as the human heart."

—KATHY HERMAN, bestselling author
of The Baxter Series

"Linda Chaikin has created a wonderful page-turner with this engaging historical novel. Her sense of time and place is exquisite, her characters so real they seem ready to step right off the page. This is a story rich with conflict, triumph over adversity, and wondrous testimony to God's grace. Your heart will sing as you read."

—DIANE NOBLE, award-winning author
of *Heart of Glass*

TODAY'S
EMBRACE

TODAY'S EMBRACE

A NOVEL

East *of the* Sun 3

LINDA LEE CHAIKIN

WATERBROOK
PRESS

TODAY'S EMBRACE
PUBLISHED BY WATERBROOK PRESS
12265 Oracle Boulevard, Suite 200
Colorado Springs, CO 80921

ISBN 978-1-57856-515-3

Published in the United States by WaterBrook Multnomah, an imprint of the Crown Publishing Group, a division of Random House Inc., New York.

WATERBROOK and its deer colophon are registered trademarks of Random House Inc.

Library of Congress Cataloging-in-Publication Data
Chaikin, L. L., 1943–
    Today's embrace / Linda Lee Chaikin.— 1st ed.
        p. cm. — (East of the sun ; 3)
     ISBN-13: 978-1-578-56515-3
   1. British—South Africa—Fiction. 2. Mothers and daughters—Fiction. 3. Pregnant women—Fiction. 4. Ocean travel—Fiction. 5. South Africa—Fiction. 6. England—Fiction. I. Title.
    PS3553.H2427T63 2005
    813'.54—dc22

                               2004021548

Printed in the United States of America

To my readers.

Thank you for your encouraging letters.
May our Lord bless and keep you.
Jude 24

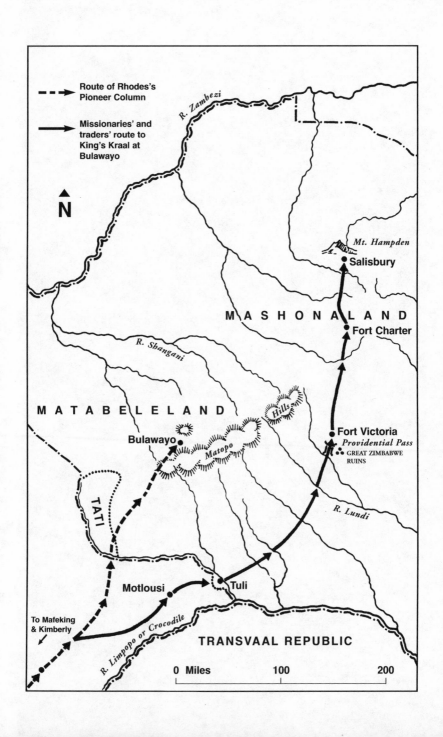

PART ONE

CHAPTER ONE

London
Marriage Dinner Ball at Brewster House
June 1900

Evy thought she would not be surprised by the tide of dissension that came rushing toward her after her whirlwind marriage to Rogan Chantry, heir of Rookswood Estate and future squire. Though the brewing storm was not of Rogan's making, inevitably it came, like large swells responding to outside forces.

Rogan had always been a controversial young man who attracted attention and made things happen—sometimes, whether he wished it so or not. Women seemed drawn to his arresting personality, as Evy had noticed from an early age. Evy saw it as both a gift and a distraction. While he was maturing as a young man, surface relationships had sought him out relentlessly enough to press him into his protective armor. Now she was finding that his solitary independence often shut her out, his own wife, causing her no end of frustration.

The storm began blowing into their lives at Lord and Lady Brewster's opulent mansion in London where a dinner ball was under way in celebration of the unexpected marriage. Her biological father, Lord Anthony Brewster, had arranged it in order to introduce his daughter to his grandfather, Lord Brewster.

Many from the aristocracy were there, some because of Rogan himself. Perhaps it was natural that he would end up "shocking" them by marrying the "rectory girl" from Grimston Way in place of Lord Bancroft's daughter, Lady Patricia—and "so suddenly, too." Those words should have warned Evy of what was to come. But being impressionable, and overflowing with happiness, she'd been unprepared for the cruel chatter instigated by Patricia against their recent union.

Evy had married Rogan Chantry at Rookswood Estate in Grimston Way a week earlier and was thrilled with the sights and sounds of the London she had never experienced. There were theaters, balls and dinners, shopping—oh, the wonderfully exciting shopping excursions Rogan brought her on, buying her everything fashionable and beautiful. And this was only the start of their honeymoon before going on to Paris!

Large chandeliers glimmered on the high-domed ceiling, dispersing light onto the wine-colored velvet draperies. Golden bowls and Italian vases were filled with fresh-blooming roses. An intricately woven rug with thick golden tassels was flaunted in the center of the room. Surrounding it sat an assortment of velvet chairs, divans, and ottomans. At the far end of the salon was a large window overlooking a sloping front lawn.

Rogan gathered with the gentlemen in the salon, where it was customary for the men to drink a glass of port and share cigars after dinner before the ball. Evy, unaccustomed to such male traditions, remained in the salon, standing apart near the window. She looked up and wondered at the outright scowl of the departing Lady Willowby, but she attributed her expression to indigestion. The dinner had been exceedingly rich.

Evy looked into the florid faces of the well-fed members of Parliament. Lord Brewster, Anthony's grandfather, stood alongside him and Rogan. Her great-grandfather was a pompous old man with a narrow forehead and wide, sagging jowls. He was in his eighties, but his small gray eyes were still clear and sharp. They beheld her with emotional distance as Anthony introduced her to him as his daughter by Katie van Buren.

As the evening wore on, Evy continued to feel embarrassed and out of place. She didn't know what she had expected upon coming here. Rogan had warned her at the Chantry Townhouse not to expect warm, family relations to suddenly sprout after all these years. In fact, he had actually wanted to decline the invitation altogether, but Evy had protested for Anthony's sake, since he had wanted to introduce her to his side of the family.

"I want you to enjoy yourself in London before we sail for Paris. Old Brewster, and those of his ilk, are pompous and overinflated. Remember, he and Lady Brewster, when she was alive, came between Anthony and Katie. They backed Uncle Julien's plans to have him marry Camilla. I'm afraid you're dreaming about butterflies and candy cane lanes, Evy darling, if you think you're going to be welcomed with open arms."

She hadn't forgotten how Lord Brewster had treated her mother, but she hoped that time had improved matters. Now she began to realize that unless God's Spirit was free to work in their hearts, real change was not likely. Rogan had dryly commented that time had mistakenly preserved old Lord Brewster in vinegar instead of sugar.

As it turned out, Rogan's observation proved to be correct. Although great-grandfather Brewster was polite and precise in their first meeting, his eyes did not soften a speck. Evy understood the reason for his indifference. He had always known that she had been raised as the niece of Vicar Edmund and Grace Havering, and that Anthony's family had held no interest in her. Evy was simply viewed as Anthony's offspring from a young and foolish lust-ridden tryst he'd had in Capetown. And Katie van Buren was the reckless girl who had allowed the unfortunate incident to happen. She doubtless, in their view, had been a shameless flirt who'd used her wiles to take advantage of Anthony.

Nor did Evy's marriage to Rogan Chantry, or the news that she was now a diamond heiress, do much to influence Anthony's grandfather. Perhaps it was just as well. If she was accepted on the basis of these sudden changes to her life, it would be a shallow acceptance at best. At any rate, time had apparently confirmed and hardened old ways. Her marriage to Rogan raised brows and created questions for already suspicious minds who refused to believe love could triumph over staunch class distinctions.

Evy's thoughts were brought back to a heated discussion going on among the gentlemen gathered.

"War," a heavy, barrel-chested man boomed to the others, "that's what it'll be. Those blasted Boers will be taught a firm lesson this time."

Rogan, in handsome black evening clothes and white linen shirt, was perhaps the one person in the salon who appeared undisturbed by either the cool social atmosphere or the heated rhetoric of war. He stood with Anthony and Lord Brewster as the debate grew between a few members of Parliament—some of whom represented the foreign secretary's firebrands for war—and certain gentlemen who were for peace with President Paul Kruger and his Dutch Boers, even if it meant calling home Cecil Rhodes from the Cape and forcing him to answer to Parliament for the incursion of the Rhodesian "rebels" into the Transvaal. The incursion had been led by Rhodes's official representative, Dr. Leander Starr Jameson.

Evy cared little for the fighting of Dr. Jameson's men. She felt that war of any magnitude might hinder her from accompanying Rogan on his return voyage to South Africa. He was already frowning each time she mentioned traveling with him to Fort Salisbury. She had learned early that Rogan had very independent ideas about his adventures. Adventures that made him hesitant to involve his "delicate" new bride. He wanted her securely entrenched at Rookswood while he pursued his uncle's murderer, the man responsible for her injury—Cousin Heyden van Buren. Evy had her own ideas about that, and staying behind at Rookswood was certainly not one of them.

"It's time we dealt with these clod farmers. Our cause in Africa is just, and at risk. It's far more important for England to succeed there than for Kruger to remain at the head of his *volk,* forever causing trouble."

"Just so, just so."

"Nonsense, gentleman," came a disdainful voice. "We all know the benefit of saying these things to the newspapers to galvanize the British people behind the randlords' war. But we can speak the facts between ourselves. It's control of the gold fields in Johannesburg that the BSA wants, and the goldbugs in Capetown are hand in hand with Rhodes. Isn't that so, Rogan?" The gentleman, Sir Gilcrist, swung toward Rogan and faced him. "You're a South African man with a gold mine. You should know."

"The Chantry mine is located in the northern Zambezi region, Sir Gilcrist," Rogan stated, keeping an equal amount of scorn from his voice. "I've no interest in the Transvaal. We've enough trouble with the Shona. We don't need to take on the Boers, too."

"The trouble in Johannesburg is that the Uitlanders are not permit-ted to vote in Boer elections," Anthony Brewster put in. "Uitlanders are what the Boers call our British miners working in the gold fields. The Boers fear they'll be voted out of office and have the British workers take over. There's graft too in the Boer police and some beatings of African workers."

The man scorned a smile, and Anthony flushed and raised his glass to his lips.

"Most of that is bosh. Oh, I don't deny there isn't a ruddy police-man now and then going into the African workers' area and causing a bit of ruckus, but they're looking for criminals. It's a good line to spread here at home to get the social workers up in arms to fight the Boers. Admit it, Rogan. You're an honest young man. There's wealth and power in the Transvaal, and that's the reason the BSA is whipping up all this war fever."

Evy glanced from the boisterous Lord George to Rogan. She already knew what Rogan thought because he'd been reading the papers each morning and commenting on South Africa news.

"I've little doubt the gold rands would like to end the Boer problem once for all," Rogan said. "Fact is, not all the Uitlanders are British. Plenty are from Australia, Ireland, and America. But why deny it, gentlemen?

The Uitlanders are beginning to outnumber the Boers in Johannesburg. They've come as foreigners disturbing the quiet farming and religious ways of the Boer. So I don't doubt Kruger would like to keep them from having the vote."

The conversation switched to Sir Julien Bley, whom they all knew. Julien held a high position among the men who formed a powerful political entity. Except for the minority peace party, they all supported London's war and Sir Julien's diamond monopoly. They'd also received shares in the mines in exchange for political favors. "The London lobby," Rogan had told her, "has organized one of the most rigid and vigorous parliamentary power blocks England has ever known. And many of them wish for war with Kruger."

What all this might mean for Evy and Rogan, she did not know. She looked at Rogan. He had told her all about the BSA and their plans to plant the British flag in the Transvaal. "They have their plans to push Kruger into war and to final defeat," Rogan had mentioned just this morning at breakfast when the London paper arrived.

"Deliberately provoke war?" She had been shocked.

"You're still a babe in the woods, sweet. Human nature remains the same in every generation. Where there is gold to be discovered, and diamonds in mines, there will be plenty of excuses for men to march to war."

Evy was well aware of the politics of diamonds and gold. Worry about this wealth going by default to the Transvaal was growing daily for shrewd politicians like Sir Julien Bley and his cronies. Talk of diamonds lit a spark, and the conversation turned. At the mention of the famous Kimberly Black Diamond, Evy tensed. She glanced at Rogan, then her father. Rogan showed nothing, but Anthony's features had stiffened.

"Wasn't it some little tart who stole it from Sir Julien Bley?" Lord George asked.

Evy thought she would drop through the floor, but tensely, she stepped forward. "No, m'lord, it was not. And my mother was a lady, not a tart."

Evy heard a gasp, then felt every head turn her way.

"My dear child!" It was Great-grandfather Brewster gaping at her in florid shock. Then Anthony stepped forward. "Evy, I don't think—"

But what he didn't think was not to be known, because Rogan came up beside her as her suddenly fearful eyes met his, expecting the worst. Amazingly, he chuckled and slipped an arm around her, proposing a toast. She stood stunned.

"Evy, darling, you just broke every rule in the book. I now celebrate not only your courage but also your delightfully refreshing spirit. To my dear bride!" He then turned to Anthony. "And to her esteemed father, Anthony Brewster." Rogan nodded to him in respect. "And to Katie van Buren, much misunderstood, and much maligned. May her departed soul rest in peace."

Silence held the room in its awkward grip for a moment. Then Lord George broke into a hearty laugh. "By Jove, I beg your pardon indeed, my dear Mrs. Chantry. I had no idea who I was speaking of when I mentioned the theft of that scandalous diamond."

Evy's throat was dry. She wondered what her great-grandfather was thinking, and Anthony. She looked at him. He stood rigid.

"No need to apologize, Lord George," Rogan was saying. "That old tale has been around for a generation. But I've new information to add to it. I've discovered the real thief of the Kimberly Black Diamond—and he, not 'she,' also murdered my Uncle Henry for it at Rookswood—"

As Rogan went on to tell the story, holding the men in spellbound interest, he quickly squelched any further discussion of Katie.

Evy was never so relieved over his charming ability to capture an audience.

Few noticed as Lord Brewster turned and left the room, his face rigid. Anthony looked after his grandfather with a tense face but did not follow. Evy came up to her father. "I'm sorry," she whispered.

His eyes softened, and he reached a trembling hand to pat her arm. He shook his head slightly. "You did nothing wrong. I should have been the one to speak out as you did."

The group was breaking up as the orchestra began playing in the ballroom and they wandered out two and three together discussing the possibility of war, diamonds, and Scotland Yard's search for her cousin Heyden van Buren.

A few minutes later the three of them were alone. Rogan leaned against the back of a chair, allowing her and Anthony a moment together.

"I'll be leaving next week for Capetown, Evy."

"So soon?" She was truthfully disappointed. "Then I won't see you for some time. Rogan and I will be going to Paris next week."

"Camilla and I will be anxious to have you and Rogan at Cape House. She's taken ill, so I'm leaving sooner than expected. I received a wire this morning from her physician. Her heart is weak."

Evy was worried. She knew a moment of frustration over being foiled in her desires. "Then I must come soon," Evy said, and turned her head to look over at Rogan, but he said not a word, maddening her. She narrowed her lashes. He raised a brow and set his glass down. Their disagreement remained. He was still set against her returning with him to South Africa, though she talked of it incessantly. He walked to the door and looked out across the hall into the ballroom. Evy noticed his expression change. He apparently recognized someone he hadn't expected and was disturbed. He left them in the salon, and Evy looked after him.

Anthony smiled. "Don't mind his determination. He worries about you. And there is good reason to think twice before leaving England for the Cape. I'm afraid the gentlemen gathered here tonight were quite right about the prospects of war. I happen to know the high commissioner in Capetown, and although he tries to conceal the fact, as does the foreign secretary, they hope to provoke Kruger into a hasty act that will seem to leave England with little choice but war. So, my dear, coming to Capetown is one thing. I doubt this war will ever reach there, but trekking with Rogan nearly a thousand miles inland to Fort Salisbury will be difficult, indeed, though I understand your reasons for wishing to do so. Katie's cousin, Dr. Jakob van Buren, is a man worth knowing.

You'd appreciate his missionary work among the Shona and Ndebele."

"That is why I must go, Father. And I want to learn about her from someone who knew her in her own family. You've told me some things, but, well, you would see Katie differently than Dr. Jakob."

He nodded and said no more. Only rarely had he discussed Katie. Evy was reluctant to ask him to talk about her, since it was unfair to Camilla for him to awaken memories of another woman he may have loved. The sins of her parents had no bearing on Camilla, and yet Lady Camilla had undoubtedly paid a price because of those sins, just as Evy had paid a price. Yet she'd forgiven her parents. Her one aching fear was that Katie might not have believed in Christ, and she was equally concerned for Anthony. While he sometimes attended the Anglican Church, was his motive merely that of maintaining traditional forms? If so, she felt that had kindled no spark in his spirit. But she did not yet feel secure enough in their relationship to seek more evidence. Camilla must know… Camilla, though a frail woman, an apparently timid woman in many ways, had eagerly attended Uncle Edmund's preaching services during her visit to Rookswood when Evy was a young girl.

"I want to come to Cape House soon," she repeated to her father. "There's so much I need to say to Camilla."

"I'm pleased you feel that way, Evy. She arranged before your wedding to send you a gift you'll appreciate, but it did not arrive in time for the wedding."

He reached inside his jacket pocket and handed her a small silver box. He did not smile.

"This belonged to Katie. It was among her things at Cape House. I'm afraid practically everything she left was given away to the poor. But Camilla found this and kept it until now."

Evy opened the box. Inside was a gold heart pendant. On the back was the inscription: *Katie.*

Evy smiled as she touched it gently with her finger. Her mother must have worn it often. Evy wondered if the embedded diamond cross had kept her from wearing the pendant the night she left Cape House with Henry Chantry in hope of finding Evy in the mission station at Rorke's Drift.

"Who told Camilla about my mother?"

"Heyden's mother. I think she was a nurse companion of some sort."

"Inga?" she asked quietly.

He nodded. "Yes, the name sounds familiar."

"She's still alive, then?"

He appeared reluctant, then nodded. "I believe she's somewhere in the Transvaal, or was it Mafeking? It escapes me. Camilla will know. She can tell you."

Then Heyden had at least told her the truth about his mother, Inga, working at Cape House.

"Inga may have taken a few of Katie's things with her when she left soon after Katie's death."

Evy's emotions churned. There were so many things she needed and wanted to do in South Africa. There must be something she could do to convince Rogan that the war should not stand in her way.

"I'll see you again at Capetown," his word came huskily. Her father bent down, kissed her cheek, gave a reassuring squeeze to her arm, and walked from the salon to join his guests, leaving her alone with her prize and her emotions.

Evy continued holding the heart pendant in her palm until coming aware some time later of women's voices. She looked up and toward Rogan, rather surprised that she'd forgotten him. He wasn't in the salon. She remembered having seen him standing in the doorway just before Anthony gave her the pendant. He had seen someone who hadn't pleased him.

She hung the pendant around her throat and managed to hook the tiny clasp. Then she placed the box inside her fashionable gilded wrist-purse, containing handkerchief, lip color, and a small powder puff. She smiled and started for the door to locate Rogan and show him her mother's pendant when the women's voices stopped her abruptly.

"Poor Rogan," came one lady's wearied tone. "I'm sure he's heart-broken over it, but what could he do?"

"Serves the scamp right if you ask me. There was Diana, too. You recall her?"

"Whoever could forget? Margaret took her on a grand tour. They always said—"

"Whatever might he have been thinking, marrying this girl?"

"My dear, you heard what Patricia said. He simply *had* to marry her."

"Then she's…?"

"But of course."

"Extraordinary. She *is* quite pretty."

"How else could she have gotten him to visit the likes of her but to invite him to the hayloft?"

"My dear!"

"I know her kind. Lord Brewster was upset with Anthony for even bringing her here. She's like her mother."

"That dreadful Boer girl Anthony knew in South Africa?"

"Mother and daughter…cut from the same piece of cloth. Except Anthony wouldn't marry *her* when she showed up…well, you know."

"But Rogan did marry Evy."

"She's a diamond heiress, isn't she? Patricia says Evy will bring him another great fortune. Oh, she was after Rogan all along. Even when a girl, she threw herself at his feet."

"Well, she got him."

"The one way she could. What could he do? It's as Patricia said; she took advantage of him."

"And she has the audacity to come here to the Brewsters'."

"Well, my dear, you can't tell yet, can you? It won't show for another month or two."

"Poor Patricia. I saw her with Rogan earlier…in the garden…"

Their voices faded as they wandered off.

The sickening feeling in the pit of Evy's stomach made her knees weak. She held to the back of the chair and lowered herself to the velvet settee. Her cold fingers sought contact with the pendant heart around her throat.

Pregnant. They think I'm expecting Rogan's baby…that he had to marry me.

The gossip stunned Evy. Never would she have thought that Patricia would stoop so low. Had she come to the ball to sow her bitter seeds?

Footsteps sounded, too solid and bold for the women. She looked up, unable to mask her feelings. Rogan stood there. He looked at her long and hard, and his jawline tensed. He came to her looking down, a frown forming. Then his warm, brown eyes noticed the gold heart with a center cross of diamonds.

"Anthony told me yesterday about Katie's pendant."

"You knew?" Her voice was tremulous, still dismayed by Lady Patricia's cruel gossip.

"It was the deciding factor in bringing you here tonight." There was a measure of distaste in his voice that was a reflection of invited guests from Brewster House. His inky lashes narrowed. "I should never have let you come here."

His low voice, hardened because of some anger, surprised her. "What did Patricia tell you in the garden?" she asked quietly. His gaze shot to hers. Had he not wanted her to know he'd spoken with Patricia alone in the garden? A sinking feeling spread over her. Rogan *wouldn't*, no, he couldn't want Patricia still—?

His mouth went down at one corner. "Nothing worth repeating."

Her gaze lowered. "That's not what I heard just a moment ago…"

"I thought it might be something like that the moment I saw your face. Patricia is gone, thoroughly castigated by yours truly. Who told you?"

She looked up quickly. Did he know about the lie?

"I don't know who they were…just two ladies. I didn't recognize their voices. They were talking outside the door. They didn't know I was here."

"Obviously. The way of all gossipmongers."

"Oh, Rogan, they think—Patricia has spread the shameful story that you had to marry me because...because—" Her eyes implored his.

"You're pregnant, I believe is the correct word," he said dryly.

She intertwined her fingers and brought them to her mouth, head lowered. "They believed it. They must all believe it. I feel so ashamed."

"Rubbish. Because of someone else's lies? Get up, darling." He reached down and, grasping her arm, pulled her to her feet. He tilted her chin. "Courage."

"Rogan, I want to leave now."

He appraised her, then his hand dropped and he folded his arms in a bored stance. "I'm disappointed in you."

"Disappointed!"

"You're willing to risk war and a spitting cobra or two in South Africa, but when the moment comes to demonstrate courage for being the daughter of Katie van Buren, you shrink away like a timid rabbit. I thought my bride was not merely the most beautiful woman here tonight but also the most courageous. I see you prefer to slink away, giving credence to the malicious talk, no doubt by the back door, through the dark and silent garden. Ah, well..." He appeared ready to go for her wrap.

Evy searched his taunting gaze. No doubt he was saying all this to put iron in her backbone. She lifted her chin.

"You really want me to stay and put on an act for them?"

"Not an act. I want you to show them who you really are—the Evy I've known as a courageous beauty since I was twelve."

She felt a smile tug at her lips. He had a way of pulling some determination out of her spirits, even when they were sagging miserably.

"Bravo, Mrs. Chantry. I see the fire beginning to brighten the green in your amber eyes—always a good sign. Now, sweet, listen to your husband. There are two things you're going to do for our *honorable* guests before we bid them adieu and abandon Brewster House to the old cats. First, we dance."

"Dance!" Was she hearing him right?

"Dance." He flashed a menacing smile, not at her, but evidently at something or someone who was on his mind. "Of course, we dance, my sweet. We are at our wedding ball. The dear 'lords and ladies' must see how charming my delectable bride really is!"

She couldn't help her smile. "Are you out of your wits? Should we walk in there now with all this talk circulating? Every eye will be on us."

"Exactly. Give me your arm, 'Lady' Chantry. You're the most fascinating woman here tonight and, by far, the most honorable. They must see it so. I won't take no for an answer," he said when she started to say something. "You know how persistent I can be when I want something," he said, giving her a slanted look, "so gracefully float forward, my love. Hark—how the waltz in our honor is about to being."

He looped her arm firmly on his and leaned over to lift her fingers to his warm lips, then waggled his brows.

She laughed, but her dismay had somehow been lifted from her shoulders as he ushered her out of the salon and across the wide corridor into the ballroom.

Evy's eyes were on Rogan's handsome face as he led her in with a devastatingly charming smile. She cast him her most demure smile in return.

The floor emptied as the guests moved back toward the walls, giving them the whole ballroom. Evy saw a familiar auburn-haired woman among the guests. So Patricia was still here. Had she come to spoil their dinner ball with a scandal?

Rogan was giving Evy a light bow, then raised her hand once more to his lips and kissed her wedding ring as all eyes fixed upon them. It was so dreadfully romantic that she knew her eyes must be shining. She felt a princess with her crown prince. They smiled, totally absorbed in each other as he led her to the middle of the floor.

"Let the music begin!" a voice from the orchestra boomed.

His eyes held hers as they began to move to the music. She was sure that in Rogan's arms she could dance as nimbly as any mystical garden fairy. Not even the special shoe she needed for spinal alignment could intervene when Rogan looked at her as he was doing now, consumed with her and oblivious to all else.

They must have made a stunning picture, for when the waltz ended someone applauded. Her brief glance caught Anthony with a proud look on his face.

"Now," Rogan said, taking her arm and escorting her toward the orchestra. "There is something you and I must do."

She wondered as he left her side and stepped onto the platform, then spoke to the conductor. The man looked at Evy, showed approval, and nodded briskly. He rapped his wand for the attention of his musicians, leaned over, and said something.

Rogan came down from the steps and escorted her to the grand piano.

"Rogan, *no,* I can't—it's been months since I've practiced—"

"I heard you just last night at the townhouse. If I can play, *you* can."

"What? You—?"

Sure enough, to her amazement, one of the musicians came forward and bowed, presenting his violin to Rogan. Rogan accepted the instrument and bowed in return.

Evy, whose heart was thudding hard enough to make her breathless, sat down at the awesome piano, taking a moment to feel the keyboard. Her eye caught the glitter of her wedding ring. The diamonds were one with Katie's pendant winking at her breast. Both seemed to urge her onward.

Rogan leaned over and said in a low tone, "Better play Paganini. That's what I last practiced."

The ballroom had fallen into stunned silence.

Lord Jesus, this is dedicated to You, Evy prayed.

She looked at Rogan. The confidence he displayed in her before all those present, her critics, along with his delight in her as his bride, gave her all she needed. She smiled at him, then glanced at the conductor, whose eye was upon her. She nodded briefly that she was ready.

Her eyes lowered to the keys. Her fingers started moving faultlessly, as though prompted by her years of practice. The stirring passion flamed, burning in her heart. All else faded as her soul and spirit arose to the demands of the exquisite concerto reverberating through the ballroom. Her heart took flight on soaring wings of gilded doves, higher, higher into splendor.

Then her fingers slowed and eased. She played softly as Rogan's strings lifted the masterpiece along with chords that turned the duet into a work of passionate love.

They reached the last note; their hands fell still. Evy lowered her head.

Silence—then thunderous applause!

Evy stood, bowing in all directions, but saw two faces in the crowd that brought her delight. Her *father,* Anthony, and another very old face, Great-grandfather Brewster. He had risen to his tottering feet with the aid of his cane, and with his free hand was wiping his eyes with a large white handkerchief. Anthony was looking at him with a smile, as though to say, "See? Do you now really *see* my daughter?"

Rogan returned the violin to its master, inclined his head to acknowledge the applause, then, turning to Evy, took her arm and led her from the ballroom. The applause continued as they departed.

As they entered the hall he said, "*Now,* darling, I'll take you home as requested."

CHAPTER TWO

Grimston Way, England
Rookswood Estate
Autumn

The rest of their honeymoon was spent in Paris, and Evy was discovering that marriage to Rogan was anything but dull. She thought she had known him, but marital intimacy opened doors to many surprises, some of which showed a romantic but rather mischievous disposition on his part—like awakening her at the light of dawn by tickling the bottoms of her feet! When she threatened to get even, he stated that he had nothing to fear, since he was confident she was incapable of awakening before him. She got her revenge, though. One evening at Rookswood she planned a surprise; she asked the servant boy to arise early next morning to collect a bucket of ice from one of the shallower ponds and had one of the maids quietly smuggle it up to the bedroom. Evy had gleefully shocked Rogan awake, dumping the ice over his bare chest before he could stop her. Oh! What *fun* to get the best of him!

Though Rogan occasionally eluded her understanding, most of the time he behaved just as she had dreamed he would: he was a sympathetic and protective husband—sometimes so tender she likened him to the groom of Song of Solomon. He accepted her weaknesses and idiosyncrasies with amazing liberality, and, of course, was the exciting lover she had anticipated.

A month after their marriage, they returned home to Rookswood. The weeks raced by. The joys of fall were yet riding the tame winds, rustling the green leaves of elm and sycamore trees in Grimston Woods, blowing through Evy's heart as well. By autumn the difficulties and surprises of newly married life visited Evy with a suddenness that left her in a quandary. She had become pregnant far sooner than she expected, bringing her smoldering coals of uncertainty back to a fiery glow. In fact, the development of her and Rogan's baby might easily appear to fit into the schedule of Lady Patricia's gossip. Evy was afraid, and dazed by it all.

If only Aunt Grace were alive! She and Vicar Edmund Havering had raised her at the vicarage with the same love and dedication as though she had truly been their blooded niece. When Aunt Grace was on her deathbed, Evy had told her that she was the only mother she had ever known. If only she, or even Uncle Edmund, were here now. So far she had not said a word to Rogan because of South Africa. This would give him even more reason to want her to stay behind at Rookswood while he voyaged to the Chantry gold mine on the Zambezi. She knew he was anxious to go—and without her.

On one of those afternoons after another inconclusive discussion about accompanying him on the voyage, Rogan told her he had to go to London without her.

"London? But why?" She looked at him, puzzled.

"Anthony wired me this morning. He's asked that I pay him a visit at the diamond business in London."

"He's still in London? How odd. He was to sail for Capetown weeks ago, soon after the dinner ball at Brewster House."

"Something has delayed him, obviously, darling. Don't worry. He didn't sound as though anything was particularly wrong. Just asked me to meet him later this evening at his office." He came up to her, taking her by her forearms. "Look, sweet, it will be late when this meeting is over. I don't think I'll have time to return tonight. I'll stay at the townhouse and return in the morning."

Rather startled, she had no answer at first. He must have noticed. He regarded her tenderly.

"Do you mind terribly?"

She did. "You never decided to go away overnight before."

His eyes glinted and a smile loitered. "I didn't realize you'd miss me so much."

Rogan gone overnight? The thought of the dark bedroom without him was suddenly unthinkable. How had she lived all those lonely nights without his arms around her? It was especially troubling that the idea did not appear to be a great concern to him. Was this a way to begin putting some distance between them so that leaving for South Africa would seem less startling?

He scanned her face, then lifted her chin. "I'll take the first train back in the morning."

Evy was quiet as he strode into their bedroom to pack a few things he'd need. It took her awhile to digest the news. What could have kept Anthony in London when he'd been so anxious to get back to Camilla, who was ailing?

She was standing where Rogan had left her when he came out with a small overnight bag.

"I wouldn't have minded going with you if you'd told me in time to prepare," she said too casually.

"You're quite right. I failed to take into account that you might want to come with me. But this is strictly business, and all that. Probably quite boring. Must be something about the diamonds. Cutting, polishing, grading...though Anthony didn't explain." He set his bag down and came to her, his arm going firmly around her waist. He drew her to him. "Look, darling, we'll go again in a few days, or whenever you like. We'll do it properly, take in dinner and the theater. All the things you enjoy."

She wondered uneasily if there was some reason he didn't want her to accompany him. Why hadn't he mentioned it in time?

He kissed her. "It's not as though I wanted to leave you." He watched her; she remained silent. "All right," he said suddenly, "I'll tell you. Anthony asked me to come alone."

Her brows lifted. "Did he? I wonder why?"

"He didn't say." He enfolded her in his embrace. He started to say something and apparently changed his mind. After touching her hair softly and lingering over a kiss, he turned and was gone.

The door shut, and she was left standing there, her heart full of unresolved questions.

A moment later she walked across the carpet of muted pink roses in burgundy, past the Chippendale furniture, to a window offering a view to the front of Rookswood. She pushed aside the burgundy drapery and peered below. The wide front garden hemmed both sides of the long drive down toward the great iron gate. The gate opened to the road that wound past Grimston Woods with many paths branching off into the thick trees. The road ran past the rectory of St. Graves Parish where she'd grown up, and into the village of Grimston Way and, for Rogan, the train junction.

Puzzled and disquieted, she watched him leave. *Will something come between us?*

London
South African Diamond Enterprise

Lord Anthony Brewster was waiting in his office at the family diamond exporting business in London when Rogan arrived on the five o'clock train. It was customary, if not a duty, to have family "sons" work for a year at the business before going to the mine in Kimberly. Parnell had put in over a year to please Julien. Rogan, too, had worked here, but he had left before his year was finished, enraging Julien, who deemed himself the family monarch. Afterward, Julien had shown up uninvited at Rogan's camp on the Limpopo River insisting that the British South

Africa Company had rights to any gold discovered with Henry Chantry's old map, a map willed to Rogan as a boy upon Henry's untimely death—untimely because he'd been murdered at Rookswood.

Lord Anthony's luggage was packed and sitting in a corner of his office. He stood from behind his large desk and nodded when he saw Rogan looking at his bags.

"Yes, my ship for Capetown leaves in the morning. My bags will be loaded aboard my cabin tonight." He explained his delayed departure by pushing an envelope across the desk toward Rogan.

"This is why I called for you to come privately. I'm worried about recent events. This letter is from your brother."

"Parnell?" Rogan was surprised. Somehow he had expected that troubling news would be from Sir Julien Bley, and why would Parnell send it to Anthony?

The letter had been sent from Bulawayo. As Rogan slipped it from the envelope and started reading, he realized it contained information that could be damaging to Julien. Rogan now knew why Parnell had not sent it to him. Rogan was independent enough to question Julien's doings, and Parnell was still trying to please him, just as he had when he was working for him in Kimberly at De Beers's mining and claims office. It disturbed Rogan that his older brother was still committed to Julien's cause above all else, as though being hitched to Julien's wagon would strengthen Parnell's position in the family and also his chances of marrying Julien's granddaughter, Darinda. Why couldn't Parnell see the obvious? Rogan doubted if his brother would ever be permitted to marry the beautiful and independent Darinda Bley.

Rogan honed in on a section of the letter that troubled him and read it again slowly, thoughtfully.

Sir Julien helped lead Dr. Jameson's troopers against Lobengula at Bulawayo. When Lobengula fled his kraal, Julien and I were some of the first to enter the savage's hut. He went berserk searching for the treasure trove of diamonds that he expected to find there. The main chest was gone. But there were bags of diamonds left behind in Lobengula's haste to flee our troopers. Yet Julien was utterly dismayed. After dumping the diamonds out onto the floor, he fell to his knees scooping them with his hands. I kept telling him to hurry. The kraal huts were bursting with fire. Julien's face was ravaged. I feared for a time that he had mentally cracked until I understood that he had expected the Kimberly Black Diamond to be in one of those bags!

He became furious. "The induna promised me it was here. Lobengula has run off with it. But I'll find him," he kept saying, but I kept trying to pull him out of the tent. "Come, Uncle," I kept telling him. "The Ndebele are coming back and will attack us." I feared for our lives, but Julien kept searching. Finally he stood, dazed. "Lobengula has the Black Diamond with him."

Julien urged Dr. Jameson's troopers to track Lobengula and his indunas. Our men were closing in when Lobengula sent more diamonds to buy them off. But they pursued him to the Shangani River. A battle ensued. Our patrol was killed to the last man. Lobengula got away. He fled to the Matopos Hills. Here he took refuge in a cave and drank poison. We captured a Shona slave of one of the chief indunas. He told us that Lobengula's most loyal induna, along with his wives, buried Lobengula in one of the secret caves, and like the ancient Egyptian pharaohs, they surrounded Lobengula with his great wealth, his assegai, and his royal cloak. There were so many diamonds sprinkled over Lobengula that the Shona now have a saying: "Lobengula glitters in his sleep. The glittering crocodile sleeps, covered over with diamonds like shiny, thick scales."

Julien believes the Black Diamond is there…

Rogan looked up from the letter, and Anthony spoke.

"The Matopos Hills—aren't they near Bulawayo?"

"Yes. You can look off and see them from Lobengula's kraal." Rogan remembered his visit there with Rhodes's delegation when Dr. Jameson and Frank Thompson were negotiating with Lobengula for right of passage through Matabeleland to dig for gold. What Lobengula had not known was that Rhodes's Royal Charter Company intended to begin a colony farther north in Mashonaland. Rogan, however, was not particularly sympathetic to Lobengula because the chieftain, though a cousin of the Zulus, had invaded land that was not his—the land of the Shona tribe—and enslaved them all.

"Then perhaps Julien is right," Anthony said. "The Kimberly Black Diamond is there on the Matopos."

The Kimberly Black Diamond. Buried along with Lobengula in his burial cave? Rogan felt the intense gaze of his father-in-law. Rogan looked up from the letter to find Anthony frowning. Just what was Anthony's emotional involvement in finding the Black Diamond?

"This spells real trouble with the Ndebele," Rogan said. "If Julien believes the diamond is there, he'll attempt to send an expedition." But could Julien locate the chieftain's burial site when the Ndebele wished to keep it secret?

Anthony shook his head. "He'll search, all right; you know that as well as I. My adoptive father's been plagued by that stone since he was a young man." He looked at Rogan sharply. "I'm not one who believes in mumbo jumbo, mind you, but there are times when I can almost think there's a curse on the Black Diamond."

Rogan lifted a brow. "I've wondered too…not about mumbo jumbo, as you aptly put it, but where it first came from. How it ever got into Julien's possession." Rogan had his own idea about that, but he wondered how much Anthony knew about the diamond's mysterious history.

Anthony was thoughtful and looked troubled. "First I heard of it was when I was a boy at Brewster House. Grandfather spoke of it, of Julien and Carl van Buren forming a partnership in a diamond hole they were digging at Kimberly."

Carl—Evy's grandfather. He'd been killed in an explosion in that diamond hole.

"Was there a witness to Carl's death in that mining accident?" Rogan asked tonelessly.

Anthony's eyes shot to his. "I don't know. Afterward, Julien says Carl lived long enough to entrust Katie to his guardianship."

"And evidently the Black Diamond. Although Henry, when he was alive, claimed the diamond was discovered by neither Carl nor Julien."

"Henry claimed many things," Anthony said wearily. "Including the *mystical* gold deposit on his old Mashonaland map."

Rogan didn't want to discuss the map he'd inherited. He ignored the dismissal in Anthony's voice. The gold he discovered on the Zambezi hadn't developed into the boon he'd hoped for. The mine was another problem facing him. He must go there to discuss things with Derwent and Mornay, but how could he leave Evy at Rookswood?

"I once heard Henry claim the Kimberly Diamond was actually discovered by his father, your grandfather," Anthony suggested.

Rogan had heard such rumors, but when he'd asked his father, Sir Lyle, he'd scoffed at the idea.

"My father agrees with you that Henry claimed some wild and woolly things," Rogan admitted. "I never placed much confidence in that idea myself, but I have often wondered if Julien or Carl might not have stolen the diamond from one of the Zulu *ngangas*."

"The witch doctors, eh? Interesting notion, Rogan. What makes you think so?"

"I don't have much to go on, except Dumaka. He came to work for Julien at Cape House. I found out Dumaka is an induna. To work for Julien would be a loathsome thing. Yet he came of his own free will. Though Heyden stole the diamond from Henry that night in the stables, Heyden claims Dumaka took the diamond from him and escaped with it. Just days later the British fought the Zulu in the war. The Zulus were defeated and Cetshwayo exiled. I've thought Dumaka took the diamond before the British arrived and fled to Lobengula at Bulawayo."

Anthony nodded agreement. "You may very well be right, Rogan. I remember the night the diamond was stolen from Julien. I'd just arrived with Camilla in time to hear of it. And that Katie had run away with the Zulu woman."

"Jendaya. She had become a Christian under the Varleys at Rorke's Drift mission. She's Dumaka's sister. Heyden seems to think she is still alive."

"Yes? I wonder. Anyway, Julien and I found Henry unconscious in the stables. Julien was adamant Henry had the diamond. He demanded I search him. It was an ugly night. I wish I'd never heard of that cursed diamond."

"This is only the beginning," Rogan warned.

"Yes, and now Heyden van Buren. I still cannot believe he actually murdered Henry and Vicar Edmund Havering. He must be mad."

"If he is mad, he's mad with the cause of the Boers. He wants that diamond for one reason—to help the Boers finance the war. They need weapons, and they hope to buy them from the German Empire. Guns, ammunition, cannons, and medicine to supply the Boer army."

"Yes, yes, so Scotland Yard tells me. Heyden was in Germany before he came to Grimston Way."

"Negotiating for armaments?"

"With friends of Paul Kruger. The diamond would then go on the international market for the best price."

Rogan looked thoughtfully at his brother's letter. "I wonder where Heyden is now. And does he know what happened at Bulawayo? Does Heyden have reason to think the Black Diamond is buried with Lobengula in the Matopos?"

"Indeed. If Heyden has heard the tale as Parnell tells it, then we can be sure Julien won't be the only one in search of Lobengula's burial cave."

Rogan hardened his jaw. Heyden was the other reason he must go alone to South Africa. Rogan had said little about it to Evy, but he was determined to hunt Heyden down for what he had done. And he didn't want her there to hear the details of what he'd do to Heyden when he found him.

"Another thing," Rogan said. "Peter will have a rampage on his doorstep at Bulawayo if the indunas find out the white men who defeated their chieftain are now poking around the Matopos to rob Lobengula's grave."

Anthony shook his head. "Something must be done. You're right."

Julien would hardly listen to Anthony's advice, Rogan thought wryly. Julien was now chief native commissioner at Bulawayo, newly appointed by Rhodes to be in charge of the conquered Ndebele. Peter Bartley, Rogan's brother-in-law, was Julien's assistant commissioner, but while Cecil Rhodes remained at Capetown as prime minister, Dr. Jameson was his right-hand man.

No, Julien wouldn't listen to any of Anthony's warnings, but the British high commissioner at Capetown might. Commissioner Milner was a friend of Anthony's.

"I'll arrange to meet with him when I arrive in Capetown."

Was Anthony willing to oppose Julien's interest in the Matopos? Rogan was surprised. Anthony had been under Sir Julien's thumb since a lad attending school at Eden, when, after Julien's wife died, he singled out Anthony to become his heir, arranging with the Brewsters to adopt Anthony. However, in return for being, as it were, "knighted" by Julien, he'd had to surrender his future to Julien's wishes in order to take over the family diamond dynasty after Julien's death. Anthony was also to assume the position of "patriarch" in charge of family monetary allowances and future marriages. Anthony hardly appeared the patriarchal sort.

"If Uncle Julien discovers you're out to stop him from robbing tombs, he's sure to come at you with both barrels," Rogan warned. "It will give Darinda opportunity as well. You're aware she wants to assume your role as her grandfather's heir. She's one young woman to not underestimate."

Anthony's face tightened. "That's the chance I'll need to take with Julien. England is on the verge of war with Kruger in the Transvaal. Her Majesty can't afford to fight on two fronts. And the last thing we need is a massacre of English settlers in Rhodesia. We cannot sit idle and allow an uprising just because of Julien's belief that the Kimberly Black Diamond is buried with Lobengula in those sacred hills."

This was one of the few times Rogan respected Anthony for taking a firm stand. His decision to appeal to the high commissioner appeared to be selfless. Rogan hoped it was so.

By the time Rogan left his father-in-law in his office at South African Diamond Enterprise, the fog had settled over London. He glanced at his watch and grimaced. He'd intended to try to return tonight, though he'd not promised Evy, but the last train passing through the junction at Grimston Way would depart in ten minutes.

He hailed a taxi carriage. The horse clipped away into the cool fall night. Rogan frowned. The Matopos Hills...the Black Diamond...even now Julien might be getting an expedition ready. Heyden could not be far away. If there was any chance the diamond was within his grasp, he would be near—somewhere, watching, waiting for his chance. There had been at least two deaths over that diamond, Uncle Henry and old, gentle Vicar Edmund Havering. Rogan felt grim as he thought in particular of the vicar. A godly man who had been needed by Evy and Mrs. Havering, and yet Heyden had arranged for his violent "accidental" death. And there was Evy's fall down the attic steps as well. Heyden was fully to blame for the damage to her spine. She might have been dead right now, all because of that diamond.

He must leave soon for South Africa. He must go without Evy. Would she understand?

CHAPTER THREE

In the dark bedroom on the second floor, Evy awoke with a start, aware of the vacant pillow beside her. She remembered… Rogan was in London. He wouldn't be back until late morning. He'd gone to see her father at the family diamond business. Then why—

She came alert and sat up, glancing toward the closed door to the sitting room. A ribbon of golden light shone beneath the door.

Slowly she drew the cover aside and reached for her silken wrapper, not troubling with her pink slippers. Like a silent wraith, her feet moved toward the door on tiptoe.

Oh come, there's not a thing to be afraid of here at Rookswood, even though—ugh, Henry Chantry was murdered on the floor above me. But that was Heyden, and Heyden has escaped to South Africa.

Nonetheless, with stealthy movement, she turned the knob and pulled the door open a crack to peer into the sitting room. She must have left the lamp burning. No, she distinctly recalled putting it out before—

She drew a breath of surprise.

He turned, still dressed from his London trip, his overnight bag on the floor near the lamp. She noticed something different about him. Was it the absence of his relaxed smile?

"Rogan darling, I didn't hear you come in." She moved into the sitting room, relieved and delighted to see him.

She felt at once something was wrong from the seriousness of his expression.

"You decided not to stay overnight in London after all."

"I managed to catch the last train—by racing after it. Ah, what sacrifices men will make for true love! I even had to walk three miles from the village junction," he said, pretending to be appalled. His warming gaze scanned her. "The thought of what awaited at home made the townhouse seem desolate."

Evy smiled alluringly and moved into his arms.

"Temptress," he said, enfolding her and delivering a kiss firmly on her lips.

Her heart was happy again. The tension between them when he had departed for London was washed away in the tide that swept over her. She drew away, gently pushing against his chest, stepping out of his reach.

"Something is wrong, isn't it? You're worried. Is it Anthony? Is he all right?" Her father's health was the first thing she could think of to explain his sober demeanor.

"He's well, leaving for Capetown in the morning, in fact." He shouldered out of his jacket and unbuttoned his shirt collar.

She wasn't satisfied but took his jacket and brought it into the bedroom wardrobe, then came back, pink slippers in hand as she stood thoughtfully. That her father was well was good news at least. She looked at Rogan. He wore a slight smile and leaned against the back of the divan.

"Then...what did he want? It must have been terribly important to call you all the way to London on such short notice."

He came to her, directing her into a tapestry wing chair. "Sit down," he said, then he plucked the heeled pink satin slippers from her hand and looked at them.

"I never could see the value of these things...totally worthless for scuffing about." He stooped and, lifting her foot, slipped one on, visibly admiring her shapely leg.

"Rogan! You're keeping things from me, you scoundrel. Do tell me what Anthony wanted."

"Yes…of course."

She latched on to the slight pause, so unlike Rogan, whose resonant voice was usually quick and assertive. Evy guessed that he didn't want to discuss the meeting with Anthony, which only enforced her curiosity. She continued to study him. His handsome face and muscled neck were still brown from the harsh elements of the South African veld, and his glossy dark hair curled slightly. The energetic rich brown eyes had taken on a far-off gleam that she often saw while he was pondering South Africa, their gold mine in the Zambezi region, or his uncle's mysterious map. During such times, which were growing more frequent, a restlessness would come over him. He might suddenly decide to take one of the horses out for a brisk ride, or he would go hiking in Grimston Woods, usually too aggressively for Evy to keep up. She'd learned it was best to turn him loose during those times, much like a wild stallion on the run.

Looking at her husband, she was now quite aware of the manner of man he was—prone to a restless, adventuresome spirit from boyhood. She knew a qualm of fear. Would the day come when marriage, no longer as fresh and exciting, would fail to satisfy and hold him?

Evy had no fear that he would break his commitment of fidelity to her. What she could envision was a day when perhaps his earthy interests would exclude her. She was determined she would show interest in all that held him—his gold mine, the Black Diamond, the map— thinking her energies in those areas would endear her to him.

"Coffee would be stunning about now," he commented. "I'll need to tell Bertha there's little need to be sending the maids up with pots of tea."

He ran his fingers through his dark hair in a mannerism she knew well. He did that when musing about a matter that either bewildered or worried him. She was wise enough to know what bothered him now was not Bertha's tea. It was the meeting in London, of course. Whatever was it about?

Patience, she warned herself. *Don't push him. You know how intolerably uncooperative he can be when you try that.*

"I'll make some coffee, darling," she said sweetly. "I've everything right here."

Evy had managed to have a small stove placed in an alcove when they'd first moved into the private suite of rooms. The suite was considered the best in Rookswood, located on the sunny west wing of the mansion, and allowed them a sense of privacy Rogan had wanted. Evy had noted at once that though Rogan loved Sir Lyle and showed him a good deal of respect as his father, they were not close. Rogan had grown up that way, she knew. Lyle, though a kindly man, lived in a world of his own. He often secluded himself inside the downstairs library with his books, where he was working on some mammoth history of Grimston Way and the Chantry ancestors. Lyle had told her he had traced the first Chantry all the way back to the First Crusade in the Holy Land.

The cookstove was perfect for Rogan's unexpected calls for "midnight coffee." How he ever fell asleep afterward was a mystery, but it didn't seem to bother him. For herself, she made a cup of Belgian chocolate. Learning of her penchant for chocolate, he had sent for the best from Belgium and Switzerland.

A short time later with coffee, chocolate, and a tin of Dutch biscuits on the low table in front of them, Evy sat on the divan beside him to try to conjure from him what had taken place in London.

"How's your coffee, darling?" she asked, again sweetly.

His eyes taunted her. "Do I detect the use of feminine wiles to wrest from a beguiled husband all she wants to know? You look like a curious kitten with glowing eyes sprinkled with green."

"I've never—" she began, then halted. She hadn't thought of herself as beguiling at all. Then, of course, she'd never been married before, so she was learning new things about herself every day.

She frowned. "Well, then, perhaps I should be completely straightforward. What did Anthony want?"

"It must occur to you that if he had wanted you to know, he would not have requested that I come privately."

"Surely you're not going to keep whatever it is from me? I never thought you'd be so atrocious as to become one of those husbands who thinks he should keep everything unpleasant from his wife lest she fall into a faint."

"Let me see—where did I put those smelling salts?" He patted his shirt pocket. "I couldn't bear the torture of you keeping me awake all night pummeling me with questions."

She gave a laugh. "As if I've ever done so."

"You're not going to threaten to torture your vulnerable husband with pond ice again?"

She covered a smile, thinking of his tough, muscled torso as vulnerable. "Of course I would, but there's no ice in the pond now."

"Saved only by the long warm days!"

"Rogan, if you trusted me, you'd share what Anthony told you."

" 'How can you say, "I love you," when your heart is not with me? You have mocked me these three times, and have not told me where your great strength lies,' " he mimicked.

"Oh, Rogan, you're a cad. How can you possibly compare me with that Philistine woman, Delilah?"

His eyes teased her. "Next you'll be asking me to put my head on your lap."

She lifted a brow. "To talk about the secret of your strength?"

Rogan gave her a ghost of a grin and set his empty cup down, refilling it from the silver urn.

"All right, settle back, my sweet. This is going to take a while."

She smiled victoriously, kicking off her slippers and tucking her feet up under her. "You may begin, Rogan, dear. I'm all ears."

He leaned back against the divan, looking up at the ceiling and frowning, as though arranging his thoughts. Finally he spoke: "Tonight, I saw Anthony at the Diamond Enterprise in London. He had a letter from Parnell with some startling information about Julien and the Kimberly Black Diamond…"

The lightness of their bantering words was left far behind as Rogan explained what he had read in his brother's letter.

Now, something quite sinister seemed to invade the room. Evy could feel the tension in Rogan, and herself as well, as it mounted with the strange tale he told. When he had finished, she leaned forward in amazement.

"What Parnell said about Sir Julien…is true?"

"What reason would my brother have to invent a fabrication? Think! What is it Parnell wants above everything—except, perhaps, diamonds?" he asked wryly.

"I suppose Darinda Bley."

"There! You're exactly right. And who controls his fate? Julien, obviously."

"From what Arcilla writes me, Darinda isn't so easily manipulated by her grandfather. She may decide she won't marry Parnell."

"That, too. She's ambitious and headstrong, that one."

Evy shot him a glance that scanned him. "You know Darinda well?"

"Well enough." He leaned forward and poured more coffee into his empty cup.

Evy arched a brow but thought better of making anything of that. It was silly to be jealous of Darinda. Hadn't Rogan left everything in South Africa and returned to Grimston Way as soon as Camilla told him of the accident?

"So you see," Rogan continued thoughtfully, "Ol' Parnell has no reason in the world to roast Julien over the fire. On the contrary, he has more reason to go on pleasing him as he has these few years. A mistake in my opinion. I hate seeing Parnell licking Julien's shoe leather."

"Yes, I see what you mean." Evy frowned. "But it took some courage for Parnell to write that letter to my father. It would seem easier for him to have written you."

His mouth curved, and he shook his head. He stood, cup in hand, to stretch. "No, I'd be the last one he'd tell about the Black Diamond."

"But, Rogan—"

"Don't you see? Parnell *fears* Julien. He has for some time now. I noticed that at Kimberly. When I mentioned, half jesting, that Julien would get Henry's map from me over my dead body, Parnell went white. I never saw him look so afraid."

Evy was horrified. Did Parnell really think his Uncle Julien would *kill* to get what he wanted?

"Then Parnell fears you'd come and confront Sir Julien over the diamond," she stated. She looked at Rogan quickly. "He mustn't want you in South Africa."

"Let's say he doesn't want me at Bulawayo."

Bulawayo had been the kraal of Lobengula, the chieftain of the Ndebele tribe. Since his defeat under the pioneer soldiers, it was now a growing town under the governing hand of the British South Africa Company. The BSA had been established by Cecil Rhodes and his diamond and gold partners after Rhodes had received a royal charter from Queen Victoria to start a trading company north of the Limpopo River.

Rogan and Derwent had joined Rhodes's pioneers for the arduous trek across the sunburnt African velds and crocodile-infested rivers, helping along the way to build Fort Victoria and Fort Salisbury, naming them respectively after Her Majesty and the colonial secretary of that time, Lord Salisbury.

Rhodes's pioneers had spread out to claim their three-thousand-acre tracts, forming a mostly European colony of dedicated farmers and, eventually, their families. To protect them from the lurking Ndebele and Shona, with their sharp and gleaming assegai, Rhodes had also hired about five hundred policemen to guard the pioneers in what was now called Rhodesia.

The farming colony had grown and expanded. Recently, Bulawayo had been incorporated, after a bloody war with Lobengula, which had defeated his army of fierce fighting warriors called *impis,* under their particular indunas, or what Rogan told her were men of "Zanzi" blood, that is, royal blood.

Evy had known about the war before Parnell's letter. Rogan had told her the lurid tale one night while they lay in their dark bedroom. She had come to look forward to the long conversations they shared and urged him to tell her all about his first trip to Fort Salisbury. He'd told her everything he could remember about Arcilla and Peter on the trek, Alice and Derwent, the men in charge of the trek, and about Rogan's visit to Lobengula's kraal and how they had to sit in the dust with their heads bent during the entire meeting while flies buzzed over their sweating faces and necks. He'd told her about his meetings with the induna who called himself Jube, who'd actually been Jendaya's brother, Dumaka, and lastly he'd told her about the war with Lobengula.

Her vivid imagination ran through the entire raid on Bulawayo as she lay in the dark in Rogan's arms. Lobengula, knowing he was defeated, had fled into the Matopos Hills to the demonic Umlimo, who spoke for the spirit god they worshiped. Whether Lobengula had found the secret cave where the Umlimo lived was not known, but he had found a secret cave somewhere in the Matopos. There, surrounded by his concubines and loyal indunas, he had killed himself by drinking poison.

What was new in Parnell's letter was the Kimberly Black Diamond, and Sir Julien's crazed obsession with it. She knew about Heyden's fixation with it and what he had done to Henry and Uncle Edmund to try to capture it for the Boer war, but she had never thought of the shrewd, tough Sir Julien Bley as so given over to the desire to get the diamond back.

"Do you think Parnell is right? That Sir Julien helped lead the soldiers against Lobengula?"

"Parnell was there with Julien. I don't think Parnell exaggerated Julien's searching Lobengula's hut. That is what he had, you know, a hut, not far from his throne wagon, though I didn't see it."

In her mind's eye she pictured the giant chieftain fleeing in the midnight darkness with his impis fighting ferociously while he and his indunas, concubines, and wives escaped for the Matopos Hills. There was Sir Julien searching madly through his treasure trove, growing more desperate as the flames grew hotter and the Black Diamond was nowhere to be found.

"Do you have any idea which induna promised him the diamond would be there?"

Rogan considered for a moment, then said, "Someone furious with Lobengula for an injustice. The son of an induna is my guess. Someone who knew Dumaka. That would explain how the person knew enough to come to Julien about the diamond. Someone who also had it in for Dumaka, knowing how he'd taken it from Heyden in the stables and fled with it to Zululand. Then he brought it to Lobengula after the Zulus were defeated."

"Jendaya?" she asked suddenly.

Rogan looked at her with curious interest. "Why Jendaya?"

Evy spread a hand. "We all know her brother, Dumaka, is against her. Even Heyden said Dumaka was searching for her to kill her because she converted to Christianity. He also insisted she knew where the diamond was. That's why he wanted to bring me to Dr. Jakob van Buren. He thought Jendaya might appear, I think. What if Julien found her first, knowing Heyden believed Jendaya knew where it was?"

"Ah! You may be right. And Jendaya said it was with Lobengula. All quite possible, my dear, but Parnell wrote that Julien kept saying, '*He* told me it was here.'"

"Could she have sent someone else in her place to tell Julien? Would she have gotten married and had a son—"

"Maybe. Good try, darling. Whoever it was convinced Julien he knew what he was talking about."

"Evidently the diamond *was* there. But Lobengula got away, bringing it with him. If it's true, that is, about his burial."

"It's true," he said soberly. "I know something about the Matopos. How sacred they are to the Ndebele, to the Shona, too, for that matter."

"Yes, their Umlimo." She shuddered thinking of demons. "Oh, Rogan, it is a good work that Cousin Jakob is doing there, bringing the good news of Jesus to the tribes."

"Indeed, an unselfish labor, Evy, darling. You may be right about Jendaya being the one. She could have a son. I'll find out when I get there."

"When *we* get there, you mean." She untucked her feet from beneath her and stood. "Rogan, you're not going to insist I stay here," she said, dismay in her voice. "Because I must go meet Cousin Jakob."

The tensing of his jaw told her he didn't see the urgency as she did.

"It's too dangerous, sweet. Even Parnell recognizes it. He's urged Anthony to appeal to Capetown to send more help to Bulawayo."

"Surely Sir Julien recognizes the danger from angering the indunas and will curtail his expedition."

"Ah, you don't know him as well as we do. Julien won't give up on anything he wants unless he's forced. Heyden is just as determined. I'm convinced Heyden's been watching Bulawayo, keeping an eye on Julien."

"How would he know what Julien's up to?"

"It's Heyden's passion. Any tale circulating about Lobengula having had the diamond will have reached him by now. That's another reason I don't want you anywhere near Bulawayo."

"But Cousin Jakob's mission station is on the Zambezi, close to the gold mine."

He walked over to her, bringing her into his arms. "I don't care for any of this, Evy. I'm convinced Heyden is there—and I must find him."

She held to him as protectively as he did her. "All the more reason to stay away from the Black Diamond. If I didn't know better, I'd believe it cursed."

"Maybe it is," he said dryly. "But not in the way you mean it. I've thought for some time the diamond may have been stolen from a tribal god, maybe even the Umlimo. It was likely the reason Dumaka went to

Capetown to work for Julien. He hated him. He was looking for an opportunity to kill him, but he had to get the diamond first. That opportunity came unexpectedly when Katie and Henry took it to ride out to Rorke's Drift to find you. Dumaka did get the diamond back, but he had to be content with that and forget about revenge on Julien.

"Heyden must be dealt with. I'm not going to forget that he pushed you down the attic stairs and left you for dead. There's Uncle Henry, too. And Vicar Havering. Heyden must be brought to justice for what he's done."

Her fingers tightened on his arms. "I wish you wouldn't. Rogan, let's forget the Black Diamond. Let's forget Heyden. We have our own reasons for going to Rhodesia: Cousin Jakob, and the gold mine."

His dark eyes hardened. "He's in South Africa. That's exactly what I want. Better there than in quiet Grimston Way. I intend to hunt him down." His eyes narrowed. "Things are different in the wilds of Africa. When I catch him there, I'll have it out with him once for all—and I won't be needing to worry about the local constable!"

She knew him too well to look surprised. He had always been independent. He had returned from Africa even more so, and sometimes hard in his thinking and manner, not that he'd ever been so with her. But his iron determination to *force* Heyden to pay frightened her. As she looked at him, noticing the hard line of his jaw, her concerns grew.

"I'm going with you, Rogan," she insisted. "I won't stay here." She threw her arms around his neck. "Darling, you've got to let me come. Don't you see? I simply must meet Dr. Jakob. You'll take me, won't you, Rogan, my love? Say you'll arrange matters so it works. Please, do."

Her sudden emotion appeared to melt some of his resistance.

"The main thing, sweetheart, is that you regain your strength." He scooped her up in his arms and carried her into the bedroom.

"I'm much stronger now. The doctor says so. And I don't need a crutch. I'll be all right, Rogan, you'll see. If I can't go with you, I shall be the most unhappy and disappointed woman in all Grimston Way!"

He smiled ruefully. "Well, we can't have that. All right, sweet, you win."

Stunned at the sudden turn of events, she simply gazed into his energetic dark eyes. As she searched their depths, his brow lifted quizzically. "What do you see?"

He was still enigmatic sometimes, even a stranger. What had caused him to cooperate?

"You really mean it? You won't change your mind?"

"No, I won't change my mind. I thought I could talk you out of it, but I see how much it means to you. If I stood in your way now," he said gravely, "I think it would do more harm to our relationship than any trial that may await us there. And be assured, Evy, trouble does await."

She shivered. His embrace tightened. "At times I still don't think I know you," she admitted.

His smile tried to tease her into withdrawing her sober remark. "Because I've decided not to contest you on this?"

"Yes, but I'm so happy you've agreed at last. The safari won't be too much for me. You'll see. I'm as anxious for Rhodesia as you are."

"And you're willing to stay with Dr. Jakob while I trek north to the gold mine to check on things?"

"Yes, as long as you're not gone for five or six months."

"Just try to keep me from you for that long. Two months, no longer, maybe less."

"That seems reasonable."

He smiled. "Then I'll see you safely delivered on his doorstep one way or another. On one condition."

"Rogan!"

"One condition," he repeated soberly. "That Dr. Jackson agrees you're up to the voyage, and the trek."

She hesitated, then smiled. "We have a bargain." She threw her arms around him. She lifted her face, her lips upturned for a kiss.

She wasn't disappointed.

CHAPTER FOUR

Further surprises of newly married life visited Evy with the first promise of the chilling autumn. Excitement tugged at her heart, and uncertainty her stomach.

Wearing her new walking habit, she came quietly down the stairs on her way to the village. She paused. Rogan's voice came from the library on her right.

"Milner no doubt already knows," Sir Lyle said in a disinterested tone.

Milner, she wrinkled her nose, who was he? Oh yes, the high commissioner at the Cape colony. What did the commissioner already know? Rogan sounded angry about whatever it was.

Evy came down the stairs and walked across the Great Hall to the library door. Sir Lyle was sitting behind his huge mahogany desk piled with books and a sheaf of paper, working on his laborious history of Rookswood. His hair was a light brown speckled with gray. He was tall and lean, and in Evy's opinion was nothing like his son in either appearance or personality.

Rogan turned from the window with white curtains and burgundy drapes and looked at his father. Rogan's rich brown eyes were as electric as a thunderstorm.

Sir Lyle frowned. "Not that Milner would admit knowing. Rhodes, as well. In public they'll pretend innocence and shock. But it's hard to believe Jameson would plan on doing such a thing without Rhodes's knowledge."

Rogan moved abruptly to his father's desk. "Milner wants to provoke a war with Kruger. I'd wager on it."

"Now, now, son, I wouldn't go as far as that."

"What more do you need? He's in with the diamond bugs. Money rules both kings and paupers."

"I didn't know I raised a cynic."

"Oh, come. The gold and diamond moguls are quietly putting the pressure on both Milner and the secretary of the colonies to deal with the Boer problem once for all. Milner is sure England will win this war. The Boers are fierce fighters and stubborn. They won't be beaten easily. But in the end, Father, as in the Civil War in America, the Confederacy could never have won regardless of how well they fought. They lacked factories and the ability to make weapons and feed their armies. Once their farmlands were burned or decimated, they would be left to starvation. The Union took the war to the backyard of the Confederates. That made the difference between victory and defeat. Do you think our government doesn't know that? The Boers will be fighting on their own farmland."

"You're right, there. I suspect Chamberlain would agree with you."

"The gold and diamond boys have always wanted the Transvaal. Provoking Kruger is a ploy. They want him to react by issuing an ultimatum!"

Sir Lyle waved an airy hand. "No use getting upset, son. You can't change politics." And he went back to his writing. "Did you know," he commented a moment later, "that your great-great-uncle rode with the Norman Bohemond against the Seljuk Turks in the First Crusade? Most interesting."

Rogan looked down at him. Then in an act of frustration he turned. "I'm going to Pall Mall," he stated and strode from the library.

Evy stepped quickly past the door before Rogan came out into the hall, apparently not noticing her.

Now, what was all that about? But she was late for the village and wanted to avoid any delay. She watched him dash up the stairway and out of sight, then she hurried out the front door.

⚜ ⚜ ⚜

Rogan threw open the door to the sitting room. "Evy?"

He heard horse hoofs through the window and crossed the room to look outside. Evy was astride the golden mare he'd bought her from a horse-breeding farm in Dublin. The white mane of the horse flew majestically as Evy rode at a gallop down the lane toward Rookswood gate. *Where is she going?* He dropped the curtain and went into the bedroom to collect the information he intended to bring to Pall Mall to show the foreign secretary. He frowned as he read again the wire from Peter Bartley, his brother-in-law.

Wait till his father's old crony in Parliament hears this!

Peter believed that Sir Julien and Cecil Rhodes's right-hand man, Dr. Leander Starr Jameson, were planning to lead armed soldiers, up to six hundred hardened fighting men, to aid the Uitlanders in Pretoria, the capital of the Boer Transvaal, where President Kruger himself had his house and where the *Volksraad,* the Boer Transvaal Parliament, was located.

The Uitlanders were feared by the Boers, who naturally saw their growing influx over the recent years as a threat to their majority rule. The Uitlanders were not allowed to vote for members of the Volksraad until they had lived in the Transvaal for a number of years. That law, however, seemed fair enough to Rogan. Though he did not have strong feelings about the Boers, he did not want a pitched battle with them. Fighting at this time would also interfere with his plan for another expedition based on Henry's map as well as his search for Heyden. The vessel he had booked passage on was set to depart for the Cape in two weeks. He intended to allow nothing to hinder his boarding of that ship.

He drew his brows together as Evy came to mind. The decisions he made since marriage must now take into account what was best for her.

In some ways, even before the marriage, he had taken her into consideration, but he now felt a frustrating pull in two directions.

He deliberately turned his thoughts back to a troubling message that Arcilla had sent by wire that morning. The Uitlanders were suddenly stirring up trouble in Pretoria, accusing the Boers of mistreatment of British subjects and calling for London to intervene, with military might, if necessary, to protect them and their rights. Arcilla had written that Peter hinted the plot was "cooked up" by the gold and diamond moguls in order for Jameson and others in the BSA to secretly ride into Pretoria. Jameson had been assured by the leaders of the Uitlanders that they would rise up in rebellion, and together they would overthrow the Boers just as they had overthrown Lobengula and taken Bulawayo.

It was insane. Did Rhodes know about it? And what about Milner and Secretary Chamberlain?

Rogan thought of his father. Sir Lyle had many important friends in Parliament. He even knew Milner and Chamberlain, and when in London, he visited Chamberlain at his country house. Even so, after reading Arcilla's letter, Sir Lyle had merely waved a hand.

"You take our dear little Arcilla's word for anything of this magnitude?"

"Yes, and for the reason you just mentioned."

His father had looked at him with puzzled gray eyes.

"Arcilla would never come up with anything this shrewd on her own. This smells of Julien and Doc Jameson to me."

His father considered, then nodded. "Maybe so. Still, son, there is nothing I can do."

"Father, you can go straight to the Parliament."

"And bring down the wrath of the government on my head? I've my work here to do." And he patted his desk. "Here, I shall stay."

"Then I'll go."

"The one thing that worries me is Arcilla. If Julien discovers she sent that wire to you—"

Rogan frowned to himself, remembering his father's warning. He placed his sister's letter inside his jacket pocket and snatched his hat from the peg. His mind was made up. Arcilla was already at odds with Julien over Peter's career. There had also been that scandal in Capetown over Arcilla's foolish behavior. Julien had browbeaten her over that fiasco.

Maybe he should contact Peter about this first.

But could he rely on Peter to tell him the truth about a plot to invade the Transvaal? He could trust his brother-in-law about Arcilla, but little else. Peter, as yet, was astride two horses, struggling to keep them in rein.

His father, Rogan thought, irritated, was little better. The old frustrations welled up inside him. He loved his father, naturally. But not much could work him up except musty history!

Someone at Pall Mall must put pressure on Milner in Capetown to drop any plans for an invasion.

When would Evy return from her afternoon ride? He looked at the time. He quickly wrote her a note about where he would be and when he expected to return, then left Rookswood for London.

The summer leaves outside the medical-office window were red and gold. Evy finished dressing and was seated on the chair when the angular Dr. Tisdale entered with a benign smile.

"Well, dear Evy, you were right. You are going to have a baby. Congratulations! I'm certain this is happy news indeed for both you and Rogan."

The smile on her face had felt glued there for the last half hour. At any other time the news would have thrilled her. Weighing heavily upon her mind now was how this pregnancy would affect her plans to go to South Africa. From her own viewpoint, nothing could change her mind except a bedridden state. But it was Rogan's view that worried her. What would he say?

Evy paused, her hand on the doorknob, and turned back.

"Dr. Tisdale, I'll ask that you please not mention this to anyone until I speak to Rogan."

He drew himself up to look an inch taller, his professional countenance showing. "My dear Evy. As a doctor I never discuss the health of my patients with anyone except those immediately involved. I would not for any reason preclude your singular right and joy of informing Rogan that he's to become a father."

She blushed. "No, of course you wouldn't, Dr. Tisdale. I suppose I'm a bit flustered over the news."

His face mellowed into an understanding smile.

"Normal, my dear, quite normal. I saw you ride in on the horse. You be careful, now."

She might have protested a bit about personal "news" getting out and about the village. After all, what of her spinal injury? Her health and treatment were freely known by all in Grimston Way. In fairness to Dr. Tisdale, however, he was not the physician who handled her injury. Rogan had searched and found Dr. Jackson, a specialist on Harley Street in London.

Evy left the doctor's cottage on Rook Lane and walked slowly, thoughtfully, to Main Street. She was thinking of doing a little personal shopping at Mildred's Haberdashery, when she saw Mrs. Tisdale coming her way with her normal rolling gate. Mrs. Tisdale saw her and called cheerily.

Evy sighed.

"Oh, Mrs. Tisdale, hello." She smiled brightly as the woman walked up.

"Hello, my dear. Doing some shopping, are you? And where's that charming husband of yours hiding? My, I should think you would shop in London now…oh, did I see you leaving Alfred's office?" she asked of her husband, Dr. Tisdale.

"Uh—no, I—was just walking. Such a lovely afternoon, isn't it?"

Evy's conscience smote her. She saw the interest in Mrs. Tisdale's eyes sharpen.

"Rather a blanching afternoon, I thought. You do look chilled, dear. Your cheeks are pink... Well, ta ta, I've got to run. Take care, Evy." She started off down the walk. "Oh..." She stopped and looked back, calling, "Isn't that Lady Elosia's coach?"

Evy looked down the street. It *was*. Mr. Bixby was coming out of the apothecary shop with a small package. He handed it inside to Rogan's aunt.

"Ah," Mrs. Tisdale said, satisfied. "She's just the woman I need to see. Martha Osgood mentioned using some of Rookswood's chrysanthemums for the fall fete..." She stopped short again and looked at Evy with apology. "Oh. I could just as easily have asked you now that you're Mrs. Rogan Chantry, couldn't I? So difficult, you know. Thinking of you as the wife of our future squire. One just automatically thinks of Elosia." And she hurried off down the street, hailing Bixby before he could drive away.

Evy entered the haberdashery, not wishing to talk to Lady Elosia until she could gather her emotions and wits together. Had Mrs. Tisdale suspected she wasn't telling the truth?

Evy stood tiredly in front of a row of buttons and pins but hardly saw them. She placed her palm to her aching head and momentarily closed her eyes. *Oh, Father, forgive me for lying like that to Mrs. Tisdale. It was wrong.*

She didn't know what was coming over her lately. She seemed to be lax in her devotions, too. *I'm doing things I'd never do at the rectory when Uncle Edmund and Aunt Grace were alive.*

A sudden longing for Aunt Grace poured over her. But what would she and Uncle Edmund say if they were alive to see how she was compromising?

Suddenly, Aunt Grace's concerned face came out of the past, as though from the rectory when Evy was a girl. "You worry me," she often said. "You can be so careless in your behavior at times." Evy had wondered back then what Grace alluded to, and when she grew older, Grace commented on her propensity for willfulness. "You must have gotten it from your mother." At the time, Evy naturally thought she spoke of Junia, Grace's sister.

Willful? Am I?

Evy had never thought so until more recently. With time and marriage and no ties to the rectory, there were moments when she felt a stubborn streak emerging from the shadows of her personality and coming to the forefront. Even Rogan had made casual reference to it. He had jested that he was to blame for bringing it out in her. *"I'm afraid I've taught you some habits Mrs. Havering would speak to me about if she were alive,"* he had said in Paris on their honeymoon.

Where had it come from? An emerging streak of willfulness could not be from Grace's sister Junia, whom Evy thought back then was her mother, but from the beautiful, willful Katie, of course.

Still, she wished Aunt Grace were here now. She could go to her and feel her motherly arms around her, sharing the joy and excitement of the news of carrying her and Rogan's baby. It would strengthen her to face the onslaught that was sure to come.

"Evy? Are you ill?"

Evy turned swiftly to face the peering eyes of Mildred, the shopkeeper.

"Oh, I'm fine, Mildred. I…I was looking for some buttons… These are nice, I'll take them, please."

The old woman hurried to write up the bill as Evy dug into her coin purse to pay for the buttons.

"And how is Mr. Rogan?" Mildred asked curiously.

"He's doing well. Thank you for asking," Evy said as she handed Mildred a few coins.

"I'm so glad to hear that. I was worried."

Evy looked up from her coin purse to meet the kindly but curious eyes staring at her. "Oh?" Evy asked carefully.

"You see, I saw him just a short time ago as I was returning from the house. I took luncheon today with Hiram. Mr. Rogan was running and nearly collided with me."

"Oh, I am sorry!"

"No, no, dear, quite all right. He was profoundly apologetic. Said he must catch the train to London."

"Oh?"

"He looked very angry—not about me, of course."

"No, of course not…"

"He had the scowl of Scrooge, he did. Well, here's your buttons, Evy."

"Um, yes, thank you. Good day, Mildred."

Evy left the haberdashery. He'd gone to London. No doubt this was related to the talk in the library with Sir Lyle. He would have left her a note, but she was sure he would be back for dinner.

Evy drew her brows together as she walked to where her mare was tied in the shade of the big oak tree. *Mildred seems dreadfully curious about Rogan…making much of his anger, and probably now wondering why I didn't know that my own husband has just caught the train for London.*

Evy untied her mare and mounted, then rode slowly toward the winding road up the hill to Rookswood. She was deep in her spiritual wrestlings and did not hear the horse-drawn coach coming behind her until Mr. Bixby slowed down and maneuvered to one side of the tree-lined roadway. Lady Elosia leaned her head through the open window. Her large fancy black hat flapped untidily in the wind.

"There you are, dear girl!" her deep voice boomed. "Get down, do. Bixby!"

"Yes, madam."

"Tie Evy's mare to the back of the coach. Hurry, girl. It looks like rain."

Evy glanced up at the sky. Ominous dark clouds were streaming in from the north. She was in no mood to endure the criticism of Rogan's aunt. Still, there appeared no easy way out of the dilemma, as she rightfully respected Rogan's family. *I may be Mrs. Chantry, the future mistress of Rookswood, but to Lady Elosia I'll always be little Evy Varley from the vicarage.*

Evy climbed down from the saddle, handing the reins to Mr. Bixby, the dignified elderly man who carried himself with the bearing of a general. She lowered her voice. "You've just come from the village, Mr. Bixby?"

"Yes, miss—madam. Lady Elosia feared she was coming down with the autumn grippe and went to see Dr. Tisdale for tonic waters and bitters."

Dr. Tisdale. Evy's heart lurched. She glanced over at Lady Elosia, who was still looking out the coach window with a pale powdered face.

"She saw the doctor before or after she met Mrs. Tisdale, do you know?"

Was she mistaken, or was there a show of sympathy in his eyes?

"It was afterward, madam."

This was the worst possible thing to happen. She couldn't explain the truth to Elosia before she told Rogan, she simply couldn't. It wasn't fitting. Had the doctor let it slip? He had said he wouldn't, but Evy did not underestimate the wiles of Mrs. Tisdale, or Lady Elosia, for that matter. Had Mrs. Tisdale roused her curiosity? Evy knew the questions Elosia would ask her in the coach should her curiosity be aroused. *"Ah? Expecting, girl? Hmm? So soon!"*

Mr. Bixby opened the door. Evy squared her shoulders and gazed up into the coach, where Lady Elosia was seated.

Into the lion's den.

CHAPTER FIVE

Clouds, gray and drooping with rain, were swirling over Grimston Woods. The wind growled and chilled Evy with unfriendliness. She placed her foot on the step, and Mr. Bixby handed her up into the shiny black coach drawn by two Chantry horses of white and speckled gray.

As she entered the coach, taking the seat across from Lady Elosia, Evy spied her face, as unsmiling as the autumn weather, and noticed her age showed more than usual, though a generous sprinkling of corn-powder had been applied. Evy thought the powder didn't help. When a woman was older, her face should be painted more moderately, she thought. She liked Lady Elosia, and had even when a young girl, but there was no denying that she was an intimidating woman, even perhaps forbidding.

Large-boned and nearly six feet tall, Elosia was what Evy thought of as "ferociously elegant." Today she wore a satiny black skirt and white blouse with leg-of-mutton sleeves with cuffs and collars trimmed with some kind of fur. She'd been lectured while growing up not to try to hide the fact of her height, but to show pride. She wore her shoulders thrown back with a challenge that dared comment and looked as though she used a backboard when sitting. Her hair was her crowning embellishment—an unusual gray-gold.

Lady Elosia had chosen not to marry. Rogan once spoke of a bitter-sweet romance that went afoul in her past. It was difficult for Evy to understand her motives, but it appeared Elosia found purpose for her life by wielding authority, a miniature Queen Victoria over Grimston Way and Rookswood. She was, for all practical purposes, the real squire in the village, for her younger brother, Sir Lyle, had gladly yielded most matters over to her after the death of his wife.

And that, thought Evy, precipitated a situation in which she might be perceived as a dark moon rising. Evy was in line to be mistress of Rookswood when Rogan eventually became squire after the death of his father. Perhaps Elosia envisioned the authority entrusted to her to be headed toward the lamentable throes of decline.

Evy settled herself on the plush leather seat, adjusting her hat and slipping off her riding gloves. In the close quarters she turned her face to the side to avoid looking directly at Elosia.

With a little lurch the coach started down the tree-shadowed road.

"A dreadful afternoon to be out riding," Elosia stated, glancing Evy over as though she'd had something nefarious to do with the approaching storm. "I'm surprised you'd permit yourself to be caught in it. I don't know how Rogan has adapted to the insufferable weather in South Africa. Dreadful heat, I'm told; insects, too. Most disturbing. I can't see why he wishes to return to that dreaded land. It must be your insistence on meeting your mother's Boer relatives. Dr. Jakob van Buren, I believe is his name?"

Evy tried to ignore the slight to her mother's family. "Dr. Jakob is a medical missionary. He was acquainted with Robert Moffat and his Kuruman mission station."

"Both fine gentlemen, I am sure, but with your spine you are hardly capable of following such mighty footsteps. Far better, if you simply must urge Rogan to the Dark Continent, to stay in Capetown and visit Arcilla."

It would have been fruitless to point out that it was Rogan who chartered his travels to South Africa and had done so from the beginning without Evy's encouragement.

"Arcilla's in Bulawayo with Peter, not in Capetown," Evy troubled to remind Elosia.

"Oh quite so, quite so. However, dear girl, if you were to stay at Cape House instead of traipsing off to that Zambezi, Arcilla would have a convincing reason for Sir Julien to let her leave that perilous place."

Evy sensed more than one conflict in Elosia's expectations. On the one hand, Evy was considered selfishly motivated by insisting upon seeing Dr. Jakob at the mission station in Zambezi; but on the other, if she did go, she should choose the comforts of Capetown instead of the treacherous mission station in order to provide Arcilla the excuse she needed to leave Bulawayo for Capetown.

Elosia shuddered with distaste. "Why England should even bother with that wretched land is beyond me."

"Gold and diamonds," Evy said with affected sobriety.

Lady Elosia, who was amply laden with both commodities, changed the subject.

"I saw Mrs. Croft in the village a short while ago. Such a hearty, consoling woman. She did say you wanted to hire her."

"Yes, I asked her to come to work at Rookswood."

"We have Mrs. Wetherly. An astute housekeeper. And Bertha has been cook for simply eons. Mrs. Croft's arrival would only cause short feelings, I'm afraid."

"I wasn't thinking of replacing Mrs. Wetherly or Bertha. I was thinking of Mrs. Croft for Rogan and me, in our suite." Evy tried to keep the tension from her voice and avoided saying *private* suite.

"Oh, I should think Rogan is quite used to things the way they are. By the bye, it is quite time for some social entertaining at Rookswood. Since you and Rogan came home, there's been no entertaining of any kind. London is beginning to talk."

Evy's heart quailed. "Talk? About what?"

"Your lack of entertaining, dear girl. Dinner parties, weekend guests for hunts, or musicals in the Great Hall. You simply must have social commitments. I do hope Rogan isn't going to take after Lyle and avoid interest in important functions. It is quite expected of him, you know. I'm sure you realize as much. As his wife you'll do your best for his sake.

Of course I realize your upbringing down at the rectory leaves you socially—well, 'unprepared' shall we say? Nonetheless, do realize it is considerably important to be accomplished at handling these sorts of social matters with a certain finesse."

Evy's cheeks warmed. "I can assure you that Rogan has hardly been fretting over a lack of dinner parties, Lady Elosia." *Though you might be.* "Actually, he's been occupied with South Africa recently."

"My dear girl! You quite miss the point."

Evy understood well enough. Disparaging comments on her lack of social graces had recurred during the last two months, though they were never heard in Rogan's presence. Evy was beginning to wish she felt more secure about belonging at Rookswood.

"One thing about Lady Patricia," Elosia continued, "although a gloomy girl, and I quite see the reason Rogan did not wish to be saddled with her, is that she does have good blood, you know. Really, quite good. Comes from a long line of lords, by the way. With, I believe, an earl in the family line somewhere...yes, Earl of Radbury. Beheaded at the time of King James. So, I daresay, she knows what is expected of her socially."

Though Evy's humble upbringing and respect for Rogan's aunt kept a few well-chosen words from spewing past her tongue, her heart was far from enjoying the untroubled peace she portrayed. She could easily have reminded her aunt that if Rogan had wanted to marry a socially adept snob, he could easily have done so.

"Evy, my dear! I hardly think you are listening to a word I've spoken," came the injured tone.

"I am sorry, Aunt Elosia, I...was listening. I'm a bit tired is all, and would like to rest in my room this afternoon."

Elosia turned prominent pearl gray eyes upon her, and for a moment Evy felt like a butterfly specimen pinned to a board.

"Not feeling well, are you? Odd."

"Not odd, when the fear of the fall grippe is prevalent."

"That reminds me—"

Evy tensed and waited for the coming onslaught. A mistake to have even hinted of illness. *Oh, Lord, I'm trapped, and I don't know how to avoid the net.*

"Guess who I ran into when I was leaving Dr. Tisdale's? Mrs. Florence Tisdale."

"Oh? How interesting." Evy kept gazing out the window. She could sense it coming now, a boiling cauldron about to be poured over her.

"She wearies me with that constant twaddle of news about Alice. Another child, she has, Florence says. That makes three now for Alice and that lanky redheaded boy, Derwent, or is it four? I simply cannot keep up with the population in Grimston Way. And of course Florence wanted to know all about dear Arcilla and Peter. She was delighted to hear of Peter's elevation. He's assistant native commissioner now. Arcilla now has a baby boy, I told her. She asked about Rogan, of course, and you, said you were not well and had been in to see Dr. Tisdale this morning." She turned her head and fixed a steady stare upon Evy.

"Oh. Did she? Extraordinary," Evy breathed. "I wonder where she came up with that notion? Um, that I was ill, I mean? Did she say Dr. Tisdale thought so?"

Evy felt her face growing hot, and her hands turning cold. She would play dumb—evade the truth.

"I gather he did say you'd been in to see him," Elosia stated.

In to see him, but he must not have told his wife the reason.

"You're not in the 'delicate' way…already?"

Evy held her breath. "Delicate way?" she asked finally, while resorting to wide-eyed bewilderment.

"Pregnant," Elosia whispered, the line between her brows deepening with impatience.

There it was…that telling word.

"Is that what Mrs. Tisdale told you?" Evy delayed.

"Florence is dreadfully curious, you know. She does a lot of shuffling around the tulip garden without actually coming out and asking directly. The topic of babies seems to fill her mind these days. And then, gossip does skitter about, you know, and Patricia thought… Well, we shan't get into that! I hardly think it would prove tasteful."

At least Lady Elosia didn't believe the malicious story Patricia had sown in London at Brewster House! Evy felt more kindly inclined toward Elosia for that bit of good sense.

"Now that you've brought up the topic, I'll go right ahead and say what I think of the horribly mean way in which she lied about me and Rogan in London." Evy felt her heart thumping and her cheeks warm again. She leaned forward, clasping her package of buttons. "How *dare* she say that I had compromised myself with Rogan in order to steal him from her? That's what her gossip is meant to imply."

Lady Elosia looked upset. "She remains bitterly disappointed about losing Rogan."

"I've taken no malicious pleasure in her loss. Why then does she cast stones at me?" She smarted, remembering how the young woman's rumor had soiled her honeymoon in London.

Elosia shrugged and sighed. "Lord Bancroft is a highly respected man in Parliament. A man of powerful influence. The Bancrofts are not accustomed to embarrassment. You'll need to learn that people can be cruel when they lose."

"I'm becoming well aware of that." Evy sank back against the leather seat with an air of weariness. "Rogan and I are married now. One would think Patricia would tuck in her claws and seek her future. Surely there are other young men who interest her. She is quite attractive— physically. It's not only unkind but a waste of her time to get even with Rogan using lies and gossip."

Elosia laid a jeweled hand against her forehead and closed her eyes. "I knew it was coming all along…the autumn grippe. I could feel it this morning when I awoke, like damp fingers of fog. I must take my tonic 'n' bitters soon as we get home. Now! What was I saying? Oh yes. Perhaps I was wrong about entertaining at Rookswood this season. It's unfortunate you've become so vulnerable in these matters. I must talk to Rogan. He will need to keep you from being devoured in the social arena." She heaved a sigh, as though the worst was about to confront them—so now she would hoist the drawbridge against invaders.

Evy knew a sudden moment of dismay. What would they think when they heard she would be having a child; would it not vindicate Patricia's gossip?

"Oh, I'd nearly forgotten. Here, my girl, this is yours." Elosia pulled an envelope from her handbag. "Bixby gave me the mail as we were leaving for the village. Perfectly silly of him. I cannot think why he did so. As though I had nothing better to do than cart about the day's post!" She shook her head. "I do believe Bixby's becoming senile. I suspect this batch was really yesterday's, and he left it on the driver's seat. He must have realized he'd left it there as we were about to leave for the village. Shameful, really… Rogan won't like it if he finds out. He's very particular about his mail. Wants it immediately upon arrival…he told me he's expecting a parcel from Derwent Brown." She looked at her pointedly. "Do you know what's so important in the parcel?"

It was the first Evy had heard about expecting a parcel from Derwent. Her own interest at the moment was fixed on the envelope she held sent from Fort Salisbury.

"A parcel?" Evy murmured.

"Couldn't be diamonds?"

Evy gripped the envelope. From Dr. Jakob van Buren. Her mother's cousin must have written from his mission station, but it was marked Bulawayo, not Fort Salisbury; why? She wanted to open it then and there, but Lady Elosia was still conversing, this time about Arcilla, and Evy preferred to be alone with her heart's emotions when she read the letter.

"Darling Arcilla, I still worry about her in that heathen land. And Peter!" She made a throaty sound of utter dismay. "Oh, what a ghastly mistake for her to have married the fellow. I told Lyle. I told Julien. Men! They never listen. It should have been dear Charles Bancroft whom she married. Dear 'civilized' Charles. Julien's infernal meddling is barbarous. By the bye—" The wintry gray eyes settled upon Evy.

"Julien is fuming about your marriage. He wrote a decidedly ireful letter to Rogan."

Learning of Sir Julien's displeasure was disturbing, but it didn't surprise her. Rogan hadn't told her about the letter.

"From the beginning, Sir Julien knew I was Katie and Anthony's child, yet he kept the truth hidden. You may not know this, Lady Elosia, but in South Africa he convinced Rogan that I was Henry Chantry's daughter by Katie, hoping to keep us apart."

"I daresay, if Julien withheld information from Rogan about your birth, it was because of his concerns. He feared you would turn out like your mother Katie, who, I was told, was a complete runaround. She made a blundering fool out of poor Anthony."

Evy doubted that was Sir Julien's reason for opposing the marriage. He had wanted Rogan to marry Patricia because Lord Bancroft had friendly contact with those in Parliament who held sway over British interests in South Africa.

As for her mother making a fool of Anthony, she doubted that. Evy believed her biological parents were equally in the wrong.

She ran away from Julien's house to find me. Evy knew the same hurt tugging at her heart as she thought of her young mother being killed in the Zulu attack at Rorke's Drift while trying to save her. In the end it was the Zulu woman Jendaya who saved her, while Katie ended up being killed. This made her think of Dr. Jakob's letter. Would he mention Jendaya? If only they would get home to Rookswood so she could escape to her room and read it away from prying eyes.

"Even so, dear girl, you will never find me defending Julien Bley. I've never trusted him. He's as thick as Michaelmas pudding with Cecil Rhodes's men, and that, according to Arcilla, has put Peter at risk."

Perhaps Lady Elosia knew about Arcilla's wire to Rogan about Sir Julien and Dr. Jameson wishing to provoke an uprising of the Uitlanders at Pretoria. Evidently, since Peter was assistant administrator to Julien and privy to any secret decisions, Arcilla must worry that Peter could be risking himself to trouble with the London authorities.

"I also think it's incredibly scandalous the way Julien's making a fool of Parnell by continuing to delay his marriage to Darinda Bley."

"Darinda is Julien's granddaughter. One would think she would necessarily have a mind of her own on the matter," Evy said. "Rogan seems to think she's quite independent. So if she were in love with his brother, nothing would stop her."

"No, no, Darinda is under Julien's thumb and always has been, though Rogan's right about her strong personality. Julien knows she wants a bigger role in running the diamond business, and to get her way she would cooperate with him."

"Everyone appears to do what Julien demands except Rogan." Evy felt a sense of pride in Rogan.

"Yes, two stags butting heads. But enough of Capetown… As for you, Evy girl, it is important how one comports oneself. You must make quite certain the villagers understand your new position as Rogan's wife. You must never let anyone think for a moment that you are still Evy Varley the rectory girl."

Except you.

"The villagers fully expect you to behave as the future squire's lady," Elosia continued her lecture. "One must not hobnob too much with the shoemaker and baker, you know. Not without reminding them who you are."

Who I am. She was God's child, that's who she was, having partaken of the one true spiritual birth that mattered.

Concerning her status as a diamond heiress through her mother, Rogan was still waiting for Sir Julien's lawyer at Capetown to send the mountain of documents from South Africa to Rogan's own lawyer that would explain how much her legacy was worth. So far, little information had been exchanged. Rogan believed that was due to Julien's influence. That was another reason Rogan was anxious to leave for Capetown soon. But Evy wondered if there might not be yet another reason why Julien did not want her at the Cape.

Evy continued to hold the envelope in her lap from Cousin Jakob van Buren. *I can't fight everyone and everything standing in opposition to me. Now I'm expecting a child. What shall I do?* Anxiety nagged at her. Change rode the winds, and what would it bring? What would it mean for her and Rogan?

And the baby—what would Rogan say? *This will change everything for him, for us, for our plans.*

And the gossip! This would be dry kindling for the flame. *So soon!* some in Grimston Way would say. *Too* soon, so London would *choose* to believe.

Evy's fingers lifted from the envelope to the diamond cross at her throat. A conviction came to her heart reminding her that she had as yet to bring all of these troubling details to her heavenly Father in prayer. She must get alone with the Lord, with Jakob's letter, and spend time before the Lord—

"What lovely blue diamonds." Lady Elosia lifted her pince-nez and zeroed in on the cross pendant at Evy's throat. "From Rogan?"

"Yes, in London, on our honeymoon." Evy fingered the cross, remembering his words. *"For my rectory girl. The girl who prayed, read the Bible, a girl of innocence and truthfulness."*

Truthfulness...

CHAPTER SIX

Finally, alone in her room at Rookswood, Evy read the letter from her mother's cousin, Dr. Jakob van Buren.

> *My dear Evy,*
>
> *Happy word has reached me of your marriage to Rogan Chantry. I send you both my heartfelt felicitations. May our Savior Jesus guide and bless this union for His eternal purposes. It is good, indeed, that you are coming to South Africa, back to the place of your birth. I anxiously await meeting Katie's daughter. I felt it was needful to correspond with you and to let you know that by the time you arrive at Capetown I will no longer be in the Zambezi region.*

Disappointment welled up inside Evy. Would he go to the Transvaal where the van Burens lived? She read on.

> *With a mixture of joy and sadness, I will be turning over the mission station here on the Zambezi to my medical partners, Dr. Nathan and Gerta Swanson from Holland. With joy, because an established work will doubtless continue to bring forth much fruit for our Lord. With sadness, because I shall not come this way again and will find it difficult to leave a people and a work I have poured so much of myself into.*

But our Lord has another purpose for me. I will journey to Bulawayo to open a new medical mission there.

There are great spiritual and medical needs at Bulawayo among both the Ndebele and Shona. By the time you and Rogan arrive, I hope to have a clinic and chapel under construction.

The letter went on in the same vein. There was no mention of Heyden, but then he would hardly seek out Dr. Jakob. He wouldn't know whether or not the authorities had been alerted to watch for him.

Evy didn't want to think of that now. She preferred to relish the news of a new mission station at Bulawayo. This was favorable, since the long trek inland to the Zambezi River would no longer be necessary. It was that arduous trip northward that had her and Rogan so concerned. She thought again of what she'd learned from Dr. Tisdale.

She was under no illusion, however. Bulawayo remained a demanding journey. But she would meet and become acquainted with Dr. Jakob and his work at Bulawayo, and Arcilla as well would be there.

A day after Rogan's return from London, Evy rode side by side with him on one of their favorite trails through Grimston Woods. Before leaving, she had told him the news of Jakob at Bulawayo, which she thought would have encouraged him, but such was not the case. If anything, Rogan seemed more concerned about her going with him to Capetown than before he'd gone to London to see Lord Salisbury.

"There will be war," he had told her yesterday after his return from London, "and I don't think anyone can stop it. And England is under the false impression it will be short. They underrate the Boer fighter, and they underestimate Kruger."

This morning Rogan was astride King's Knight, upon which he'd once won ribbons at the Dublin horse show. The horse had fully recovered from the glancing bullet wound it had taken from Heyden van Buren, which Heyden had intended for Rogan.

Evy rode her golden mare with a shiny cream-colored mane. She was proud of the beautiful horse, and she remembered fondly when Rogan had brought it to her.

She felt the wind that bore the first promise of a chilling autumn, yet hardly noticed the cold. Her dilemma still burned in her heart. How would she tell Rogan the news that he was going to be a father much sooner than he'd anticipated?

Rogan seemed in no easy mood. Could it be because he was expecting a parcel from Derwent, a report on the gold mine? They were to sail for Capetown in two weeks. Passage aboard the *Venture* was bought, and plans were made. Oh, how could this happen now? And yet—was not her loving heavenly Father in control of so wonderful a miracle as a human life? Should she not be happy with her plight? A sweet baby—*Rogan's* baby! A smile tugged at her mouth. At any other time the news would have thrilled her.

But *now*. Now! After the wicked lies that Lady Patricia had spread in London. She gripped the reins too tightly. Patricia would now be able to convince herself she was right, that Rogan had rejected Patricia, not because he hadn't wanted her, but because he had no choice but to marry the village girl! Patricia would console herself among her friends, thinking she'd been vindicated, especially after Rogan had shown pride in Evy at the Brewster dinner ball, parading her up to the piano to accompany him. That must have gnawed at her.

And Rogan—Evy now needed his support, his strength, but would he give it selflessly? Though he'd agreed that she could sail with him to meet Cousin Jakob, Rogan still had reservations, nor did he hesitate to occasionally voice them.

She looked over at him, biting her lip, unable to feel that she could reach through the armor to make him agree with her wish to sail. She would have liked to lay her hand to his heart and feel it beat as one with her own, and with *their* baby's.

Rogan had never previously been called upon to surrender his plans for the good of another. And now, he found himself joined to her. His thoughts were not for himself alone, but for her, and now there would also be…their child. How would he react?

She watched him intently as they rode along together. She sensed their thoughts were miles apart. Those rich brown eyes she loved so much were full of energy when his mind moved into troubling areas, areas that recently excluded her: thoughts over the Boer war, the gold mine, the Black Diamond, the Matopos Hills, and the Umlimo, as well as Julien and Heyden…

This morning, before she'd suggested the ride after breakfast—a breakfast she had not eaten but secretly disposed of—she had seen Rogan looking at his Uncle Henry's old map again. Why, she did not know. She was so absorbed with her own dilemma that she had little reserve acquisitiveness. Thus, again, their minds and hearts were not uniting. Why must she bear this worry alone? Why could she not simply tell him about the baby, and how she feared he would tell her to stay behind?

But she believed she knew what he would say. He would quickly determine that her pregnancy had tilted the scale in favor of caution. He would point out the importance of her remaining safely at Rookswood. The most depressing thing was that she could see some wisdom in that decision.

And yet she knew she must be aboard the ship when it left the port for Capetown and Cousin Jakob van Buren. The rendezvous with Katie's relatives had to proceed. She would visit Rorke's Drift, Katie's grave—it must be out there—and Dr. Clyde and Junia Varley's resting places as well.

They rode along the musky autumn trail through the thickening wood. Fir trees were predominant here, and woodpeckers and squirrels were racing up and down the trunks.

Her loving gaze took Rogan in, but with a bit of worry as well. Rugged and forceful as ever, he was wearing a hunter green jacket over an open neck shirt and a jaunty brown felt hat. He brought his black gelding with an easy grace to the stream facing the ascending hill with encrusted boulders and fir trees. The ends of his dark hair ruffled in the pleasant pine-scented breeze.

"You're as enigmatic now as you were before we were married," she complained.

"Indeed? Why so?"

"You don't share things with me. You don't discuss your concerns."

"You've said that before. Look, sweet, it makes no sense to be chattering like magpies without saying anything."

She smiled ruefully as he looked over at her with a ghost of a smile.

"One kiss," he said meaningfully, "is worth a thousand words."

Evy laughed. "I don't mean that sort of thing. I think you know what I mean, about explaining and sharing things. You keep me locked out of your mind, your plans, *our* plans."

And it makes it more difficult for me to tell you things. Troubling things.

His smile was crooked. "Yes, I know. You want me to become talkative and cuddly."

She drew back, feigning distress. "Cuddly! *You?*"

"Cuddly," he repeated with mock gravity. "By telling you every detail of how I *feel* inside about everything from Aunt Elosia's meddling—as you perceive it—to whether Heyden will hang, or," he added firmly, "whether I intend to shoot the Boer clod soon as I lay my eyes on him."

Evy twisted her lip into what was meant as a benign smirk. "You forgot to add the rumor of Dr. Jameson's invasion of the Transvaal on behalf of the Uitlanders at Pretoria, or Sir Julien's expedition into the Matopos."

"I told you all about that the other night. You know what I think of Julien and the Matopos. It's insanity," he scoffed. "He knows he can't get by with that kind of action without bloodshed. Julien is not a fool when it comes to the Ndebele tribe and what they believe. If he insists on seeking Lobengula's burial spot, he'll place Arcilla, Darinda, and others in danger. He knows they are right there in the thick of it, at Bulawayo."

She lapsed into immediate silence. Any mention of women in the thick of danger spoke with pointed emphasis to her own "delicate" predicament. Discussing Bulawayo now would not do.

"Julien thinks too much of his granddaughter, Darinda, to start out on a reckless expedition now," Rogan said in a thoughtful voice. "He'll need to think of some shrewd way to move without the Ndebele knowing what he's up to. That will require patience on Julien's part, and the delay is to my benefit. If only the ship were sailing tomorrow instead of in two more weeks."

His fiery gaze swung abruptly to hers. She sensed resistance to her going and quickly changed the subject.

"Cuddly," she repeated with a short laugh. "You make sharing our thoughts sound a bit squishy."

His brow lifted. "Squishy and cuddly. I don't like either."

"It isn't either one, and you know it, Rogan. You're deliberately being difficult. Aunt Grace and Uncle Edmund discussed everything."

"Did they? Vicar Edmund was a talkative fellow, as I recall. He often overran his sermons. Never seemed to run out of words." A smile danced in his eyes as he looked at her.

"And you should have listened—but instead you sat in the pew with your book on Africa."

"I heard every word he said when he stayed with Scripture. Most times he wandered."

She ignored that. "Uncle Edmund talked to Grace about everything interesting in the *London Times,* or about whether to plant vegetable marrow or turnips."

"That's where he went awry."

She wasn't progressing very well—she had better just jump in all the way. "Why, Uncle Edmund even discussed—Grace's pregnancy." She glanced at him sideways. *Pregnancy.* Would he pick up the verbal gauntlet?

"Names, I suppose…shall we call him Harry or Harriet. Arthur or Anabelle."

She narrowed her eyes. He was deliberately teasing her. "No. Not names." She grew sober, about to unleash the secret. "He discussed her pregnancy. *Their* pregnancy, actually. Uncle Edmund saw it that way."

"Very astute of him."

"There! You see?" she half accused. "You didn't even ask me, 'What pregnancy?' You know they never had any children. Why didn't you ask what happened to the baby?"

"It's rather obvious, darling. She had to have lost it."

"She did. Aunt Grace was depressed for years about it. I think that was one reason Edmund took me in."

"Undoubtedly. Good thing he did, though." He looked at her with a winsome grin. "Just think, there'd have been no girl at the rectory for me to fall in love with. Think of all I'd have missed if ol' Henry hadn't brought you back from Africa on the ship."

"Yes, like teasing and taunting me all those years."

"I much preferred to have been courting you, but you made that a challenging effort."

"Mostly because of what I learned from Aunt Grace and Uncle Edmund," she said cheerfully. "About her miscarriage… It was very serious to her." Evy looked at him intensely.

Rogan leaned over and patted the strong neck of his black horse.

She continued. "So Uncle Edmund told her how he felt inside about it all. By talking about their loss, he strengthened her. It was a sorrow they shared."

His face was unreadable.

Her fingers began to move more quickly over the reins she held. "How would you feel, Rogan?"

He scowled. "About a miscarriage? Good grief, Evy! How do you think I'd feel?"

"No, no, not a miscarriage, about a baby—our baby. That is," she hastened, "if God should give us children?"

"I surrender," he said glibly, throwing up his hands in a gesture of dismay. "I assume I'm failing in some way, and it has to do with communicating. I agree to do better. We're talking now, are we not?"

"Well yes, but—" She stopped.

"There, you see? I'm right."

"About what?"

"Just this. I'll wager you hardly know yourself what you want from me when it comes to understanding you. And that's what you really mean, isn't it? About talking? You're saying I lack understanding about how you *feel*. You want to *share* heart to heart."

"Yes, Rogan, oh yes!"

He grinned. "Bravo, Rogan! I've come out of the fog. But, Evy, of course I understand you. I've always understood you. Even when you were a girl, I knew you secretly adored me—since we were fourteen."

"Oh, what conceit!"

"Not at all. Because I felt the same way. We usually hid it, but you more than I."

"I wouldn't say that…"

"I understand you now, much better than you think."

She looked at him swiftly. But he was fussing with the horse bridle again. Deliberately?

"It's not just about understanding *me*. I want to understand you better too," she said. She tried to judge his reaction again. "And the plans we have for *our* future."

"That's just the problem, sweet. Right now things are so unsettled with war, and all. We sail in two weeks, but who knows? That ruddy Jameson and Milner might do something foolish, and guns will begin blazing. A pity Her Majesty doesn't know what's going on in South Africa. I'm sure she hears only what the prime minister wants her to hear." He looked over at her, and his gaze became tender. "You would hardly be interested in war and politics, darling. Haven't you preferable things with which to concern yourself? Elosia claims you don't take enough interest in the social life at Rookswood."

Evy's temper spiked. "That's another thing, Rogan. You don't help me with Lady Elosia. I've mentioned before how she's part of the problem."

"Elosia has always been a problem, and no doubt will remain so," he stated lightly. "She's an old bear, and her cub is Rookswood. She will do whatever to protect it."

She looked at him, surprised. Then he did understand the tenseness between the two women over running Rookswood.

"Thank goodness I don't need to run the estate now," she said. "I hardly think I'm ready for that."

"It's not mine until my father passes on. Let's hope the Lord keeps him around for many years. I'm not ready either. The last thing I want now is to take on the added role of squire. There will be plenty of time later on to settle down with all those responsibilities."

Her heart shivered. He did not want the added burden of responsibility yet. A baby would change everything.

"Even so, your aunt treats me like a child."

"She treated Arcilla that way. Arcilla warmed to being coddled. There's the warm, fuzzy word again. No—it was cuddly, wasn't it?"

"I'm not Arcilla. Your aunt adores Arcilla. She doesn't adore me."

"Of course she does. Who would not adore my beautiful Evy?"

"Lady Elosia—and Lady Patricia, for two," she murmured dryly.

"Ah, *that*. Forget all that nonsense. It doesn't matter about Patricia. Her chatter is meaningless to anyone with sense. And those who have no sense will believe anything. There's no convincing them of your character. Jealousy can only see through distorted vision."

She smiled softly. "Thank you for saying that, Rogan."

He looked at her quickly, regarding her with some puzzlement. "I would have thought you would know how I felt without my saying it. It's so obvious. Your character, I mean."

"I like to hear you say it anyway."

"I'll remember that."

"If I did take a greater interest in running Rookswood the way your aunt claims I do not, she'd be on me as fast as a crow in the standing corn."

He laughed. "Don't let her ever hear you compare her to a crow, darling. I should hate to come to loggerheads with dear old Elosia."

That's just it. No one does, Evy thought.

"Oh, don't misunderstand. I do love her," she said. "I really do, but she can be—well, cruel, if you want to know."

He looked startled and thought about it.

"Cruel? I can hardly imagine that. She means well. She came here after Mother died and took over."

"Exactly, and she doesn't want to surrender the reins," Evy might have said, but she felt as though she might have already said enough. It was clear that Rogan didn't see his aunt as she did. The trouble had only begun in the last few weeks. Lady Elosia appeared to go out of her way to make her feel inadequate, and even inferior to the Chantry name. Her mind went back to the conversation in the coach, but Evy would not bring that up, for Rogan might ask what she was doing in the village.

Keeping the truth from Rogan is leading to some complications, she thought uneasily.

Evy remembered when Rogan's mother, Lady Honoria Chantry, died when they were children. Arcilla had taken her mother's death terribly hard, and Sir Lyle had sent for his older maiden sister Elosia, a dowager in London society. Elosia had tried to fill Honoria's shoes, and Rogan's father had been pleased.

Rogan maneuvered his horse closer beside her, took hold of her arm, and squeezed it.

"Darling Evy, you've no reason to feel insecure at Rookswood around my aunt, or around anyone else. You are my wife. I'm proud of you. That's what matters. No one is running me, least of all dear old Aunt Elosia. She's no threat, believe me. So why should we get up in arms about the dear old mistress and her imperious ways?"

That he was proud of her, regardless of the various insinuations, warmed her heart. She could have told him that his aunt's fussiness smothered her, but she held back out of respect for his family.

She was Rogan's wife, yes, but exactly where did she fit into this old, established household? Anything she may wish to accomplish at Rookswood must first pass muster with Lady Elosia. And Evy was sure that whatever it was, even if perfectly fine, would be deemed inadequate by his aunt.

Sir Lyle was another matter. He treated her kindly, and while he, too, had wanted, or at least expected, his younger son to marry into the Bancrofts, Lyle did not lament or fuss over it. He was much too indifferent for that sort of behavior. Sir Lyle was indeed the very opposite of his sister Elosia. As Rogan told her when they first came home to Rookswood after their honeymoon, "Don't expect much from my father. He doesn't take much concern over what goes on as long as he can work with his myriad books and musty histories in the library."

Evy knew that and respected his individuality, but she did wonder, as she had for years, how he could have produced Rogan. Sir Lyle's indifference had been clearly shown a day earlier when Rogan had gone to the library to urge him to act on Arcilla's letter.

"I don't think Aunt Elosia has forgiven me for what she believes was my coming between you and Patricia. She liked Patricia and wanted you to marry her."

He smiled. "You *did* come between Patricia and me. You quite overshadowed her. But I think you're too sensitive when you say Elosia doesn't like you. She thinks highly of you."

Sensitive or not, it was not her imagination. Rogan just didn't see the change in Lady Elosia when he was not around.

"Elosia wasn't against our marriage, if you remember," he went on. "Nor was my father, so forget your fears, Evy. Fact is, every one of us must do some adjusting. You, too, my sweet. I cannot very well order Elosia back to London—or is that what you want me to do?"

"Oh no, that's not what I meant," she hastened, feeling suddenly beastly because it had entered her mind to wish she might go of her own will. After all, she had come years ago to nurse Arcilla out of her grief, and those days had passed. But Evy could see that Rogan was not ready to hear that.

"I suppose it would be very audacious of me to expect such a thing," she said.

He looked at her a long moment. "Not audacious, exactly. You are to be mistress of Rookswood when I inherit the lands and title after Father dies. But perhaps it would be unbecoming of you should you insist. Odd, I never thought of any of this before we married. It's not pleasant to think about now." He scowled to himself.

"That's just it," she said suddenly. "I need you to think about it. Not just Elosia, but other things as well. What is my place? What is expected of me?"

His lines of impatience showed. She could see that he'd had more than enough of all the new things he needed to consider.

"You should know your place. By my side. Do you want me to bore you with details?"

"Yes," she challenged.

"What I'm thinking!" The spark of temper suddenly showed in his eyes.

"Yes. About you and me, marriage…Rookswood, having a baby…" She glanced at him. "Would you be very disappointed if we did have a child?"

He turned in the saddle to look at her long and hard, until she felt the warmth in her face.

His inky lashes narrowed. His jaw set. "Are you trying to tell me something, Evy?"

"Well…yes." She did not know why, but she blushed, which seemed silly, but she could not control her reaction. "What if, after all the nasty gossip on our honeymoon, I—we were going to have a baby much sooner than we anticipated?"

He looked at her in stern silence.

"People would talk," she said in a choked whisper. "They'd feel they were right. Wouldn't they? They'd say it was awfully *soon.*"

Rogan made no comment.

What is he thinking?

"And, of course," she continued a moment later, "it would be soon, I mean too soon. I mean—that Arcilla and Peter didn't have a baby for two years—and Alice and Derwent, as well."

The wind blew around them, rustling the yellow and golden-red leaves.

His fingers enclosed around her arm again, while his gaze held hers.

"Are you?" he asked quietly.

Her eyes faltered under his penetrating, heated gaze. Now was the moment. She must tell him. But why this way? She wanted to cry. The news should be a joyful moment as they embraced and loved each other, relishing what the great Creator had done, performing a miracle of life in her womb.

She felt his intense gaze, his fingers tightening on her arm, and her own desperate desire not to let the news ruin her plans to go with him to Capetown.

"I...I don't, I hardly think so."

"Then why bring it up?" he clipped, his hand releasing her arm, as though irritated she'd introduced something so emotionally disturbing when there was no need.

"I don't know..." She was very tired now. She had withheld the truth from him and compromised. Now she felt disillusioned with herself and depressed.

"You've never mentioned how you'd feel about it if...if I were." Her voice was but a whisper.

His lashes narrowed. He studied her carefully. "How do you think I'd feel?"

"How should I know? You've never even hinted you knew babies existed." She was getting angry now. Nothing was going as she wanted.

Their relationship was already tarnished. She had withheld something precious that Rogan had every right to know.

"My dear," he said in a labored voice, "I assure you I know babies exist and where the sweet little bunchkins come from. That doesn't mean I want one this instant."

A pain flashed through her heart.

She looked at him, searching his face, seeing little except frustration. She had done this to him; she knew that. She had handled matters badly.

"I know you don't," she said stiffly. "Anyone can tell that."

"Now, wait a minute. What do you mean to suggest by that?"

"I mean that you think I'm burden enough." Feelings of self-pity bubbled up from her heart. "Me and my limp, my silly chatter, my inconsequential difficulties with your oh-so-beloved aunt. Oh yes, I know it all very well."

"Evy, what has come over you?" he gritted. "You're…different."

"That's not true." Was she? More sentimental perhaps? Was it physiological?

"You like provoking me into conflicts, is that it?"

"Conflicts? You think I want to have conflicts with you?"

"I'm beginning to wonder," he said coolly. "You keep pushing me against a wall, Evy, and if there's one thing I don't like, it's being pushed."

Stunned that he would think that was what she was doing, she felt tears fill her eyes.

"I'll tell you what *you* want, Rogan Chantry. You want to be independent. You want marriage as it suits you. When it ceases to be that, you feel trapped. You want to go to South Africa without me. You have from the beginning."

The muscle in his jaw twitched. "Yes. Because what I need to do can best be done on my own without worrying about your safety."

"You will always find an excuse to need to do something on your own without wishing to deal with a wife and baby! I know that now."

"You know nothing of the sort. You're hurling accusations wildly and not thinking about—"

"I am thinking!"

"Don't interrupt me," he gritted.

"I think you're sorry you married me!"

"Evy, you're being unreasonable and childish."

"Oh! So now I'm unreasonable and childish."

He heaved a sigh and ran his fingers through his hair. He looked away toward the boulders, and she saw his jaw flex. Her heart thumped loudly in her ears, and her hands were sweating. She was on the verge of bursting into tears but felt that would only reinforce his accusation that she was emotional and unreasonable. She swallowed hard, easing the cramp in her throat.

"You're wrong," he said at last in a controlled voice. "I want to go to the Zambezi, yes. That's certainly no secret. But you're not holding me back. We have already agreed that if Dr. Jackson says that you're strong enough, you'll be coming with me. I married you now instead of waiting until matters in Rhodesia were concluded because I wanted you. I still want you—I will always want you. But it's troubling that you are suddenly analyzing my thoughts in new areas that you've never wanted to discuss before—especially on babies."

"You're wrong." She sniffed loudly, because a few tears had broken through after all. "I did…"

"How interesting…when?" He took a handkerchief from her jacket and handed it to her.

She dabbed at her eyes. "It would have been very forward of me to say so, don't you think?"

"I would have found your interest in the stirrings of my mental processes on the subject quite stimulating. Do you want to discuss babies? Is that my great failure? I'm not talking enough about babies—"

"I didn't say that. It's merely one of several topics we've never discussed, that's all."

"All right, then. Let's talk about babies."

"No, not now," she said stiffly, hurt.

"Wait a minute. You've just made it clear I don't talk enough. I don't tell you how I *feel* about things, including babies. Then we're going to *talk* about it now."

She glared at him. "I won't talk about it now. You're unfeeling and hardhearted. And you're being derogatory about babies."

"Derogatory!"

"You don't want a baby. My baby, your baby. You don't want it."

He stared at her. "What is this? Have you gone daft?"

"Forget it, Rogan," she gritted, gripping the reins tightly and staring straight ahead. "You don't understand. You don't even try to understand. There will be no talk about babies."

"No?" His eyes narrowed.

"No!"

He leaned toward her. "Is that a challenge? I wouldn't go around repeating that too often, or too firmly, Mrs. Chantry. But if you want to know what I think, neither of us is ready for babies, not for a long, long time."

She must have blanched, for he looked startled. He reached a hand toward her, but she avoided his touch and turned her horse sharply away.

"Evy, I'm sorry. This is no good, raising our voices like this—"

Before he could see the tears in her eyes, she flipped the reins, and her horse sprang forward. She rode back toward Rookswood. The tears wet her face and dried in the chill wind. Her heart stung, as though slapped.

CHAPTER SEVEN

Rogan held his mount steady as the wind ruffled the shiny black mane on King's Knight. With his face set grimly, he watched Evy ride off in the direction of Rookswood.

Things had gone wrong between them again. He had thought he understood her. He was confident he did. Then why couldn't he figure out what was lacking? What did she want him to do? He was committed to her. Didn't she realize that? He'd do anything to make her happy, to make her feel satisfied and fulfilled, and yet—he was irritated that she wasn't happy. Was it his pride? He had given her everything he could think of. He'd even taken the first diamonds he'd bought at Kimberly and had them made up into a cross pendant, thinking the cross would tell her what he thought of her character growing up in the rectory. From her childhood she had been faithful to her Christian standards, and she'd made more of an impression on him than she had understood. Hadn't she realized what the pendant meant?

What does she want of me? he wondered again.

"You don't share your feelings," she had said.

Frustrated, he gripped the pommel and stared after her, deep in thought. What kind of overly sweet nonsense was that? "Sharing feelings," like old teddy bears and gumdrops.

And what was all this about babies? He scowled. Why was she intent on talking about it now? Did he like babies? What a question!

That gossip in London at the Brewsters. That's where it all started. Pregnant! Evy Varley Chantry!

He had said nothing to Evy, but after she'd gotten upset over the gossip, he'd gone to his close friend Charles Bancroft, Patricia's brother, and told him to straighten out his sister, or else he would do so himself. Fortunately, Charles was a young man of good sense. He'd also been angry with his sister's behavior and promised he'd try to put a stop to her venomous talk.

Clouds were moving in, scudding across the sky.

King's Knight shied a little, his head jerking upward, a snort blowing through his nostrils. Rogan thought of his father. No use trying to have a man-to-man talk with him about marriage. He was harder to get advice out of than a gold mine.

There was Vicar Osgood, but...Osgood always wanted to delve deeply into Rogan's dedication to Christ. That made him uncomfortable.

Too bad ol' Derwent isn't here. Putting up with Alice these last few years should have given him a pound of wisdom.

The wind gusted against him. He felt a droplet of rain on his face. Higher up on the hill, above deep green fir trees, a white face of rock looked as though it had just snowed. It was a tranquil picture. How misleading appearances could be. The tall brush around the boulders swayed as a startled deer emerged, ears pricked nervously, its soft brown eyes alert. The deer suddenly leaped forward, bounding toward the thicket on swift, sure feet, disappearing into the security of darker, denser woods. A moment later Rogan saw why. A wolf dropped silently onto the boulder, whiffed human presence and went down from the boulder into seclusion.

Be vigilant...your adversary the devil walks about like a roaring lion, seeking whom he may devour.

Rogan hesitated, then turned his horse back onto the trail and rode toward Rookswood.

When he reached the estate stables he dismounted, tossing the reins to the groom. He didn't see Evy's horse.

"Mrs. Chantry return yet?"

"No, Mr. Rogan, 'less she tied the mare up front by the house. She does that sometimes, and I send one of the boys after it."

Rogan nodded and strode purposefully across the field toward the castlelike mansion with its menacing gargoyles glowering from the roof. He checked the front of the house. No horse. He suspected she had ridden to the rectory. Evy didn't think he understood her, but he did, far better than she knew. The vicarage was a safe haven for her, a reminder of less complicated days in the spring of their lives. He didn't mind her going there to have tea each day with old Mrs. Croft and to see the vicar's wife, but it did surprise him that she appeared to be running away from Rookswood whenever things upset her. He had thought her more persistent.

He scowled and lowered his hat. She was acting odd. More emotional than he had ever seen her. Little things brought her to tears. This was not as he remembered her. She was looking tired, too, and didn't have much of an appetite. When they were visiting Paris on their honeymoon, she had devoured the French cuisine, and he had even teased her about gaining weight if she wasn't careful.

He neared the front of the house, thinking of another married man, his brother-in-law, Peter Bartley, who was married to Arcilla.

Poor ol' Peter, he thought grimly, then smiled to himself as he considered the antics of his spoiled, sometimes empty-headed sister. Peter must have gone through the wash after he first married Arcilla and took her to South Africa. For that matter, what poor ol' Peter must still be going through.

Rogan squared his jaw. Well, he himself wasn't going to follow in Peter's footsteps.

His conscience jabbed him. In fairness to Evy, she was not spoiled like Arcilla. Evy had always been serious and astute, with a streak of wisdom that had often surpassed her age. His admiration for her had grown with time, as he had come to appreciate her faith in Christ, her love for good and holy things, her personal virtue. While growing up she'd been the one girl he hadn't been able to lure into the garden. And now all this absurd talk that he'd *had* to marry her.

Again he scowled as he ducked under a low-hanging branch on an apple tree. He resettled his hat. What does she want of me? That she was disappointed in him stung and agitated him, leaving him bewildered. He felt irritated with himself over his apparent ineptness. He ought to be able to handle this easily enough. Hadn't he been able to deal with the rigors of South Africa, the dangers besetting him and those with him?

And yet—marriage, the blending of his and Evy's desires, the resistance, the need to bring two hearts together, was presenting him with difficulties that loomed as large as ol' Lobengula.

Evy tied her horse by the rectory gate and came up the walkway through what had been a flower and rose garden. It had first been embellished with new rose rootings by Aunt Grace. Feeling unduly melancholy, Evy felt moisture rise in her eyes. Oh, to go back to those warm days of youth when all the world resided in little Grimston Way and her greatest worry was standing up to the young scoundrel Rogan Chantry.

She sniffed. Now he was her husband. And he was more arrogant than ever! She sniffed again and felt a little wave of dizziness as she came onto the familiar front porch.

Inside the rectory hall she stood quite still, remembering, gazing up at the photographs that hung over the landing at the top of the first flight of stairs. There they were, Dr. Clyde Varley and his wife, Junia, who had been killed at Rorke's Drift in the Zulu War of 1879, the missionary couple who had wanted to adopt her from her mother Katie van Buren. Evy recalled how as a young girl she liked to convince herself that she resembled them, even to green flecks in their eye color. A little smile touched her lips. Well, they were not her parents, though they had wanted to be. They were safe with the Lord Jesus now.

Missionaries—Dr. Jakob van Buren came to mind again, and her heart beat faster with a longing and enthusiasm to go to his mission station in Bulawayo. He was her mother's blood cousin, and she longed and prayed to reach out and feel the warm, human clasp of her own family, albeit he was a distant cousin. *I will go to South Africa,* she affirmed. *I will see Cousin Jakob and learn about my mother. Maybe I can even meet Jendaya, the Christian Zulu woman who saved my life at Rorke's Drift.*

And there was Heyden…Heyden the murderer, who had killed Henry Chantry, arranged Uncle Edmund's tragic accident in the carriage, and pushed her down the attic steps. She shuddered. Heyden, too, was in South Africa somewhere, perhaps seeking Jendaya. Heyden was sure the woman knew where the Kimberly Black Diamond was hidden.

Evy lifted her chin as she stared at the photographs on the wall. Vicar Edmund Havering and Grace; Vicar Brown, Derwent's widowed father, who'd served a short time as vicar after Uncle Edmund; and now Vicar Osgood and his wife, Martha.

Rogan won't stop me from going with him to South Africa.

Then she stepped back emotionally. What had she come here for except to talk to the gentle Martha about the role of a Christian wife? She must be teachable. But she had so many questions about what true submission to one's husband meant!

Must I be wishy-washy? with no will or interests of my own? Must I give in to everything Rogan demands? But was that a fair question? Rogan was not doing that. He did not want to put her in a box.

Evy could hear Mrs. Croft's nasal voice singing loudly in the big rectory kitchen, where she still worked as cook for the new vicar and Martha. Dear Mrs. Osgood had an ailing heart and could not be too long on her feet lifting heavy pots.

Evy went to the kitchen, knowing she was always welcome. "No need to knock, my dear," Vicar Osgood and his wife often told her. "Just come in and be at home. This is your home too."

Rookswood was her home now, or was it? She felt like an unwanted stranger, except when she was in Rogan's arms. Rogan scoffed over her feelings of not belonging. Was he right, was she too sensitive, or was he the one out of tune with Rookswood, where he'd grown up?

"Everything is exactly the same at Rookswood," he had said, *"except you are now with me instead of down at the rectory."*

Her gaze traveled the huge stove, long sideboards, and floor-to-ceiling cupboards stashed with dry foodstuffs, chipped dishes, and great beat-up pots and pans that had served numerous generations before her.

Mrs. Croft was beating some batter with relentless dedication. She was a tall, bony woman, with white hair skewed from its bun, and a rather pointed nose below sharp, beady eyes. If Evy had any family at all, it would be Mrs. Croft, whom she had known since she was a small child, and who had become her adopted "Granny."

"Grab a chair, child. I'll pour you some good Indian tea. Just made scones, too. Thick with cinnamon and sugar."

Evy nearly gagged at the thought and shook her head as she slipped into the hard-backed chair at the huge wooden table against the wall.

"Just tea, Mrs. Croft—and no milk in it this time."

Mrs. Croft's prickly white brows shot up like arrows.

"Pah! What's this, my girl? No scone, an' it being your favorite, too. What's come over you, eh? A bit of early fall grippe coming on, is it?"

Evy grimaced. "No, I feel fine, just a bit nauseous. Make the tea very hot."

Mrs. Croft lowered the small metal spectacles on her nose and eyed Evy suspiciously. Evy looked away.

"Hmm…" Mrs. Croft poured a cup of tea and brought it to her, then went over to a big calendar and stood looking at it, floured hands on her hips.

"Mrs. Croft, please don't do that!"

"You been married over three months now."

"I know, I know—and oh…" She rubbed her forehead. "You know what all those nasty cats are going to say."

"Can't keep 'em from howling among the trash cans, dearie, and them that know you since you were a wee little girl isn't going to believe a word of it. Did you tell the happy daddy to be?"

Evy groaned. "That's just it. He doesn't want any. Not now, anyway. He's going to be very upset with me."

"Upset with you? Well, ain't that too bad! That scoundrel can be told a few things, an' I'm just the tongue to do it too."

"No, no, Mrs. Croft. You mustn't say a word to him, or anyone else. I'll handle this—eventually."

Mrs. Croft gazed at her over her glasses. "Hmm, now what could you have in mind, I'm wondering?"

Evy remained silent.

"Humph. Well, you'll have to say something sometime, and soon. There's no keeping this from him long, or anyone else for that matter." She walked over to Evy, the wood flooring squeaking under her heavy shoes, pulled out a second chair, and lowered herself with a grimace. She rubbed her elbow.

"Getting old."

Evy felt a surge of melancholy. "No, *don't* say that. You've got to stay around a long time. You're all I have."

Mrs. Croft's callused hand covered Evy's on the table. Her eyes were so kindly they sparkled. "Now, what is this about I'm all you got? And after the biggest wedding Grimston Way saw in many a generation? What's that rogue doing to you that you feel like this? Where's my frying pan? I'll conk him on his hard head, I will!"

Evy smiled, envisioning Mrs. Croft going after Rogan with a black skillet, then her laughter turned to unreasonable tears.

"He'll leave me behind and go to South Africa if he knows. And I just received a letter from Dr. Jakob. He's opening a new mission station at Bulawayo. He wants to become acquainted with me there. For the first time, Mrs. Croft, I'll have a blood relation. So you see why nothing must keep me here at Grimston Way?"

"Sure I do. But remember, it's no great haroosh to go atravelin' when you're expectin'. Can be dangerous, too."

"Oh, Mrs. Croft, you sound like Rogan!"

"Hokey-pokey, not saying you ought to stay home 't'all. Just uncovering the basket of worms so you'll know before you go."

"He said no babies—he didn't want *any*."

"For double shame. He said that to you?"

"But I am going to South Africa," Evy gritted, blinking away the brief show of tears. She leaned across the old table, squinting her eyes with determination. "We both are. You're coming with me."

Mrs. Croft raised her brows again and drew back against the hardbacked chair. "Well, 'course I am, Evy. A team of wild foxes won't keep me here now. It'll be the day when I leave that rogue to look after you without my keeping a sharp eye on him to make sure he does it right. Just remember, you'll be hampered down with the precious thing for months of nursing and such, and 'twill be a good year before the baby's proper weaned." Mrs. Croft scrutinized her face. "You're aware of all that, Evy girl?"

Evy did not want to think about it now. "I'll manage."

"'Course you will." She patted her hand again. "Now you just stay calm. Have you seen Dr. Tisdale?"

"Yes. He said—that I was."

Mrs. Croft nodded, satisfied. A tender, reflective smile spread across her face. "A baby. Your own little one. To think I'll live to see a new generation come along." She counted on her bony fingers. "Around July."

Evy discussed matters more closely, then made Mrs. Croft vow to silence.

"Well…if you insist."

Evy then inquired about Martha Osgood.

"She's doing dandy, she is. Out in the sunshine garden doing her embroidery."

"I'll go see her."

Martha Osgood's thin, veined hands worked tirelessly with her needle and pink thread on the rosebuds sewn onto a dresser scarf. She sat in the garden chair in the sunshine with a big hat shading her face and shoulders. With the sparrows chittering and the late mums blooming, Martha was the homily of all that was gentle and unassuming. For a time Mrs. Osgood chatted about village news. Evy listened without much comment. Somehow, just hearing her calm voice at peace with the God of all circumstances was soothing. Here was a woman who'd throughout her life had small portions of earth's vaunted goods, so coveted by small and great so as to lead to all manner of vice, even murder. Yet Martha was not striving. Her health was weak and growing more so by the month. She had lost her only child when newly married, and the Lord of Grace and Good Gifts had not seen fit in His wisdom to give her another baby, or reward her in this life with goodly possessions, though she had remained faithful through her loss.

Evy mentioned this to her, and Martha smiled and nodded thoughtfully.

"Well, it has been hard sometimes. It is so difficult to wait on the Lord, isn't it? When we feel we *need* provision *now.* We can't *see* what He is going to do, and oh, how we wish we could." She shook her gray head and clucked her tongue, as though remembering her own youthful struggles. "Ah yes, we want so desperately to *see,* don't we? But we must 'walk by faith, not by sight,' as Scripture tells us. For me, dear, life is like walking through a valley with high mountains. We walk just one step at a time, trusting His Word, and as we progress, sometimes we see very little of what lies beyond the valley's high mountains. But God has promised bountiful blessings. He will always be faithful. Faithful and True are two of His names."

When Evy remained quiet, Martha looked up from her embroidery. "And what of you, my dear? Are you adjusting to married life at Rookswood? Such a beautiful mansion, I always think. Except those ghastly gargoyles." She clucked her tongue again. "Whatever were folks thinking in those days, I wonder? One would think angels would be so much more attractive, don't you agree? And Lady Elosia? Is she doing well with her back pains? Such an energetic woman! I've always thought she would have made a wonderful twin of Queen Victoria, don't you think?"

Evy smiled but realized Martha was innocent of any double meaning.

"So determined is dear Lady Elosia, so here and there and every-where."

Evy put her fingers to her lips to keep from laughing. *Here and there and everywhere,* yes, that was Lady Elosia, putting her tuppence in every situation. *Oh, goodness! What will she be like with Rogan's child?*

"Do you have a headache, dear?"

"Um—oh, well, I suppose I do, rather. You were saying?"

"I noticed you were massaging your forehead. And you do look most distressed, Evy. Perhaps another cup of Mrs. Croft's tea with a tweak of herbs added will make you feel more relaxed. The weather, you know."

"Yes?"

"Warm days, chilly evenings. I daresay we'll soon have our first frost." She looked about the garden and drew her shawl closer about her shoulders. "Fall makes one double-minded. You're having second thoughts about Rogan, are you?"

Evy looked at her, surprised. She hastened, "No. Oh no, I am very much in love with him."

Martha nodded and worked her needle. "Yes, I can see that. I am so pleased. It's the adjustments that pose problems. Two very different people suddenly joined together in everything from morning tea to sharing the same bedroom, seeing each other in the worst possible moments and the best, differing on things great and small. There are bound to be conflicts."

Evy sipped the tea Mrs. Croft had brought to them. The taste of tarragon was typical of a Mrs. Croft tea for "tired nerves," as she put it.

"It hasn't been quite that for me, not yet. It's clashing over plans. Rogan feels strongly one way—and, well, I feel the opposite. And Rogan is, shall we say, determined."

Martha nodded. "Ah yes, I see, very much so. Very protective of you, I would think. Very much the squire's son. A delightful young man. Very opinionated, I should think. Then as you say, so are you. Yes, I can see the potential for struggle. Then again, many women would be thrilled to have a husband so interested in their doings, so as to have strong opinions about them. Some husbands don't care a bit about what their wives do as long as it doesn't interfere in their own desires."

"You think Rogan is interested in what interests me?"

"Oh, good gracious, yes. I have seen how Rogan is quite interested in all you do. Being a strong-willed man, he would have opinions, naturally, because he cares so much for you."

"Trouble is, his opinion and my opinion differ considerably," Evy repeated in stronger emphasis.

"Yes, yes, that can be quite discouraging. And you have made your wishes known quite clearly and wisely, I gather?"

Wisely?

Again, Evy kept silent.

"What I mean, dear, is letting him know you reverence him, that his ideas on matters that disturb you are nonetheless esteemed by you?"

Evy sipped her tea to keep from answering.

"That will go a long way toward ensuring you of mutual consideration and respect. I always think of what the Scripture says about Sarah calling Abraham 'lord.' Whose daughters we are."

This was not want Evy wanted to hear.

"He loves you dearly. Anyone can see that. I should think he would do anything he thought was right to please you and make you contented."

"He doesn't want children," Evy blurted out.

"Oh, you don't mean it, my dear."

"It's true."

"Never?"

"Well, at least not *now*. Not for years and years."

"I see." She had stopped embroidering and turned slightly in her chair to look at Evy thoughtfully. "And you want a baby now. Is that the problem?"

"It wasn't that I *wanted* a baby *now*. It's just that—"

Evy's eyes welled with tears. In great gushing words she told Martha what had happened earlier on the ride in Grimston Woods when she had clumsily tried to prepare Rogan for the news that she was going to have a baby.

"And all he did was make light of what I was trying to say. It was obvious any baby now will make him unhappy. It comes at an inconvenient time, and he sees me and the baby as a dreadful burden."

"If he really thought that, I would be most surprised. I'm sure, yes, quite sure that he is simply a normal young man who didn't have the foggiest notion of what you were hinting at. He is quite practical, I should think. And you're coming at him on a strictly emotional plane. You'll simply need to come out in plain everyday English and tell him, my dear. What I would advise is tell him as soon as possible. I'm sure you will see a complete change in him once he understands the situation."

"Having a child now, this soon, was not on our itinerary. It…just happened."

"Yes."

"You see, if I tell him now, it will give him the excuse he needs to insist I stay at Rookswood while he leaves for Capetown. And I don't want to stay. I want to go. I've Cousin Jakob to meet at the new mission station at Bulawayo, and Arcilla has had her baby—a boy."

Evy stood, setting down her empty cup. "There's something else, as well. Something awful."

Evy told her the gossip first begun at the Brewster dinner ball. She concluded: "So you see, expecting so soon also allows the gossip to continue with renewed fervency."

"I see. This can raise problems. I was reading just this morning about the birth of Jesus."

Evy looked at her. *But it's not even near Christmas,* she wanted to say but caught herself.

"Birth of Jesus? What has His birth to do with this, Mrs. Osgood?"

"With your situation? Oh, none, considering he was virgin born. But Nazareth, where He grew up in the home of Mary and Joseph, was not always a pretty place, Evy. Those who rejected his virgin birth could have whispered all sorts of evil, including his own half-brothers. I suspect Nazareth was even worse than Grimston Way about gossip. Remember what Nathaniel said, 'Can anything good come out of Nazareth?' If you ever want to read about Jesus's boyhood, read Psalm sixty-nine. Jesus said He was the song of the drunkards."

"What!" she gasped, growing indignant.

"Indeed. Imagine, singing ditties about Him and His mother. I suppose, dear, what I'm trying to say is this. That if the holy birth of the Son of God was the object of vicious tongues in his hometown, then we, who *do* have some manner of sin in our lives, should not be shocked to discover we are not immune to scorn, whatever the cause." She shook her head. "Can you imagine what Mary must have gone through in the small village of Nazareth?"

Evy stood looking down at her, feeling her heart enlarge with compassion. Yes, to some small degree she could. How bitter it could have been at times when Mary saw glances cast her way, or when the whispering suddenly stopped as she walked up to the well for water, or took the child Jesus into the village to barter for the family. For many, Jesus was believed to be illegitimate, when all the time He was the legitimate Son of the living God.

They had both lapsed into silence for some time, then came aware together as a drop of rain splattered on the brick garden walk.

"Oh dear, looks like a storm is blowing in, doesn't it? Do help me gather my things indoors, will you?"

Evy hurried to put Martha's sewing things back inside her big knitting bag and, holding her arm, aided her across the garden path toward the rectory.

"There is one thing you and Rogan must agree upon."

Evy glanced at her, feeling wary. She wanted the truth, but at the same time she wanted the truth not to interrupt the fulfillment of her wishes.

"Yes?"

"You both must agree that your expecting a child much sooner than anticipated did not come as a surprise to your heavenly Father. God controls life. He is in control of your life, and Rogan's, is He not?"

"Yes, I believe that with all my heart, Mrs. Osgood."

"Then, as I see Scripture, dear, it is God's will that He guide you in all things and that both of you, as individuals, and as partners in marriage, yield yourselves to His gracious hand of providence. He's created this child for a special purpose."

Evy nodded. She had been so upset recently that she had almost forgotten the providence of her gracious God. *All things work together for good to those who love God, to those who are the called according to His purpose.*

But would Rogan agree that God wanted them to have this particular baby at this time in their marriage, their lives? And that she was meant to accompany him to Bulawayo?

Or was she meant not to go there? The idea that it might not be God's purpose for her to journey there at this time met her with difficulty. *But I want to go now. I can think of many good reasons to go. I can even help Dr. Jakob at his mission station while Rogan treks north to check up on the gold mine.* She could serve Jesus there, so why would the Lord not wish her to go now?

"And if Rogan and I don't agree on the trip to South Africa because of this unexpected blessing?"

Mrs. Osgood was quiet a moment too long, and Evy looked at her, then swallowed uneasily at the sadness in the older woman's eyes. Evy thought she already knew the answer. Perhaps she had known all along. All of her racing about in an agitated state of what to do was merely a front. She *knew*. She was no stranger to the Scriptures, to God. She was to yield to Rogan.

Evy tensed and resisted again what felt to her like a smothering pillow thrust over her face.

"Then," Martha said quietly, "if God and His will and purpose have no seat of authority in your lives as a married couple, Evy, you and Rogan are in for a very difficult marriage. And a very unhappy life."

Evy's eyes filled with tears. She believed this too. It was one of the reasons for her agitation. Obedience, yieldedness, was of great value to God. She had believed this long before she ever permitted herself to fall in love with Rogan Chantry. There were years gone by when she had deliberately avoided any emotional entanglement with him because she had not been sure of his commitment to Christ. And now to be confronted with the shocking possibility that she herself was not fully yielded to the will and purpose of the Lord Jesus, whom she claimed to love and honor!

Yes, what of her decision to obey His Word? Tested and tried—would she come through?

"You are right, Mrs. Osgood," she murmured after what seemed a very long silence. "I see."

Without Jesus Christ, they had no foundation on which to build their life, their "house," as it were, and without Jesus Christ, their future family, goals, and ambitions were naught but ashes blown about by every conceivable wind.

Evy helped Martha into her favorite chair, one that Evy recalled Uncle Edmund sitting in years ago.

"My dear, I fear I've not been much help to you. This has all been quite difficult for you, I can see."

"On the contrary, you have helped me immensely, Mrs. Osgood."

"I should like to pray for you and Rogan before you go, if you'd allow me."

"Please."

As Evy bade her good afternoon and left the rectory, she was still not at peace with herself. *I simply don't want to yield my plans,* she admitted firmly. *It's that simple, that difficult, and that painful.*

Evy mounted her mare and rode away sorrowfully. *What has happened to me that I think I cannot completely trust my Lover, Provider, and Protector?*

And yet it was so. At least in this matter.

CHAPTER EIGHT

The rain was just beginning to fall when Evy dismounted at the front door of Rookswood. She gave the reins to Hank the groom, who led her horse to the stables. Once indoors Evy walked tiredly across the Great Hall and began climbing the wide staircase to the second floor. Her head was aching, and she wondered if Arcilla had felt this badly when she became pregnant. Perhaps it was just her own worries that weighed her down so heavily?

Bring your burdens to the mercy seat and leave them there, Evy. He has never yet forsaken you, has He? Has He brought you this far on the path of faith? Yes. Then why do you think He's looking in another direction now? That everything will fall apart into a thousand pieces?

Her sense of hopelessness must be physical, she told herself.

Was Rogan back? She braced herself for a difficult meeting. He must not notice that she felt ill. He might suspect something. He had already made an agreement with her that her trip to Capetown should be contingent upon Dr. Jackson's assessment of her health. Dr. Jackson! She must keep him from discovering that she was going to have a baby.

She had climbed more than halfway up the stairs, when she noticed Rosie and Midge huddled together in the upper hallway. Rosie, holding a mop, was as short and round as Midge was tall and slender. Rosie was recently hired by Lady Elosia from her house in London. Midge, who had just turned sixteen, was related to the housekeeper, Mrs. Wetherly.

Rosie was speaking in a whisper that reverberated through the hall as audibly as if she'd conversed in a normal tone.

Evy paused, her hand gripping the banister.

"Such a pretty girl, she is. That thick, tawny hair. All wavy natural like, too. An' amber eyes with green in 'em, too. I should be so lucky. An' raised sweetlike in the vicarage, too. Oooh, but that limp. D'ye see that shoe? Black, it is. And thick soled."

"Oh, twaddle, I seen her awaltzin' with the master, that's a fact. Ha, and what's a wee limp when she's a diamond heiress, eh, Rosie?"

"Ducky, eh? The limp matters, though, it does, to Master Rogan. Bet he's already regretting he didn't marry Lord Bancroft's daughter."

"Why'd ye be sayin' that?"

"'Tis as plain as the nose on your face, ain't it?"

"Not to me—"

"I heard talk."

"What kin'?"

"Oh, you know. That Master *had* to marry her."

"Pah! Not Miss Evy! I knowed her all my days. Why, she'd ne'er be bad! Vicar's niece? Pah! No one like her in all the village when growin' up. Can't be."

"Heard it from Lady Patricia Bancroft!"

"Hoity-toity!" interrupted a twangy voice from behind them.

The maids jerked away as though stung. Rosie's mop was instantly moving across the floor, while Midge's feather duster flew up to the painting of a scowling Chantry hanging over a gilded hall table.

"So!" came Lizzie's voice. Mrs. Croft's niece marched up, hands on hips, jutting out her chin.

"So!" she repeated. "Slothing on the job again, both of you. And nasty toothed you are too! For shame, Rosie, talkin' like that. An' you, Midge, for listening to such cackle. You best get on with your work and never mind the young mistress. If the master hears your talk, you'll both be turned out on your ears."

"Oh, Lizzie," Rosie whined, clutching the mop to her heart. "We didn't mean nothing. We surely didn't—"

"Don't you 'oh, Lizzie' me. An' after Lady E just got you the job here, too. Should have left you in London, that's a fact." Lizzie wagged a finger under her nose. "I'll quote the good Vicar Osgood." She drew in a breath and straightened her shoulders, looking off into space. " 'The north wind brings forth rain, and a backbiting tongue an angry countenance.' From Proverbs, it is," she spoke, as though having memorized the verse.

Lizzie leaned her face toward Rosie until the girl backed against the hall table. "D'ye see my angry countenance, eh? You'd better! An' if I hear such gibberish again about the mistress, you'll both be out of a job. I'll talk to the master himself, I will! Then you'll see how ducky it'll be."

They gaped foolishly and took off their separate ways, Midge dusting furiously, and Rosie moving the cleaning pail and slopping water.

Lizzie looked after them, satisfied, with a sharp nod of her head. Mumbling to herself, she strode down the hall.

Evy, out of sight on the winding stairway, hardly contained her laughter. *I didn't have to say a word in my defense. Thank you, Lizzie.*

Moments later she went on up the stairs. Despite the humorous scene she felt grieved in spirit. Even the Rookswood maids knew the cruel tale Patricia had spread in London. So Rogan was sorry he'd married her, was he? Well, that was their wishful thinking. Their fancies entertained the notion that the handsome future squire secretly found all the Rookswood maids attractive.

Evy recalled growing up in the village where all the girls were infatuated with Rogan. But now, it seemed, they still were. She saw how women noticed him when they went into the village together. At first it simply amused her, but later on she felt some irritation.

The town whispers, unlike Patricia's lies, could be overlooked, considering that his marriage to the "rectory girl" had come as a shock to the entire village. Everyone had anticipated his union with Lord Bancroft's daughter. That expectation had gone so far as to prompt Patricia to order a wedding trousseau. And when Rogan was in South Africa, he had received a rather threatening letter from Lord Bancroft suggesting he was "trifling" with his daughter. Sir Julien had used the situation to attempt to persuade Rogan to marry Patricia at once. Rogan, however, had scoffed at the notion of betraying Patricia. "I never proposed marriage to Patricia," he had told her on their honeymoon. "She assumed marriage, as did everyone else, without ever asking me what I thought. Then, when I chose the only woman I ever really wanted, I was suddenly accused of betraying Patricia. She and her father formed expectations that were not of my making. I suppose it's face saving to blame me."

Evy climbed the stairs and tried even harder not to limp. They had noticed the shoe Dr. Jackson wanted her to wear. She loathed it. She no longer needed a cane, thanks to Rogan's insistence on managing her exercise program.

Evy was ready to turn down the hall to her and Rogan's private suite when a tug of emotion tripped her heart. She wasn't ready to face Rogan yet. Not after hearing Rosie's gossip. Soon her waistline would change. Many would be surprised and consider the gossip to be true. They would say Rogan had been a scoundrel, and perhaps it was because Evy had lost her Uncle Edmund and Aunt Grace at a crucial time in her youth. Yes, even the rectory girl could go astray with a handsome rogue like Rogan Chantry.

Instead of going to her room, she climbed to the third floor, where she'd once lived with Aunt Grace during those few years after Edmund's death. Grace had been Arcilla's governess back then. Evy walked down the quiet hall and opened the door.

The past reached out to her like perfume, filling her head with fond memories. She entered and shut the door, looking about, a gentle smile on her lips. She ran her fingers along the dresser Aunt Grace had used.

"Wish you were here," she murmured. "You'd know what to do."

I AM here, a thought ran through her mind. *The Lord never changes. Jesus Christ is the same yesterday, today, and forever. Come to Me, all you who labor and are heavy laden, and I will give you rest.*

As though Jesus Himself stood in the room, Evy rushed to fall on her knees, leaning the side of her cheek against the soft comforter on the bed.

"Lord, what shall I do? You heard Rogan this morning. A baby now would ruin all his plans. And if he knows he'll insist I stay behind. I don't want to stay behind to face the gossip alone. I want to go with him to South Africa. I want to meet your servant, Dr. Jakob. Lord, give me strength and wisdom. Work in Rogan to be what You want him to be, to accomplish what You will. Oh, Lord, help me to trust You, to believe You're working in our lives, that You brought us together in holy matrimony."

The rain beating softly against the windowpane kept time with her heart. Peace began to settle over her soul.

Her knowledge of Scripture flowed through her mind, bringing order. Her frustration ebbed. *He is in control. Do you believe Him? Nothing takes Him by surprise. Certainly not the new life He created in your womb. Rejoice! Don't falter. Your plans—Rogan's plans are all subservient to His greater plans. You don't know what a day will bring forth do you? Then why fret and fume? Rest in the Lord's provision. Wait on Him to act in His way, in His timing. You ought to say, "If the Lord wills, we shall live and do this or that!" When you can't understand it all, Evy, then trust Him to work everything out. Trust Him through uncertain days and scary nights. Trust Him especially when it is difficult.*

She was relaxed and nearly fell asleep on her knees, her cheek resting on the comforter, until a strong and gentle hand touched her hair. Her eyes fluttered open. She started, until she knew Rogan's touch.

He slipped down beside her, his arm going around her shoulders, drawing her head against his chest, his fingers caressing her hair. She looked at him, knowing her eyes revealed her expectations. His gaze was tender, and she could not doubt for a moment the love and respect in his warm, brown eyes. A smile came to her, and she reached her fingers to run through his dark hair.

He lifted her hand with his, raising it to his lips. Looking at the wedding ring, he straightened it on her finger, the diamonds sparkling.

"I'm sorry I was thickheaded this morning."

"It was my fault, too. How did you know I was up here?"

"I was watching for you when you came home." He regarded her intently. "Still troubled by old Mama Bear?"

She smiled at his term for his Aunt Elosia. "I feel a bit like Little Red Riding Hood."

He smiled. "Then I must be the big bad wolf."

"Maybe it's silly of me, but sometimes I feel intimidated by her."

"That's not too surprising. I've been thinking about what you said earlier when we were out riding. I've tried to see things from your perspective."

She looked at him quickly.

"I suppose there's a reason why she never bothered me much with her dominant ways. By that, I mean the things she wants to do usually don't affect me." He smiled crookedly. "Truth is, I care very little about the issues she gets boiled up about, so I've seldom found myself at emotional odds with her. The main source of trouble for me has been Julien, whom I consider ruthless. I've been in a battle of wits with him for years. But for you, I can see how Elosia could invoke a similar sort of conflict."

She smiled. "It is comforting to realize that you understand. Perhaps I've been overreacting."

"Not if it troubles you, and apparently it does. Evy"—and he drew her to him again, leaning his head against hers—"your security at Rookswood is not at risk, certainly not with me, anyway. It's you and I together, my love. The day will come when Elosia is gone, and we'll still be here together."

"Well, now that you've understood things, it doesn't seem so important anymore."

"Oh no, my dear, you're not getting out of this that easy. Didn't you tell me this morning I failed to take enough interest in matters that are important to you? I took what you said to heart. I've been debating with myself all afternoon. So now you must *explain* things to me."

She was pleasantly amazed at the willingness he showed to understand. It was as though he'd decided to pick up a heavy load and shoulder it because it was his masculine calling to accept the God-given role as husband. At that moment she was experiencing overwhelming delight in her beloved bridegroom.

She tossed her hair from her shoulder and hoped she sounded reasonable.

"All right. I'll give you an example. I wanted to ask Mrs. Croft to come here to Rookswood. She had mentioned last week she would like to work for us. I thought she might be able to use these rooms until a governess or nurse is needed for Arcilla and Peter's return." *If they ever return,* she thought. "Mrs. Croft wouldn't interact with the rest of Rookswood help, just with you and me."

"Seems reasonable."

Evy tried to keep her voice mellow. "Elosia dismissed my decision as unnecessary. Perhaps it was to her, but I wanted Mrs. Croft to come, especially now."

His gaze was questioning. "Especially *now?*"

She felt her cheeks warming and looked away at the fringe on the comforter. She plucked at it.

"No reason, except she and I have always been close. She's more like a grandmother to me."

"I understand about Mrs. Croft. Fact is, I want her to be with you. If Elosia doesn't realize that, then I'll just explain to her."

Could it really be that simple? Rogan thought so.

"But she said you wished things to remain just as they are."

His brow arched. He reached over and brushed a tawny section of hair from her throat. "So you want Mrs. Croft?"

A flood of emotion, so untypical of her, bubbled over with a show of tears. "Yes…"

Rogan drew her into his arms, holding her against his chest and kissing her forehead and her cheeks.

"Then my little girl shall have Mama Croft to bring her tea and crumpets, and dry her tears. Cheer up, darling, I'll take care of it. If this is the worst I'll need to deal with, I'll be pleased."

She looked at him, grateful that he hadn't made a flippant remark.

"What about Elosia's feelings?" she asked quietly. "I don't want a strained relationship with her. What could be worse than two women vying for supremacy at Rookswood by striving for your loyalty?"

"Sounds sticky," he said with a grimace. "Look, don't worry. No one is going to manipulate me," and he cupped her chin playfully, "not even you."

"I don't want to manipulate you," she said loftily. "All I want is a fair chance for us to become what God intended when we made our vows to each other, and to Him."

He smiled. "Bone of my bones and flesh of my flesh. Therefore a man shall leave his papa and his mama—and the forbidding Lady Elosia—and be joined to his one and only." He planted a quick kiss on her chin. "Consider it done, my Eve. I'll have a cozy little chat with Auntie."

"Oh, Rogan, the last thing I want is trouble. You won't be too hard with her, will you?" She knew a sudden wave of guilt. "You know I actually like her a great deal and want to form a bond."

"Bonds come in good time. Don't fret, Evy. I'll treat her with a satin glove. I've been dealing with Mama Bear since I was a boy. Now, get rid of that crease in your brow." He rubbed between her brows with his thumb. "That's it, smile for me."

"Oh, Rogan…" She put her arms around him, and he cradled her in his. She relished his understanding as he simply cuddled her.

After a minute he said, "Give me your left hand, Evy."

Left hand? She did so, curious as to why. He held it firmly, his face determined.

"This morning you said I never prayed with you."

"I shouldn't have said—"

"Let's try it now," he said tonelessly. "I'm not one who likes to speak my mind and heart out loud to God, but I'll do it, since you want it. Maybe I'll learn to appreciate it."

Amazed, she stared at him for a while. She had no doubt that he believed in Christ, prayed at times, and read the Bible, but he seldom shared those intimate thoughts with her. Indeed, until now, the only time he shared anything of a spiritual note with her was on Sunday worship at the rectory chapel.

He had already bowed his dark head and was praying. Evy listened to his resonant voice talking about *her* and her *needs* to the heavenly Father. *This is Rogan, and he actually means it. He's reaching out to God about meeting my needs.*

Her heart warmed. He looked so wonderful praying beside her, more masculine than ever as he yielded in submission to his Head, Christ.

When he had finished, he looked at her calmly, and she smiled. He stood and pulled her to her feet.

Dizziness assailed her. He caught her swiftly, drawing her against him. "Darling," he said swiftly, worried.

Evy held to him tightly as the room spun round.

"You're not well," came his concerned voice.

"No, I'm all right," she murmured, keeping her eyes closed.

"I can see that isn't so. You've been looking pale for days now. You're not yourself, Evy. I know you, and you're not the same recently. Is it something seasonal? Should I call for Tisdale?"

"Rogan...no, don't." She wet her lips and kept her face downward, her fingers plucking at his shirt front.

He scowled a bit and tilted his head, looking at her, questioning.

Now was the moment. *Go ahead,* she urged herself, *tell him. You must tell him. If plans are to be altered, then give him time to think about them. Remember what Martha told you? "Tell him the truth."*

But the words lodged in her throat. *After all, why cannot I go to*

*Capetown expecting a child? Other women have sailed the ocean and sur-
vived, why not me? That's it. That's the answer. I'll just go and tell him
aboard ship.*

"Evy…?"

"It's nothing, darling," she said with false cheer. "Just a bit light-
headed is all. I didn't take lunch, and I think that funny tea Mrs. Croft
makes for headaches was too strong. I'm fine now. I…I stood too
quickly."

She sensed his relentless gaze and deliberately avoided it, looping
her arm through his.

"Shall we go down? The post should have come by now. Weren't
you expecting a report from Derwent?"

For a moment she thought she wouldn't get by with her facade, but
when she glanced at him, she saw suspicion slowly change to puzzlement, as though he was not sure about things.

"All right, we'll go down. This reminds me, I've arranged for Dr.
Jackson to come from London tomorrow. I want to make certain you're
up to all this before we sail for Capetown. I know that land, Evy. It eats
up little girls who are frail. I won't let that happen to you. You're too
important to me."

Now was not the time to resist. He was being too wonderful. He
was the man of strength and tenderness she always imagined he would
be with her.

She maintained her smile as they walked to the door. Better Dr.
Jackson than Dr. Tisdale. She'd been lucky there. If Dr. Tisdale came, he
would surely mention her "delicate" condition.

"I wish, though, that we could just get on with making our plans
for the voyage."

"We will."

"Arcilla's so anxious to see us," she continued, overly enthusiastic
with the use of *us*. "To show off her baby boy to his uncle Rogan. Baby
Charles, she says, is adorable."

"All babies look the same for months after they're born." He stopped on the stairs and turned to her, frowning. "Charles! You did say she named the baby Charles?"

"Why yes," Evy said, puzzled by his reaction. "Charles Rogan—you see? You're favored over Parnell. Why? Charles is a perfectly dashing name."

He shook his head in disbelief. "That sister of mine. It's a wonder Peter allowed it. Unbelievable!"

"What is? Why are you—"

"Because dear Charles was her first love."

Evy now understood Rogan's reaction. "Oh," she said, lamely.

"Yes," he said dryly. "*Oh,* is right."

Charles Bancroft, of course, the one young man Arcilla had wanted to marry. "I see what you mean. Maybe Peter didn't notice."

His mouth curved. "Come, darling. Well, if the ol' boy didn't, it goes to show he's working too hard. Charles," he repeated wryly. "That will go over very well in Grimston Way when they eventually come home—and it will cause a few tongues to wag."

Evy withdrew into uneasy silence at his mention of wagging tongues.

"Dizzy again?"

"What?"

"You look pained. Here, sweet, I'd better carry you to our rooms."

"No, it's all right, Rogan, really."

"No, it isn't." He swung her up into his arms and carried her through the corridor of the second floor. "One thing about you, Evy, concerns me. You don't want to admit your weaknesses to me. You should, you know."

Because you'll want me to stay behind if I do. And I'm determined not to be left at Rookswood while you sail over the golden horizon.

CHAPTER NINE

It was late afternoon when Rogan left Evy asleep and came downstairs. He would be relieved when Dr. Jackson arrived tomorrow. She must still be suffering the effects of her fall down the steps… That Heyden van Buren! Rogan just itched to lay hold of him.

He left the house and walked around the side of the mansion into the rose garden. The rain had stopped and dewdrops were on the roses. He paused. Yes, Elosia Chantry was there as he'd expected, strolling among her beloved roses, her large hat shielding her from any lingering sprinkles.

Rogan watched his father's maiden sister. She had left an aristocratic life in London to come to Rookswood to assume the role of woman of the family soon after Rogan's mother died. Rogan had never needed Elosia, nor had Parnell. Their younger sister, Arcilla, however, had needed her desperately. She was the coddled baby in the family and had taken her mother's death painfully hard. Elosia was considered of the old school, pompous, autocratic, and haughty, or as Rogan affectionately called her, "Mama Bear."

She hadn't seen him as yet and moved along the brick walk to pause before a favorite red rose bush. She bent over to sniff it appreciatively, gloved hands folded behind her.

He smiled as he walked to join her.

She straightened and turned.

"Oh, Rogan, dear boy."

"Look, Auntie, I've got to talk to you about Evy."

She lowered her pince-nez to regard him with lofty demeanor. "Aha, I thought it would come to this eventually. Well, you should have listened to me and married Patricia. She understands you, you know. She's of your kind. Evy is a sweet girl but totally unprepared to assume the role of mistress of Rookswood—"

Rogan sighed and folded his arms across his chest, regarding her with tilted head. He knew just how to handle her. He'd been getting around her autocratic ways since he was thirteen. There was an understanding between them. He came straight on, always had, and she knew it. When she saw his narrowed gaze, she stopped in midsentence.

"You know I love you dearly, Elosia, but things have gone far enough where Evy is concerned."

"What?"

"You know what I mean. All this rot going around London circles about my needing to marry her because she was pregnant. It's all a sickening dish…served out by our darling Patricia. If it keeps up, I'll need to confront her in London. You tell her that, will you? Tell her if she wishes to continue discussing my wife, I may do a bit of discussing myself—about her."

She looked stunned. "You're serious."

"Quite serious."

"Well, I never believed it about Evy for a moment. I told her so this afternoon."

"Even so, the talk has her upset. It's got to end. That means you, too."

"Me? But really, Rogan, whatever do you mean?"

"You know what I mean, old dear. It's time to draw in your claws and get used to the undisputed fact she's my wife. And"—he smiled to soften the impact of his next words, for he had no desire to hurt—"she is the future mistress of Rookswood."

"What—whatever do you mean, dear boy, draw in my claws? Why, I've been quite gentle with the girl."

The girl. "Aunt Elosia, the girl, as you persist in addressing her, is Mrs. Rogan Chantry."

"If you had only mellowed toward Patricia and married her. How much simpler things would be."

"For you perhaps, and dear old Julien as well, but I made up my mind years ago I would marry whom I pleased. You best know my devotion to you, Auntie, will reach its limit should it come to a choice between the two of you. So please don't try to make me choose. That goes for Julien, too. Though I think he knows better now."

"You know how outraged Lord Bancroft remains over your betrayal of his daughter?"

"There was no betrayal of Patricia."

"Well, then, dear boy, I believe you, but it does make things most difficult for *me.* How can I attend the upcoming socials when I will need to come face-to-face with Lord and Lady Bancroft?"

"I've married Evy Varley, and there's no more to be said about it."

"Van Buren, dear boy. She's no more a Varley than I am."

"She's a Chantry now, so forget Patricia. I don't want her name mentioned again to Evy. I don't think she's well. I want her left alone." He narrowed his lashes, smiling. "Understood, Auntie?"

She looked dismayed. "Well, I—I'm sure I can't possibly promise not ever to mention Patricia—"

"Yes, you can, old darling, and you will. Evy is to be treated with the respect she deserves. She's unhappy, and I'll go to London over this if I must. I've already talked to Charles, but I want it stopped here as well. Granted, she has plenty to adjust to. She was raised in the vicarage, not at Rookswood, but she's more than capable of learning what's needed. She'll be a stunning mistress of the family estate one day, and it's important that family and acquaintances understand that."

"My dear boy! I'm sure I don't understand what has you so upset. Of course she will be an asset to you and Rookswood. I never thought otherwise."

"Evy seems to think she's treated as an odd piece of china."

"What a strange idea!"

"Yes, isn't it? And we won't have *Mrs.* Rogan Chantry feeling that way, will we, Auntie?"

"Perish the thought, my boy. I didn't realize I had upset Evy so. Tush! I shall try to be more careful henceforth. We must *do* something. Yes, something to make Evy feel perfectly comfortable in the family. Now let me think…what should that be…"

Rogan smiled wryly. "Begin by inviting Mrs. Croft to Rookswood to look after Evy's interests."

"Yes, she did mention Mrs. Croft. I thought Mrs. Wetherly was quite enough."

"Mrs. Croft will stay on the third floor in the governess quarters. Do you wish to express any other reservations?"

"Well, naturally she needs to *learn,* and there are so *many* things she doesn't know yet. And Rookswood and the family reputation are important. But if you think Mrs. Croft is necessary."

"Evy feels she is," he said smoothly.

"Then I'll tell Mrs. Wetherly to have the rooms ready."

"I knew I could count on you." He put his arm around her shoulders and walked with her through the sea of red blooms toward the side door that opened into an afternoon sunroom.

"Oh, by the bye, dear boy, have you heard anything more from Julien since the letter he sent about your marriage?"

Thinking again of his uncle's lecturing monologue rekindled Rogan's temper. Julien had threatened to cut him and Evy both off from the diamond mine. Rogan wasn't worried so much about that as he was about Evy's acceptance at Bulawayo with Julien. Rogan didn't like the idea of leaving her there under his authority while he went off to the Zambezi gold mine.

"No, I haven't heard back from Julien. He must not have appreciated my response."

"I suppose you told the old one-eyed lion how your choice of Evy was your own business."

"I did."

"That must have wrangled him. He so wanted you to marry Pa—" She stopped at once and glanced at him.

Rogan covered a smile. He opened the door and let her pass through into the sitting room.

"Ah, well," Elosia was saying. "Arcilla has her troubles with Julien as well. She's written that he's now chief native commissioner or some such title at some dreadful sounding place."

"Bulawayo," Rogan said absently.

"Yes, Evy told it to me as well. Sounds like a dry, dusty place full of charging bulls."

Rogan was still considering Julien. What if he went on the expedition into the Matopos looking for Lobengula's burial cave while he, Rogan, was hundreds of miles to the north from where Evy was?

"Arcilla's worried sick over Peter."

He looked at her. Had his sister told her about the plan to attack the Transvaal? In her wire of the other day, she'd said she had told no one else. If Julien found out she'd wired him—

"Worried? About what?"

"About Peter's position as Julien's assistant."

"What else did she write you about? Anything important?"

"If you're asking whether she mentioned that foolhardy Dr. Jameson and his plan to start a war with the Boers, no. She did not. She wrote about Peter's dreadful situation, trying to appease all those naked savages. My poor, precious Arcilla—"

"Then how did you find out?" he asked pointedly.

"My dear boy! If you think it's a secret after that conversation with Lyle in the library the other day, well, you have another thing coming. I'm quite aware you stormed off to see Lord Salisbury in London. But don't worry. I doubt anyone else paid attention. So what did his lordship say to you?"

"To mind my own business," Rogan said wryly.

"Did he really!"

"He might just as well have."

Rogan thought of the meeting in Salisbury's office at Pall Mall. Salisbury said he would wire the high commissioner at Capetown, even though he personally rejected such nonsense, saying it would be a fiasco of the worst sort for Jameson to sponsor a raid into the Transvaal with England and the Boers teetering on the edge of war. Salisbury had cynically asked Rogan if he was fool enough to think the British government actually wanted war with Kruger.

"I've not said that I do, sir," he had answered.

Salisbury had huffed over his insult but assured Rogan that Her Majesty's government did not want a war with the Boers. They would never secretly sanction Jameson's raid into the Transvaal. "And Milner is working day and night for peace."

Rogan had been pointedly silent about that…

"So," continued Elosia, "Arcilla is worried over Peter. I do hope he's not fool enough to allow Julien to dip his hands into blood."

Rogan turned sharply to look at her.

Just then one of the new maids entered with a bob of her skirt.

"What is it, Rosie?"

As he spoke to her, she twittered and blushed.

"Oh, Master Rogan, sir, a good afternoon to you, sir!" came her nasal twang. "Yes, a package for you. The post brought it just a wiggle ago," she tittered. "And here it is, for you!" She presented it as a gift from her hand to his. She beamed. "You see, sir, I just *happened* to be looking out the window here"—she gestured to the window facing the rose garden—"and saw you walking over from the stables, so I ran to get the package from the hall table."

Rosie must have caught the bored, unamused eye of Lady Elosia. She blushed and bumbled out of the room.

Rogan felt sorry for her. It was nothing new to have girls titter in his presence. When he was young it amused him, and he would deliberately give them his most devastating smile. Evy was the only one who hadn't acted that way. The only girl who had presented a challenge to him. And when she finally did smile at him, he hadn't shown it, but he had dreamed of kissing her. He'd only revealed that recently—on their honeymoon. *"I had that effect on you?"* she had gasped, delighted, clapping her hands together. *"Oh, if only I had known!"*

"Which is the very reason I didn't tell you, you heartless creature."

He looked down at the package. It was from his friend, Derwent Brown. He'd been expecting a report on the gold mine, and any other happenings. Rogan thought Derwent was swimmingly good about reporting the news. He might have made a respectable newspaperman. He was anxious to get alone and read it.

The postmark caught his eye. Why was he not at Fort Salisbury, but Bulawayo?

"Is it about diamonds?"

Rogan came back to his aunt's curious voice.

"No. This would be the report on the Zambezi gold mine. Though the postmark looks as though Derwent mailed it from Bulawayo."

"The van Buren man is there as well. Did Evy tell you she received a letter from him?"

Rogan became alert. "Heyden?"

"A doctor. Some uncle, or other, to Katie."

"He's a cousin, Dr. Jakob van Buren. No, I didn't know he had written her. He's in Bulawayo?"

She looked smug. "I must say I'm surprised Evy hasn't told you. Extraordinary!"

He tried to keep his irritation from showing. "She mentioned it to you?"

"No, I saw it. The postmark on the envelope was the same as Derwent's parcel. You know...Bullswayo."

He ignored her unwillingness to learn the name. He wanted to ask her when Evy had received the letter, but that would reinforce his aunt's enthusiasm over discovering Evy's "secret."

"If you'll excuse me now, Elosia, I've work upstairs."

"Yes, of course. Is Evy feeling any better? Rosie said earlier that she was lying down asleep. I'd heard that Mrs. Tisdale saw her leaving Dr. Tisdale's a few days ago."

He turned and looked at her.

Her eyes gleamed.

Tisdale? "Nothing to worry about. We agreed that she'd be checking in with the doctor to make sure she's up to the voyage to Capetown. And Dr. Jackson will be here tomorrow to give his opinion."

Elosia appeared satisfied…and perhaps faintly disappointed at his response. If it was disappointment, it couldn't be over Evy's good health.

He turned and left the room. His jaw set. So she went to see Doc Tisdale? And, just like Jakob's letter, she hadn't told him. And his aunt had taken notice.

He dashed up the wide staircase to the second floor on the west side of the mansion to their suite.

He entered and saw the bedroom door was still closed as he'd left it with Evy asleep. All was silent, and the rain tinkled on the windowpane.

Forget it, Rogan. So she didn't tell you she went to see Tisdale, or about the letter. We're newly married, and both of us are used to independence and privacy. She forgot, is all. It's not important.

Had his beloved old aunt wished to cast suspicion between him and Evy? Why had Evy gone to Dr. Tisdale?

Rogan frowned over his concerns and walked into his small office next to the sitting room. The rain clouds made the cloister dark. He lit the lamp and dropped Derwent's report on the desk, removing his coat and rolling up his sleeves. He undid his tie and tossed it aside—then his frown deepened. He remembered that Evy picked up after him. He snatched the tie from the table and looked around for a place to hang it. He finally folded it up and impatiently stuffed it in his jacket pocket. Single life on the veld had some advantages!

It was a relief to get away from all the gibberish of maids and the small talk. It would be refreshing to read Derwent and Mornay's report on his gold and learn what was happening with the British South Africa Company. He longed for the masculine world he'd left behind.

He opened the package and removed Derwent's letter, followed by a heavy report. Some of the first words in the letter hit hard—

Depressing news, Mr. Rogan. I'll get straight to it: Mr. Mornay and two other good miners died in an explosion at the Zambezi mine this July. Before Mr. Mornay died he asked me to bring some gold he had to Dr. Jakob van Buren, who is here at Bulawayo. That's where I am now, staying with Dr. Jakob. Mornay came back to his childhood faith in Christ through Dr. Jakob. So Mornay wanted his belongings to go for the new mission that Jakob's opening here about a mile from the old Lobengula kraal.

After I buried Mr. Mornay on the Zambezi, I left the geologist, Mr. Clive Shepherd, in charge, and I took off for Salisbury. A stage is running from the fort now, down to Bulawayo, so I traveled on it. Guess I'll be staying here with Dr. Jakob and Alice and the children. At least until you and Miss Evy arrive. Don't know what your plans will be now. I think you'll want to see the mine, though it's shut down since the explosion. Mr. Shepherd and some armed Uitlanders are keeping watch. The BSA has yet to look into matters. Sir Julien seems preoccupied with other things. He asked one of the men with me if he'd lead an expedition into the Matopos, but the old Uitlander wouldn't do it. Don't know why Sir Julien wants to go up into those hills. There's rumors that Chief Lobengula had the Kimberly Black Diamond.

Things don't look good here at Bulawayo, Mr. Rogan. The Ndebele are looking with curses on the English who built Government House at the old kraal. They don't take much to Dr. Jakob, either. They say among themselves that the white god is poison to the Umlimo. I don't like Alice and the children being here much, or your sister and Cousin Darinda. Miss Darinda is determined to stay to work alongside her grandfather. As for Miss Arcilla, she'd leave today if she could. Mr. Peter is grim. I shouldn't say this, but Alice told me the marriage is going poorly. Captain Ryan Retford is working for Peter. He's much like you, I think. But he and your brother, Mr. Parnell, don't seem to like each other. They remind me of two big lions circling each other.

Not good news about the mine either. Before the explosion Mr. Shepherd told Mornay he was convinced the gold had run to a dead end. It's all in the report I'm sending, with my own report as I see it, along with the professional report from Mr. Shepherd.

Mr. Mornay thought the mine had gone bust, too, but he wanted a chance to go deeper into the ridge first before the report was to be sent to you. That's when the dynamite brought down too much dirt and rocks. The cave-in was a sad hour, Mr. Rogan. I got some bruises, which is nothing, and Mr. Shepherd took a bad injury in his arm and shoulder. Dr. Jakob looked at it and says he might not be able to use it much in the future. The other two miners lost were an Australian and a new lad from Pretoria, both Uitlanders from the Transvaal. One Shona died, another has an injured foot. We also lost two good mules. All in all, it's been the worst of times.

Derwent T. Brown

Rogan slowly folded the letter and set it aside. He took time to remember his friend Mornay. The loss, on a personal level, hit hard. There were none better as a hunter-guide than the old Frenchman, except perhaps his father before him. Rogan had lost a friend and ally. He had hoped they would sit around the campfire together and discuss his most recent ideas about Henry's map upon his return. Now it would never be.

Death. It was often sudden and surprising, though every previous generation had passed through its doorway. No one should be shocked by it, but they almost always were. As for men under the sun, with death came the end of every dream.

Rogan opened the desk drawer and took out his small Bible and flipped to Job. If he could find those verses again... He'd come across them on Sunday while sitting with Evy in chapel as they waited for

Vicar Osgood to step behind the pulpit. Those verses were being reinforced in his mind, because of Mornay's death.

He found them in Job chapter twenty-two and read slowly, starting at verse twenty-four: "Then you will lay your gold in the dust, and the gold of Ophir among the stones of the brooks. Yes, the Almighty will be your gold and your precious silver; for then you will have your delight in the Almighty, and lift up your face to God. You will make your prayer to Him, He will hear you, and you will pay your vows."

He pondered. Pondered their wisdom, their warning, their invitation. He remembered Mornay. He considered his own heart.

Now Mornay was gone. He had left everything behind, including his skills, so treasured by others. But Mornay had showed more than benevolence by giving his possessions to Dr. Jakob for the mission station work. He showed a trust in God's Word that rules beyond death.

It was good that Dr. Jakob was able to direct Mornay back to his Christian faith. Though Derwent hadn't said so, Rogan believed Derwent's consistent life had even more to do with Mornay's decision.

Thunder rumbled over Grimston Woods.

Derwent might not know as much about mining as the geologist, whom Rogan hired to work with him, but Derwent's keen discernment was something Rogan held in quiet regard. If Derwent sensed trouble stirring on the veld at Bulawayo, then he was likely on to something.

Julien was shopping about for someone to lead that expedition. Where was Heyden? Somehow he didn't think the Boer was very far from Bulawayo.

All this troubled him even more because of Evy. If only there were some way to get her to stay home and allow him to proceed on this dangerous venture alone.

Yes, he'd made a wise decision in arranging beforehand for Dr. Jackson to see her tomorrow. Now, if he could just convince Jackson to tell Evy that she was not strong enough to make the trek to Bulawayo...

CHAPTER TEN

Evy awoke from a long, restful nap, got dressed, and came out into the sitting room to find a lovely candlelight supper awaiting her.

"Rogan, what a delightful surprise. And I slept through the entire preparation!"

He came to her, took her face lightly between his hands, and kissed her. She looked at him, and he smiled, a dark flash to his eyes that could surprise with its intensity. He grew serious, studying her face.

"Are you happy being my wife?"

Her brows lifted. "Why, what a question." She wrapped her arms around him and hugged tightly. "Wonderfully happy."

"That's how I want you to stay. You're feeling rested now? No more dizzy spells?"

"Oh no," she hastened. "It…was nothing."

"Nothing," he repeated, regarding her.

"You're looking at me…strangely."

"Am I? It's your beauty. It never ceases to stun me."

"Mmm, nice…but it wasn't the stunned look of breathlessness that I saw just now, Rogan, dear."

He winced. "Never call me *dear*. Sounds feminine. *Darling, the one and only man of my dreams*—anything casual will do," he teased, "but not *dear*."

She laughed. "I'll remember. How about Prince Charming?"

He pretended to consider. "It's all right, but not very original. Tell me, love of my youth, why did you see Dr. Tisdale?"

The smile on her lips froze. *Who* had told on her? Lady Elosia? Mrs. Tisdale?

He drew her against him, holding her face against his arm as he buried his face in her hair, and his embrace so tightened that for a moment it cut off her breathing.

"Who's been spying on me?"

"Spying?" He held her away by her shoulders, his eyes flashing. "Doesn't your husband have a right to know if there's something wrong?"

She felt her cheeks flame. "There is nothing wrong with me!"

His lashes narrowed. "Then why did you go?"

Her breath came rapidly. "This is quite unfair of you."

"*What* is?"

"This." She spread her arm toward the lovely table with sparkling crystal and dinnerware and gleaming candlelight. "Do you need this to spring questions on me as though I...I were hiding things from you? I suppose it was Lady Elosia who told you."

"It was. She was worried about you. As am I. You nearly passed out upstairs this afternoon. Do I not have a right to know why you went to see Tisdale?"

She turned away, miserable. How quickly the lovely gesture of a romantic supper had turned into a conflict.

"Yes," she said wearily, "you have a *right*. If that's what means the most to you, *your rights*."

"Seems to me you're responding to this with exaggerated defensiveness. Which tells me there's something you wish to hide."

"You want to know why I would want to hide anything?" She looked at him intensely. "It's your response I worry about. If you think I'm not well, you'll use it against me."

"Against you? Is that how you see my love and concern for you? As something selfish on my part that wants to deny you something good?"

She felt a pang of regret and guilt. She rushed toward him. "Oh, darling, no, that's not how I feel. I'm sorry…"

"Evy…"

She closed her eyes as his arms enfolded her warmly and his lips were on hers, fierce with passion and frustration. She clung to him.

"I love you," she whispered against his neck. "Trust me, Rogan. Will you? Just trust me? I'm up to the voyage to the Cape. Believe me, I am. I'm strong. I've always been strong. Until the accident I rarely had a sick day in my life." She looked up at him, her eyes pleading with his intense gaze. "If I didn't think I could handle the voyage and the trek to Bulawayo, I wouldn't insist on going with you."

For a long moment she didn't think she had gotten past his armor. He looked at her, studying her carefully, until her lashes began to waver. Then he merely gave a nod of his dark head, and his arms released her slowly, as though she might sway dizzily.

"All right. You're asking me to trust you. I will. If you don't think I have a need to know why you saw Tisdale, so be it."

She cringed inwardly. *Oh God, what has happened to me? I can't believe I'm doing this.*

"Of course you have a right to know." She wet her lips. "It was the dizzy spells… He said it was—nothing. Too much excitement recently. Or maybe I wasn't getting enough rest."

She walked slowly to the table where the glow of the candle seemed hypnotic. Her fingers on the back of the tall chair tightened convulsively. She winced at the long silence.

"I see."

Did he? Did he see through her?

"I just didn't want you to be concerned, is all," she murmured. Her appetite was gone. But if she didn't eat…

"I could easily have a talk with Dr. Tisdale."

She stiffened her spine. That would be the end.

"But I won't," came his quiet voice, surprising her with its ability to release her from its grip.

"Do you want to know why I won't go to him?"

"Because Dr. Jackson will be here tomorrow afternoon." Her voice was tired.

"No, that's not the reason. I won't go to Tisdale because I respect you. I won't 'spy' on you, as you stated a moment ago. If I went to him, I'd be saying I didn't trust you to tell me the truth."

She shut her eyes.

"So we'll let it go," he said. "If and when you care to share what's on your mind with me, you'll honor me with your trust. Until then, Evy, I shall respect your privacy. I'll gain nothing I want from our relationship by forcing you."

Oh, how that hurt. How wonderfully mature he was being, and how poorly she was behaving—and she was the one who'd grown up in the rectory. What did that show except perhaps that only genuine faith and not religious ritual could change the heart, her heart? While Rogan had been the rascal, he seemed to be learning and maturing faster in the closeness of marriage than she.

She would make it up to him aboard ship. Yes, that was an answer. And once this was all over, she would never again keep anything back from him that concerned them both. She would do so just this once. It wouldn't do any damage ultimately to their relationship.

He walked up behind her, and for a moment she could sense his pensive stare. But he said not a word and pulled back the chair for her. She sank into it, her knees feeling shaky, as he went to his seat.

She avoided his gaze at first, trying to quell her emotions. She would say nothing more about her visit to Dr. Tisdale for fear of adding to her earlier defensive reaction. Actually, it was partly true that she'd gone to see Dr. Tisdale because of dizziness. And it was true he had mentioned she might not be resting adequately, and that too much excitement from their travels to Spain and Paris may be affecting her stamina. But…he had also said—

Rogan began to talk too casually about other things that had nothing to do with their immediate conflict, and slowly the tension eased, and her conviction began to ease as well.

She took a bite of the tender sirloin. What would have been simply delicious earlier was now absent of taste. Even the champagne seemed flat. Guilt did amazing things to the body...as well as the soul.

Soon afterward Rogan shared some of the dark news from Derwent's report. Another mine explosion? She remembered her grandfather Carl van Buren had also died in such an accident. At the time Carl was partners with Sir Julien Bley in what would turn out to be a rich diamond hole in Kimberly. That big hole was still producing diamonds today.

Evy could see how Mornay's death sobered Rogan. He told her his old French associate had, like the prodigal son, come home to faith in Christ before he died.

"You'll be pleased to know it was Jakob who influenced him."

"Did he? How wonderful." Somehow she felt connected.

"Derwent tells me Mornay left his gold to Jakob's missionary work."

"Yes, so he wrote me. He left the Zambezi station with another medical couple in charge and went to Bulawayo."

Rogan was watching her; she wondered why.

"So you did receive a letter from him."

Evy should have known Elosia wouldn't omit that bit of news, not that Jakob's letter needed to be another secret. She explained, showing him the letter, relieved she could share it with him.

"Interesting how Jakob agrees with Derwent about something stirring at Bulawayo."

She saw that Rogan was restive.

"More trouble?"

"Trouble, always. Trouble with the BSA...trouble with Uncle

Julien. You know about the Kimberly diamond and Lobengula's burial cave."

"Yes. Does Derwent know about it?"

"He mentions it. Julien tried to hire an Uitlander familiar with the Matopos region to get up an expedition. If he does, it will light a fire under Lobengula's impis. They're already drawn as tight as a bowstring. Now there's a drought, and the Umlimo told them it was white man's doing—the result of Lobengula's death as well as the white man's rule. They believe we've brought a curse on their cattle and land...no surprise there either. The British are blamed for everything these days."

She thought about that. "I wonder how it will affect Cousin Jakob's missionary work there."

"It won't help any, not with their Umlimo warning them against the *English god.*"

It was as though they were satanically deceived. For centuries the tribes had been limited to nothing but dark ideas, resulting in spiritual bondage. Satan did not want to give up control over this people.

"If that isn't enough, the Zambezi gold mine has gone bust."

"Oh no!" She was disappointed for him, not that it meant much to her, even though she shared his part of it. "So soon?"

"Too soon, if you ask me. But my geologist is sure." He took a turn up and down the room. "A bit odd. I wouldn't have thought Henry's big gold find would have come up dead already. Mornay didn't either. That was the reason he wanted to go deeper."

She knew not what to make of it all.

"Maybe the geologist is mistaken," she consoled.

Rogan ran his fingers through his dark hair. "He is too smart to make a mistake like that. And I trust him; no deviltry on his part either. Makes me wonder about the map." He looked over at his desk, where the map was carefully pinned out for study.

Evy, wishing to show that she was interested in matters that captured his interest, walked over to the desk and looked down at the old map. She had never been much of a map reader. All the squiggly lines crossing here and there amid strange sounding names told her nothing. What did interest her were the symbols Henry Chantry had drawn. One was a great bird, another a lion, and then a baobab tree.

"What do these pictures mean?"

He joined her at the desk. "I wish I knew. Perhaps nothing at all. But recently I've been thinking otherwise. I doubt Henry wanted to pretty up the map with African symbols."

"There's a message in them, you think?" The very mystery sparked her interest.

He leaned his hands on the desk, frowning down at the drawing. "I'm inclined to think so. That's another reason I'm anxious to return as soon as possible."

She thought of the books he'd brought up from his father's library, all of them on Africa, its tribes, and tribal emblems.

"African tribal symbols often tell a story, and they generally use animals. I've been doing research on those drawings. That bird, for instance. Notice the way its wings are spread. It could be significant. It's the bird that holds my interest. What does the bird remind you of?"

She studied the drawing carefully. "At first I would automatically think of an eagle, or a hawk."

"My first thought also, but not anymore."

She was curious. "Some bird unique to South Africa?"

"What else could it be? Remember, the tribes have never been out of their own environment. So what is it that the Africans see in this bird?"

"First, I would consider which tribe."

"Exactly!" He looked at her, a sparkle in his eyes. "The Zulu? Ndebele? Shona? Since Henry went to the Zambezi before the Zulu war, it could be any of the them, or even another group altogether..." He frowned again as he stared intently at the bird. "Someone familiar with the tribes and their lore might offer a bit of wisdom. I thought I'd have a talk with Dr. Jakob. He's been in that region longer than any of us, including Mornay." He gently rolled up the small map. "It will be easier now that he's at Bulawayo."

She was excited and pleased. Jakob was becoming an important part of the venture.

"Don't forget Jendaya," she told him. "Heyden thought she was still alive and wanted to see me. She, too, may be able to shed some light on the symbols."

There was no enthusiasm in his gaze at the mention of Heyden, or Jendaya.

"But what do the symbols have to do with the gold mine going 'bust' as you put it?"

"I've been thinking about it for some time now. Maybe we were just a bit lucky, stumbling onto a mine the way we did after reaching Fort Salisbury. Even back then, I wasn't convinced we'd found Henry's deposit…these symbols kept me wondering. There was nothing within several miles of the spot that even resembled the symbols. The tempting conclusion to come to at the time was to think they had no meaning."

"But you no longer think so?"

"It's not like Henry to be duplicitous. He wanted me to succeed with the map. And the find has gone bust too quickly. Henry was convinced of something much more dramatic. Later on, Julien realized his error of not funding Henry's expedition. If Julien weren't obsessed right now with the Kimberly Black, he'd be breathing down my neck again. That also holds true for Rhodes. He wouldn't have bothered with me as he did, coming to my camp on the Limpopo River, forcing me into the Company to get his hands into such a small gold mine. No, they believed in something bigger, and so did my uncle."

Evy knew that Rogan had always believed Henry had discovered a mammoth vein of gold back before the Zulu War of 1878. A lode so rich as to be on par with the historic discovery of Witwatersrand in the 1880s.

"There's more to Henry's map. And I've got to discover what it is."

"Another trek?" She was uncertain how she felt about this sudden new possibility.

She had always understood he would go to the gold mine while she stayed and visited with Dr. Jakob, but Rogan was suggesting much more now, a trek that could become expansive as he resumed the search for Henry's secret—an expedition that could last many months, even a year. She felt her brows nipping together.

"Another trek like the last one may not be possible, or wise," he said casually. "If the Boers take up their rifles, there'll be war. Even if they don't, Doc Jameson could act rashly on his own, and there may be no way to stop the killing. We'll all get involved. I don't see how it can be otherwise."

"But Jakob is a missionary. Neither the British nor the Boers would attack his mission station," she said hopefully. "Both sides are Christian."

"In war very little is sacred, darling. I'm not suggesting either side would deliberately attack the station, but regardless, Jakob is bound to be in the midst of trouble at Bulawayo. If I bring you there and go off on a new expedition, you'd be left on your own. Jakob's a rough man, Evy, a just man who's used to doing without, an old bachelor. His mission on the Zambezi was little more than a few huts and a chapel. I've no reason to think Bulawayo will be much different."

Evy had no wish for Rogan to begin an extensive new expedition, especially if there was some question of her safety at the mission station. Even so, she decided it would do no good to press the issue now. She would wait for Dr. Jackson's report on the morrow. Somehow she must keep the doctor from suspecting her pregnancy. That should not be too hard to do. He was a specialist on the spine. If she kept silent, he wasn't likely to discover the truth.

CHAPTER ELEVEN

The next day Dr. Jackson arrived by train from his office on Harley Street. With the discussion and exam behind her, she sat on the brocade settee in the sitting room and glanced at Rogan through narrowed lashes. *I've gotten by with it.*

Evy blinked aside the prick to her conscience. Keeping the news of the baby to herself for another three weeks shouldn't hurt anyone, and her secret was for a good cause. Her departure from Rookswood would solve many of her present difficulties. The baby would be born long before they returned to Grimston Way. By then Patricia Bancroft would have found a new love (perhaps even married), the gossip about Evy would have faded, and Elosia would have mellowed, not keeping such a tight grip on running the estate.

All I need to do, thought Evy, biting her lip and watching Rogan, *is to delay informing him for a short time. In the end all will be forgotten.*

"Tell Rogan the truth as soon as you can," Martha had said.

Well, Evy would tell him as soon as she *could.* But to keep from having her plans unravel, she had to wait until she was far enough out at sea, with no possibility of turning back. *I'll tell Rogan aboard ship.*

Evy loathed resorting to such tactics, but it was partly Rogan's fault. If only he weren't so resolute about making the present state of her health such a deciding issue. *It's not like I'm being unfair to Rogan just by delaying the announcement. And besides, had I conceived only one month later, Rogan would not receive the announcement until aboard ship anyway.*

And that would be exactly the same situation as far he was concerned, and there would have been nothing deceptive about it.

She made a sweeping dismissal as guilt sprang up like a stinging thorn. It was Rogan's fault, actually. Because he was too controlling. He was forcing her into this deceit. *Look at the way he's carrying on now. Insisting we must have Dr. Jackson's approval for the journey. Just as though I were still a schoolgirl, needing permission from the headmistress before leaving the school boundary.*

It was sweet of him to worry about a spine problem causing too much fatigue, but she would be resting most of the time anyway, either aboard ship in a cabin, or in a wagon or stagecoach when they crossed the frontier on their way to Bulawayo. *He's determined to use my weakness as his "reason" to keep me "safe and secure" in Grimston Way. And then he can have his big adventure with Derwent without having a woman along to be responsible for. Well! This woman has her dreams of adventure, too, and with good reason, and she isn't going to stay in Grimston Way if she has anything to say about it.* Yes, she should be submissive to Rogan's wishes, but this trip to see Cousin Jakob van Buren meant too much to her.

Evy had practically worked herself into a simmer as she watched Rogan speaking in sober tones with Dr. Jackson. She squirmed on the settee. It was all she could do to keep silent—as though she were not even listening. *I'm supposed to sit here, hands folded calmly in my lap, a demure expression, leaving them to decide everything about me.*

Dr. Jackson prepared to leave for the trip back to his office in London, having been paid a great amount to come here. He stood thoughtfully, fingering his gray Vandyke beard. "Whether the journey will be too much for her at this time is difficult to say with certainty, Rogan."

Evy's brows lifted in shock. *Ha, my darling Rogan, your plan isn't working, is it?*

Somewhat gleeful, she wanted to stand, quite willing to give Dr. Jackson a hug, but she quickly managed a demure face.

"As I've already said, I see no reason why Evy couldn't go on this trip to Capetown."

Rogan looked displeased. She knew he'd been expecting the doctor would recommend that she stay in England. Rogan seemed to be avoiding her gaze, but when he looked over at her, she rested her chin on her palm, covering a smile as their eyes held. His mouth turned wryly.

Rogan spoke with determination to the doctor. "I'd say it's near a thousand miles from Capetown to Fort Salisbury, and even if she stayed at Bulawayo with my sister and her husband, it would be nearly as long a trek. We'd go partway by frontier stage through Matabeleland, then by covered wagon. A trying ordeal any way you look at it, Doctor."

Evy narrowed her gaze. He should have been a member of Parliament the way he liked to present matters to influence and change minds.

"Yes, your point is well taken, Rogan. It would be difficult for almost anyone, I imagine. It could indeed prove too much for her, although she's heartily improving. The rehabilitation has gone very well in her case. As I've said, I commend you for your discipline. Your work with her each day on the exercises has done wonders. And if she continues to improve, I foresee a day when she may no longer need to wear the corrective shoe."

True enough, Evy thought, ashamed she'd criticized him. Rogan had been wonderful. He was supportive, tender, and even humorous at times just to make her laugh at her trial. But that didn't make up for what he was trying to do now. She drummed her fingers on her knee.

Rogan was walking Dr. Jackson to the door. "Thank you, Doctor. You've been very helpful to us in this decision. I can see Evy and I will need to have a little more discussion before we decide what's best."

Quite so, thought Evy with a sweet smile.

Rogan opened the door for the doctor, then followed him out into the corridor, avoiding her gaze and closing the door behind him.

Evy jumped to her stocking feet and hurried to the door, listening, but could hear nothing except muffled voices, followed by footsteps along the hall to the staircase.

She waited at the sitting room window as she saw Rogan escorting

Dr. Jackson to the Chantry coach. Mr. Bixby, who had previously brought Dr. Jackson from the train junction, opened the coach door as the doctor stepped in. Rogan saluted him good-bye.

Evy watched as the coach headed down the path toward the gate and Rogan walked back to the porch steps and entered the mansion.

She left the window and took her place on the settee to replace her shoes, one of which was the loathsome, heavy corrective shoe that had been made for her in London. She grimaced as she tied the laces. At least her skirt covered it when she stood. Her hemlines were a smidgen too long for today's finest fashion, but it was better than seeing the shoe. The idea that she would not need to wear it permanently lightened her burden for the moment.

She smoothed her thick, tawny hair into place and looked up expectantly as the door opened and Rogan entered, shutting it behind him.

He stood, his hand resting on the doorknob, looking across the room at her.

Evy forced a dignified face, chin lifted. His dark hair waved slightly across his forehead, and his energetic dark eyes drifted over her thoughtfully. Virile and pleasing to the eye, he was hard to resist. She smiled.

Rogan's hand dropped from the doorknob, and he came into the room. Walking up to the settee, he looked down at her. He was dressed casually in a brown tweed jacket, with his shirt unbuttoned at the neck. He looked the future squire and less the South African pioneer adventurer—something she knew he would have preferred, though he'd settled with Squire Lyle for Rookswood and its title rather than more shares in the family diamonds, as Parnell had done.

She'd been waiting for this battle of wills, and her emotions were as taut as a tiger ready to spring. She stood, arms crossed in a show of contest.

A smile came to his mouth, and his brow arched.

"Ah, the withering glance. The prince will surely be turned into a frog again."

"And next time I shan't kiss you and turn you back into a prince."

He laughed. "Darling, I adore you, but you know you ought to stay here at Rookswood. You heard Dr. Jackson. He doesn't advise your going."

Evy gave a mirthless laugh. "I heard nothing of the sort. You're willing to hear only his words of caution, just because it suits your purpose."

"Your safety suits my purpose. Look here, Evy, I've been there. I know what it's like, what's ahead of you."

"Meaning you don't believe me when I say that I'm quite up to the journey?" she challenged.

"Sweetheart, I believe you," came his assuring voice.

"Then—"

"But you're anxious for the trek just to meet Dr. Jakob. I think you'd do almost anything to get your way in this."

Evy felt her face turn hot. "So that's what you think of me?"

He ignored it. "I know it was our plan from the beginning that you might be able to go, but it's also true that desires can color our thinking and deceive us. You may think you're ready for this when in fact you're not. The land can be quite brutal. I was against Arcilla going there, if you remember, but I had no choice in that decision. However, you're my wife."

"Arcilla and the other women are there, regardless of the newspaper headlines. She has a baby too, and Alice has three. They are no stronger than I am."

"I disagree. Alice turned out to be as strong as an ox. And Arcilla is constantly wailing in poor Peter's ear to come home. Anyway, my plans have changed," he said seriously.

His plans. That's what troubled her. She desired his plans to be *their* plans. It seemed as though there were places in his mind, his soul, that bore the label: "Rogan only—Evy keep out." Rogan denied her complaints.

"It's all for your good, my sweet. Just be as cooperative and submissive as you are charming and beautiful."

"Exactly," she said, feeling rebellious, "and therein lies the problem, dear husband. The garden you want to confine me in is fragrant and lovely, but my spirit chafes at being bound by security. I want to *share* in your adventure." She felt nettled that she couldn't reach deeply into his heart. "We made a bargain, Rogan. You said that if Dr. Jackson approved, you'd no longer contest my going with you. You can't say he recommended I stay in Grimston Way, because he didn't say so—unless you're going to be a perfect scoundrel the way you were as a boy."

He grinned. "Well, I'm not quite as odious as all that, I hope. I think I've learned a few things—about my charming wife, as well."

"What do you mean?" she asked quickly. Had he guessed after all?

He looked over at her, smiling. "She is an exciting, determined young woman," he said gently. "One who doesn't want her wings clipped. That, I readily understand. And I'd be the last one to want to do so."

"Then we've a bargain, Rogan Chantry?"

His mouth tipped down at the corner. "We've a bargain. But know that I don't approve."

"You're willing to let me go?"

"Allowing you to accompany me across dusty velds where irate savages can pop up at any moment from behind every bush and tree with their assegai, is not how I want my sweetheart living. No—" And he held up a hand to her protest. "Spare me the saga of Arcilla again. You might as well know I don't share Peter's mind about such matters. I don't think Arcilla should be there, but in Capetown. That land is naked and raw. If you're not strong, Evy—"

"But I am *strong*, darling!" She threw her arms around him, smiling. "You promised me… It's settled, then."

"Vixen." He kissed her. "Yes, I did say if Dr. Jackson gave the nod you could come. All right, Mrs. Chantry. Have it your way. But when the dust blows, the spiders jump, and the crawlies come creeping under your blanket, don't come squalling to me."

She laughed airily. "I won't. I shall have your cousin Darinda teach me how to shoot a pistol."

"Not a chance. *I'll* teach you how to use it…and when. And if you ever need to, I want you to be a dead shot. We'll start tomorrow. War is ready to break out with the Boers." He snatched up the *London Times* he'd been looking at earlier and thrust it toward her, tapping the black headlines:

WAR WITH BOERS LIKELY, FOREIGN SECRETARY SAYS

"The foreign secretary is a pessimist. You said so yourself just last week," she said with forced cheerfulness.

"It will be a dangerous trek to Bulawayo, regardless. If the stubborn Boers don't start the war, the bitter and resentful Ndebele will."

"Was I safe when you left for South Africa last time with Heyden here, in Grimston Way?"

"Yes, but we know Heyden is in South Africa now. Both Parnell and Derwent bear witness to that. If you stayed here it would be different for you this time, sweet. You're at Rookswood under the watchful eye of the imposing Aunt Elosia and Sir Lyle. So nothing can happen."

"And what happened on the third floor of this house when your uncle was *murdered* for the Kimberly Black Diamond?"

"That was different."

She looked into those dark eyes and saw the unmistakable love in their fiery depths.

"Sometimes I think the real reason you want me here is so you can hunt down Heyden," she said soberly.

"An excellent idea!"

"I'd better come along—just to keep an eye on you," she said gravely.

He laughed.

"We'll need to have Mrs. Croft here tomorrow to help us pack."

"So soon? We've almost two weeks, don't we?"

He smiled. "No. You'll be happy to know we sail on Wednesday morning. I was able to book passage on an earlier ship."

"Oh, Rogan, this is wonderful! And you didn't tell me. Even though you expected me to sail with you all along. Oh, I forgot to tell you, Mrs. Croft is coming with us."

"I was expecting that as well. She has a cabin next to us."

Evy breathed a sigh of relief. Faithful, steady Mrs. Croft. Knowing she would be near made Evy feel relieved. She laid her forehead against his chest a moment.

"You won't be sorry I'm along."

"I don't know about that," he said dryly. "I think you'll be a great cause of worry." He lifted her chin, and he wasn't smiling as he searched her eyes.

This wasn't the first time their strong wills had come into conflict, and she knew it wouldn't be the last. He was letting her go, but not because he preferred to. What would he say aboard ship…when he learned she was going to have his baby?

PART TWO

CHAPTER TWELVE

Bulawayo, South Africa

The Matopos Hills glowed an eerie dark red in the setting sun. This was no longer Matabeleland, but Rhodesia; and Bulawayo, the kraal of Chieftain Lobengula, was now part of the British South Africa Company's charter lands, a British town under British government. Arcilla Chantry, now Mrs. Peter Bartley, walked along the crooked path that led away from the dusty garden of what was lightly named Government House toward some distant bungalows belonging to the Charter Company.

Arcilla glanced warily about, trying to peer into the rosy dusk descending like a secretive veil. The wind from the veld blew through the acacia trees. Did she hear a twig snap under someone's stealthy foot?

She licked her dried lips and pushed ahead on the path toward the bungalows, which were still out of view. The bungalows lodged officials working under Dr. Leander Jameson for the BSA. Arcilla drew her lacy shawl about her shoulders and swallowed her fear. Then— She stood rigid on the path, her heart pounding thunderously. After the horrid death of Major Tom Willet...

A peacock strutted out and stood in the middle of the path, looking in her direction, its tail fanning into colorful splendor, as though to say, *It's me, proudly showing off the handiwork of God. You should rely on Him more.*

A breath released from Arcilla's lips. Everything about Africa frightened her. And those hills… She gazed off toward the Matopos again. If she wasn't careful, as Peter had said, she would soon come to believe the "extraordinary nonsense" about those mountains and hills, which were held in superstitious reverence by the Ndebele and even some Shona. An evil spirit abode there, according to Derwent, possessing a girl called the Umlimo, who gave forth oracles to the tribe.

A ghostly breeze brushed against her skin, as though conjuring up from the dust a power to impede her way. She could almost hear the clacking bones of the demonic *nganga* "doctors."

Arcilla hurried along the path through the narrowing line of acacia trees, glancing behind her. Catching her slipper on an embedded rock, she lost her balance and nearly fell. She regained her footing and hurried on.

How often she had asked Peter to tell the workmen to clear out the rocks. Was it too much to ask? But Peter!

Arcilla clutched the front of her shawl. Peter was busy with more important things for the Charter Company than to pay heed to her complaints.

The BSA! How she loathed the Company—Uncle Julien Bley, too. And that laconic Dr. Jameson, Rhodes's chief spokesman here in Rhodesia. Yes, she loathed them all. Her dislike reached out to include her cousin Darinda Bley, Julien's granddaughter. She disliked her because, like some wild, malicious flower, Darinda opened her petals and warmed to the ruthlessness that was Africa. Darinda was not afraid of anything this wretched land threw at her, and Peter too often noticed her courage while showing impatience with Arcilla.

I can't help it, I don't belong here. I belong to England, to its soft greens and gentle fog, to Rookswood and Chantry Townhouse.

With her fingers still grasping the front of her shawl, Arcilla walked more carefully along the serpentine path. *Peter is unfair and selfish. Peter doesn't really love me. I know he doesn't. I should have married Charles— and Peter should have married Darinda.*

Dear God, whatever am I going to do? I shall die here! I shall! I know it—

Arcilla half stumbled along the bumpy path again. This time the strap on her dainty slipper came off her heel. She stooped and slipped it back. She sniffed loudly and brushed her golden hair from her face. Peter had insisted she wear sturdier shoes like Darinda, but the very mention of her cousin provoked Arcilla's stubborn streak. If Peter would just stop comparing everything she did to Darinda—

Miserable pathway. The workmen couldn't even level out the dirt! The BSA had taken her husband from her, had stolen her peace of mind, had taken her life! *I'm trapped here in this savage land with heathen and poisonous snakes and stinging centipedes and flying spiders—all of them are one and the same!* Her loathing of everything around her shot adrenaline through her body, giving her the drive to press ahead down the darkening, constricting path.

Derwent had kindly told her to pray more, but what could she say to God when she hardly knew what God was like? Oh yes, she'd heard about Jesus. After all, hadn't she grown up going to church in Grimston Way? But she couldn't remember much of anything Vicar Havering had said. She had a Bible, but she hadn't learned it well enough to know where to read. In those times she did turn to it, she seemed to lose interest upon reaching a list of "begots." Oh, and Peter was no help at all! None. Peter didn't know how to pray, either. Once she had asked him to pray before they retired to bed for the night, and he looked at her as though she'd suddenly developed green skin.

Beyond the trees, not nearly as far as they now seemed at dusk, stood a group of bungalows where members of the Bulawayo government were living. *Oh to be home in England, safe.* To raise her son at Rookswood under the secure counsel of that bastion of strength, Aunt Elosia.

A thought flashed through her mind. She remembered what Dr. Jakob van Buren had said when she'd attended his Sunday service once. Dr. Jakob had been invited to speak at Government House, and his message had not gone over well with those present. Uncle Julien had

LINDA LEE CHAIKIN

looked as though he wanted to toss him in the river while the crocodiles were feeding. And Peter had sat straight in his chair with an expression as leaden as the statues in the British Museum.

"Most people," his voice had boomed, with a ragged Boer accent, "prefer their sin clothed with the latest style of sophistication. Pride puts on a pretty face and sits in the theater enjoying a symphony, and we say, 'Oh, these are the *good* people of the civilized West.' Oh, the raw sin of the naked savage with his doctrines of demons offends our finer natures—as well it should—and so we missionaries come with torches of light, which is God's Word. A Word that reveals His Son Jesus Christ. For we are darkness in and of ourselves. We have no light apart from Him.

"Witchcraft unearths the rotting corpse called sin, and we sophisticates are offended! It is well we should be. But are we equally offended with our own sin? We are all sinners before a holy God, whether that sin is raw, and dark, and openly evil—or hidden behind silks and perfumes, lordly titles, and ambitious national goals for Her Majesty. And the sin of hypocrisy was firmly denounced when our Lord was on earth, but He had words of mercy for the woman taken in adultery!

"Ah yes. It took the willing death of Jesus on the cross to pay for our sin. Christ is the door to God, and that door is open wide for all to enter. If you come through that door, you will find that the Father of all creation has made you a new creature in Christ. That new spiritual birth is yours through faith in Jesus Christ."

Arcilla shuddered. Oh! How Uncle Julien was offended! His face had been flushed with high blood pressure.

She hadn't liked Dr. Jakob's bluntness either. Imagine, comparing her little sins to the spooky brutality of witchcraft with bones, gizzards, and snakeskins!

Arcilla drew the shawl closer and lifted her chin, aware that her golden hair shone. She imagined herself a white princess in the starlight, slipping along the trail, waiting for the silvery moon to send moonbeams through her hair.

But the princess must now watch the dark, crooked path that

tempted her feet to go astray. Yesterday she had come across a four-inch band of army ants. If she'd been careless and stepped on them, she would have been stung mercilessly. There might be a snake, too, one of those banded cobras, or the spitting kind that blinds with a stream of venom. She could never become used to such things, never. And to think Derwent Brown had said that the biblical Garden of Eden may have been in Africa! Bah! Everyone knew it had to have been in England. England, with its cool, misty weather and fragrant roses. Probably quite near Buckingham Palace, too, very close to where Queen Victoria ruled.

Here, on the Dark Continent, she must always be wary. Not merely of wild creatures, but worse. Oh, indeed, much worse. The Ndebele, those fearsome, sullen-faced cousins of the Zulus, whispering of the great days when Lobengula was their king leading them to great victories, were a constant threat.

Now the dark, naked giant was buried somewhere in the Matopos Hills, covered in piles of diamonds.

Arcilla loathed the sight of those mountains with their lower hills so near to Bulawayo. Derwent said the demons once had their way here at the kraal, and they now held cruel hatred toward those building a chapel where the name of Jesus was praised. That name, he said, could easily send demons fleeing in fear.

Was that true? It was all too much for Arcilla to fathom. Trying to make sense of it all made her head throb. Why must life be so difficult?

"All I want is a British cup of tea and a scone—as only the British servants at Rookswood can make them."

And now, her baby son, born here. Sweet, precious little Charles Rogan Bartley! Eight pounds and thirteen ounces of sweet British baby fat! Ah, he was a *Rhodesian!* Oh…what would that mean when he grew up a handsome young man? Would he talk funny when he went to England? Arcilla could imagine all the ladies laughing behind his back.

My poor baby. My Poor Charles Rogan Bartley!

How Aunt Elosia wrote of her desire to hold him in her strong arms. Oh, for the nursery on the third floor of Rookswood.

Arcilla stopped so quickly her curls bounced on her forehead. She widened her blue eyes into circles.

A dozen crows, their black wings scarlet from the blazing summer sunset, cawed plaintively as they flew from the field alongside the path and disappeared into the thick grouping of acacia trees farther across the veld. The cawing and the beating of their black wings dried her mouth with sudden fear. *Something was ahead that frightened them.*

The crows settled into silence, bringing back the same dense African stillness across the veld that she loathed. The stillness closed in about her, smothering her. *Someone is out there. Yes, someone on the path ahead just as it circles out of sight behind those monkeypod trees—*

Voices!

Arcilla stood still on the pathway where a hedge towered above her. She was unable to see what lay beyond, but she could hear voices. She listened as angry speech cut the twilight—

"You have stolen my rights."

"My dear, that is something you'll need to discuss with Julien."

"I have. He has this notion he's made a promise to you he can't go back on. That promise is unfair to me and my sister."

"Cannot go back on his promise? Since when has Julien been concerned about keeping his word?"

"I resent that! He's my grandfather—"

So, that must be Darinda Bley. But who was she arguing with?

"You are very much like *him.*"

"I take that as a compliment. My grandfather built the diamond dynasty with his wit and hard work. And I shall follow in his footsteps."

"There are those on all sides of the family who would disagree with your assessment about who started the diamond business, or that Julien even deserves to be in control. One of those who could have been used in court if he were still alive was Carl van Buren, Katie's father—and Evy's grandfather. Evy van Buren, now Evy Chantry, has more right to the business than you, if the truth were known."

"Lies. She won't cheat me out of what's mine, and neither will you!"

"No one wants to cheat you of anything that's truly yours."

"No? Then what do you mean to suggest?"

"I suggest you ask your grandfather. Now, if you'll excuse me, I'm late for a meeting."

"You won't get by with this. I won't let you push me aside and take over for your *illegitimate* daughter!"

"Is that some sort of threat?"

"You can take it to mean anything you wish. I won't be disinherited. Somehow I'll make my grandfather see he must change his will in my favor, not yours."

"I have no doubt you'll try. Good evening."

There was a crunch beneath his shoes as he turned and left.

It was Anthony. Anthony Brewster. He'd arrived unexpectedly this morning to meet with Uncle Julien. Arcilla stepped behind a thorn tree and waited for Anthony to walk past on the path to Government House. She waited, but his footsteps faded instead of coming nearer, faded into an uneasy silence.

Arcilla drew her brows together. After another moment of waiting—where had he gone? Back to the bungalows? And where had Darinda Bley gone? At least one of them should have appeared on the path. Arcilla waited another minute, then assured that neither would appear, she stepped out from behind the thorn tree and continued on her way toward the bungalows.

Now, what was that argument between Darinda Bley and Lord Anthony Brewster about? Diamonds, I daresay. What else? It's always something about family control over the beautiful, glittering diamonds.

She breathed deeply to settle her nerves. The fragrance of native flowers mingled with dust, filling her nostrils. The mixed fragrance brought a grimace, as did so much about Africa and its history, its beauty and brutality mingled.

Arcilla rehearsed in her mind the cool tension in Anthony's voice, and the hot emotion in Darinda's.

Upon the arrival of Lord Anthony Brewster, Arcilla envisioned a reprieve that would brighten her world of despair. Lord Anthony Brewster was bringing new orders for Peter from the British high commissioner's office in Capetown. Looming in her mind was the expectation that Lord Milner would reassign Peter to home duty now that his father was ailing.

Arcilla had written the Home Office, requesting Peter be sent home. She was expecting Peter's father to also request his son's return. She'd written him twice, begging him to do so. She believed Anthony's arrival was at least partly due to those letters.

She had written quite a different letter to Rogan, warning of Julien and Dr. Jameson's plans to aid the Uitlanders in the Transvaal. She was sure Anthony had come to see Uncle Julien about that as well.

When Anthony had arrived that morning, she had been so hopeful! But as the day wore on, and there was no word from him, the waiting became excruciating. When she could endure no more, she had decided to come to Anthony's bungalow to speak with him herself.

She hurried along the pathway between clumps of flowering shrubs and trees, thinking of Anthony…Anthony Brewster who was Evy's father. What a shock that bit of news turned out to be! Anthony and Katie van Buren were her parents. And to think Anthony knew about Evy during those years in Grimston Way and never told her. Uncle Julien, too.

Was Darinda fearful of Evy or Anthony?

There was too much wind this evening. The vast stretch of the land lay dusty brown in the twilight. Even the birds were silent.

Julien had appeared positively stunned this morning when Anthony walked through the door. *There must be a letter from Lord Milner,* thought Arcilla, trying to understand what Anthony's unexpected visit would hold.

Uncle Julien had good reason to be alarmed, plotting the way he did with Dr. Jameson. And then there was the whispering about the Black Diamond.

What would Peter do if he knew she'd sent that wire to Rogan about the meeting between Julien and Jameson? Would her action become the final wedge between her and Peter?

The path came to an acre of reddish-brown earth, now in shadow, and twisted past six widely spaced bungalows, where jacaranda and pepper trees grew. Beyond the bungalows was an incline of knee-high grasses and wildflowers that led down to a watercourse, where, at sundown, animals of all kinds congregated to quench their thirst.

Arcilla wisely stayed far afield from the watercourse.

She hurried across the swept yard to one of the bungalows that she'd learned was assigned to Lord Anthony while in Bulawayo. It was the empty one that sat farther back, with a rocky path down to the watercourse. She climbed wooden steps onto a screened porch. The lamps were on as twilight descended like a mantle. The door into the small drawing room stood open to let the breeze blow through and out the back windows.

Arcilla stopped on the porch, surprised. Darinda stood inside with her back toward the door, busy with something on Anthony's desk. Arcilla glanced about the room and did not see Anthony. Had he returned here with Darinda? Had he gone on to the big house to keep his appointment—a meeting with whom?

"What are you doing, Darinda?"

Darinda turned quickly around from the table.

What was she doing back in Anthony's bungalow after they had parted so angrily? Darinda was a lovely young woman who dared to wear riding pants and carry a pistol. Her smooth dark hair was pulled back and pinned up. Her eyes were a cool, self-possessed gray. Those eyes widened now as she stared at Arcilla, who realized she must look wild and wind-tossed, her face flushed from hurrying.

Should she let Darinda know she'd heard her arguing with Lord Anthony? Perhaps not.

Darinda quickly regained her poise.

"Hello, Arcilla. I'm surprised to see you out alone at twilight. I came to welcome Lord Anthony to Bulawayo. He's not here. He went to keep a meeting."

So she was willing to fib about getting on well with him.

Members of Dr. Jameson's body of officers were living in the other bungalows. Which one did Anthony meet? Did it have to do with the Uitlanders?

"And you?" Darinda continued, her voice calm. "Why did you come? Is anything wrong?"

Arcilla sensed that something was all wrong somehow. Darinda was standing there so outwardly calm, when a short while ago she had struck with venom at a man who stood in her way to assuming the power she sought.

Arcilla was bemused. Things certainly weren't at all what they appeared. Who had said that to her recently? Derwent?

Darinda was like a river flowing peacefully by its banks, while beneath the surface it was teeming with hungry crocodiles with large white teeth—like diamonds, reflecting the sun's glitter. Like the Kimberly Diamond, bringing a curse to all who tried to possess its beauty, its wealth. If one clutched that diamond too closely to one's heart, it turned into something alive, slithering, black, and deadly.

Life suddenly was upside down, blurred, and deceptive—

"Are you all right?" Darinda asked sharply. "You're as white as a lily."

"Yes, oh, I'm fine—*No!* I am *not* fine." And she sank into a chair and foolishly giggled.

Darinda stared, frowning, as if Arcilla had gone balmy. "Better have some tea," she said crisply. Tea was Darinda's answer to any upset.

"You ask what's wrong *now.* My point exactly—something's *always* wrong in this horrid place."

Darinda's lips turned with impatience. "You're not making a bit of sense."

Parnell had written Anthony about Uncle Julien's attack on Bulawayo and the routing of Lobengula and his impis. Arcilla suspected her older brother had not written the news to Rogan, for fear he would come straight here and get involved in trouble. Parnell didn't know that she had wired Rogan about Jameson's plan to attack the Transvaal.

Arcilla reached for the teapot. Her fingers shook. The cup and saucer rattled. The same hysterical laughter bubbled in her chest as she gazed at the delicate pink rosebuds on the china cup. She giggled. How ridiculous it seemed. Delicate chinaware in a savage land. *We'll never bring British civilization here.*

She added sugar and stirred with a small golden spoon, spilling the tea onto the delicate saucer. She giggled again.

"Stop it."

She ignored Darinda's directive. Darinda had little patience with her idiosyncrasies, and Arcilla knew it. She was smiling as she swallowed a calming pill Dr. Jameson had prescribed for her, trying not to laugh.

"More pills? With Parnell, it's liquor. Why can't either of you pull yourselves together?"

Arcilla set her cup down with a rattle. "We're not as hardheaded as you are," she managed to say with a cynical smile.

"Hard? Am I? Just because someone needs to hold things together in this family?"

Arcilla giggled loudly.

"Hold—the—family—together—"

Darinda looked exasperated.

A third voice interjected: "Protecting us more feebleminded? From *what?* Anthony's rule, or maybe Julien's *sjambok?* Extraordinary notion, either way!"

The cynical question reaching Darinda from the doorway startled Arcilla. She turned her head sharply. Her brother, Parnell, stood on the porch, his mouth tucked into a bitter smile.

He's been drinking again, worried Arcilla. There would be trouble.

Parnell L. Chantry was a slim, agile young man, an inch shorter than his younger brother Rogan, with curling chestnut hair and a dark mole on his chin that women appeared to think attractive. He was considered vain by Rogan, and rather imperious, though Arcilla thought with amusement that both her brothers were the imperious sort.

Parnell, who usually dressed impeccably in shirts of white Irish linen, Italian silk cravats, and British hats, now looked somewhat dowdy. Arcilla thought he appeared mussed and harassed, as though he might have drunk too much the previous evening and was still feeling dull-witted. She felt awash with sympathy. *It's Darinda's fault. She leads him on, deceptively.*

"Well?" Parnell repeated to Darinda. His smirk challenged her. "Who are you protecting us feebleminded from—Anthony's rule or Julien's sjambok?"

Arcilla watched Darinda's anger grow as her color darkened and her gray eyes flashed.

Darinda's ways were well known to Parnell. He once told Arcilla that Darinda's "pushing" to attain the fulfillment of her ambitions clashed with his less dominant approach to dealing with Uncle Julien. Parnell's ego chafed under her aggressiveness. Darinda didn't appear to worry about Parnell's ego, however. "In my mind that proves she doesn't love him," Rogan had once commented.

Darinda placed hands on hips and stared at Parnell.

"If you've come to see Anthony, he's left for a meeting."

"What of you, why are you here?"

"I came to welcome Lord Anthony to Bulawayo."

Arcilla cast her a quick, doubtful glance, but Darinda didn't notice.

"Ah yes, dearly beloved Lord Anthony. Your grandfather Julien's heir, the head of the family diamonds!" Parnell chuckled. "How does that make *you* feel, Darinda?"

Arcilla glanced at Darinda. Parnell was being foolish to goad the woman he wanted to marry. He would only anger her. Everyone knew that Darinda resented Anthony Brewster. Her grandfather Julien had chosen him as his male heir when he married Camilla. Darinda now argued to her grandfather that he should choose an heir of *blood* to run the family diamond business after his death, meaning herself and the man she would marry.

Now that Anthony was here, Darinda wanted her grandfather to choose between them. The argument Arcilla had overheard on the path between Darinda and Anthony promised more dispute. Peter had said it was a grave mistake on Darinda's part.

"Julien will never make Darinda his heir as long as he has Anthony. Julien doesn't think it wise for a woman to have the top spot over the family diamond mine, even if she's his own granddaughter. The more she pushes Julien, and shines the light on Anthony's mistakes, the more Julien is going to undergird Anthony, whom Julien accepted as a son when Anthony married Lady Camilla."

No, Arcilla thought, *Uncle Julien is not a man who admits his mistakes or Anthony's. His arrogance prevails. And if he didn't have something on me that he could tell Peter about, I wouldn't stay here in Bulawayo.*

Miserable, she swallowed her tea and set the cup down, her hand shaking as the mournful cry of a distant hyena sounded upon the evening breeze. She felt the taste of fear in her mouth and jumped when Darinda spoke to Parnell.

CHAPTER THIRTEEN

Darinda Bley, unsmiling, faced Parnell Chantry inside the bungalow belonging to Lord Anthony.

"You've been drinking again." Darinda's gray eyes flashed hot.

"I didn't know you were here," he said, excuse in his voice as he stepped across the threshold.

Arcilla, watching the moment play out between her brother and Darinda, moved uncomfortably on the divan, where she sat watching tensely.

"I asked you, Parnell, not to come around me with liquor on your breath. I can't stand it."

Darinda's father had been killed years ago while riding horseback after drinking heavily. The horse had thrown him, and Sir Bley died with a broken neck.

Parnell rubbed a hand across his chin. "What meeting did Anthony go to, did he say?"

"No." Darinda's voice was curt. She turned her back toward him and sipped her tea.

Arcilla stood quickly. "Sit down, Parnell. I'll get you tea."

Parnell plopped into a chair, looking strained and exhausted. "Coffee, if you've got it, sis."

"There isn't any," Darinda cast over her shoulder.

Parnell glanced at Arcilla and tossed up his hands. "Tea then…no sugar, no cream."

Arcilla poured the tea as she held the cup, noticing again the delicate pink English rosebuds. How ludicrous everything seemed. She sobered her emotions as she brought the tea and saw Parnell's hand shake when he took the cup and saucer.

Peter was absolutely right. Something must be done about her brother's incessant drinking. Peter had warned of it last night after Parnell left the others to take after-dinner brandy and cigars while she and Peter had gone up to their room.

Arcilla agreed with Peter's conclusions, but the problem was too much for her to cope with and added to her own burden of discontent and growing fears. What could she do? Parnell never listened to her advice.

If only Rogan were here. He would be all over Parnell for turning to drink. Peter might do something, but he was too involved with the BSA to talk sense to his brother-in-law. Not that Parnell was inclined to listen to Peter; only Rogan could really take him on.

At the time, however, Arcilla's reaction to Peter's remark had come as a retort for bringing up the burdensome matter when she'd wanted to escape unpleasant things. All during dinner she'd had to endure talk of war with the "stubborn Boers" from Uncle Julien and the others, including Dr. Jameson. War was the boring topic most evenings.

Well, her brother hadn't drunk when he lived in Grimston Way, she'd told Peter, as though the Charter Company were to blame for Parnell's unwholesome change. Laying the blame on Peter's pride and joy allowed her to hit back at what he held in honor, for she believed he put his work ahead of her, his infant son, and their happiness. Her remark wasn't totally in error. Parnell hadn't drunk at Rookswood, and she couldn't understand the change that had come over him here at Bulawayo since the war with Lobengula. Parnell was with Julien when the troopers under Jameson first entered the chieftain's kraal. What had happened there to affect Parnell so, or was it just coincidence?

"You've a bit of a right to your hysterics, Arcilla, ol' girl. We're all balmy for staying here. We're just dupes, waiting to be slaughtered like the Shangani patrol. And for what? So dear ol' Julien can get his fingers on the Black." He put his fingers to his lips and kissed them. "Well, he won't get me crawling into the Matopos caves."

Darinda turned her head. "Must you be so harsh on my grandfather?"

"He's been making plans, and now he's just biding his time. Waiting for the moment to form his expedition—the one that will get us all killed."

"You're being unfair, Parnell," Darinda said with wearied distaste.

Arcilla disagreed. Her brother was right about Julien. He would go to any lengths to get what he wanted, even if it meant putting others in danger. Darinda preferred to wear a blindfold concerning her grandfather's greedy ambitions.

Arcilla's mind went back to something Peter had mentioned after the attack on Lobengula, about Rhodesian troopers getting trapped at the Shangani River by Lobengula's impis. Yes, that was it. The Rhodesians had followed after Lobengula, but later on they'd been outnumbered, fighting to the last man before being hacked to death by the dreaded assegai.

Arcilla shuddered. "You think Bulawayo will be another massacre?" Her voice sounded rough with fear.

"With Julien planning an incursion into their sacred hills to enter Lobengula's burial cave? Use your head, Arcilla. We'll be lame ducks among the crocs."

Arcilla's fingers felt tight and clumsy as she moved them to her throat.

"Can't you see you're frightening your sister? She's still recuperating after giving birth."

Parnell took a mouthful of tea and choked on it. "Better scared than dead. Horrible tea…like dirty river water."

"Pay him no heed, Arcilla. I don't see the situation being as dire as you Londoners do. I love this land, and I'm going to stay." Darinda walked about the room, looking thoughtful. "We have six hundred armed men drawing police pay from the Charter Company. The Ndebele know that. They're not fools."

Parnell squinted at her over his cup. "No, they're far from fools. That's my point, beautiful."

"Don't call me that."

"But think, *my dear.* What if there's war with the Boers? And what if our precious Six Hundred must be sent into the Transvaal to fight with the British?"

Arcilla looked sharply at Darinda to see her response. He was right. All the more reason to have sent that wire to Rogan about Dr. Jameson's plan to aid the Uitlanders in the Transvaal. *This may be why Anthony is here in Bulawayo. Could the high commissioner at Capetown have sent him?*

But if she mentioned that now, in front of Darinda, would she run with it to her grandfather? That was always a risk with Darinda. One never knew where she actually stood. Arcilla shuddered to imagine Julien's anger if he ever found out about her wire to Rogan. No one suspected her. It was fortunate Uncle Julien thought her too frivolous to have taken that action. *Well, I'm not so frivolous as they all think!*

Oh Rogan, if only you were here to help Peter.

"Remember what Willet said before he was killed?" Parnell jostled their memories. "It's not the Boers we need to worry about, but a tribe whose defeated hearts burn for revenge."

"Grandfather says the attack on Tom Willet came from a lion."

"Nonsense! You're too sensible to believe that, Darinda. Willet was killed with an assegai."

"The assegai is banned."

"That doesn't change the fact—he was killed with an assegai."

Arcilla choked on her insipid tea. Major Tom Willet had been killed a week ago while out on patrol in the bush near the Matopos. Uncle Julien had an assegai on display in his office at Government House. The sight of the short Zulu stabbing blade, adopted by their cousins the Ndebele, was fierce and dreadful to Arcilla. When she'd mentioned how tasteless she'd thought it was for Julien to display the weapon on his wall, Peter told her it was Julien's prized souvenir, taken from Lobengula's hut on the night of the fighting.

"Look, darling," Peter had said. "Think how many hours of conversation that blade will evoke in London one day when old colonels gather over their pipes and brandy to discuss past assignments."

"Is Tom's death worrying you, Parnell?" Darinda asked.

He stood. "We should be worried. Savages, that's what they are. Sooner cut out your gizzard an' hang it up to dry as look at you. Best face it."

"But they're not all savages."

"Only takes a few to go on a spree. Dip their assegais in blood, as they like to put it, so they can take a wife. Those young men are itching for their initiation as warriors. Do you think they want to be rounded up by Julien's police to build roads? Their honor has been lashed and bloodied. They want it back."

Even Darinda looked tense, but Arcilla could see she was trying to hide it.

"We know all that. But there aren't any impis in Bulawayo now," Darinda objected. "If any of the indunas are suspected of having weapons, Grandfather's police will confiscate them. Grandfather's law is firmly held to—no new weapons."

So Peter had also said. This did not fully alleviate Arcilla's fears. Parnell was right about Julien's police using the young Ndebele men as conscripted laborers. Uncle Julien, as chief native commissioner, had come up with the law, a boon to farmers and builders, so Peter said. "But neither do we allow them to make their traditional raids against the Shona." Yet he'd told her gruesome tales of the Ndebele stealing Shona cattle, Shona women, as well as strong young Shona boys for slaves.

Parnell was grim as he paced the floor, teacup in hand, still glowering at its contents. "If we believe those sullen indunas don't have plans to forge weapons and arm their warriors, we deserve what we get. Tom Willet wasn't mauled by a lion, like the Company men are saying. His death should alert us all. Those cut marks were from a blade. Even Retford says so."

At the mention of Captain Ryan Retford, who worked for both Peter and Julien, Arcilla glanced toward Darinda. One woman *knew* another. As Arcilla expected, the mention of his name brought a slight pink to Darinda's face. For someone who rarely if ever showed her feminine fluster, Darinda revealed emotions she undoubtedly wished to conceal.

"Captain Retford believes Tom Willet was killed with an assegai?" Darinda asked uneasily.

Parnell's cup paused midway to his lips. A smile came to his haggard but still handsome face.

"Does that change things for you, darlin'? The gallant captain's word is to be trusted, but not mine?"

Darinda's flush deepened. "Not when you're always drinking that awful poison like it's water."

Parnell banged the cup down on the table. He pointed at her, eyes narrowing. "I'll tell you something else ol' Retford thinks. He knows what the indunas are doing. I heard him telling Peter just yesterday he smells trouble."

"Trouble? What did he mean? What kind of trouble—"

"Retford heard it from that young Ndebele impi—the son of the induna that Lobengula had his council 'smell out for witchcraft,' so he could have the induna chopped to death for betrayal. The boy, the dead induna's son, told Retford, 'The sacred bird images flew from the ruins of the Great Zimbabwe. There can be no peace in Matabeleland.' That's what their Umlimo is telling all the indunas."

Arcilla drew her lacy pink shawl around her bare arms and huddled on the divan. Her eyes went from Darinda, who looked tense and determined, back to her brother, who had fallen silent.

The wind whispered around the sides and roof of the bungalow. The Umlimo, somewhere in the Matopos in a secret cave, was giving forth oracles that were believed by the Ndebele. They were perhaps guarding Lobengula's burial cave. Her teeth chattered. She must go *home*. She *must*.

Arcilla stood. "Captain Retford's right. I wish Peter and Uncle Julien would listen to him. And what of all the evil things that are happening in the house? I tell you we must leave for Capetown."

"Perfect nonsense," Darinda said shortly, but even she looked uneasy.

"Not at all," Arcilla argued. "Malicious, frightening things have been happening recently."

"You mean Grandfather's office burglary?" Darinda scoffed. "Some pesky boy looking for something to steal and sell."

"It was nothing of the sort." Arcilla was irritated by Darinda's brave fronts. "Isn't that so, Parnell? You don't think it's all nonsense, do you?"

"I don't like what's happening," he agreed, "if you're talking about Uncle Julien's office."

"Peter said it was the wind, but the wind doesn't blow books about," Arcilla persisted. She frowned at Darinda. "Uncle Julien's office window was *closed*. But someone or something scattered all his things about in the dead of night."

"The window was found unlocked," Darinda soothed. "Someone crawled through and left the same way. He closed it after him. It has nothing to do with tribal superstition. All that talk about the Umlimo is exaggerated."

"Is it?" Parnell countered. "Not according to Derwent and Dr. Jakob."

"And that splatter of blood across the wall in Peter's office," Arcilla jumped in.

Darinda winced. "It was red ink, dear. One of the Shona servants spilled it when cleaning Grandfather's desk and feared to admit it."

"Is that what the Shona house servant said?" Parnell asked doubtfully.

"Of course the servants aren't going to come out and admit it. Or the cat knocked the inkwell off the desk."

Parnell turned to Arcilla, a mocking smile on his lips. "Mere coincidences, Arcilla, my dear. So get over it, my girl." He whipped back toward Darinda, his smile gone. "But no one can yet explain how a bottle of red ink tipped over by the cat ended up on the wall some twenty feet away! I'm with you, Arcilla, and so is Retford. The ngangas are up to no good."

Ngangas. Mere medicine doctors, some say, but not Dr. Jakob van Buren or Derwent Brown. They say most ngangas seek advice from dark spirits.

Arcilla stole a wary look toward the porch, where the doors stood open. The breeze entered, stirring the curtains on the other windows like the passing of ghosts.

"Now you're giving me the jim-jams," Darinda said. "Really, Arcilla, sometimes I think you're deliberately playing all this up just to get Peter to leave Bulawayo. You must stop dwelling on the war with Lobengula. That's all over now."

"Is that a false bravado I hear in your voice?" Parnell's lips turned back from his white teeth in a wolfish smile. "Ask your gallant captain if he thinks the repercussions of war are all over."

They stood looking at each other evenly.

"Maybe I will," Darinda challenged.

Parnell will never win her like this, Arcilla thought.

"If Julien follows through on his expedition to locate Lobengula's burial cave and the Kimberly Black Diamond, there'll be more than just red ink splashed on the wall of his office. Julien's got to be stopped."

Darinda's gaze swerved accusingly. "So it was you who contacted Anthony in London!"

He walked to the teapot and refilled his cup. His face was testy.

"Julien isn't himself recently. He's obsessed with the Black Diamond. He'll never give up his search, no matter what Capetown has to say about the expedition. The diamond has a power all its own. It will destroy anyone who is determined to possess it!"

"I hope you're wrong about why Anthony came," Arcilla interjected. "I hope he came to tell Peter about a new position in London."

Parnell gave a short laugh. "Is that why you came here to the bungalow to see him? None of us will go anywhere that Julien doesn't want us to go, regardless of Capetown or London."

"Do stop it, Parnell," Darinda said wearily. "You're free. You can leave anytime you please." And she turned her back and walked over to the open door, then stood there looking out at the sunset.

"Am I…," he asked in a husky voice, "free?"

Arcilla felt a twang of pity. Her temper flared toward Darinda. "We both ought to go *home*, Parnell," she said daringly. "No one appreciates us here."

Darinda cast her a glance but made no reply.

"Anthony's come about the Black Diamond, all right, that's clear," Parnell stated.

"There's no proof Lobengula had it, only some wild rumors," Darinda said.

"Julien thinks there is more to it than rumors. And if he gets up an expedition for the Matopos, we'll all end up like Tom Willet."

Arcilla's skin crawled, then she turned toward the window on the other side of the room. "What was that? Did you hear something—out there?"

"You imagined it. Parnell, can't you talk about something else?"

"Heyden van Buren wouldn't mind getting his hands on the Black Diamond either," Parnell murmured thoughtfully.

"Don't worry about Heyden. He's nowhere around Bulawayo," Darinda insisted.

"I wouldn't be so sure. Remember, Dr. Jakob, one of his relatives, is here."

"Next thing, you'll be agreeing with Arcilla that some nganga's put a curse on the house."

"Derwent says Satan can't hurt us if we have Christ's Spirit living in us," Arcilla said, then turned to the window again, where a rattan blind tapped the wooden frame in a gust of wind. "He says that the evil spirits can suggest things to our minds, but they can't control a believer or what he thinks—we have a new Master, Jesus."

"Well, well, little sister. What's happened to you? You're sounding like 'Vicar Derwent.'" Parnell's lopsided smile was far from antagonistic.

Arcilla wasn't used to talking about such things, and she wasn't inclined to now. But the possibility of evil frightened her and made her more aware of Christian values. She sometimes felt like the lost sheep wanting to find the protection of the Shepherd.

"Well, it wasn't some dark spirit who threw that red ink on the wall in Peter's study," Darinda said dryly. "If there is anything going on around here, it's humanly inspired."

Parnell scowled at the bumping rattan shade as the wind kicked up. "The other night I could have sworn I surprised Uncle Julien—it looked like he was casting bones in his office."

Casting bones...a dark ritual of the ngangas...

Two hot red spots formed on Darinda's cheeks. "Absurd! Grandfather? Whatever for? We're all Christians here."

Arcilla rubbed her arms. "Please close the window, Parnell."

"Dark spirits eavesdropping?" He smiled wryly and walked over to the window. He drew up the rattan shade to shut the window. "I doubt they need open windows, but—"

Arcilla watched him glance out into the deepening twilight. As he did, she saw him stiffen, then momentarily pause.

Arcilla stood slowly, hugging herself. "What is it?" came her uncertain whisper.

Parnell shook his head. Darinda edged up beside him and looked out, but Arcilla drew farther away.

"I could have sworn something was crouching below the window," Parnell murmured, surprise in his voice.

Arcilla strained to hear the rustle of leaves on the trees and vines.

Darinda shut the window with a bang. "You must have seen a shadow. It's windy. Twilight is always a difficult time to see clearly."

Arcilla glanced toward the veranda. The slowly setting sun had painted the western sky ablaze with reds, golds, and violets.

"Who…who would wish to eavesdrop on us?" Arcilla's weak voice encouraged her own fears.

Darinda turned, scowling. "There was no one there. Don't imagine things. You'll soon have yourself worked up into a dither."

"I'm not imagining things! And not every woman wishes to feel safe by toting a .45 around her hips. You seem to forget that!"

"Look here, you two," Parnell scolded. "This is no time for a cat-fight."

Darinda's mouth turned. "Huh, most catfights, as you call them, are between tomcats."

"I wish Derwent were here," Arcilla stated suddenly. "He and Dr. Jakob always have wise answers about the Umlimo. I think I'll ride out to the mission tomorrow and see how the chapel is coming. Ryan is helping them build it on his time off."

Darinda looked at her with an arched brow. "Ryan?"

Arcilla smiled sweetly. "Captain Ryan Retford. You do know who he is, Darinda?"

Parnell shot Darinda a dark look. "Oh, quite," he stated acidly. "By all means, Darinda knows who the dashing captain is. He seems to be hanging about Government House like a stray cat looking to be fed."

Darinda shrugged. "You seem to have cats on your subconscious today. Is Captain Retford about? I hadn't noticed. But if so, it's because he's working for Grandfather and Peter."

"He's a guard, too," Arcilla said, still being too sweet. "That makes us feel so much safer, doesn't it, Darinda?"

Arcilla believed Darinda had an eye for Ryan Retford but pretended otherwise.

"I can take care of myself," Darinda said. She glanced at Parnell. "After that spitting cobra incident, I knew that if I didn't learn to use a gun *myself,* no one else was likely to come to my aid."

Parnell remained silent.

Arcilla fumed. "If I recall, Captain Retford shot that snake for you."

"All this silly talk," Darinda said. "I've more important things to do. I'm going back to the house. Are you coming with me, Arcilla? It's getting dark."

"I'll walk back with Parnell," she said loftily.

"Have it your way."

Darinda walked to the open door and left through the screened porch without a backward glance.

CHAPTER FOURTEEN

Darinda left Anthony's bungalow and walked along the path back toward Government House. Twilight deepened, bringing out faint noises of the wild. Arcilla might make disparaging remarks about the pistol she wore, but with dangers from animals and poisonous snakes, along with rumors of unrest among the Ndebele, Darinda felt it wise to be armed. It gave her a sense of independence. After frightening chatter from Arcilla and warnings from Parnell, the pistol was comforting.

Who had Anthony gone to meet? He'd left after their argument, and she'd thought he was on his way to see Parnell, yet that couldn't have been, since Parnell had come to the bungalow looking for him. Maybe Anthony had gone back to Government House to confront Julien? But somehow she didn't think Anthony would confront Grandfather. Julien had always told Anthony what to do, and she didn't think that had changed, even if the high commissioner had sent Anthony here with a letter for Julien.

Darinda slowed her steps on the trail, listening. The breeze was up, and she brushed a strand of her dark hair away from her cheek and glanced about. Her instincts were on edge. That silly Arcilla! She was beginning to affect even Darinda's own steady nerves. *I wish she and Peter would be sent back to London. Arcilla is an embarrassment to womanhood. Giggling, primping, fainting, screaming, always dressing improperly. Silks and lace, and the absurd shoes she'd worn tonight, obviously designed for a ball. Whatever did Peter, a sensible man, see in her?*

Diamonds. Arcilla was a Chantry, and that meant a sizable inheritance in the family diamond mine.

Darinda thought of her own inheritance. She was by far the greatest of diamond heiresses. Whoever married her would become tremendously rich and politically powerful. Did Parnell actually think Grandfather Julien was seriously dangling her before his eyes? Grandfather wouldn't give his granddaughter in marriage to any man unless he had something to offer in return that her grandfather felt was crucial to the family conglomerate. Grandfather had gained influence in Parliament through Peter's marriage to Arcilla.

It didn't seem to her that Grandfather was actually planning to have her become Parnell's wife. Parnell had the impression that Grandfather had promised her to him, and so Parnell was serving him dutifully. Julien best utilized Parnell by continuing to let him think Darinda would become his without ever following through.

Darinda would have been outraged by this, except that Parnell's avid interest in her had not been based on love. The one man Grandfather might have wanted to let her marry was Rogan Chantry, and mostly because Rogan always contested him and in many instances had gotten the best of him. Grandfather Julien would have been pleased to get Rogan on his side, but Rogan had surprised them by returning suddenly to England and marrying the illegitimate daughter of Katie van Buren and Anthony Brewster. Oh! How furious Grandfather had been about that turn of events!

"He did this behind my back," he had shouted. "It will never stand! I'll see to that."

What her Grandfather had meant, she didn't know. But Julien had seen the marriage as a cunning move on Rogan's part to undermine his control.

The last rosy flush of sunset in the western sky was turning the polished rock of the distant, brooding Matopos Hills to a marbled pink.

She walked slowly along the path with a dark stand of trees on her right.

She shuddered when a bat, noiseless in flight, swooped and flittered past the Rhodesian wisteria. Now in October, the lilac-blue flowers were in bloom in a showy display, while the tree was leafless. She paused to take it in, for she had always loved nature.

She passed on, nearing a wait-a-bit tree, of which there were many across the land, with what she considered curious hooked clutching thorns. The multistemmed branches drooped with hairy leaves that had two thorns. It was the thorns that caught her interest—one thorn went straight up, while the other thorn was curved, coming up from the leaf base. There were fruits on it too, round and dull red. They were edible, and some animals liked to browse on them, but she hadn't found their taste particularly exciting. Derwent Brown was often suggesting that "the Great Creator designed all these things for His glory and the good of His creatures." Darinda wondered. She hadn't been raised to believe in a good and loving God who had concern for His creation. She didn't know what she believed, actually. She had never read the Bible that Dr. Jakob van Buren taught at his mission. She had prayed several times in her life, though she had no clear concept of to whom she was speaking.

She studied the thorns again. Derwent had said a crown of thorns was mockingly placed on Jesus's brow. He called Him the Savior of mankind. Just what had Jesus come to save mankind from? Derwent had said sin. *Well, there is plenty of that to go around,* Darinda thought wearily.

The sun was now behind the Matopos, and the reddish horizon shone behind a handful of rose pink clouds. A lone planet that was as yet no more than a polished silver gleam caught her eye.

It was a pleasant evening, breezy and yet quite still of sounds. She glanced down, seeing something odd from the corner of her eye. What was *that* lying there all sprawled out—

She gasped. Just off the beaten pathway was what looked very much like a body lying in the tall, swaying grasses. Were her eyes deceiving her? It could be a dead or wounded animal from the creek below.

Yes, that's what it must be. An animal.

She moved forward cautiously, aware that it could still be alive and dangerous in an injured state. She might need to put it out of its misery. She couldn't stand to see helpless animals suffer.

She drew her pistol. Her heart was beating heavily. It was unnerving to discover she'd been standing so near something sprawled in the grass. It was like discovering someone watching you when you'd thought you were alone.

Darinda approached with her pistol drawn. She could see better now. Her mouth went dry. It was a human body, a man, and he wasn't moving.

She approached, still wary, lest it be some sort of deception.

She studied the body from a safe distance and sensed the man was dead—it was Anthony Brewster.

She rushed to where he lay, hoping against reason that he could still be alive, that she could do something, when footsteps on the path caught her attention.

She turned to see Captain Ryan Retford in uniform. He was walking toward her and must have caught sight of the body near her feet. He came swiftly. He saw the pistol in her hand, looked at her, then down at Anthony Brewster.

"Don't touch anything, Miss Bley. And don't step in or disturb any scuff marks in the dust."

He stooped beside the body, appearing to take in the scene.

"Did you hear or see anyone as you approached?"

"No." Her voice sounded ragged. A touch of shock was gripping her.

A few moments later he stood again and faced her grimly. Captain Retford was quite handsome and very precise. He hadn't discovered that it was she who had recommended him, first as Peter's assistant in military affairs, then more recently as assistant to her grandfather. She had first noticed Ryan on a trip to Capetown to see Arcilla, and had later used her position with her grandfather to gain access to his records.

His reputation as a soldier was impeccable; his schooling was traditional at the Honorable East India Company's Military College in

Addiscombe. He had served with honor and received a brevet for courage in the fighting in the Sudan. If he had come from a family of distinction, or had wealth, she could easily interest herself in him. As it was, he was merely a career military attaché from a poor family. His father had been killed in the Sudan, and he had a mother and sister in London who were making ends meet, partly on his wages. His generosity for them showed admirable responsibility, nothing more.

She had also learned within the last month that there was a girl he was writing to, and who in turn wrote him, a girl by the name of Ann Parker.

He looked at the pistol in her hand. His eyes, she knew, were a flinty blue, his hair a sandy color. He was muscular and browned.

"It—the gun is mine. I wasn't sure it was safe to approach him." She looked to the ground, where the hand was thrust forward. A wave of remorse for the harsh words she'd spoken earlier to Anthony washed over her.

"He was *alive* just a very short while ago, and now *suddenly* he's dead."

The reality of the brevity of life was glaring, painfully so.

Captain Retford gave a nod. "You can put that gun away now, Miss Bley," came his quiet voice.

She tightened her lips. Her gaze sprang to his, searching. "You don't think that I—" Under his level gaze she bit her lip and dropped her eyes first to Anthony, then to the gun in her hand.

"He didn't die from a bullet wound. And see those marks in the dirt? Looks to me like he was dragged here after he died."

She glanced about in the last vestige of twilight. "Can you tell how he was killed?"

"Concussion, at the back of his skull."

She didn't move. She tried to steady her breathing from coming in gasps. She envisioned someone creeping up from behind with a heavy club.

"Then…he was taken by surprise."

"Where were you coming from just now?"

Darinda realized how suspicious it would sound—"From his bungalow." She turned and looked back toward the circle of bungalows, pointing, though in the settling shadows they could just make out the outline of the huts.

"I have witnesses. I was with Arcilla—Mrs. Peter Bartley. Parnell Chantry was there too. I just left them about ten minutes ago."

"They must still be there. A lamp's just been lit."

Darinda saw the yellow light flickering wholesomely in the front windows.

"Did you hear anything as you came along the path, Miss Bley?"

"Just the sounds of evening coming on, and the wind."

He nodded thoughtfully, glancing about. "I didn't think you would hear anything. Whoever did this has probably been gone for a while. Lord Brewster's been dead a good hour."

"How would you know that?" Her voice was strained. She kept thinking of when she'd met Anthony—and where they had argued.

He glanced at her thoughtfully. She had the notion he was weighing her emotional stability.

"Ants," he stated simply.

He need not have said any more. She gritted her teeth to keep from giving away her shock. Why it seemed important to her that Captain Ryan Retford thought her strong, unlike Arcilla, she couldn't say. Perhaps she dare not think why it mattered.

"Let's step away from here," he said, and she passed before him onto the dusty path. She walked a few feet and stopped, looking off toward the bungalows. Captain Retford came up behind her.

She placed her palm against her forehead and shook her head again.

"It's so awful, isn't it, Captain? Two deaths in a week. Do you think they could be related?"

He appeared to regard her calmly. "What makes you ask that, Miss Bley?"

She shook her head, looking about for answers in the breezy darkness. "Doesn't it seem obvious?"

"Perhaps it is. Major Tom Willet, you're talking about?"

"Yes. A nice man. A gentle man. He had a family."

"Yes. My sister is a friend of his wife."

He seemed curious as he looked at her. Did he wonder how she knew about Major Tom Willet?

He was looking at her with the same military grimness she so often noticed on his face, a mental attitude of calm discipline that she found somehow comforting, so different from Parnell's emotional upsets. The captain seemed to be a man who could handle crises with cool resolve. In that, he reminded her of Rogan. She had liked that about Rogan. Rogan didn't need a drink for his courage. She had never seen Captain Retford with liquor, either. Even on his time off from duty he seemed to stay alert. Was it true what Arcilla said? That on his time off he'd gone to Dr. Jakob's mission?

"Who could have wanted to kill Anthony?" she wondered aloud.

"The authorities will sort through the facts on that, Miss Bley. But there were no trumpets blown at Government House in celebration of Lord Brewster's unexpected arrival."

She turned her head sharply, but it was getting too dark to see his expression. Was he including her grandfather among those disturbed by Anthony's arrival?

"Why? Because of the talk of an expedition into the Matopos?"

"I'm inclined to think it had to do with Lobengula and the Kimberly Black Diamond."

"Because Anthony brought a letter from Capetown to my grandfather?"

He remained dutifully silent.

"Was it a cease and desist order?" she persisted.

"I left the room before Sir Julien read the Capetown letter, and before he and Lord Brewster entered into discussion."

Discussion. A diplomat's language. Had they argued heatedly?

"You're not suggesting that my grandfather had anything whatsoever to do with Anthony Brewster's death?" she asked tersely.

"I'd be a fool to suggest that, Miss Bley. But I do know your grandfather is determined to search for Lobengula's burial cave to find that diamond, regardless of what Capetown or London may say."

"How would you know my grandfather's plans?" she challenged.

"He's already suggested that I lead his expedition."

She looked at him quickly, surprised, though she could see why her grandfather would want to choose Captain Retford for the task.

"Are you going to do it?"

"I am opposed to any such effort. I believe it's unwise at this time. There's nothing I can say to Sir Julien to change his mind, but perhaps he will listen to you."

So Captain Retford agreed with Parnell. The expedition, if her grandfather went through with it, would be dangerous. The silence between them lengthened.

"You say Parnell and Mrs. Bartley are at the bungalow?" he said in a professional tone.

"Yes," she stated tersely. "That is, they were there when I left a short time ago."

"Then you'd better wait there, Miss Bley. I'll need to go to Government House for help."

She permitted him to walk her back to the lighted bungalow. He was silent and looking thoughtful.

Was there anything to what Captain Retford had said about the poor reception at Government House? She tried to think, but her mind was fuzzy.

"And you didn't see anyone in the area? Coming or going?" he asked again quietly.

She gave him a cool glance, noting how well his uniform fit, and how straight his shoulders.

"No one until *you* appeared, Captain." If he wanted to cast doubt upon her grandfather, Captain Retford wasn't above suspicion, either! "One could ask, Captain, why you unexpectedly appeared from the shadows. Might it not be said you could have been there all along?

Having brought the body there? You could have watched me a moment from the trees, decided it was better for you to come out in the open and cast doubt upon others."

Naturally, Darinda wasn't inclined to think Captain Ryan Retford had bashed poor Anthony, but—

"I see," came his casual response. "Looks as if I'd better do some explaining," he said. "I would hate to think you believe me a possible murderer."

There followed an obvious lapse, in which she could have hastened to deny thinking so dreadful a thing about him, but she deliberately kept silent.

"So if you will, permit me to explain what I was doing here," he said. "Sir Julien sent me to escort you back to Government House. It was getting dark, and he didn't want you out alone after Major Willet's death. I don't think he or Peter realized Mrs. Bartley was here as well."

Her curiosity was baited. "How did Grandfather know I was here?"

"Did you tell him before you left?"

"No."

"Then he must have seen you leave the house, or perhaps someone told him where you were headed."

She hadn't told anyone at the house where she was going. Her grandfather would have been upset if he'd known she was coming to talk to Anthony about the diamond business. She wondered how he would take Anthony's death.

"I walked over earlier this afternoon," he said. "I didn't see you until I rounded the corner of the trail. When I caught sight of you, I wondered why you were just standing beneath the tree. It didn't seem a conducive spot to meditate. At first I thought you might have turned your ankle, and that I would be coming to your rescue."

She glanced at him, having noted the smile in his voice. "I've never sprained an ankle just walking trails, Captain," she said dryly.

"Most fortunate, Miss Bley." He smiled. "But a man can hope."

She felt absurdly pleased and quickly put a damper on her emotions.

"The wait-a-bit tree," she said thoughtfully. "Interesting that Anthony's body was placed there."

Captain Retford looked quizzical. "What did you say?"

"The tree, Captain. It's called a wait-a-bit."

He nodded politely and continued to look puzzled, as though he wondered what she was suggesting.

"Do you suppose that's why Anthony—Lord Brewster's body—was placed there? The murderer was telling us something?"

They walked on toward the bungalow. "What might that be, Miss Bley?"

"You did say the body was dragged there."

"It appeared so. We'll set up a search unit to follow the marks in the dust. It could lead us to where the murder took place."

"Why was the body brought here?" she asked. "To the wait-a-bit tree? Is there a message to us in the choice of the tree?"

She feared he might be amused with her imagination, but either he was too polite to show his feelings, or he thought her question worth considering. He was grave as he regarded her, then looked back into the shadows they had come from. Darinda followed his glance. The odd-looking tree stood darkly etched and sinister against the backdrop of the Matopos, still faintly silhouetted by glowing crimson in the last light.

"Meaning, I suppose," he said thoughtfully, "that there will be more deaths to come if we just wait?"

"Precisely. I know it sounds silly, but—"

"Not silly, actually. The answer to your question depends on who killed Lord Brewster."

"Meaning?"

"Meaning, Miss Bley, that we both know the African tribes set a great store by symbols."

"Yes." Darinda thought of some of the things Arcilla and Parnell had said earlier about bizarre happenings in Government House. Could there actually be something to Arcilla's hysterics?

"Yes," she repeated, "especially if a nganga were involved to give advice to the killer." She was aware of the night around them, the wind, and the otherwise ominous silence. She must put some restraint on her runaway emotions, or she might end up on a precipice with Arcilla.

He gave a short nod. "If Lord Brewster was attacked by a Shona or Ndebele warrior, there may be some imagery to the tree. Unless…" He looked off toward the trail once more, as though it might produce an answer.

"Unless," she offered, "someone wanted to divert our attention away from the murderer, onto a superstitious tribal warrior?"

"Entirely possible. The police will have some work here. Let's hope they do it wisely and not stampede to judgment."

"You think they might blame one of the Ndebele without searching deeply for the truth, Captain?"

His gaze became unpleasant. "There is that tendency among us. I hope this notion of yours about the tree symbolizing something doesn't set the hounds off on the wrong scent."

Her grandfather was the head of native affairs in Bulawayo, and he had authority over Company police.

"You're not implying Sir Julien won't be fair and just in his approach to this terrible crime?"

His face took on the expression of a military man carrying out orders.

"I, for one, will take nothing for granted when seeking who murdered Lord Brewster. That goes as well for Major Tom Willet."

Was he saying that others might do so, even including her Grandfather Julien? Her temper was kindled. She was aware that the thaw between them, which occurred so naturally in their discussion of the tragic circumstances, was chilling up once more.

"Parnell believes the Ndebele are planning an attack. He mentioned you don't believe Tom was mauled by a lion."

"I'm inclined to agree with Parnell about the tribe. And I've said before that Major Willet was killed with an assegai."

She felt a shiver. "But you're the only one in Government House who feels that way, Captain."

"I spend time out with the regular troopers and police. Those inside government may convince themselves of what they prefer the facts to be, Miss Bley."

"You don't like my grandfather, do you?" she accused suddenly. "I hadn't realized that until now, but it's plain to see."

"It's not within my professional responsibilities to decide whether or not I like the men I take orders from. Sir Julien is chief native commissioner here in Bulawayo, and it's my duty to serve him. That goes for Peter Bartley as well."

"Yes, but you must surely have an opinion."

"If you care to know my personal opinion on their judgment of matters concerning the tribe, I believe Sir Julien is too harsh with the indunas. His use of their blooded warriors for road building is likely to lead to trouble. Peter has more insight into this, but he fears to stand up to your grandfather."

Darinda stared at him. She should have been furious, but somehow she was not. Perhaps because she had heard Dr. Jakob van Buren saying much the same, but in the spiritual arena. Still, she felt it was her duty to take up arms for her grandfather's reputation.

"Sir Julien Bley is a very important gentleman in South Africa. I am sure you know that, Captain Retford."

"I do, Miss Bley. I fail, however, to see that his importance as a diamond magnate augments his wisdom for dealing with the tribe."

She narrowed her eyes. "Mr. Rhodes and Dr. Jameson seem to think my grandfather is a man of knowledge and ability. He wouldn't be native commissioner if he weren't," she said shortly.

"Mr. Rhodes is also a very rich man in diamonds, Miss Bley. One could suggest that perhaps that is the chief reason for his being politically powerful in South Africa, as well as in London. And one diamond magnate would tend to think highly of another. But common sense where the Africans are concerned doesn't necessarily come with riches or the ability to form a conglomerate of diamond mines into a monopoly. That kind of knowledge may be related not to wisdom but to shrewdness and greed."

She sucked in her breath, staring at him, searching his face for signs that he simply *must* be joking. But there was no ironic humor in those blue eyes, or the tanned, rugged face.

"That sounds outrageous," she stated. "You should know, Captain, that I could wire your commanding officer in Capetown and request that you be removed from service to Peter and my grandfather."

He looked back calmly. Something in his unwillingness to cower was surprisingly refreshing. She was accustomed to Parnell, who until quite recently attempted, above all else, to please her.

"Yes, Miss Bley, I am aware that you are a very wealthy diamond heiress. Your complaint to the War Office could have me called up."

"And yet, you'll still say these things about my grandfather?"

"Would you think better of me if I flattered him? You asked for my opinion, and I gave it. If that upsets you, then I suggest you don't ask, or ask only those who are willing to please you."

Her cheeks burned with a rush of temper. She tightened her mouth and stared back evenly. As their standoff solidified, she turned and went up the steps to the screened porch.

"Please tell Mrs. Bartley and Parnell not to leave the bungalow for any reason until I return with the police."

She looked back, still angry. He touched the brim of his military hat in a polite, gentlemanly salute, then turned and walked back to the trail and Government House, disappearing into the evening shadows.

Darinda was left alone with the unpleasant burden of telling Arcilla and Parnell that Anthony was dead. Murdered, in a most brutal fashion.

She felt suddenly tired and hesitated on the porch. This was no time to allow her weariness to take control. Arcilla would most likely scream and perhaps faint, and Parnell, in emotional weakness, would reach for a decanter. She sighed and squared her shoulders in determination. She stepped into the lighted drawing room, aware that both Arcilla and Parnell turned toward her, surprise on their faces.

I must look awful, thought Darinda.

Arcilla's blue eyes widened, and she reached a hand, sparkling with diamonds, to her throat.

"Something's happened," Arcilla whispered in a cracked voice as she studied Darinda. "Not another killing?"

Parnell took a step toward Darinda, shocked, then stopped. "Who?" he asked. "Not—?"

"Yes, I'm afraid so. Anthony's been murdered."

Darinda wondered just why Arcilla had braved the twilight to walk here alone. It was so unlike her. In the days following the death of Major Tom Willet, she had refused to go outdoors after sunset even to walk in the immediate garden around Government House. Arcilla had said that she came here to the bungalow to see Anthony about Peter being sent back to the Home Office in London. Was that the real reason?

Though her arrival at the bungalow could be viewed somewhat suspiciously, the idea that the frivolous Arcilla would commit murder seemed preposterous. She didn't have the fortitude to step on a bug, much less the strength to swing anything that had struck Anthony.

And why had Parnell shown up looking so dreadful? He'd said he had come from his own bungalow not far from Anthony's. Was Parnell concealing something?

Someone at Government House had contacted Anthony in London about her grandfather's plans for an expedition into the Matopos. Had it been Parnell? If so, Parnell should have *wanted* Anthony here in Bulawayo.

And what about herself? Darinda grimaced. She was known to be strong and bold. She had argued with Anthony about her inheritance just before his death on the very trail where he'd been discovered—and by her! What if someone had heard her threaten him? Nor was it lost on her that she would be seen as having a motive. For she, more than anyone, had much to gain by Anthony Brewster's death. The one obstacle that had kept Grandfather Julien from making her his primary heir had now been eliminated.

CHAPTER FIFTEEN

The news of Lord Anthony Brewster's murder reached Government House with a thunderous crack. Sir Julien Bley was dressed for dinner, and Sir Peter Bartley began searching for Arcilla. Arcilla, who Darinda was most worried would become hysterical, had surprised her. After Arcilla's initial shock, she had turned a sickly white, but she merely sat down slowly and uttered not a word until Captain Retford returned with Peter, Sir Julien, and a handful of the Company police. At once they secured the area and began a meticulous search of the compound grounds and bungalows, though it wasn't clear what they were looking for. Darinda thought that whatever was used to strike the deadly blow must have been carried away.

They gathered in the drawing room with Sir Julien in command of the Bulawayo police. As the detailed interrogation began, Captain Retford entered quietly with Julien's chief police sergeant, Mr. Harry Whipple, a young and rather brutish man with broad features and blond hair. He was wide across the chest and shoulders, which gave her the impression he was a fighter or a wrestler. His pale, watery eyes were bold, sometimes disrespectful in the way she caught him watching her and Arcilla.

"We've found the weapon that bashed his lordship's head in, Sir Julien," Harry Whipple boasted. "Got blood on it too. Here it is, sir."

Darinda was careful not to wince as Whipple produced a sturdy section of hardwood that looked solid enough to crush rock. Arcilla made a sickening sound, revealing her horror, as expected. A look of satisfaction showed on Harry Whipple's face, as though he enjoyed her feminine shriek. He squared his shoulders, cleared his throat and said, too gravely, "My apology, Mrs. Chantry."

"Never mind the theatrics, Whipple," Sir Julien dictated. "Where did you find it?" Julien asked.

"We followed the tracks to where the murder looks to have happened, Mr. Bley. Looked like Lord Brewster was jumped by more'n one, knocked down, and struck from behind before he could get up."

"Do you agree, Ryan?" Sir Julien's one good eye swerved to Captain Retford.

Ryan stood apart from Harry Whipple near two Rhodesian policemen and three armed Shona. The Shona police were despised by the Ndebele, who thought of them as former slaves. Using Shona to lord it over the Ndebele had cultivated resentment, but Whipple insisted he trusted only Shona, and Sir Julien let him have his way. Another handful of Company police were outside.

"The footprints were such that one can't be sure, sir."

"Really, Retford," Whipple said with a laugh. "It does appear there was more than one who met his lordship. You said so yourself."

"True enough, Harry, concerning the number of footprints, but it looked as though they were placed intentionally, after the fact."

Whipple scowled thoughtfully. "Maybe, Retford, but you admit they were bare feet, not boots. That tells me all I need to know."

"Go on, Ryan," Sir Julien said.

"The prints looked deliberately placed, sir."

Julien's black brows shot up. "You don't think the Ndebele are involved in this?"

"I'm not suggesting they weren't. You know what I think about Major Willet's wounds, sir. But in Lord Brewster's case, there's an unnatural look to those footprints. I think they were intended to be noticed."

Darinda scowled. "But you did think the same person or persons killed Major Willet?"

Captain Retford looked across the room at her. "An assegai was used. And the major's death took place near the Matopos. But in this present case, sir," and he looked back at Julien, "no Ndebele warrior would jump a man from behind and use a club. That has the white man's feel to it."

"You're too easy on the tribes," Harry Whipple said with disgust. "Trying to make excuses for 'em. Any of 'em would as soon kill Brewster as look at him. Anyhow, who do you think would want to murder Lord Brewster? Certainly none of us. But the savages? They'll strike anytime, anywhere. We've confiscated the assegais, so they used a club."

"You're likely to be right about Tom Willet," said Retford. "It was not a lion that got him, but probably an induna. A leader could still have had one of their weapons buried somewhere."

Darinda felt the tension in the room. There was a ripple of unease as the others glanced about the bungalow. Darinda saw her grandfather reconsider his earlier decision of blaming Major Tom Willet's death on a lion.

"Whipple, I want more of the troopers on duty to avoid trouble. I want a strong show of force. We'll ride to Jube's kraal tonight. I want to know where he's been. That includes his impis. All of them. I don't care if they're asleep or not. Get them up! We'll talk to them. I'll join you and the others on the road in thirty minutes... Darinda, my dear, I want a few minutes alone with you before I leave. Captain Retford will see you back to the house. Parnell? Come with me, my boy, I have good need of you!"

Parnell looked a ghastly color. He seemed to be worried about more than Anthony's death. Was he fearful Julien might discover he'd been the one who'd sent a letter to Anthony, bringing him here to Bulawayo...to his death?

Darinda did not look toward Captain Retford again until the bungalow began to clear. Did she see a bit of displeasure in the set of his jaw?

"I find it difficult to believe anything this wretched could actually happen to Anthony," Peter said with a shake of his head. "Come along, Arcilla, my dear. This has been dreadful for you."

Peter left with Arcilla for the house, and Whipple and the police hurried off on horseback to round up more troopers. Within a few short minutes, Darinda was left alone in the bungalow with her grandfather. *Captain Retford must be waiting outside,* she thought.

Julien strode up to her and enclosed her in a grandfatherly hug. "I'm sorry you were the one to have found him. Wretched business! But whoever did this to Anthony will pay severely!"

She could readily see the deep emotion he felt. She understood better how attached he'd been to Anthony. Her conscience smote her. *He bullied Anthony, no doubt of that, but he loved him. Ryan is wrong— Grandfather would never do anything to bring Anthony harm, regardless of the rebuke he might have brought from Capetown about the Matopos expedition.*

"Grandfather," she whispered, "Anthony was found under the wait-a-bit tree just up the path—did Captain Retford say anything about that to you?" She glanced toward the open windows, with curtains shuddering in the breeze, not that she expected Ryan would ever eavesdrop.

"Wait-a-bit?"

"The name of the tree… You know, where I discovered Anthony's body… Captain Retford didn't tell you?"

"Oh? What was he to tell me?"

"Well, perhaps it's not important, but it could be." As she explained, his fingers tightened on her shoulders. An odd leap of fear reflected in his one eye.

"Witchcraft," he repeated. "It's possible, Darinda. By the time we've dealt with Jube, we'll know what they're up to."

"What are you going to do?" She remembered Ryan's concerns.

"Leave it to Harry Whipple."

Julien paced the room. She watched him, wondering.

"Is there something more you wanted to tell me, Grandfather?"

"Yes." He stopped his pacing and turned toward her. "What happened tonight is just the beginning of trouble. I need your help, my dear."

Her senses were alerted. He needed *her* help. What better words could she possibly hear, though they came on the heels of dark and ugly tragedy?

"Grandfather, of course I'll do all I can to assist you. Has it to do with the loss of Anthony?"

He waved a hand doused with diamonds. "Never mind Anthony right now. I must talk to you about the Boer war. A matter has arisen of some concern."

Mention of the possibility of war between England and the Boers was not what she'd expected. He glanced at her, and she noted the thoughtful glint in his eyes.

"It's necessary you stay in Bulawayo indefinitely, Darinda. I'll need you here with me."

She'd had no intention of leaving, but she was pleased to hear her grandfather admit he needed her.

"You won't mind, my dear, will you? Captain Retford will prove an interesting conversationalist—and a gold mine of information for our cause."

She stared at him. "Captain Retford? Information for our cause?" She searched his face with its wily smile. His bristly black brow shot up above his eye patch in a characteristic look that was almost an amusing trait.

"Yes, our *loyal* British Captain Retford is a traitor! Surprised, my dear?"

Darinda was bewildered. "Captain Retford—a traitor?"

His smile fled as his eye hardened like glass. "He surprised me, as well. I don't enjoy being made a fool. The man, I believe, is a spy for the Boers. For President Paul Kruger."

Stunned, she simply stared at her grandfather. For a moment her mind was blank. Ryan Retford a Boer spy?

"You're not afraid of the man, are you?" he asked.

She found her voice. "Afraid? Hardly that, but I don't understand—"

"Splendid, because I want you to find out what he's up to here in

Bulawayo. He doesn't know it yet, but his orders have been changed. He'll be going with me on the Matopos expedition. I'll make it appear as though I trust him. Make him my bodyguard. I'll be trekking there as soon as matters are fully arranged. And I want you, Darinda, to find out what he's up to. Your presence will suit our cause very well indeed."

She continued to watch him, her confusion growing. The last thing she wanted was to play the spy, and with Captain Ryan Retford. What had all this to do with the family diamonds? The murder of Anthony? *Ryan*, a Boer *spy?* And what for?

"Grandfather, I don't see why any of this is necessary."

"Make no mistake about it, my dear. The Kimberly Black Diamond is rightfully ours, a family treasure. There is no way I'm going to let it remain buried on the Matopos, wasting away in the dark confines of a grave!"

He reached for his cheroot, struck a match, and lit the end.

"Grandfather, if you don't explain I shall burst."

"It's necessary you play the spy, my girl, not just for the family, but for England. You're the one person who may have an opportunity to unmask Retford."

Unmask him…

He looked at her insidiously. "He's as cool a gentleman as I've come up against, and I don't like it."

"But I thought you actually trusted him," she said, aghast. "Captain Retford mentioned just tonight that you wanted him to lead your search in the Matopos."

"Did he? Well, I did trust him until word arrived through Anthony that he's not merely a Boer sympathizer, but working against our plans to aid Uitlanders in the Transvaal." His countenance darkened with anger. "He's betrayed me. Anthony had proof—a letter Retford had written to the high commissioner in Capetown. I can't go into all that now. Just believe me when I say he poses a threat to the success of our plans."

Was this true, or was her grandfather exaggerating as he sometimes did? "What letter?" she asked quickly. "About the expedition to find the Black Diamond?"

"That, too. But I speak of another matter now. A secret plan to aid the Uitlanders. Jameson's Troopers, we call them. Six hundred soldiers to invade Pretoria and help the Uitlanders overthrow Boer injustice!"

She stared at him. Invade the Transvaal!

"You now, Darinda, are another matter. He may appear aloof, but I've seen the way he's looked at you. Now, now, I'm not asking you to commit yourself to Retford. Just be friendly with him. It's information I need, and you can ask the sort of questions that I cannot."

She was shocked, but should she be? "You want me to spy on Retford?" she asked in a choked voice. "But what can he possibly tell me that's so important?"

"I want to know what Retford knows and what he's up to, whether he's working for Kruger at Pretoria, and what he wants for himself. Has he spoken to you in any way about the Boers?"

"He's said nothing to me about them. And he talks very little about himself."

"Then learn what his game is. I think you're the woman to do it."

Was she? Using underhanded tactics hadn't benefited her on the pioneer trek to Fort Salisbury. She'd tried to get Henry Chantry's map from Rogan by using Parnell. When he had failed her, she'd considered using Captain Retford. It embarrassed her even remembering what Retford had said that night in Rogan's camp along the Limpopo River. He'd seen through her tactics almost at once and warned her against them. No, not warned, "lectured" her on becoming a lady of Christian principles. He had dared to suggest she'd have a tendency to be a common thief if she'd been raised on London's East Side instead of being the rich, favored granddaughter of Sir Julien Bley. Though that had infuriated her, later she'd thought about what he said. She still thought about it, in fact.

"I'm not sure I want to play the spy, Grandfather—"

"Darinda, need I tell you how crucial this is to our success in expanding the frontiers of Rhodesia? Those gold fields in the Transvaal are successful because of British and colonial miners—Uitlanders, if you please. If the Uitlanders rebel against the government of Pretoria—and Jameson and his six hundred ride in to their aid—we could produce a full-scale uprising. He'd soon be ready to talk peace with London. The high commissioner is even now preparing to meet with Kruger and discuss peace. We can't afford to allow a turncoat among us to alert Kruger about Jameson's raid!"

"You're not saying Dr. Jameson's troopers are going to invade the Transvaal—"

"When it happens, my dear, we'll assure an astonished London that we had no previous knowledge of Jameson's plans. Rhodes, too, will maintain his innocence."

"Does he know?" she whispered uneasily.

Julien waved a hand. "I'm not quite sure, though it's hard for me to imagine Doc doing something on this level without Rhodes's knowledge. But afterward, Jameson would have to say Rhodes was not involved. Rhodes is now prime minister of Cape Colony. The stir would be so great he would need to resign as an embarrassment to Her Majesty."

Darinda was skittish about muddying her hands in anything of this magnitude. Invading the Transvaal in a plot with the Uitlanders to rise up against the Boer president would bring serious consequences.

"I don't think Captain Retford would tell me whether he knows such a thing is planned," she said, "nor the name of any who could be passing information to him. Wouldn't it be better just to step away from all this?"

"When you're spying for the future of the Charter Company? We want a monopoly on the gold fields in the Transvaal in the same way we control the Kimberly diamond mines. This is crucial, not for us only, but for England. Would you prefer to have the German Empire sign a pact with Kruger?"

His words cast in the uniform of British patriotism encouraged her. This made it sound more like a noble cause. Still, Captain Ryan Retford was no fool. Could she learn what Julien wanted?

"What if he sees through my efforts?"

"That's what bothers me about Retford. He leads me on a hound's chase after a rabbit that isn't there. But you, my dear, have something I do not—feminine wiles and beauty. Now, now, don't protest. It's true. Though the perfect woman for this task, if I had my choice, would have been Arcilla—"

"Arcilla! That silly goose?"

"She's flirty and without scruples—it comes naturally to her. But she's not the slightest bit malicious and has no interest in politics. That is why I couldn't trust her with this, though I think she would do it if I offered to reward her with a ticket home on the next ship with Peter."

Darinda couldn't help but smile. "You are an old conniver, Grandfather. But I suppose that's what's gotten you where you are today."

Julien's eye gleamed. "And you and I, my dear Darinda, are cut from the same piece of cloth."

She didn't know quite what to think about his comparison. She felt somewhat offended, though she couldn't say exactly why. Perhaps Dr. Jakob's preaching was having an undue effect upon her conscience.

She was pleased Grandfather Julien believed her capable of helping broaden the family dynasty from diamonds into gold.

"I do think that I may be more like you than Anthony was," she said with a rueful turn of her lips.

He sobered. "Yes, much more so… I made a mistake years ago with Anthony, but that was before you were born. I had thought I could develop him into the right man to take over after me, but Anthony never showed the iron that was necessary to make decisions to benefit the Bleys, Chantrys, and Brewsters. He was sensitive and worried too much, especially toward the end. I couldn't have that—could I?"

Darinda's gaze swerved to meet his one cool, hard eye.

"One must learn to quench one's conscience to get ahead in this world," he continued as he poured himself a small, precise amount of liquor in a jigger.

She watched. Somehow it didn't trouble her as much as when Parnell used liquor. Maybe because Grandfather never let it make him vulnerable. He seemed to be in control of how far to go—without getting snared by his sin.

"One should be willing to take the initiative when necessary, regardless of what others may think. Anthony was weak in that way, troubling his mind with what others thought. He worried when he'd given up Evy to the Haverings. And he always seemed to have a guilty conscience about Katie van Buren."

"That he'd deserted her when she became pregnant?"

"He didn't desert her! It was necessary he marry Camilla. He knew that. So did she. What happened to Katie was the result of their propensities toward stubbornness. I had warned Katie on several occasions to stay away from Anthony, that there could never be a marriage between them. She wouldn't listen. I fear her daughter Evy followed in her mother's footsteps marrying Rogan."

Darinda lapsed into silence. She didn't want to feel sympathy for the memory of Katie van Buren, but somehow she did. A woman could understand how her fellow sister had fallen in love with Anthony and trusted his intentions before he had made a permanent commitment. If Anthony had actually wanted her for his wife, then he should have been man enough to choose Katie regardless of Grandfather Julien's plans. Yet—how could she think this when she was willing to do a very similar thing to gain control in the family diamond business?

Darinda smiled, but she felt a hardness stealing over her emotions. "I'll play the spy for you, Grandfather, but I want something in return."

"My dear, you know very well I shall leave you most of my accumulated fortune—even the Kimberly Black Diamond. I've no doubt it's buried with Lobengula, and I'm going to get it back." His eye flashed. "It's mine…it's always been mine. And no one is going to rob me, or you and your future children of the right to own it!"

His pronouncement gave her a chill. She admired him, yet there were times when his determination seemed more like an obsession. *But I'll be different. I won't totter on a precipice of ruin. I'll always leave a way back to safety.*

"All that is fine and good, Grandfather. But I want to contribute to the family business and take the place left vacant by Anthony to follow you as head of the family dynasty."

Julien smiled, but little joy or warmth came through. His thoughts appeared to be elsewhere. He patted her shoulder.

"First learn what I need to know about the Boers and whether Kruger suspects we're going to aid the Uitlanders at Pretoria, and I will make you my partner, Darinda. I'll train you to follow my steps, and change my will to stipulate that you'll take over after me."

She sucked in her breath. "Grandfather, do you mean it this time, really mean it?"

He gave her a little shake by the shoulders, still smiling. "Yes, I've decided. I invested years on Anthony, only to be robbed of him in the end. You're already inclined toward my way of thinking. You'll go a long way, Darinda. Just make certain you don't allow your heart to overrule your head when it comes to Captain Retford."

"Never. I'm quite content at this stage of my life. Marriage and family can always come later. About Parnell…"

"Bah! He's not worthy of you. He'd be unnecessary baggage for years to come. Parnell could work as your husband only if you were in control of the marriage. I suspect he would submit, my dear, but—"

She pulled away, shaking her head. "I don't want that kind of man. I'd not respect him, and I'd lose my own respect. I don't love him…and his drinking problem—"

"Parnell is useful to me now. As long as he has hope that he will eventually marry you, he'll cooperate with me. I need him right now to accomplish some things."

She nodded. Parnell was to be strung along for the foreseeable future. At the right time he would be dropped. She pushed the thought from her mind. *Why should I feel guilty just because Grandfather's taking advantage of him?*

"Aren't we risking a good deal by sending troopers into the Transvaal?"

"It's a chance we must take, but we are in great danger of having a traitor, one who's allied with Retford while pretending to cooperate with Doc Jameson. I need you to find out who that person is. The sun never sets on the British Empire, my dear. There is a reason for that. The British were made to rule. It's in our blood."

"You sound horribly arrogant, Grandfather, like Mr. Rhodes and his dream to make the Dark Continent 'all red' like the Union Jack."

He waved a hand. "Never mind that. Since you hope to take over after me, you must guard your emotions from the missionary lobby. You're not here on a crusade. We've England's interests, and those of our own family, to put first. Loyalty to Her Majesty must inspire us both. Your ability to learn what the Boers are up to is essential."

"Why should Captain Retford trust me? He'll see through my questions at once."

"I've taken care of that. You'll tell him you've been sent ahead to prepare business matters for me. We're in a race to win South Africa. And the Boer Republic is the one we must defeat."

She nodded, wondering if she could prevail.

"From Retford you can learn much, but most important, I want the name of the turncoat who is working with Rhodes and Jameson."

Could she accomplish that?

Her thoughts must have shown on her face, because he slipped an arm around her shoulders. "You can do it, and you will. If we can route the turncoat into the open and reveal him, it will give Jameson's Troopers enough time to move into Pretoria and overthrow the Kruger presidency. We'll beat them at their own game."

A rush of excitement rampaged through Darinda's brain. There was a turncoat, a spy for Paul Kruger who was known to Ryan Retford. But why would Ryan find it in his heart to support the Boers over his own British ancestry?

"As for Retford, we'll need to be shrewd. We need to play along with him for the present. You're the bait."

She looked at him. He gave a short chuckle.

"Don't worry. If I didn't know he was a gentleman, I wouldn't let you take him on. It's Retford who is in trouble—I've confidence in you, my dear."

What of me? she thought, unexpectedly alarmed. Was not there great risk to herself? Captain Ryan Retford was one man she found attractive.

"Once I'm through with him, Rhodesia will offer many interesting prospects for seeing to his demise."

Her eyes swerved to his. "What do you mean?"

"Don't look so concerned. I'm not speaking of his death. You just learn everything you can about what he is up to with the Boers. Who knows? This may have a blessed ending after all."

A blessed ending, Darinda thought. Was there such a thing?

Chapter Sixteen

Julien left the bungalow to meet up with Harry Whipple and the Company police on the road to the induna's kraal. Darinda waited inside the bungalow for Captain Retford, moving restlessly around the room as she mulled over her Grandfather's words.

What's come over me lately? I never worried unduly about the consequences of my actions before.

The reason for her concern was simple: Captain Ryan Retford. She did not wish to admit it, but she cared unreasonably about Ryan's opinion of her. And so far, thanks to her past behavior over Rogan's old map, Captain Retford's opinion of her was not exactly admirable.

She suspected he found her attractive, just as Grandfather had shrewdly noted. What Julien did not understand, and underestimated in importance to the success of his plans to use her, was Captain Retford's own solid character.

Over the past year she had discovered that Captain Retford also considered character to be of chief importance in a woman. Arcilla seemed to know something about the woman he was writing to back in London; she was involved in works of charity.

Darinda mused about that, absently lifting a pair of spectacles from the rattan table where the oil lamp glowed brightly, fingering them while her thoughts drew a mental image of the woman, Ann. Probably very sweet and full of humility.

Unreasonable irritation took control. No doubt he thought she was without scruples. Ryan Retford had been keeping company recently with that freckle-faced Derwent Brown! And, no doubt, hearing all of his little lectures. Now there was a scrambled-brain boy, if she'd ever met one! And Alice, his wife, was nothing less than a catastrophe. If Arcilla was a hysterical crybaby about wanting to go home to Grimston Way, Alice Tisdale Brown was a sour bit of goods that wanted to stick it out in Bulawayo until she had her hands on a pile of gold. It was almost humorous. As though Derwent was somehow going to come home to their bungalow one evening pushing a wheelbarrow full of shiny gold coins.

She played with the spectacles. Was Arcilla right when she said Ryan was helping to build Dr. Jakob van Buren's station not far from Bulawayo? With interests of this sort on Ryan's mind, he wasn't likely to become involved in passing secret information to her about a spy in Rhodes's camp. Bridging the social and romantic divide that stood between them wasn't a likely task for Ryan to wish to accomplish anytime soon. He'd more likely remain standing at attention behind his uniform.

So how to win his trust and gain the information Grandfather wanted?

What would winning mean to her in the end when Ryan discovered her attention had all been a ruse for Julien to gain the upper hand?

She would have what she wanted most—a leadership role in the family diamonds, perhaps even a partnership with her grandfather that would eventuate in her assuming control when he passed on.

What else? Certainly, she would not have Captain Ryan Retford. The question was, did she really want him? There were other men, plenty. Parnell, of course, plus a host of wealthy and powerful men in both London and Capetown, many of them members of the British nobility. They were also partners with Rhodes and others in diamonds and gold.

Darinda used the tips of her fingers to massage her aching temples. She felt a terrible headache coming on. One of those rare ones that put her to bed for twenty-four hours.

Oh how frustrating choices could be.

I've got to make up my mind, and soon!

If she let Grandfather Julien take the helm of her little ship, he would direct her life's course into gigantic swells of turmoil. If she survived the storm, she could be very successful in business. But if not—or if she learned that what she really wanted in life was a man like Captain Ryan Retford—then it would be too late for her to change course.

I must think carefully about this. I need time. No matter how urgent Grandfather says it is.

Ryan intrigued her. Was she falling for a man of unusual character? The idea maddened her. How could she admire him when it was her grandfather she most admired? Did not Julien's shrewdness impress her? No sentimentality affected his plans, just hard, cold facts on the balance sheet.

It seemed to her that lack of character made it simpler to make choices. As Julien had often told her when she was growing up at Cape House, "Just choose what benefits you most and forget all the rest."

But what if Dr. Jakob is right? What if there is a God who keeps an accurate record of one's life? A righteous Judge who cannot be bought off with diamonds and gold?

Darinda shuddered. *I won't think about that now.*

For a moment or two, she listened to the wind fluttering the shrubs outside the bungalow like little rats running here and there. *Rats—the world is full of them. Like the ruthless human kind that can be far worse than ordinary rats. Rats do what rats are supposed to do, but mankind is shrewd in its sin.*

Why am I thinking this? She rubbed her forehead. *Don't be a fool, Darinda. This is your chance to be the first woman to head up the family diamond business. Think of the notoriety you'll get in London. Think of the powerful men, even earls, who will see you in a new light. How important you'll be, and how intelligent you'll appear.*

Where was Captain Retford, anyway? It was rude of him to keep her waiting.

She set the spectacles down on the table and turned to leave. She paused, looking back at them. Whose were they? Not that it mattered. Anthony didn't wear spectacles, nor did Arcilla—she was too vain to do so, even if she really needed them. Parnell? Not that she recalled. She picked them up again, wrinkling her nose, turning them over several times. Gold rims, expensive, with the initials, *JB.*

Of course, Grandfather's. She placed them inside her pocket to return to the house.

Driven with impatience, she decided to leave the bungalow. She didn't need to wait for Captain Retford to escort her back to Government House! That was more in line with what Arcilla would expect, or even that religious girl from a vicarage in England somewhere, Evy van Buren, now Mrs. Chantry. She vaguely thought about the wire that arrived some time ago from Squire Lyle Chantry in Grimston Way, telling his stepbrother, Julien, that Rogan and his wife had sailed for Capetown weeks ago. Their arrival would mean little to Darinda now that Rogan had married.

She went down the dark bungalow steps. Dust lifted around her booted feet as she entered the moonlight from the shadows of the bungalow.

The moon had risen over Bulawayo from the foreboding Matopos Hills. Sharply etched branches and the tops of distant thorn trees on the veld showed black in the bone white moonlit world that lay spread out before her. On the far side of the clearing, a candle glowed in a bungalow window. A small dim light…from bungalow thirteen.

Her memory was nudged—*Number thirteen is vacant.*

Hadn't there'd been some meandering discussion at lunch about putting Anthony there? Arcilla had said something about thirteen being larger and more comfortable. Someone had joked about its "luxury." Then someone else—was it Peter, she couldn't remember—had suggested it was too isolated, requiring a long walk to Government House each morning and evening for meals and meetings, and that Anthony had recently developed some sort of heart condition.

Darinda vaguely thought how sad that Camilla must be told about her husband, and when Evy arrived, she would find out that her father, whom she'd only recently come to know, was dead.

Darinda stoically stared off toward the flickering light in bungalow thirteen, refusing to allow the pain of others to depress her.

The breeze danced about her like a satyr.

Yes, thirteen was vacant. In fact, Parnell had jested that he was so alone in bungalow twelve that he hesitated to go out at night for fear of prowling lions.

Then what was a light doing in the window?

If Captain Retford was a Boer spy, might he have gone to that vacant bungalow tonight for a clandestine meeting with the other man in the Company getting information for President Kruger? How many other such meetings had been there? Had Parnell ever noticed that little light flickering?

Although Retford had known he was to escort her back to Government House, Julien had been with her discussing matters, and Captain Retford may have thought he had enough time to meet with his contact. What better time for a meeting than when Julien and Harry Whipple were gathering troopers to ride off to question the local induna? Sometimes the secrets were best kept right under the noses of those who sought them. Grandfather was right.

She glanced round about her again, assured that Ryan was nowhere at hand, and rallied her determination. If she was going to serve the Company, this was an opportune time to begin.

She brushed her fingers against her pistol, confident she could use it if she needed to protect herself, but equally confident such would not be necessary with the honorable Captain Retford.

The evening was so quiet that Darinda could hear the faint sweep of wind on the brush near the creek. The grasses quivered. Perhaps an animal crept along on silent paws to quench its thirst, or a python slithered by, hoping for some small creature to appear. Some men were like that: they could swallow up the vulnerable and say, "I have done no wrong. A man must eat any way he can."

She must stop listening to Dr. Jakob van Buren, allowing his beliefs to take root in her mind.

She started along the path toward the distant bungalows, watching her steps as she went. The moonlight slanting over the hills shone onto the thatched bungalow roofs, turning them into a golden amber while the shadows of trees swayed on the walls.

She approached bungalow thirteen. No wonder Parnell thought it lonely down here at the end of the row of huts. From the back of the bungalow, a slope went down to the watercourse. She could hear the water rippling over stones.

She came near the side window. The candlelight glowed. She drew yet closer, cupping her ear and listening. There were no voices, only murmurs from the wind.

She drew quietly away and backed…into something.

"Good evening, Miss Bley."

Captain Ryan Retford's voice caused her to whirl around.

His gaze dropped to her hand as she clutched her gun. Embarrassed, she quickly returned it to the holster.

In the silver moonlight she could see he was displeased.

"You're kind of easy with that .45, Miss Bley. Let's hope you keep a clear head when you're startled."

Her face burned. "You mean when a man sneaks up behind me after a murder's taken place."

"My apology, Miss Bley. Sorry I frightened you. You do well to be on guard. I heard someone and circled around to see who it was. What are you doing down here?"

Very casual indeed. "I saw a light in the window. I thought it was a candle. Since thirteen is empty I wondered."

She eyed him. He looked quite handsome in the moonlight in his uniform. What would he think if he knew his superior had confided in her that he was suspected of being a Boer spy? He looked so British, so apparently loyal to Her Majesty's throne that it crossed her mind that Grandfather Julien must be wrong.

"Don't you think, Captain, we should have a look inside the bungalow to make certain no one is hiding there? I mean, wouldn't it be quite clever of Anthony's murderer to hide in a vacant bungalow while the Company police are out searching for him? Then, while everyone is preoccupied elsewhere, he could simply slip off unseen."

"Yes, quite clever of him, if that were the case. However, I'll need to confess, Miss Bley, that this is my bungalow."

Startled, she stared at him. "Yours?"

He smiled. "Mine. As of four o'clock this afternoon. Your grandfather's orders. I came here to have a look about while you were meeting with Sir Julien."

She looked at him a long moment. She could let the matter drop, but… "Do you mind if I have a look inside? I was so sure I heard voices."

He paused, then smiled. "Not unless I talk to myself. But if you don't mind being late for dinner in the pleasant surroundings of Government House, Miss Bley, then I'll not hurry you. Welcome inside Lucky Thirteen."

Did he know she had not really heard voices? She went up the steps onto the screened porch, and he followed. He reached over and opened the door. Darinda entered. The bungalow was nearly identical to the one Anthony had been given, except it looked larger.

"The builders must have gotten carried away on this one," he said lightly when she commented on it being larger.

She looked toward the window facing the path, where the candle glowed and flickered.

"The lamp was out of oil," he said, following her gaze.

He walked over to the window, opened it to let some breeze in, and moved the candle to another table. "No one else wanted this bungalow, so when Sir Julien asked me, I grabbed it up. I'm not one to turn down a comfortable bed just because it's assigned the number thirteen." He smiled and turned to look at her.

Darinda was watching him curiously. He must have noticed, for he looked as though he was wondering what she was thinking. For an awkward moment they stood facing each other.

She didn't know what to say. She glanced toward a closed door. She must be bold; she wasn't the kind to blush and withdraw. She walked daringly across the room, opened the door, and stepped into the small bedroom. It was too dark to see. To her surprise, Captain Retford came up behind her with the candle, and the room came into view. There was nothing of particular interest, certainly no spy. The small closet stood open and empty. She took the candle from him without meeting his eyes, walked in, stooped, and looked under the bed. Nothing. Feeling a bit foolish, she got up and walked past him into the main room.

"A very adequate bungalow," she said, her cheeks burning as she set the candle down on a small table.

"Quite pleasant, and much quieter than the barracks." A smile in his voice.

He must think she was daft.

"My grandfather asked you to stay here?" She tried to keep too much curiosity from her tone. She turned to look over at him.

Perhaps his hair was the color of sand, she decided. It contrasted well with his tanned skin and flinty blue eyes.

"He wanted me to be within closer call."

So he could keep an eye on him, no doubt.

Captain Retford stood looking the perfect soldier, and it was only by chance that she noticed the flicker of something like wry humor in his eyes.

She gave him a cool appraisal and turned away. She wasn't doing well at all in thawing the ice between them. How could she ever expect to learn his secrets when he was on guard? As long as it was "Captain Retford" and "Miss Bley," what could develop?

"Well," she said airily, taking in a breath and moving easily about the room. "The mystery of voices and lights in the window is solved, at least."

"And no bodies under the bed, either."

She turned sharply to look at him.

"Sorry," he said. "I shouldn't have made light of it after Lord Brewster's death."

He had mistaken her quick turn in his direction as offense over his jest, assuming her pain over losing Anthony. Little did he know her true feelings, or that they had argued hotly just before his death.

"You need not apologize," she said flatly. "I didn't have a lot of affection for Anthony Brewster. And not only that, Captain, but I benefit from his death." She turned and looked at him again evenly to see his reaction to her blunt honesty. Now, why was she doing this? She was risking alienating him further.

To her surprise—or was it relief?—he did not look shocked or disapproving.

"I had a terrible argument with him on the path about my inheritance," she confessed, still gauging his response. Would he be repulsed? Would he sympathize?

In her brief pause the bungalow creaked in the wind.

"Why would you be telling me this?"

She shrugged and walked about slowly, thoughtfully, touching things cautiously, as though she might get burned.

"I don't know..." She honestly didn't. She looked up. He watched her. "I suppose you're bound to find out," she said. "So will Harry Whipple. I was one of the last people to see Anthony before he was murdered."

He gave a nod. "When did you meet him on the path?"

She considered. "It must have been around 5:30. About an hour before I found him under the tree. I told him he had no right to control the diamond business after my grandfather died."

"You need not tell me what was discussed, Miss Bley."

"I don't mind. I told him that I was the rightful blood heiress because I'm a Bley." She couldn't tell what was moving through his mind. "He didn't like what I said. I didn't think he would, but it was truthful." Her eyes sought his.

"You'll need to tell Sir Julien about this," Retford said. "I would advise you not to go to Whipple."

That interested her. "Then you don't like him, either?"

"I don't know about that, but I wouldn't trust him if he thought he could get something for himself out of an unpleasant situation. You'll admit, Miss Bley, yours is a unique and unpleasant situation. But don't be alarmed. I can't see you bashing his lordship on the head when he turned his back to you, and I don't think anyone else would, either."

She walked over to the open window and interlaced her fingers tightly, wondering why she had admitted this to Ryan. This is not what she had come here for. There was no need to have mentioned her meeting with Anthony. No one else knew about it.

Captain Retford walked up. His next words surprised her. "I already know much of what you're not telling me, Miss Bley."

She studied his face, trying to make sense of what he'd said. "You knew I'd met Anthony? But how?"

"I didn't know you'd argued with Lord Brewster. I did understand about your strained relationship with him."

She delicately lifted her eyebrows.

"It's hardly a secret you two were at loggerheads," he explained. "You let your opinion be known on Rhodes's pioneer trek to Fort Salisbury."

"Did I? Was I that transparent?" She offered a rueful smile.

"You've made it clear, I think, that Lord Brewster stood between you and your desire to assume headship over the family diamond enterprise. So your argument with him this afternoon would not be considered surprising."

She thought about that a moment, then walked away, stopping to rest her hands on the back of a chair.

"What is curious to me, however, is why you came back to his bungalow," he said. "I understand he went on to keep an appointment with someone. Just who that individual was, no one appears to know. You'd already told him what you thought, so why didn't you just return to Government House?"

She hesitated. Her fingers dug deeply into the soft backing of the chair. She'd come back to find the letter the Capetown authority had sent her grandfather regarding his plans for the expedition to the Matopos. She suspected it was a sharp reprimand, and she'd wanted to read it for herself. Anthony had insisted on meeting alone with her grandfather upon his arrival with that letter. She'd been looking in the table drawer for it and hadn't gotten far in the search when Arcilla had interrupted her.

Silence settled. "I had wanted to talk with him again," she said. "I was going to wait for his return." Did he accept that explanation?

She turned to look at him. She changed the subject: "Do you think it was a native who killed him?"

"If it wasn't, then perhaps it was one of us, Miss Bley."

The breeze through the open window caused the candle flame to flicker, its light growing uncertain.

"Parnell believes the indunas are on the verge of sending their impis to attack us."

"They may like to, but their shields were burned, their assegais broken in two. They've no weapons that would stand against our Maxim guns. They know that and are not that foolish."

She agreed. She thought of the ngangas. "Arcilla is worried about happenings in the house. Witchcraft—do you believe in such things?"

"In the sense that it can be diabolical, yes, I believe there is some power behind it, and that evil spirits are real. I do agree with Parnell Chantry that the indunas feel they have grievances against us. I'm hoping we can work with Dr. Jakob to solve some of those problems. If I were in control here at Bulawayo, I'd ask the men to send their wives and children to Fort Salisbury until tempers cool down over the cattle issue."

The cattle issue—was it about Ndebele cattle?

"Parnell said their Umlimo blame the growing drought on the white man's presence."

"That, and a few other things. Their superstitions run rampant, I'm afraid. And the policies enforced under Harry Whipple and his Shona police aren't turning the indunas into stalwart friends."

"Do you blame my grandfather?" she challenged.

"He's the one who made Harry Whipple head over the police. Whipple is hated by the indunas, and with good reason at times. He has a weakness for being a thug and a bully."

She agreed with that, but linking her grandfather to some of the ugly incidents she'd heard about recently was unfair.

"The talk of the Black Diamond, too, has done harm," Captain Retford said quietly. He came close to her, his eyes serious. "I know you don't care to hear this. You're devoted to your grandfather, and that's normal. I understand he was the father in your life."

She stiffened at the mention of *father*. She didn't want to talk about her childhood and its lack of parental guidance and love.

Retford went on: "The indunas have heard whispers that your grandfather is searching for the Black Diamond. You can imagine how upsetting this is to them. Lobengula was like a god to them. If the Umlimo, whom they trust as the oracle, warns them that the white man is out to steal and plunder, what do you think will be their reaction, Miss Bley?"

"That's beside the point! They're wrong."

"Yes, they're mostly wrong. That's why Dr. Jakob is here. To reach them with the truth of Scripture, with the news of a God of light and mercy, who has given His Son for their redemption—but it confuses them when the white men in charge steal their cattle, conscript their young men to build their roads, and occupy too much of the cattle land."

"You sound like the ever-complaining missionary lobby in London, Captain. They're always going before Parliament declaring the 'evils' of the British!"

"In some cases they are very right."

"And of course the natives are mistreated, taken advantage of, and lorded over like slaves!"

"You asked what I thought about future trouble, Miss Bley. I'm telling you my honest thoughts. If Sir Julien searches the Matopos for the royal burial cave of Lobengula in order to retake that diamond, then he's putting the colony of farmers at risk. He won't listen to Dr. Jakob van Buren. He certainly won't listen to me. But *you* he might listen to. You just might be able to stop an unnecessary bloodletting."

She was horrified but quickly restrained herself. "Then—you think it will come to that?"

"I've told your grandfather I do. I requested he send for reinforcements and ask the women to leave. He is of another mind, Miss Bley."

"And so am I," she stated coolly. "I won't run away, Captain. Not now, not ever. And after what's happened to Anthony, my grandfather will need me here beside him more than ever."

Captain Retford looked at her long and hard. Darinda felt oddly embarrassed and turned her gaze away.

"I've no authority to order you and Mrs. Bartley to Fort Salisbury. So your wish to stay is likely to be upheld by your grandfather."

She moved away from the chair and walked to the window. A gust blew against her, prompting her memory. The window in Anthony's bungalow...the *open* window from which Parnell had claimed to see a fleeting figure crouching near the bushes. At the time Anthony was already dead...at least, he should have been, if he'd been dead an hour by the time she'd discovered his body. Anthony must have been attacked almost immediately after he'd left her on the path. Yet, she had heard nothing—or had she?

And the figure outside the window—*if* there'd been a figure, could have been Anthony's murderer.

Tap, tap, the rattan blind bumped against the edge of the window in a stronger breeze.

The breeze rippled against her face, her neck, moving her hair. Darinda ran a palm over her dark hair, thinking, looking into the night's shadows, seeing nothing as her thoughts rolled on.

She turned suddenly. "Parnell may have glimpsed the murderer."

"What was that?" Ryan walked up.

She explained quickly. Then: "But if it was Anthony's murderer he noticed, why would the person wait around afterward?"

"Yes...whoever it was took the chance of being seen in the vicinity. Was the conversation between the three of you important in any way?"

"No. Arcilla and I chatted about her fears, and I tried to calm her. Maybe ten minutes later Parnell walked in from his bungalow."

"Ten minutes, you say?"

"Yes, I'm sure it was."

"He said he came from his bungalow?"

"Well, no."

"You assumed that he came from there?"

She narrowed her lips. "I suppose you think—"

"I think nothing in particular, Miss Bley. But I'll need to report this as new information. No one mentioned this to your grandfather earlier."

"None of us felt at the time that the murderer was loitering about the open window," she went on briskly. "It was just something that Parnell thought he'd seen. Arcilla had apparently heard something earlier. She was nervous and asked him to shut the window. That's when he may have caught a glimpse out of the corner of his eye of a crouching figure."

"It's a very risky thing for the murderer to be eavesdropping."

She looked at him for an explanation.

"Whether or not it was the murderer, I can't say. But it was likely someone who knew about the murder and was trying to listen to your conversation."

"But nothing of importance was discussed. So why go to so much trouble to listen to Arcilla's hysteria?"

"Well, then, his purpose might not have been to eavesdrop at all, but to enter Anthony's room for some reason."

Darinda snapped the window shut. "Yes, that is possible."

Her eyes were busy as they moved slowly about the room, taking in every piece of furniture, every object on the tables, as though she were seeing not Captain Retford's bungalow, but Anthony's.

"Perhaps the murderer hadn't expected anyone to be inside the bungalow," she whispered.

"The murderer would know that Anthony wasn't there. The three of you may have hindered him from entering after Lord Brewster's death. You can imagine his frustration as the discourse you mentioned dragged on."

"In fact, he never got inside Anthony's bungalow," she said hurriedly, "because—"

"Because even after we all left, you stayed on to speak alone with your grandfather."

"And after Grandfather left, I still stayed and waited—" She looked at him; his eyes reflected understanding.

"And he could not have gotten in until I left and saw the light burning in your window. And—"

Captain Retford rushed to the door and out in a flash.

Darinda followed him down the porch steps and along the path toward Anthony's bungalow. She arrived a minute after Retford and rushed inside, where the oil lamp still glowed. She stopped in the bedroom doorway. Retford stood looking about at the confusion.

"We're just minutes too late," he said.

The chest drawers were all pulled open and empty. The closet was disheveled, and the bedding had been torn from the mattress. Anthony's baggage was dumped on the floor, its contents, mostly articles of clothing, scattered.

"What could they have been after? Money? Diamonds—"

He shook his head. "Information is my guess, either from the Home Office in London, or Capetown."

Darinda laid a hand on the wall to steady herself. She glanced at him, but he wasn't noticing her reaction. She must take a chance.

"What do you mean? What information?"

Captain Retford turned to look at her. A curious light shone in his eyes. Darinda felt her face betraying her. She wanted to tear her eyes away from his, to escape that clear glance.

"Someone wanted something pretty badly," he said quietly. "Your guess is as good as mine, Miss Bley. What was it that Lord Brewster brought with him here to Bulawayo?"

She knew it was the letter. Did he? Had he been in Government House when Anthony arrived? And had Retford also been in the inner circle when Anthony took Grandfather into his office?

She walked into the main room and sank tiredly into a chair.

A moment later he came from the bedroom. "I'll need to report this at once. Can you walk back with me to Government House?"

She stood abruptly. "Yes. I'm fine. You didn't think I was going to faint?"

A smile came to his face. "If I were a betting man, Miss Bley, I'd say you'd be the last to falter."

A compliment, or not? She guessed the latter. She walked to the open door and down the steps. He followed, then led as they took the path back to Government House. A path that had seen murder and deception in the hours just before sunset of this very night. If the trees and bushes and bugs could talk, what story would they tell? What would the wait-a-bit tree say about someone dragging Anthony's body to the base of its trunk for her to accidentally discover?

Darinda followed, tired and worn, longing for her room, a bath, a strong cup of tea.

They did not speak further. She guessed he was trying to piece together the events of the day and what they might mean.

She, too, was thoughtful; her thoughts were anything but comforting. She was not the only one interested in that letter. She had been merely curious to know the extent of any reprimand upon her grandfather. There must be something more to this. Something more important than she had suspected.

The moon had set behind the mountains. The stars were glowing. Her heart felt cold.

Chapter Seventeen

A hyena warbled and sobbed in the darkness.

Arcilla's flesh prickled as she looked behind her into the night. The leaves on the bushes lining the walk up to Government House shimmered in the windy moonlight. Peter had been delayed from returning with her, as they'd met Dr. Jameson. He'd heard about Anthony and ridden out to get all the facts. Afterward he'd wanted Peter to attend a meeting at his house. Arcilla had gone with Peter and had been served tea while Peter went with Jameson and some other officers into the meeting. Finally, she'd had to send a message to Peter through the cook that she needed to get back to Baby Charles. Dr. Jameson had insisted one of his aides safely escort her back to Government House while Peter stayed to finish the meeting.

This time, surely, after what had happened to Anthony, Peter would keep his promise to come home early to cheer her and cuddle his baby son.

Arcilla opened the front door and stepped inside the big rambling bare wood room everyone called the common room. Here, attachés working for Julien, Peter, and the Company police had their desks and chairs lined around the walls. One of those desks belonged to Captain Ryan Retford.

A few small oil lamps were burning on several of the desks to cast a secure glow. She grimaced, for the light also revealed bugs that disappeared into the cracks when she approached. She walked slowly to give them time to scurry away. Anything to avoid them. Little lizards walked the ceiling. She liked the geckos; she thought they ate lots of bugs. Some bugs didn't run away, but seemed to run *toward* her. Before the rainy season there were spiders, lots of spiders. Some were flying spiders—to her, at least, they appeared to fly. Peter claimed he needed calming pills as the rainy season approached just to endure her screams. Peter always exaggerated. Her screams weren't loud, just little shrieks. At night she would make him wake up and lead the way safely to the "powder room." Sometimes he would need to carry her.

"My *dear,* can you not just ignore them?"

"You're heartless. How can I? They squish if you step on them."

Standing in the common room, she looked along the floor before walking. She picked up the hem of her straight skirt and tiptoed across to some steps.

There was a square woven matlike rug in the center of the floor. She moved as quietly as she could toward some crude wooden steps that led to the top rooms used for private sleeping quarters. She'd complained loudly to all that one small bedroom was not enough with a baby, so Peter had bribed the workmen to add a second small room and a "powder room."

She was climbing the steps when she noticed a sliver of light under the door of Uncle Julien's office.

They had left Julien at the bungalow with Darinda. From there he was supposed to have ridden with Harry Whipple's police and Shona guards to question the induna at his kraal. Arcilla could never remember how many indunas there were, nor how many kraals. *Anyway, I don't care.* Perhaps Julien had not gone to question the induna after all.

Anthony must have told Uncle Julien whether the Colonial Office wanted Peter transferred back to London. In the letter she'd written Camilla, she'd begged her to intervene with Peter's father in London to see that his son was brought back to work for the colonial secretary. It had taken nearly a year, but at last Camilla had written her, saying Anthony promised to do what he could to get them back to England.

Had Anthony mentioned something about Peter to Julien this morning in their meeting?

She made up her mind. She was going to ask Julien straight out!

She turned and came back down the steps. Perhaps now was not the best time to see Julien, with the vicious thing that had happened to Anthony, but the horror of his murder only inflamed her urgency to leave this loathsome land.

Arcilla hurried to Julien's office before her courage thawed into cowardice. Outside the door she smoothed her mussed golden hair back into its bun and rubbed color into what must look an anemic face. What a horrible day! A draft came from somewhere, and on the air wafted the smell of supper cooking on the other side of the house. The very thought of food turned her stomach.

The door to Julien's office was already open an inch, as though the latch hadn't clicked. The lamp was burning. The window behind the desk was open, and the rattan blind was drawn partway up, bringing the draft. Her fingers shook as she took hold of the door edge and pushed it open.

Julien stood by a tall table with his straight back toward her. For a moment she thought he was striking a match to light one of his square, stubby cheroots. He turned sharply, startled by her entry. It wasn't a cheroot he was lighting. It was a sheet of paper. It was burning in the big ashtray on the table, turning to gray ash. The odor of burned paper and smoke gently drifted past her nose.

He walked toward her, effectively keeping her from approaching. He motioned to a chair.

"Where's Peter?"

"In a meeting with Dr. Jameson." She sat down, looking up at him as he towered over her, unsmiling. His black eye patch gave him a hawkish look—his one bright eye somehow impressed her with the notion of a bird of prey.

"I know it's a horrid time to bring this up, Uncle, but it's about Peter's father. He's so sick, you know. In that last letter I showed you from Lord Bartley, he spoke of being confined mostly to his room now, in London." Her fingers kneaded the arms of the chair. She felt she couldn't tear her eyes from his steady gaze.

"Cousin Anthony—poor Anthony—he'd promised Camilla to see that Peter and I got home for a spell to stay with Lord Bartley."

"Peter has mentioned none of this to me."

"He should have." Her frustration flared. Excuses, always excuses. As though she had no right to want to take the baby and go home with Peter for a time.

"Then, naturally, Aunt Elosia wants to see Baby Charles Rogan…"

"Yes, of course she does."

"And, well, I didn't get a chance to talk with Anthony alone about what Lord Bartley wanted." *Because you hovered over him, not allowing it.*

"How charming of you, Arcilla, to be so worried about the ailing old father of Peter. Very generous of you, my dear."

She felt her cheeks scorch with heat. He saw through her like an owl eying his prey at midnight.

"Peter worries about his father." It was all she could do to keep her voice calm and civil. Julien was a scavenger!

"I know Lord Bartley well, my dear. You must not worry so about him. He wants what is best for Mother England." Julien's lips drew back, showing his white teeth in a derisive smile.

"Ah, my poor lamb, Arcilla. How I am disappointed in your stamina. I worry about you and Peter getting on!"

She stood, trying to measure her breathing. "I want my son raised at Rookswood!"

"Of course you do. A worthy ambition on your agenda."

He was mocking her!

"I…I wondered if Cousin Anthony had brought any new orders for Peter about serving in London in the Colonial Office."

Why was he smiling at her like that? She always felt uncomfortable when he smiled that way. She could see no humor in the situation. And especially now with Anthony lying dead. She believed Julien considered her a foolish child, as though he must either threaten her, or soothe her bedtime fears of darkness.

"No, Anthony did not mention any new post for Peter. Peter is needed here in Bulawayo, you see. Has Peter talked to you about returning to London soon?"

"No," she admitted slowly. "I thought Anthony may have mentioned any future plans to you when you met with him this morning after he arrived."

"I'm sorry, my dear, he did not. But you mustn't fret, you know. As soon as this nasty business about his death is resolved, and we deal with the Boers, you and Peter will have plenty of time to visit Rookswood with Baby Charles." He walked to where his decanter sat on a tray, pulled the stopper, and poured himself a drink. "To British South Africa." He emptied the jigger.

Her hands clenched, and her nostrils flared. She had the urge to fly at him like a mad, fluttering crow and peck out his eye.

"Why must Peter stay here until the murderer is found? That's the job of Harry Whipple!"

"Now, now."

"And the Boers? I daresay if there's a war, it will last for years! And there will be a war if you and Dr. Jameson have anything to say about it."

He turned sharply on his heel and looked at her. All mocking playfulness was washed clean from his swarthy face. Alert and determined, he approached her.

"Why did you say that?"

She saw her mistake. She had come close to giving herself away. If he discovered she was aware of their plans for a strike into Boer territory to rouse the Uitlanders—

The front door opened boldly and shut. Voices sounded. With relief she heard Darinda, then Captain Retford.

Julien took his attention from her and looked toward the doorway into the common room. He walked there and called out. "That you, Darinda? Captain Retford?" Julien stepped out of his office.

There followed an exchange of words, then the calm voice of Captain Retford took over.

Probably discussing Anthony's death… Arcilla paced, frustrated. Nothing had gone well. With Uncle Julien it never did. She was no match for his shrewd devices.

She rubbed her arms in distaste and moved about the office. He had no right to say Peter couldn't leave until the Boer situation was cleared up.

She wandered about the room until she'd ended up by the table where the large ashtray contained the ashes of the paper he had set a match to. The remains looked to have been a letter. In fact, she knew it was, because the envelope was intact on the table. He must have forgotten it was there. Her entry must have distracted him.

George Trotter, Cape Mining Fields, Capetown, it read. Then in florid handwriting: *Sir Julien Bley, Chief Native Commissioner, Bulawayo.*

A small section of charred paper remained in the ashtray. The smudged words lazily looked up at her.

—R's and J's plans for—Uitlanders should proceed—

The voices in the common room continued. Arcilla glanced there over her shoulder. Her deft fingers quickly retrieved the section of sooty paper from the ashtray. She blew it off and slipped it down the front of her blouse. The envelope she reached for—then decided against it. No, he might remember he didn't burn it. He might look for it, and if it was gone, he would know she was aware. She moved back across the room to where she'd been sitting.

Another voice joined the discussion outside the office door. Peter! With relief she swept from the room into the hall.

Julien stood with Darinda and Captain Ryan Retford. Arcilla came up beside Peter.

"Something more has happened?" Arcilla asked.

Peter nodded. "The bungalow was searched."

"What do you think was behind the search, Captain?" Julien was asking Retford.

"Diamonds, perhaps, Sir Julien."

"Diamonds, Captain?"

Arcilla noticed that Darinda looked briefly surprised, then her face went blank.

"And gold, too, perhaps," Captain Retford added.

"You think this was a common burglary of Anthony's bags, then?"

"It could have been more, I suppose. If you're thinking this is connected to Lord Brewster's murder."

"Evidently, Captain, you do not?"

"I really couldn't say either way, sir."

Arcilla looked at Darinda, but she remained expressionless.

Peter frowned. "Someone was dashed bold, I daresay. Entered the bungalow beneath our very noses, you say?"

"Indeed, sir," Retford said.

"And after Harry Whipple's out with a dozen police, too," Peter said with disdain. "It doesn't say much for our murderer being a native, then, does it?" He looked at Julien, brows raised, questioning.

"Captain Retford doesn't think it was a Ndebele," Darinda said.

Both Julien and Peter looked at Retford for an explanation. Arcilla thought he looked a trifle reluctant. He smiled, however, and turned straight to her, knowing she was exhausted and under duress.

"I'm sorry to have to ask more questions, Mrs. Bartley, but earlier, when you were at Lord Brewster's bungalow with your brother and Miss Bley here, did you see or hear anything unusual outside the open window?"

"Open window? Oh." Arcilla just remembered. "I'd forgotten. I thought I'd heard something outside, footsteps, or maybe just the bushes moving too much."

"You mentioned it to Parnell Chantry and Miss Bley?"

"I did. When Parnell went to close the window, something startled him. He made the comment he thought he'd seen a figure crouching. Remember, Darinda?"

Captain Retford nodded. He looked at Peter and Sir Julien. They were sober.

"Eavesdropping?" Julien asked doubtfully.

He pondered. "I don't know what else it would be, sir. Lord Brewster's murderer wouldn't have dared hang about the bungalow. Your granddaughter, Miss Bley, said their conversation went on for thirty or forty minutes."

"Yes, I see what you mean, Retford," Julien stated. "Foolish, indeed, for the enemy to hang about eavesdropping for that long. Makes no sense at all."

Arcilla waited, and when no one else commented, she turned to Peter. "Do let's go up, Peter. The baby is awake by now, and Marjit can't feed him. He must be crying, poor dear. I think I hear him."

Peter accompanied her across the common room to the steps, and they went up together.

Arcilla thought of the scrap of paper she had. She ought to show it to Peter. She was sure it was part of the letter Anthony had brought Uncle Julien as a reprimand from Capetown.

She glanced at Peter. He was deep in his own troubling thoughts. The only problem with showing it to him was that the words on the scrap seemed to approve Julien and Dr. Jameson's plans to aid the Uitlanders, not rebuke them. Could she safely assume that from those few words? What would Peter say? He looked as though something was disturbing him. From the top of the stairs, he looked down at Captain Retford.

CHAPTER EIGHTEEN

Dinner was served late. Parnell arrived from his bungalow looking tense.

He's probably still thinking about Anthony, Darinda thought. He kept glancing around the table at those present.

Her grandfather had encouraged Captain Retford to stay and dine, which he accepted, confirming to her that she should follow through with the plan to spy on Retford. Darinda frowned into the amber contents of her teacup. The idea that Ryan Retford was a Boer spy still seemed ludicrous to her. Grandfather had yet to give her any solid reasons why he was convinced Retford was sympathetic to the Boer cause.

Arcilla did not come down. "She has her hands full with Charles. He's been doing an inordinate amount of fussing," Peter said.

Darinda felt a smile tug at her lips. Even when discussing his newborn son, Peter retained a certain haughty sophistication, while Arcilla, before coming to Bulawayo, was usually a bag of giggles. Seemingly, a mismatched couple.

"The day has been extremely rough on Arcilla."

"The poor girl," Parnell commented of his sister.

Grandfather's lip dragged at one corner, apparently over the brotherly strain of sympathy in Parnell's tone.

"We all humor Arcilla too much. One baby is enough in this house. We have a great deal of business to attend to."

Darinda glanced from the corner of her eye at Peter, who was sitting at the end of the long table. His shoulders drew back, but he kept silent.

The evening meal crawled by. No one appeared to have much appetite, and all reined clear of discussing Anthony's untimely death. Darinda said she had learned that Dr. Jameson sent a wire to Capetown to Lady Camilla, treating Anthony's death as a random attack from the African tribe.

Parnell splintered the awkward moment by suddenly bringing up the Matopos expedition.

"I realize we're all reluctant to talk about it, but there's little use in continuing this blindman-dumbman game. Look here, Uncle Julien. That Zulu savage isn't likely to forget that you're here in Bulawayo. And he has a stake in the Black Diamond."

Every head turned toward Parnell. He made use of the moment in the lamplight by leaning closer to the table. "We've all heard the story of Dumaka and his sister, Jendaya?"

"Jendaya was the Christian convert, wasn't she?" The question came from the calm, quiet voice of Ryan Retford.

"And despised for it by Dumaka. Some think he killed her."

"Not Dr. Jakob," Darinda said. "He thinks she is still alive."

"That may be, but Dumaka stole the family Black Diamond from ol' Uncle Henry in the stables at Capetown, and he won't surrender it to Uncle Julien now that it's finally buried with their king."

"What do you mean 'finally'"? Peter asked dryly. "You're not suggesting that Dumaka and the tribe have legitimate rights to the Kimberly? I think Uncle Julien will contest the idea." Peter looked past the candles down the table at Julien. The wick flames dragged and flickered.

It was unusual for her grandfather to remain this quiet in any discussion of the Black Diamond, and Darinda was curious as to why.

"Dumaka is dead." Julien tasted his wine with utmost satisfaction.

The others looked at him. Parnell was clearly stunned by this abrupt announcement.

"But—" began Parnell futilely, then stopped.

"I know, I know, my boy," Julien told him. "You thought he escaped

Lobengula's kraal the night we fought his impis. I did too. But Harry Whipple claims otherwise."

"Excuse me, sir," Captain Retford interjected in a moment of silence. "This is news to me. I wasn't riding with Jameson's Troopers in the war with Lobengula. I was north of here at the Zambezi. You say Dumaka is dead, sir?"

Clearly there was doubt in his voice, and Grandfather Julien smiled tolerantly and took another sip of his wine.

"I shall be pleased to explain." And he smiled in his superior way at each of them around the table and began a lofty tale of adventure that he enjoyed only too well.

Most of the story Darinda had heard before, except the part about Harry Whipple and Dumaka. Though she disliked and did not fully trust Whipple, she listened.

"Lobengula and his warriors withdrew from Bulawayo, the site of his kraal. I entered Lobengula's hut in search of the family diamond, which had been stolen by Dumaka and protected by Lobengula's witch doctors. Dumaka, who was one of Lobengula's indunas, had fully intended for the diamond to be brought to the Matopos as a gift for the Umlimo; however, Lobengula had not surrendered it. This bothered Dumaka and became a point of tension between the two men for about a year. Lobengula was then told that Dumaka was disloyal. It was our luck to attack on the same night Lobengula intended to have the spell-casters 'smell out Dumaka' for betrayal and witchcraft against Lobengula. Dumaka escaped but later returned to look for the Black when Parnell and I"—he gestured his wine glass toward Parnell—"were in Lobengula's hut searching. We had little time. Everything was going up in flames, but I knew I must find the Kimberly. Then Dumaka appeared with his assegai and would have killed me except for Parnell."

Darinda was stunned. *Except for Parnell?*

"Parnell shouted a warning. I was just able to turn and fire my gun. I missed Dumaka, but Harry Whipple heard the shot and came running.

Dumaka fled with Harry after him. With a handful of troopers, they tracked Dumaka to the Shangani River. Dumaka was hiding in the tall grasses when Harry spotted him. He fired. Dumaka was trapped. Rather than surrender he jumped into the river." Julien finished his wine. He smacked his lips and smoothed his mustache, his hand flickering diamonds. "Unfortunately for Dumaka, the river houses some of the biggest crocodiles in these parts."

The silence settled. Darinda stared at her plate, the food mostly uneaten and now cold. She pushed it away.

"And the Kimberly Black Diamond, sir?" Ryan Retford asked.

Julien set his glass down with a dull thud. "Lobengula managed to have it on him when he escaped. We hunted him, but he fled to the caves in the Matopos. He's dead. Buried with his precious things." He looked up, his eye glimmering in the candle flame. "The diamond, my diamond, the family diamond is either on him, or in the sacred cave of their Umlimo. Regardless, it will be confiscated."

Again silence fell.

Parnell cleared his throat. "Then, Uncle, what's this talk of the diamond being first stolen from the Zulu chief by either you or Carl van Buren many years ago?"

Julien's fist smacked the table. The dishes rattled.

"Grandfather!" Darinda said, alarmed.

"Rot!" Julien leaned toward Parnell, his fist still clenched. "I found the Black Diamond. Carl and I were partners in our own mine in Kimberly. "

"The day of the mine explosion?"

Julien's dark head whipped in Retford's direction. "Months earlier, I say, months earlier." He leaned back and reached for his empty glass. Schubert, her grandfather's personal servant, produced the bottle and poured. Darinda saw Schubert's slim hand tremble.

Julien took a drink. "Now," he said more calmly, "where was I, Darinda?"

Darinda felt cold and rubbed her arms. "We are ready for coffee now, Grandfather."

"Ah yes…coffee…Schubert! Bring in the coffee!"

Darinda glanced about the table. Peter watched her grandfather. Parnell was staring at his plate, but Captain Retford was looking at her. There was a grave look of sympathy in his eyes. She knew then that he understood. Peter did too. Perhaps they all did. Sir Julien was not well emotionally. When she had first noticed it, she could not say for sure. It had come like a creeping vine upon a tree, growing, growing, until finally it was obvious the ivy was starting to take over and would soon smother the tree. Most of the time Grandfather was normal. But this was the first time that his emotions had overflowed in public. Perhaps all he needed was a rest. Somewhere away from Bulawayo.

"Ah, the Matopos," Julien was saying heartily. "Beautiful hills. You'll get your chance to see them, Parnell, my boy. I'm only waiting for the right time to get the expedition together." He looked at Captain Retford. "I'm still depending on you to help lead that expedition, Retford. I've a map I want you to look at after dinner in my office. You too, Parnell— Darinda. Peter? You'd better spend time encouraging little Arcilla."

"I had planned on that." Peter's tone was stilted. He looked strained and haggard. He pulled out his vest watch and looked at the time. "If you will all excuse me?" He stood and nodded toward Darinda, then Julien.

A short time later Julien also stood. He looked almost elated. He rubbed his palms together. "If everyone has finished their coffee, let's have a look at the Matopos map. It arrived with Anthony. A fine, detailed map."

"Anthony?" Parnell asked, standing.

"Yes, he brought it to me. A precious gift. I shall miss Anthony. Almost like a son to me." He looked at Darinda. "I suspect a charming young woman may slip into his position." He smiled and laid a hand on her shoulder, then walked toward his office.

Parnell offered a wry, mocking smile. "So now it's Queen Darinda," he said, looking after Julien. "Uncle's forgotten about our dear Boer cousin."

Darinda, confused, turned and looked from Parnell to Ryan Retford, but Retford wore a military countenance. Then she realized Parnell was speaking of Heyden van Buren.

"I have my doubts about Dumaka's being dinner for the crocs. Ol' Harry Whipple will say anything to get in with Julien. But even if Dumaka was consumed, Heyden's still likely to be sneaking from tree to tree watching us. Gives one the jim-jams."

Retford showed immediate interest. "Heyden van Buren," he stated. "I wonder…"

Darinda was curious. "Why do you think he'll come here?" she asked Parnell.

"Think, my beauty. He has kin here in Bulawayo, doesn't he?"

She had forgotten that. Both Jakob and Heyden were cousins of Katie, Evy Chantry's mother. Carl van Buren, whom her grandfather had mentioned at dinner, was Evy's grandfather. Evy, Darinda decided uneasily, had quite a claim on the family diamonds.

"Dr. Jakob will never hide Heyden," Retford said. "Heyden's wanted for murder. Jakob knows that. If he shows up, I think Dr. Jakob will contact me."

She noticed he'd said contact *me,* not Harry Whipple.

The mention of murder brought the chill back.

"Heyden murdered my uncle Henry," Parnell told Retford. "Then there's Evy. She's married to my brother Rogan. Sorry I missed that wedding… Anyway, Heyden's responsible for Evy's fall. Rogan says she has a spinal problem now."

Darinda hadn't known about her injury, and her sympathy sprouted. Would she like Evy?

"Then I hope Heyden shows up in Bulawayo," Captain Retford said. "I would like the privilege of arresting him."

"You'll have some competition, there." Parnell wore a smirky smile as he looked thoughtful. "You know Rogan—he has his eye set on catching Heyden."

Retford nodded. "Derwent sets a great store in Rogan Chantry. What I remember about Rogan, I can appreciate. Does Sir Julien know your brother and Mrs. Chantry are on their way here?"

Parnell smiled. Darinda thought she could see a touch of satisfaction on his face.

"No. Actually I've done all I could to keep Rogan away from Uncle Julien, and since we know what Rogan's like when his mind is settled on something, we should see a jolly time here in Bulawayo when he arrives."

Suddenly someone screamed—

Darinda gasped and turned toward Grandfather Julien's office. A tense and quivering awareness of danger choked her.

"What—" Captain Retford pushed past them and ran ahead into the common room.

"That was Uncle Julien," Parnell breathed.

Darinda ran after Retford. She heard Parnell quickly behind her.

As she entered the common room, which was full of shadows and weaving displays of light on the walls, Peter appeared at the top of the steps. "Was that a scream I heard?"

Parnell stopped and looked up. "Julien!"

"Julien!" Peter repeated in a stunned voice. He clambered down the steps.

Darinda reached the office door, which stood ajar. She pushed through, but Retford stepped in front of her to block her way. His flinty eyes told her to stay out. She shoved against him. "Let me in—"

"It's all right, calm down. He's alive, just frightened."

"What?" Her eyes searched his, bewildered, yet relieved. She then caught a glimpse of her grandfather standing in the middle of his office as if in a trance, his face reflecting stark fear. Darinda pushed past Retford.

"Grandfather! What—?" Darinda neared his desk, her skin taut with uncertainty.

Her eyes transfixed on a spot of blood on Julien's desk...then many

spots. Her eyes followed them like pebbles on a trail. She lifted her gaze
to the ceiling. A slaughtered chicken hung from the ceiling. Beneath, on
the desk, were bones and other hideous things that made her turn her
head. Retford took her arm and drew her aside.

"Witchcraft," he explained in a low voice. "The various ngangas use
them. This looks like the work of a spellcaster."

Peter rushed in, alarmed, was met by the odious scene, then stopped
and stared.

"Who did this? A bunch of absurd nonsense!" Peter said with dis-
gust. He strode to the open door and shouted in the Sindebele language.
A moment later one of the young Ndebele guards working for Harry
Whipple came running. He stopped in the doorway and saluted Peter.
Then he saw Retford and saluted again.

Peter spoke brusquely, pointing and glowering. The young man's
eyes widened, and he backed away, shaking his head, speaking rapidly.

Captain Retford left Darinda and walked to Julien's desk.

"He says he knows nothing about this," Peter told Retford.

Darinda recovered from her initial shock and went to her grandfather. The consternation on his tanned face frightened her more than
the demonic ritual. This was the first time she'd witnessed fear carved
upon his face. His lips were pulled back, baring his teeth in a wolfish
display. His one eye had sharpened its gaze like a bird of prey, fixed on
the scattered bones on his desk. For a moment she thought he was going
to sway on his feet.

Peter looked surprised by Julien's reaction. Gripping his arm, Peter
steered him to a chair. He went to the doorway and called into the common room: "Detlev, tell Schubert to bring Sir Julien brandy!"

"Yes sir."

The blond-headed Dutch guard returned with Julien's valet. Schubert was pale and shaking as he fumbled with a decanter he'd brought.

"The Umlimo," Julien rasped, taking the jigger of brandy from
Peter's hand. "A nganga has done this. The spellcasting nganga's been
sent here—to—me—"

"Dashed nonsense, Uncle Julien," Peter clipped. "Pull yourself together, man. Surely you don't give credence to this cauldron of mish-mash? Here, now, drink that brandy. You're in shock."

"Peter's right, Grandfather. Pay no heed," she said. "It's like an awful joke someone has played on you."

"Bones, sir." Detlev was at the desk with Captain Retford.

"They're *hakata* bones, divining bones," Retford said. "If Dr. Jakob were here, he could explain better than I. He's informed about this divination. While he's taught the Ndebele about the redeemer Christ, he's learned some of their occultist entrapments."

"Hakata bones?" Darinda repeated. "They look like wood."

"They are, from the *mutarara* tree. Sixteen to the set, I think. The ngangas throw them the way a gambler tosses dice."

Peter called for the young Ndebele guard again. Jo came back reluctantly, cautiously circling the hakata. He said something in a hushed whisper to Captain Retford. Then Jo looked over at Sir Julien.

"Out with it, Retford. What's he gibbering about?" Julien asked.

"He says the *ngwenya* bone is pointing upward. Means the future is black."

"No," Detlev said. "No one can say such things but God."

Julien sat stiffly in a chair.

"Absolute poppycock," Peter agreed.

"It may look like a mixture of nonsense, but don't underestimate the nganga's witchcraft. It's demonic," Retford stated.

Peter scowled. "Are you trying to tell us, Retford, that the ngangas have power to cause some sort of impending doom?"

"Demon worship is rampant in the tribe's religion. The Umlimo, who they think speaks the oracle, is a girl possessed with an evil spirit. The tribe believes in their nganga witch doctors as well as their divining bones, and if the Umlimo tells the warriors to rampage and kill, they will. It's wise to stay away from the nganga. You may remember, sir, that when King Saul of Israel visited the witch of En Dor, Samuel the prophet informed him that he would lose his life on the next day."

"Balderdash, my good fellow. You're not telling us this hocus-pocus is real?"

"As real as Satan and his demons. But that's no reason for undue alarm. The Scriptures record that demons are subject to Jesus Christ. He cast them out whenever He encountered them. You may remember reading of the madman of Gadara? Jesus freed him from a legion of demons, also seven evil spirits from Mary Magdalene, as well as many others."

Peter straightened his gun belt and looked uneasy. "No, I've not read that, Captain, but I will." He looked over at Julien.

Julien downed his jigger of brandy and shuddered.

Captain Retford gestured to Detlev to get the divining bones and chicken parts out of the room.

"Leave the hakata," Julien said huskily. "They belong to me."

They turned to look at him. He was measurably calm again, having his wits about him.

"Yours?" Darinda was shocked. "Grandfather—"

He stood, swaying a little, so Peter steadied his arm, but Julien shook off Peter's hand, turned, and walked out of the office.

Parnell followed at a distance and watched Julien climb the steps to his room. "He's snapped out of his fear," he said. "I didn't believe I'd ever see the day that Uncle Julien was as scared as a rabbit over a cauldron of mishmash."

Darinda heard the wood bones click together as Detlev gathered them up from the top of the desk.

"What'll I do with 'em, sir?"

"My advice? Burn them," Retford stated.

Peter came out of his thoughtful scowl and looked over at Detlev, who was clutching the pieces of wood. "You heard Sir Julien. Better dump them in his drawer, I suppose," Peter said crisply. "If we burn them, he'll rant at us all."

"Yes sir."

The bones clattered as Detlev dropped them into the drawer and shut it. Detlev looked up at the dead remains.

"A waste, sir, if you ask me. Woulda gone for a good smoke pit back home."

"We agree on that," Retford said with a wry smile.

They left the office for the common room, leaving Detlev to clean up.

"My good fellow," Peter said to Retford, "who do you think was behind this?"

"I wish I knew. I'll have another talk with the Ndebele guards. Someone is either trying to frighten Sir Julien into leaving for Capetown, or worse...perhaps even wants him like Lord Brewster."

Though not intended, Darinda had overheard the two men talking. Julien's fear had notably affected her, and she clamped her jaw to keep the men from noticing her teeth chattering.

"But why?" she asked.

She found sympathy in Retford's eyes. "Why don't you go up to your room, Miss Bley? I'll see that matters are taken care of here. It's been a long day for you."

"For all of us," she said. "Yes, thank you, Captain. Coming, Peter? Arcilla will be on pins and needles by now."

"Yes, I'd best get up to her," Peter said.

She turned to Retford and smiled ruefully. "Good night." She looked away from his steady gaze.

Parnell looked too upset to be thinking of anything else except the evening's events.

"I'm with you, Retford," Parnell was saying. "I'm not walking back to the bungalows alone. I understand you have the one next to mine now."

"Yes, Bungalow thirteen," Retford said as a faint smile touched his lips.

"Dumaka," Parnell murmured again. "I wonder... Maybe he's not dead. He has plenty against Julien. All this talk about the Matopos and the Black Diamond being there with ol' Lobengula in his burial cave. If Dumaka thinks Julien is going on that expedition, then he could be as riled as a banded cobra. But Julien won't listen. He's obsessed with the Black Diamond."

Detlev appeared from the office. "Jo wants to see you, Captain. Something about the way the hakata bones were arranged."

Captain Retford and Parnell went with Detlev as Darinda went upstairs with Peter.

"Peter," she whispered. "If it isn't Dumaka, who else wants Grandfather—dead?"

Peter's craggy face was reflective. "That isn't the question, Darinda. The real question is, who doesn't?"

CHAPTER NINETEEN

Arcilla walked to her vanity table and placed the paper scrap from the ashtray in Uncle Julien's office inside her decorative letter box. After putting the box back, she closed the drawer. She left the bed chamber and went to the next little room.

Marjit, Detlev's wife, was dozing in a chair while Baby Charles slept in his cradle. Arcilla smiled for the first time and gently rubbed her infant's back. She made a kissing sound. "Hello, my sweetie."

Marjit stirred awake. Seeing Arcilla, she rubbed her eyes and sat up straighter.

"Thought you'd have supper first, Mrs. Bartley." Marjit stood and stretched like a skinny cat.

"I wasn't hungry. You can go now, Marjit, and thank you."

Marjit looked at her kindly. She and Detlev had a farm, but when their only child, a girl, died of what Dr. Jameson had called blackwater fever, Marjit abandoned the farm and came to Bulawayo with Detlev, intending to return to Fort Salisbury. Arcilla had begged her to stay with her for a few months and help look after the baby. Peter had then offered Detlev a job working as Captain Retford's assistant. Arcilla and Peter offered the couple a good salary, and they'd decided to stay indefinitely. Marjit was a wholesome woman who liked her and said so.

"Sound asleep," Marjit said of the baby. "Would you like some tea before I go find Detlev, Mrs. Bartley?"

"Yes, please do, Marjit. I'm done in. It's been a horrible afternoon."

"So I heard. Gruesome and positively frightening. Who could have done such a thing to his lordship? Was it the Ndebele? Just like poor Major Tom Willet?"

"Oh, Marjit, I can't bear talking about it anymore tonight. All I want is that hot cup of tea. Just to hold Charles Rogan in my arms when he wakes is enough… Could you let that rattan shade down, please? I think I'll just lie down awhile till Peter gets here…"

Marjit, a tall, thin woman with braided yellow hair and lashless blue eyes, looked at Arcilla concerned, and nodded.

"Yes, you do lie down, my dear. You look ill. I'll get that tea."

Arcilla sank into the narrow cushions and lay on her side so she could watch her baby sleeping so sweetly. She found comfort watching him. Soon, tired tears blurred her eyes. *My poor, poor darling baby. How can I get you to Rookswood safely?*

The cold cup of tea was sitting on the table when Arcilla sat up in the semidarkened room. How long had she napped? Baby Charles was not in his crib.

Lamplight filtered in from the main bedroom. She heard heavy footsteps moving about and knew it was Peter. She arose, smoothed her hair, straightened her skirt and blouse, and stepped through the doorway to the next room.

Peter was relaxing in shirt sleeves, collar unbuttoned, pacing leisurely with his son asleep in his arms.

Arcilla watched soberly. Peter saw her, and he paused, their eyes meeting for a long wordless moment.

He looks dreadful, she thought. *He's worried.*

He went to put the baby in his crib and rejoined her a minute later, drawing the door partly closed.

He was strained, tired lines showing beneath his eyes.

"Oh, Peter."

He held her quietly, rubbing and patting her back much the same way he did with Baby Charles.

"It's horrible," she cried. "Someone bashed in the back of poor Cousin Anthony's head. They snuck up behind him and—"

"Enough, Arcilla. You'll make yourself ill. Try not to think about it."

"I can't get it out of my mind."

His mouth tightened. "There's been more trouble since dinner. Someone played a nasty bit of goods on Julien tonight. A taste of witch-craft in his office."

"Oh no, not again?"

"It was more serious this time."

She suspected he left out the hideous parts in his explanation, but even so it was all quite ghastly.

"Who could it be? Who is doing this? The same person who killed Anthony?"

He held her from him, his craggy face looking a bit stern. "If we knew, we'd handle the blithering fiend at once. Arcilla, until this is solved, I don't want you out on your own."

"Then let's leave Bulawayo now. We'll go to Capetown, to Camilla. She'll need help after what's happened to Anthony."

"We cannot leave now, Arcilla. You know that. I have my duties here."

"What of your duties to me and your son? Parnell says the natives will attack all of us. Don't you care?"

"Need you ask so cruel a question of me? You and Charles mean everything to me."

"I wish I could believe that."

"Parnell drinks too much, I've told you so. He's destroying himself. If anyone should leave Bulawayo, it's Parnell. He should forget Darinda. She's only toying with his affections for her own ends."

She watched him walk over to the window and stand tall and straight, hands clasped behind his back.

"Darinda again," she scoffed. She sank into a chair, leaning her head back. Peter turned his head.

"Why do you speak of her so disparagingly? It isn't becoming of you."

She leaned forward. "Because you speak too well of her."

He turned about. "Don't be ridiculous. She's only one more matter for you to seize upon to criticize me. I would think a husband is entitled to a bit of respect from his wife."

"I would respect you more if you stood up to Julien. Tell him you're taking your family and returning to England where we belong."

He snatched up his pipe and tensely filled it with tobacco. He was frowning as he struck a match and lit it. He bit the end and looked at her with narrowed eyes.

Arcilla was sorry she'd spoken hastily. She did respect him. She stood and began to walk across the room to him, hands extended, but he turned his back and looked out the window into the darkness.

Her shoulders slumped. The baby began to cry. She went to see to his care. When she returned ten minutes later, Peter was sitting in the large chair smoking his pipe, his long legs crossed at the knees. He looked at her soberly.

"Everything all right?"

She nodded and walked over to the window. The cry of some animal stabbed through the darkness. She whipped the curtains closed and turned to look down at him where he sat.

"Did Anthony mention your father this morning?"

Peter shook his head no.

She tightened her mouth and plucked at her hair. "Uncle Julien said we couldn't leave until the Boer situation is resolved."

Peter remained silent, puffing his pipe. She gave a short laugh. "That will be years. I told him so. Charles will be four or five and have never met his grandfather Lyle and Great-aunt Elosia."

"You imagine the very worst, then become depressed."

She looked over at him. "Peter?"

He looked at her more tenderly. She said, "The letter from the authorities in Capetown—what was in it?"

He lowered his pipe and curled in his brows. "Letter?"

"You know, the letter Anthony brought to Julien. Would you mind telling me what was written in it?"

"Just government business, I suppose." His brows curled even deeper. "That Matopos map…I wonder now. Anthony mentioned no map. Seems out of character for him to have brought something he so heartily disagreed with. That expedition means nothing but trouble. I wish Julien would come to his senses about the Kimberly."

"You don't know what was in the letter Anthony brought him?"

"No." He bit the stem of his pipe again.

"Weren't you in the meeting with him and Julien this morning?"

He shook his head. Arcilla noted a strange expression of wariness on his face.

"No. Just as we were entering Julien's office, Doc Jameson called me away."

She paused, thinking. "He's always calling you away, like tonight. Don't you think that's suspicious?"

"I doubt if the high commissioner at the Cape had much to say to Julien in that letter. A small reprimand was in order, I imagine. The lofty hinky-dinks would not want a big haroosh to rile the Ndebele over an expedition into the Matopos. Not that Julien will pay heed. Parnell's correct on one point. Julien is obsessed over the Kimberly. I suspect that's why Anthony came. To argue face to face in hopes of getting him to see reason."

"Darinda would say it's not like Anthony to argue with Uncle Julien over anything. Julien controlled him all his life."

He waved his pipe. "Why are you asking about the commissioner's letter?"

With all the attention on the Capetown letter, why shouldn't she ask? She debated whether to tell him of the scrap of paper she had hidden. She had no one else to turn to except Parnell, and he was nearly as frightened over things as she. She had a choice to tell Peter or wait for Rogan. By the time her brother arrived it could be too late.

"Peter…suppose that letter wasn't from the commissioner. I don't think the letter talked about Matopos and the Black Diamond at all."

His pipe became still. His alert gaze flicked over her face. He bit the stem. "Hmm. Odd you'd say that. What makes you say so?"

"Anthony came about the Transvaal. About Dr. Jameson's plan to invade Johannesburg and aid the Uitlanders and provoke the Boers to declare war. The British government wants war."

Peter gaped at her. He leaned forward.

"How—how did you find out!" He stopped, stood, and stared at her, his face turning slowly into a scowl. "Have you mentioned this to anyone?"

At his low, urgent voice, she turned her head to the side.

"I had to. I sent a wire to Rogan."

"*Rogan!* Great Scot! If you wanted to stir up the cobra's den, then why not just sound the trumpet and send a wire to Kruger himself?"

"Yes, well, Kruger wouldn't have come to Bulawayo, and I wanted Rogan to come. I think Rogan might have gone to London about it."

"Rogan? *Rogan?* But of course *he* would go to Pall Mall! Do you think he wants a war? It would interfere with the Zambezi gold discovery!"

"Peter, you're upset with me! Do *you* want a war?"

"Great Scot!"

"Stop saying that, darling. You're not a bit Scottish… Look, Peter, I simply had to *tell.*"

"You sound like a girl in a dormitory anxious to spread gossip about her competitors. Do I want a war? Naturally not! I'm working to stop—" Peter rubbed his forehead as if to calm himself. "Do you know what you've done in going to Rogan?"

"But of course." She widened her eyes. "That's quite why I did it, darling. He must have gone to London with my information, and jolly London must have sent Anthony to warn the high commissioner at Capetown. Somehow or other a Mr. Trotter found out too, who in turn simply must have written Uncle Julien that the monkey was out of the bag, but to go ahead anyway because 'R' agrees. It's got to be Rhodes, darling. Rhodes and Jameson and Julien."

Peter groaned. He set his pipe down in the ashtray and came to her, grasping her shoulders. His worried face frightened her.

"My dear, you should never have interfered like this. This is none of your concern. Don't you see how it can be used against you?"

"None of my concern? Peter! If Dr. Jameson's troopers invade the Transvaal and there's fighting…?"

"You don't understand—"

"I do understand what war means. I'm not as silly as you and everyone else think I am."

"So I've discovered."

"In my own way I'm as clever as Darinda."

"Quite. I don't think you're silly. You're my wife. And I expect and desire you to show more discernment. I do think, however, that you are wholly gullible at times. You should never have told Rogan without coming to me first."

"You would have stopped me," she said naively.

"Of course!" His tone showed frustration.

"Well, then?" She blinked. "Naturally, I didn't come to you. I wanted Rogan to know."

He looked at her askance, then gave a short laugh. "Darling Arcilla, you cannot know all of what you're suggesting about Rhodes. And whatever was that you said about 'Mr. Trotter and "R" agree'? Wherever would you have heard that? At any rate, say nothing of this to anyone here at Bulawayo. Is that understood?"

"I won't, Peter, but I think more people than Julien and Dr. Jameson know of the plans to aid the Uitlanders at Johannesburg."

"How did you discover that?"

"I overheard a discussion about Doc Jameson's troopers. People do have a tendency to talk rather loudly, you know, when they think it's safe to boast."

His hands dropped from her shoulders. He looked dismayed.

She walked quickly to her vanity drawer and opened it, taking out the charred scrap of paper. She brought it to him and explained how Julien was burning a sheet of paper when she walked into his office, surprising him.

"I was upset and didn't knock. It was right after the hideous business with Anthony. The sheet of paper he was burning in the ashtray was a letter, I think, one of the letters Anthony brought from Capetown."

She watched as his face grew alarmed. "Don't worry, darling," she whispered. She patted his arm and even managed a smile. "Julien didn't guess I knew what he was burning. There is an advantage to being underestimated sometimes. People do things they think are safe around me, or they say things they don't think I'm clever enough to understand."

Peter clapped a palm against his forehead and sank into the chair. "That can be dangerous. Very dangerous…" Peter stared at the scrap of paper. After a moment he looked up at her.

She was surprised by the look of concern in his eyes.

"Does he have any reason to suspect you took this?"

She shook her head. "There was an envelope, too. Clearly marked from George Trotter, Cape Mining Fields, to Chief Native Commissioner Julien Bley. I started to remove it, then thought better of it."

He shook his head again as though overcome. He reached for a match, struck it, and held the scrap to the fire.

"Peter!"

"Hush." He dropped it into the ashtray and stirred it about until it was gray ash.

"But 'R' is Mr. Rhodes—"

"You won't mention any of this to anyone, Arcilla. Is that clear?"

She was sobered by his deadly gravity, the tremor of his voice. "Of course not, Peter, if you say so. I said earlier I would not. But I don't see why you're so worried. He doesn't know I took it."

"My dear, you don't understand. It's not that you took the letter scrap." He stood and came to her. "You are clever, but there's more to this that you wouldn't know. It's the fact that he had the letter at all. Anthony *never* gave Julien that letter."

She looked at him, feeling muddled. "But of course Anthony gave the letter to Uncle Julien. I just explained how Julien burned it. You saw the scrap. I told you about the envelope sitting there to the side…"

He gave her a small shake. "Listen to me. Yes, it's the letter! But remember, Retford and I were at Government House when Anthony and Julien met at Julien's office. And when the meeting broke up, Retford saw Anthony leaving in a hurry, clutching his briefcase, and heard Julien shouting that the letter was his. I doubt Anthony even realized at first what Trotter wrote. Cape Mining Fields is connected with Rhodes, De Beers, and the Charter Company. Anthony must have thought it was a reprimand to Julien about Matopos. He must have thought those in Capetown authority supported London in rebuking Uncle Julien and Dr. Jameson for their plans to enter the Transvaal. But at the meeting with Julien he learned otherwise. That scrap you found dealt with the plan to have Jameson's Troopers ride into Johannesburg to aid the Uitlanders. So Capetown knows about the plan and secretly supports it. Anthony must have snatched up the letter as proof and fled the meeting with it."

She twitched her nose. "Proof?"

"Yes, as a weapon to use against Julien and the others involved if they proceeded with the raid. And if it went badly and London demanded answers, Anthony would then have proof that people at the top were privy to the plan."

"And what would that mean—?"

"Prison, my dear—if the incursion turned into a bloodbath. The British public's outrage would demand it!"

Arcilla lapsed into silence. "Someone entered Anthony's bungalow tonight and searched through everything," she said.

"So now you do understand." His hands tightened on her shoulders until she winced. He drew her to him, embracing her so tightly that she couldn't breathe.

"Say nothing about this—nothing about what you know, or heard, or about finding that scrap of paper, understood?"

She gasped, trying to breathe, and nodded.

"I love you, Arcilla—"

She was confused, yet his unexpected violent emotion in telling her he loved her was also thrilling. It was so unlike Peter.

"Oh, Peter, my love! You really *do* love me and—and our baby."

"You silly. Darling, of course I love you and our son." He held her tightly again. "How could you ever question it?"

She looked at him. No…she wouldn't say it. She wouldn't make her desire to go home to Rookswood the *proof* of his devotion.

He held her. Then he kissed her with such emotion that she lost her breath. She pulled her lips away and giggled. "Why, Peter!"

He grabbed her and kissed her again. "You'll not mention any of this to anyone." He gave her a shake. "It's dangerous. Promise me. Go on, promise me, Arcilla, please."

"Oh, Peter, I promise." She stroked his worried brow. "Don't worry, love. They'll find Anthony's murderer, and then everything will be all right." She offered what she thought was a brave smile. But Peter wasn't smiling. He was looking off in the distance, as though considering something that seemed to upset him dreadfully. Yet, he didn't speak his thoughts. He continued to hold her protectively.

Later that evening, when he thought she was asleep, she saw him get up quietly from bed, check the door, then the baby's cradle close beside the bed. Then he went to his desk.

In the moonlight shining through the window, she watched him open a drawer and remove his pistol. He checked it, then brought it back to bed with him. She lay still, heart thumping. She was sure he put the pistol under his pillow.

Arcilla was afraid again. Peter knew something more. His mind was grappling with something that he hadn't wanted to tell her.

She finally fell asleep, her fingers entwined through Peter's. *Peter actually loves me.* A small smile touched her lips as the moonlight stole across the bed toward the cradle.

CHAPTER TWENTY

The steamship *Endeavor* creaked and groaned. They'd been just a few days out to sea when Evy awoke from a nap feeling as though she had been adrift amid moving mountains and canyons. She couldn't eat much, she couldn't sleep, and last night Rogan had tied her into her bunk to keep her from falling. She was cranky and miserable.

Evy watched as the cabin door opened and Rogan entered, looking offensively cheerful and strong, and carrying a small tray. He encountered her gaze and smiled disconcertingly.

"At your service, madam," he said with a bow. "I've brought my true love some food."

"Go away—I think I'm going to be sick again."

"Optimism, my little rosebud, always optimism." He set the tray down. "Just a wee bit of soup and a dry biscuit."

"No—"

"You'll feel stronger after you've had something to eat."

The small cabin dipped and rose, tilted, sank, and steadied again with an endless sickening rhythm, and the soup in the thick china mug slopped over the rim onto the tray.

"You can count your blessings, sweet, that we've had wonderful weather until now."

"We've had nothing but ups and downs since last night."

Rogan grinned. "Well, I warned you, didn't I?" he said cheerfully.

"Where's Mrs. Croft?" she moaned.

"Sick. In her cabin. Poor creature. I've just left her."

She turned her head and looked into his earthy brown eyes, alive with mischievous good humor. "You're looking after Mrs. Croft, too?"

"Alas! But aside from the old plum's embarrassment at being down, I think I've won her eternal affection."

Rogan sat down beside her. "You'll soon settle down and get sea legs, as they say. Captain says we've good weather ahead too. Here, take a little sip—that's it."

The uneasy motion of the ship seemed to be lessening, or perhaps it was true that the soup had benefited her.

As the days passed, the weather did clear. At times the sea was as smooth and glittering as topaz, and the nights unveiled a shimmering display. On a number of occasions, Evy prepared herself to tell Rogan she was going to have his baby, but each time she broached the subject, something always seemed to interrupt. Mrs. Croft scolded her, wearing a perpetual, worried frown between her gray brows.

"Evy, dear, you've simply got to tell him. There's no cause now to keep it secret. There's no turning back even if you wanted. It's straight to the Cape we're going."

"Yes, yes, I know, and I'm so miserable in not telling him."

"Then why aren't you doing it, dearie? Waiting won't make it any easier now."

They were on deck, for it was a pleasant afternoon with a clear sky and calm sea. Evy sat on a chair on the shady side of the ship sipping tea while Mrs. Croft attended her embroidery.

Evy made up her mind. She looked across the deck to where Rogan was having a conversation with the captain of the ship. She watched him go down to the cabin, probably to get his books and maps.

Evy stood. "I'll tell him now," she said firmly.

"That's the way. Get it out in the open. He'll soon forget all about your itty-bitty secret and be the beaming father-to-be." Mrs. Croft was the one who beamed, looking at Evy with an endearing smile. She turned back to her work, embroidering the baby blanket.

Evy walked through the narrow, dim passageway and entered their cabin.

Rogan turned his head. "Captain wants us to dine with him tonight. Are you up to it?"

"That's very nice of him." She stopped short and looked at him with a moment of alarm. "What are you doing?"

He pulled a trunk out from under the bunk and was opening it.

"Odd...I can't seem to find the trekking book written by Mornay's father, Bertrand. I thought I'd packed it—"

She hurried to stop him, her hand on the lid as he began to lift the trunk lid.

"It's not in here, Rogan."

He looked at her, a curious gleam in his eyes.

"All right."

She offered a quick smile and drew her hand away, smoothing her hair. Under his gaze she felt her cheeks warming. She turned away, casually, she hoped, and began glancing about the small cabin. "Let's see...where might you have mislaid the Mornay book..."

"I'm wondering now if I might have been in too much a rush to include it in the box of books. By the way, what do you have in here, gold or the Black Diamond?"

The casual talk of his books, followed by the smooth reference back to the trunk and her reaction when he'd started to open it, brought a qualm. She was irritated with herself for reacting so defensively. Even if he saw the baby things, she could say they were gifts for Arcilla's and Alice's new babies.

She turned to look at him, trying to appear amused.

"The Black Diamond? Yes, darling, it was me all along who stole it and concealed it."

His mouth turned into a brief smile. He looked down at the trunk, his hand toying with the lid, yet not lifting it. He looked at her again. "Now, what could be in here, my sweet? I'm almost afraid to look...

Instead of the diamond, maybe it's the head of Great-great-aunt Hortense."

"Very funny. I don't know why you're making so much of the trunk."

"Because you nearly had a fit when you saw me about to open it. It cannot be feminine—what's the word?—*modesty*, over bits of lace and such?"

"Don't be silly." She was getting upset. She walked over to the trunk again and dusted an imaginary speck of dust from the lid. "You're making much out of nothing, Rogan. Would you mind either *opening* it, or putting it back under the bunk please? It's already too crowded in here without it sitting here staring at us."

He smiled lazily. "I'll open it. You have me extremely curious."

She shrugged and folded her arms. "Go right ahead."

"Thanks, I will. It's always pleasant that two people married, sleeping in the same bed, have no undue secrets between them, don't you think?"

She fluttered her lashes. "I'm pleased you see it that way."

He opened the trunk lid. She held her breath. He stared without saying a word.

She bit her lip, feeling the heat growing in her face. Now what?

Slowly he removed baby's booties, gowns, blankets, diapers, baby powder, baby lotion, baby bibs—

He held up the baby bib with an embroidered bear. He looked at her.

As she looked back, she saw his eyes darken with something that was uncommonly like anger.

"What is all this, Evy?"

Her throat went dry. She had imagined that keeping the secret from him until they were far at sea would upset him, but what she immediately felt frightened her with its reality. Gone was the warmth of passion and teasing amusement that he so often displayed when showering her with attention. She now saw something she had never seen before, and it caused her heart to constrict.

"I asked you an honest question, Evy, and I expect an answer. Or is that too much to hope for?"

She gasped. "What do you mean by that?"

He pulled out blankets and diapers and held them toward her. "Wasn't this the trunk you begged to take, even though we already had one too many?"

"Well, yes, but I don't see why that should suddenly make you angry."

"Don't you?"

"No," she fibbed, and grabbing the things from his hands, she tossed them back into the trunk.

"Why did you find it necessary to bring a trunk full of baby things?"

"Isn't it obvious?"

"If it was I wouldn't be asking."

"You're being insulting—"

"All I want is the answer. I think I deserve the truth, though you, evidently, think not."

"Rogan," she gasped. "Don't say that." Her eyes pleaded with his. She suddenly felt sick and swayed slightly. He caught her, and she held to him, shutting her eyes, feeling miserable. He sat her down in the chair and stood looking down at her. His face was grave and his eyes cool and unsympathetic.

She pushed her hair from her neck and swallowed.

Very calmly he poured a small glass of water and handed it to her, still watching her evenly as she drank. He studied her like a physician might a stranger.

"I'm waiting," he said.

"They're gifts," she murmured, looking down at the glass.

"Gifts?" His voice was expressionless.

"Yes, for Arcilla and Peter—for Baby Charles, or have you forgotten you're an uncle now?"

"What I want to know is if I'm going to be a father."

She finished the water in the glass so she wouldn't need to answer at once.

"And some of the things are for Alice and Derwent. This is their third, I think—or is it their fourth?"

"Are you pregnant, Evy?"

The blunt but quiet question was such that she could not avoid it. Her eyes faltered, and she set the glass down.

"Yes."

Her voice was so quiet that if he hadn't responded by a small intake of breath, she might have thought he hadn't heard.

The moments ticked by excruciatingly slowly.

The awful silence seemed to her to be laying brick after brick, raising a wall between them. Somehow she had to get through to him, to stop the wall from coming together, but how? It all seemed too late. As she realized this, she could see more clearly how foolish she had been. In wanting to have her way, no matter what the cost, she had put their relationship last.

She began to talk. He held up a hand to stop her rush of words. "How long have you known?

What would she say? In a moment she saw the obvious string of deceit and knew he would as well. Was it to be the truth now, or did she continue with another lie?

"When you went to see Dr. Tisdale?" he asked.

She let out a breath and lowered herself on the berth. She nodded. "Yes. But, Rogan, I—"

"So that's why you acted so strangely on the ride in Grimston Woods. Now I see."

"I was going to tell you then, honestly I was, but—"

"But you decided to withhold it from me because you had other plans? You wanted to come to South Africa, and you didn't trust me to handle the truth."

"That isn't true. I did trust you, but—"

"But. You didn't tell me."

"I knew you'd insist I stay at Rookswood. I had to come! I had counted on this trip for so long I couldn't risk losing it."

"So you risked our relationship because you couldn't trust me to at least try to do what was right for you, for *us?* I see. You trusted your own decisions and put our baby at risk."

She sucked in her breath and stared at him. "Put the baby at risk? That's uncalled for, Rogan! That's completely unfair—"

"Well, what do you call it? Your plans and wishes mean more than mine or the child's safety. You may not understand this even yet, but we're going into danger. I set aside my better wisdom to let you come now because I knew how much it meant to you, but at no time did I ever fool myself into thinking there wouldn't be risk, a cost with this decision. We're headed into war, Evy. And you've decided nothing, not even our trust of each other, or the baby's safety, means as much to you as meeting Jakob van Buren and learning a lot of musty history about your mother! I'll tell you this." And his eyes snapped with anger. "You've emerged more like the willful Katie than you have Mrs. Grace Havering or Vicar Edmund. Your careless indifference proves your relationship is not so vital after all with the God whom you've always said meant more to you than anything else."

Evy slapped him. Then her hand flew to her mouth. She stared at him. But soon the tears dimmed her vision, and she could no longer see him. The last glimpse she had was a cool anger mingled with rejection.

"Can't handle reality, Evy?"

She turned away, trying to hold back the emotional devastation.

"Well, you've gotten your way, Evy. You've made certain of that— we can't turn back to England. Now you'll have to bear the burden you've created. When we reach Bulawayo, Dr. Jakob will be all yours— for just as long as you want."

She whirled. "What do you mean by that?"

"Just what I said. You've gambled everything we had going for us to sit at his table. You preferred Jakob to me. Now you can have him, his mission station, and anything else there you want."

"Rogan, you're not deserting me?"

"Don't sound so melodramatic, my dear Mrs. Chantry. I'm merely going to live up to your expectations. I'm an adventurer, remember? I can't be trusted with some of the most important information affecting our lives. So I'll be proceeding with my expedition to find Henry's gold—for as long as it takes me!"

She searched his face, seeing a hardness and stubbornness she had never come up against before. This was the Rogan Chantry others came up against, but he had never treated her this way.

"You blame me for everything," she said bitterly. "Well, what of you? You're allowing your hurt pride and anger to make you stubborn and…and…and yes, immature! You're running away!"

His eyes narrowed. "Hurt pride? Maybe. But maybe just a realization that when a relationship isn't based on mutual trust, there isn't much to work with. You didn't trust me. That, Evy, has damaged our relationship more than anything you may say now. Immaturity on my part? All right, have it your way. If I had known you thought all this about me when I dropped everything at Fort Salisbury and came rushing back to Rookswood, I wouldn't have wasted my time."

She swallowed the pain cramping her throat. Everything was falling apart around her. She had never dreamed he would react this way. She had thought he would be irritated she hadn't told him, but not take it so devastatingly hard.

"So," she said with trembling lips, "you're—leaving me—and my baby."

"*Our* baby, Evy. You've seemed to ignore that. The child you carry is as much *mine* as yours. I'll be around. But according to your own plans, you'll have everything you need with Dr. Jakob at the mission station. It won't make much difference if I'm away."

"I never said that, Rogan—"

"You said that louder than words when you decided it was really none of my affair that you were pregnant. When you set out to deceive me, so you could have your way. I don't think you're in love with me at all, if you want my opinion."

"What!"

"You heard me. A woman who loved her husband would have run with joy to tell him she was expecting his baby."

"But—you intimated you didn't want a baby now. You shrugged it off and made light comments. You—"

"Then you don't really know me, do you? What I said about someone else's child is not the same as I think about *ours*."

"You're being unfair, cruel. You've been hurt, and you want to hurt back. I—"

"Well, you won't need to suffer from my cruelty and indifference any longer."

"Where are you going?" she cried as he went to the cabin door.

"To leave you in peace," he said flatly.

She went after him, taking hold of his arm. "Rogan, can't we work through this?"

He looked at her for a long moment. "No, not now. I'm not ready to forgive you yet."

"Rogan!"

"I'm being honest. Painfully honest. You've angered and hurt me more than your glib ability to understand. The fact that you simply want to kiss and make up right now tells me you don't really understand the damage to our trust, our oneness. And right now, I just don't have it in me to get over it. Someday, maybe, but not now."

Flabbergasted, she simply stared. She could not be hearing this. He opened the door and went out.

Evy stood there, devastated. She covered her face with her palms and burst into tears. She sank to the bunk, burying her face in the pillow, and wept. "This can't be happening. He'll change his mind. Before we reach Capetown he'll change his mind. I'll make him understand. He'll forgive me and realize that—"

Realize what?

The indifference from Rogan continued through dinner and breakfast the next morning. Not that Rogan treated her badly. Oh, far from it. He was courteous enough, too courteous, especially when she wasn't feeling well, but he remained distant, his emotions far from her reach. Their conversations continued much as normal, except he appeared detached, apparently less interested in the little things that he had once paid attention to. He was no longer warm and playful with her as he had been, but grave, and she missed the Rogan she thought she knew and had fallen in love with. She was depressed, angry with herself for what she'd done. If she'd only had the good sense that came so naturally to Aunt Grace and Mrs. Osgood. Mrs. Osgood's words came back to haunt her. "You must tell him as soon as possible," she had said. Even Mrs. Croft had seen it.

Sometimes she thought that if she tried a little harder she might possibly break through his barrier, but even when he held her in his arms, his emotions were kept behind armor, or so it seemed. Evy also withdrew and pretended her own cool indifference, building a structure of defense against the pain his behavior brought to her. It all seemed a vicious cycle that led nowhere, except to frustration and emotional exhaustion.

He's stubborn. She narrowed her eyes. *He's trying to punish me. I never realized just how stubborn Rogan Chantry can be! I'll show him I don't need him at all.*

Unaware that an order had been issued from the captain for passengers to stay below, she left the cabin and made her way up the companionway steps onto the deck, greeted by refreshing wind and an expanse of gray sea.

She breathed in deeply and watched the sun setting behind a reddish-gray horizon. She noticed the clouds, but the sea was still calm. She watched the sunset and prayed for Rogan and herself, but after a while, she became aware of increased rolling and pitching as the wind seemed to be strengthening. As the ocean swells seemed to be rising rather swiftly, she turned back toward the companionway steps but found herself grasping hold of the ship's rails as the deck beneath her feet rolled steeply. She feared she wouldn't reach the companionway in time when she saw the first waves starting to reach the height of the deck. She was grasping a post when she spotted Rogan rushing up from the steps onto the deck. A look of relief swept over his face when he saw her, before settling into frustration. The wind whipped his peacoat, and he scowled beneath his hat, somehow keeping his balance as he strode toward her. He latched hold of both her and the post, and they swayed together with the rolling of the deck as she felt the wind and cold sea flowing over her ankles and rising, then sucking her backward as it withdrew. Panic began gripping her as she clung to Rogan.

"Are you mad?" he cried in the wind. "Why did you come up here against the captain's orders?"

"I…I didn't know—"

"You could have been washed overboard!"

She mistook his fervency for anger and felt even more miserable. With waves of self-pity washing over her heart, she cried back, "That should please you!"

"Don't be absurd!" He clasped hold of her and waited a moment. "Now," he shouted, then they fled toward the companionway door before another swell flooded the deck. She went down the steps, and he quickly closed the bolt as some water splashed in and dribbled down.

Mrs. Croft was waiting at the bottom of the steps, wringing her hands. "Thank God you're safe!"

Soon Evy was safely back in the cabin with Rogan, and Mrs. Croft had returned to the cabin she shared with two other ladies who were traveling companions. Evy and Rogan were both wind-tossed and wet. He held her tightly, almost fiercely.

"I might have lost you," he gritted.

She winced from the strength with which he held her. Was he angry? He looked at her, narrowing his eyes, sea water dripping from his hair. She was confused. Was it anger, or was he actually frightened that he might have lost her?

As she looked up at him, trying to see beneath his armor, he released her and whipped off his hat and coat, turning away from her scrutinizing gaze. He grabbed a towel and dried his face.

"I'm sorry," she said. "I didn't hear about the order to stay below."

"It's my fault. I should have made certain you knew."

The tense silence grew between them. Her heart thudded. She longed to throw her arms around him and vow her undying love, begging him to forgive her for hurting him over the secrecy of their baby. She tried to speak but bit her lip, finding such words stuck in her throat.

"The captain had heart failure sometime this afternoon," Rogan said woodenly. "We found him on the floor in his cabin."

"Oh no, how dreadful for him!"

"For all of us. I doubt he'll pull through."

"Then who will take over?"

"The first mate. And there's been another change. We're headed for a stop at the nearest port. I hope it's short. This brings a delay we could certainly do without." He tossed the towel on the stand and looked at her. His gaze took her in with one sweeping glance, her windblown hair and her wet frock. His expression changed to one that she could not easily read. He walked over to her.

"Feeling all right?"

She looked at him quickly, hopefully, searching his face for what she needed to find, but it was smooth and blank. The emotion that had enveloped him only minutes ago had ebbed.

"I'll be fine."

His hand dropped from her arm, and he turned away, reaching for a dry tunic. "Better get out of those wet clothes while I'm gone," he said flatly. "I'll see what I can dig up to eat from Cook—if I can bring back the treasure without spilling it all. That sea is getting rougher by the minute."

Evy looked after him, her hopes wilting. The ship's timbers creaked and groaned like an arthritic giant. She wouldn't give up. Rogan must still care! Had not the fear she'd seen in his eyes told her so, or had she imagined what she desired to see?

The storm eased during the night, but Mrs. Croft still remained upset when she came to Evy the next morning.

She entered with a sigh, reaching down to massage her knees. "One must learn to stiffen the wobblers. I came near being washed overboard myself yester eve before I found Master Rogan."

"Then you sent him on deck to find me?" She kept the disappointment from her voice, but Mrs. Croft knew her too well to be deceived, for Evy could see the look of sympathy in her sharp, beady eyes.

"Tush, it was me, dearie. When I didn't find you in the cabin, I knew you must've gone on deck as usual and not heard the warning to stay below."

"Well, I'm truly sorry you got knocked around searching for Rogan."

"Nary a thing to worry about. Seems we're to dock this afternoon at some heathen port called Tangier. There's talk of a new English captain, or even a change of ships, for some who want to get speedily on with the voyage." Her tufted brows lowered in irritation as she peered down at Evy over a pointed nose. "Tangier, my foot. A nest of vipers. Thieves on the prowl, I should say. A mistake getting off in a heathen place like that. I thought Africa was dangerous enough." She looked at Evy with shifty eyes. "You won't be having any outrageous idea about going ashore now, will you, dearie?"

Tangier...Casablanca... Evy felt a ripple of excitement dance along her spine. She looked off dreamily. "How thrilling to visit a bazaar."

"Now, *now*—"

"Aha, Mrs. Croft, no use to prickle and frown like that. Tangier is perfectly safe, I assure you."

"Safe, my foot. No place's safe outside Grimston Way, I'll be bound."

"Naturally I want to go ashore." Evy heaved a sigh and looked around the small cabin. She threw up her hands. "I'm sick of these four walls closing in on me tighter and tighter. I want to see a few things while I've the chance to get my feet on solid ground again."

Mrs. Croft's voice changed to a whiny protest. "But, dearie, with your being in the delicate way as you are, don't you think it's prudent to stay here in a nice deck chair?"

"No," Evy smiled sweetly. "I don't. I'm going ashore to shop. There's bound to be wonderfully exciting things at a bazaar. Spices, perfumes, silks—"

"Beggars and thieves, I daresay."

"We'll have Rogan to escort us."

Mrs. Croft tilted her gray head with a birdlike look. "Master Rogan's not likely to want you roaming bazaars. Not when he was so upset with you wandering the deck with the wind and waves rising."

"That was different." She refused to feel mollified. She told herself he was merely worried about the baby—not her.

"My mind's made up. I'm going ashore. It's a perfectly logical thing to do. I'm not worried about thieves."

When the ship had docked, she waited for Rogan to come for her. Her excitement grew at the prospect of seeing Tangier. Rogan didn't come but sent Mrs. Croft. On first glimpse of the victory reflecting in the woman's gray eyes, Evy folded her arms and tapped her foot, waiting for what Mrs. Croft would announce. Two spots of color tinted Mrs. Croft's face.

"The master says he thinks it best you stay aboard until he returns."

"Where is he?" Evy asked stiffly.

"Gone ashore to see about getting us passage on a different ship for the Cape. Said we can't afford to waste time on this delay. I must say I agree. I'm sure we're missing nothing on shore."

So he had gone off and left her, knowing full well that she had wanted to visit a bazaar!

"Better get your hat and a cloak, Mrs. Croft. I'm all dressed to go ashore—and I'm going."

"But, Miss Evy, dearie—"

"Don't *dearie* me. Are you coming with me or not?"

Mrs. Croft frowned. "Speaking about mules—"

"Which we were not," Evy stated airily, catching up her hat, hand-bag, and short-waisted coat.

"But you and the master can both be just as stubborn."

Evy smiled, unperturbed. She looped her arm through Mrs. Croft's. "Come along, my dear Mrs. Croft. There's no time to squander."

The topaz waters of Tangier glimmered in the white sunlight. A wither-ing gust whipped at Evy's hair and blew the hem of her skirtline. The bazaar near the harbor was teeming with Arabs, Frenchmen, and Span-iards. Groups of mercenary soldiers, legionnaires, jostled one another while camels grumbled beneath their heavy loads. Thin donkeys flick-ered their pointed ears to chase away the flies. Arab women wore long, hooded robes of dark cloth called *haiks*, balancing water jugs or fruit upon their heads, or holding them on their hips. A section of cloth called an *itham* covered their faces. Evy and Mrs. Croft were enveloped in the throng of hawkers and traders.

Evy found herself pursued by Arab vendors robed in dusty *djella-bahs*, their brown faces as baked and cracked as dried mud in the sun. They gathered around her like a flock with their wares. Competing voices shouted in a hodgepodge of Arabic, French, and Spanish. They pushed and shoved, waving baskets and trays of green sweet figs, ripe oranges, lush dates, and bright melons. Everywhere there were big, lazy flies that clung to cut fruit, the smell of Arab tobacco, along with *cham-poraux*, an Algerian drink of strong syrupy coffee, thick with sugar and throat-scalding brandy. Drugs were sold boldly—cannabis, mixed with tobacco, and hashish. The various ship passengers were in a consuming mood, and English pounds, French francs, and Spanish pesetas were passed back and forth as fast and loose as chips on a gambling table.

There were still more passengers jamming the cabanas in the *souk*, the market, vainly hoping to find a lavatory. In the crowd and confusion, Evy became separated from Mrs. Croft. She stopped and turned back, but Mrs. Croft was nowhere to be seen.

Oh no! Where could she have gone? She couldn't have gotten that far behind.

Then Evy remembered Mrs. Croft's arthritic limp, and she berated herself for such thoughtlessness. She had rushed on her way without so much as a glance behind to see if her dear friend was keeping up. Mrs. Croft had once called out to her, but Evy thought she was pausing to look at blue beads at one of the stands. But Mrs. Croft knew Evy was going to the silk stall, and she would surely go there to meet. Evy gave one more searching look around before turning once again toward the cabana at the far end of the souk. Surely Mrs. Croft would show up if Evy just waited there.

It was terribly hot and dry, despite the nearby blue water of Tangier Bay. The sunlight was glittering and hurting her eyes. Her throat grew dry with thirst, and she looked about for water to buy. She proceeded forward, determined to find the bolt of silk she wanted.

Evy made her way through the sluggish throng toward the other end of the souk to one side of the harbor. She paused when she saw some Arab men watching her. Had she not seen these same men before? When she had disembarked from the ship? Were they following her?

A French legionnaire standing just ahead was questioning some uncooperative Arab traders with camels. The men were seated in the dusty shade of a tamarind tree. The presence of the French mercenary soldiers made her feel a little safer. She walked on in search of Mrs. Croft and the silk cloth.

She came near the whitewashed walls at the edge of the souk. Here some Berber women sat on the hard, swept ground, wearing striped blankets and straw hats adorned with black pompons—a remnant of old Spain that had once ruled the Sahara before France. The women were guarding their piles of eggs and dried *medejul* dates. Evy paused, dug into her handbag for some English coins, and handed them to one of the

Berber women in exchange for the dates, but she was too thirsty to eat them now. She wondered if Rogan would enjoy them aboard ship.

She walked forward, glancing in all directions for a sign of Mrs. Croft. She couldn't have gone far. She hoped she would suddenly appear. What would she tell Rogan if she lost poor Mrs. Croft amid the bazaar?

She stood in the dusty square, her concerns becoming as heavy as the bag slung over her shoulder. She tried to assure herself there was little reason for alarm. So they had somehow separated from each other; that was no cause for panic. Even now Mrs. Croft might already be at the cabana, among hats and bolts of cloth, waiting for her. Yes, that surely must be. After all, Mrs. Croft knew she wanted to buy silk, so she would move toward that spot. Evy quickened her steps.

An Arab walked by hawking his drinking pitcher and his tin cup. Water! If she didn't get some soon, she'd begin seeing mirages! Mrs. Croft—and water—that was it! Mrs. Croft had gone for water…

She called for the Arab to stop. "How many English shillings?"

The stoic-faced trader held up five fingers. He suddenly grinned at her, showing a missing tooth.

"Five shillings!" She didn't have that much loose change. "That's robbery," she murmured, sure he couldn't understand her English.

"For you, two shillings."

"One shilling and these dates." She pushed both toward him.

"Allah will reward you."

"Um—I'd prefer not. Just the water, please."

As he poured she looked about uneasily. "Tell me, have you seen an English lady with gray hair, tall, rather large, wearing a flowered hat and carrying a straw bag—oversized?"

He poured the trickling water into the tin cup. *I don't care if a camel drank from it, I'm thirsty,* she thought.

She took a chance in drinking from the cup, but she felt feverishly hot. Her lips were dry and cracked and her throat such that she could hardly talk.

"Veery beeeg lady, mademoiselle? Like thees?" He held his palm up a foot above his own head, grinning amiably.

"Well…yes, I suppose, that is rather overdoing it, but…and wearing a blue frock with large puffed sleeves?"

"Ahh!" He nodded vigorously, watching her with the same hungry smile, his shiny black eyes fully expectant. He pointed behind him. "I see madam go that way—behind the *hanootz*." He pointed to one of the now empty bazaar stalls. "I bring you there, yes?"

"Evy! *Don't* drink that!"

She whirled, stunned by Rogan's shout. He was pushing his way toward her through the throng, his dark hair damp beneath his hat as he rushed up.

"It's drugged, no doubt," and he grabbed it from her and whiffed it, tasting it. He spat it out, threw down the cup with a clatter, and grabbed the Arab by the front of his djellabah.

The man pleaded for mercy as Rogan shoved him angrily to the dust. "I ought to break your neck."

The Arab groveled in the dust, covering his head with both arms and rolling up into a knot. Evy grabbed Rogan's arm. "Mrs. Croft. She's disappeared. He was going to lead me to her."

Rogan's eyes flashed. "That's an old trick. He hasn't seen Mrs. Croft. She's waiting for us back near the front of the souk. This ruddy camel trader was going to drug you and sell you to an Arab trader. You'd have likely wound up in some Arab sheik's tent somewhere. Slavery is rampant around here."

"Slavery—" She gasped and stared at him, a cold chill running through her blood. *A harem.*

Rogan steadied her, drawing her into the safety of his strong arms. "Darling, didn't I ask you to stay aboard ship and wait for me?"

"You didn't tell me anything," she protested. "You told Mrs. Croft."

His dark eyes flickered. His jaw tensed. "All right, I was a little arrogant in not explaining to you myself, but I was in a ruddy hurry. An English ship is leaving for the Cape in the morning, and it was important we had space on it. Look, Evy," he said more gently, "I apologize. I didn't take you seriously about wanting to see the souk."

She clenched her jaw to keep from crying. She had almost been taken into slavery to be sold into some Arab's harem! *Oh, Lord Jesus, thank You for looking after me in my ignorance. Thank You for sending Rogan in time. I should have listened to him and not willfully pushed ahead with my own wishes.* A tear welled up in her eyes and suddenly, despite the throng, she found herself in Rogan's embrace. He was holding her so she could hardly breathe.

"Evy, darling, if anything had happened to you—"

Mrs. Croft came rushing up, sweating and breathing hard, her face flushed red with heat and anxiety.

"Oh, thank God he found you, Evy, dear lamb. I was so afraid. I turned around, and you were gone. I didn't know where you'd disappeared to. I went straightaway back to the harbor and saw Master Rogan coming this way. He was like a mirage. I was so happy to see him."

Rogan watched the Arab, who was crawling away under one of the stalls. "Come, let's get out of here. I don't like the looks of him. He's likely got a ring of thugs waiting on the other side of the souk."

He took Evy's arm and Mrs. Croft's and led them toward the harbor. He looked down at Evy. "Shall I carry you?"

"No." She smiled nervously. "I'm all right now. But I don't think I'll ever get over shuddering when I remember what could have happened to me."

Some of the same gravity and irritation sparked in his eyes. "Now do you see why it would have been wiser to stay at Rookswood and good old Grimston Way?"

Evy looked away. She knew he still had not fully forgiven her deception of withholding from him the conception of their baby.

Chapter Twenty-One

The HMS *Horatio Nelson* docked at Capetown weeks later. "You'll want to stay at Cape House for a few days with Camilla," Rogan told Evy after they arrived at the Cape. "She'll be able to share facts about Katie. You can even tour her room and have a look at the now infamous stables where Henry was knocked unconscious by Heyden when the Black Diamond was stolen."

They left the ship, and he hailed a coach to bring her and Mrs. Croft to the house.

"You sound as though you won't be staying at the house."

"I have business to take care of before the trek. I should be back in a week or so."

She reached a hand toward him. "Rogan, I—"

"I'm sure Camilla will have a doctor you can see while here."

She slowly withdrew her hand, which he had not taken, and turned her head away from his laconic gaze. A glance toward Mrs. Croft in the back showed her unhappy face. The trouble between Evy and Rogan was impossible to hide.

Cape House was as she had expected: a white two-story mansion with a red roof and encircling verandas. There looked to be several acres of land with stables. She had always thought that coming here would in some way touch her heart. As she stood looking at Cape House, knowing Katie had grown up here under Julien's rule, Evy surprisingly felt very little. Nor did the long anticipated meeting with her father and stepmother bring her joy. Mrs. Croft had been ushered off by the house-keeper. Rogan, who had been about to leave after bringing Evy to meet her stepmother, stopped short in the hall and turned sharply when Camilla announced in brutal honesty, "There is no good news with which to greet you, Evy. Your father, Anthony, is dead. He's been murdered at Bulawayo. No one there knows who did it, or why."

Evy felt the emotional blow. Anthony, dead? *Murdered?*

She must have turned ashen, for Rogan came quickly beside her, holding her, and leading her to a chair.

"I shouldn't have shocked you like this," Camilla said remorsefully. "I'm beside myself. I fear I'm not thinking well."

"Evy is expecting a baby," Rogan told her. "After this long voyage, I think we should call for a doctor."

"I'm all right," Evy interjected.

"Do you have a doctor you respect?" Rogan asked Lady Camilla.

"I'll call Dr. Morris at once." Camilla hurried off, and Rogan looked down at Evy with concern.

"Darling, are you all right? Can I get you anything? Tea, maybe?"

Darling. He hadn't called her that in weeks.

"I'll be all right," she said. "Oh, Rogan, *murdered.* How could this have happened? Do you suppose there's some mistake?"

"Stay calm. We'll find out. I should be able to wire Peter." He turned as Camilla came back.

"He's on his way. I've asked Tandy to bring tea."

"How did it happen, Camilla?" Rogan asked. "Are you sure it was murder? Not an accident on the trek to Bulawayo?"

"No, Rogan, murder. It was horrible, horrible…"

"How do you know this?" Evy cried.

Camilla gestured to the desk beside the window. "All the papers and letters are there, Rogan. I've gathered everything together for you. At first Julien wired from Bulawayo that Anthony had met with an accident, but later new information came to me from Captain Ryan Retford.

Darinda, too, wrote me. You can read all the details yourself. I don't understand how this could happen, but it has."

Camilla turned to look at Evy and held out a hand to her, her eyes full of pity. "And you, poor child. No sooner did you learn who your father was and reconciled with him, than you lost him."

Evy in turn tried to comfort Camilla, but her own heart was like a tomb. "I still have a stepmother," she said, "and…I'm going to have a baby."

"If only we had happier news about Anthony. He would have been thrilled to have a grandchild—"

"Oh, Camilla—"

Rogan did not leave Cape House that day as he had planned; the departure for Bulawayo was delayed. With Evy receiving a clear bill of health for traveling from Camilla's doctor, Rogan arranged to leave the next day. There was a train to Kimberly, he told her, and something new had been added since he'd left. There was now a stagecoach line that made a run between Kimberly and Bulawayo.

"You'd better turn in early, Evy," Rogan told her. "You won't be able to do much sleeping on the train. It's a dusty journey and none too comfortable. I'll do what I can to get you both an extra seat so you can lie down."

"I'll be all right," she said briefly.

He glanced her over, then, nodding good night to Camilla, he turned and left the house. Where he went, Evy had no idea. She saw Camilla look a bit surprised, but she didn't ask questions. Evy noted, however, that she treated her sympathetically.

As Camilla led her upstairs to the bedrooms, Evy told her the truth. "I've blundered terribly. You see, I wanted so much to come that I feared to tell Rogan I was going to have a baby until we were out at sea, too late for him to ask me to stay at Rookswood."

"Oh, dear…I see. So that's why Rogan seems a bit distant toward you. I noticed it at once. It surprised me because I knew how much you meant to him before he left for England. It was cruel and beastly for Julien to have lied to him, telling him you were Henry's child." She shook her head. "Julien is a hard and cruel man. I'd put nothing past him, mind you. Absolutely *nothing*."

Evy looked at her, feeling a shudder run through her. Rogan had said that once as well. She believed he and Camilla were right. But *surely* Camilla didn't think Julien had killed Anthony? Julien had made Anthony his chief heir in the diamond business. All that had changed now. Who was next in line? Darinda?

"Why would anyone wish my father dead?"

Camilla looked drawn and thoughtful. "I've lain awake nights wondering. Money is the first motive that comes to mind, but Anthony has left most of the wealth to you. No—don't look embarrassed. I knew all along; we had talked it over. You see, I have enough income from my side of the family." She looked at Evy. "You were very gracious to accept Anthony as your father even after his weakness and failure to tell you all those years."

Evy looked at her rather surprised. Camilla seemed stronger than she remembered. Perhaps it was Anthony's death that roused her.

"So his inheritance has not benefited any who could have murdered him. The other motive that's come to mind is politics," Camilla said thoughtfully.

They had reached the landing. It was a magnificent house with Viennese crystal and lots of polished wood.

"You mean the Matopos Hills and the Kimberly Black Diamond?"

"So you know about that? I suppose Rogan told you. Well, it's not much of a secret now, is it? The fear of an uprising among the natives, if Julien proceeds with his expedition to find Lobengula's grave, was much on Anthony's heart when he left," Camilla admitted thoughtfully. "However, I think there was another reason that burdened him. You see, Anthony had no intention of going to Bulawayo. He wanted to be here when you and Rogan arrived. He had talked so much about you when he came home from London. He was so sure you and I would become friends."

Evy slipped an arm around her stepmother's waist as they walked down the spacious hall toward the bedrooms.

"But something important came up in the last hour before leaving," Camilla told her. "He didn't explain the details, just told me he must go and reason with Julien and Dr. Jameson. One thing Anthony did accomplish before he left was to pay an unexpected visit to Sir Cecil Rhodes. What they discussed, Anthony didn't say, but he was worried when he left, even angry."

Evy looked at her. They had stopped outside a bedroom door.

"Angry?" Evy asked, wrinkling her brow.

Camilla mused a moment. "Yes, I would say he was angry about something." She sighed. "I wish now I had asked him more questions. I wish I had…" She stopped. "Wishes are too late now. There comes a time in life when it's too late."

She wondered what it was that Camilla wished she had done differently with Anthony?

Evy considered herself and Rogan. It couldn't be too late for them. There had to be a way to work through this situation, to gain Rogan's trust again, to make him see how much she loved him. But what? What could she do, when Rogan was still determined to reject her overtures?

"This is Katie's old room," Camilla said softly. "I knew you'd want to see it, to be alone here for a time." She looked at Evy with sympathy. "Don't think that you must stay here tonight, though. If it bothers you, we've another room."

Evy walked into the pretty room with its lace and satin. She walked over to the grand bed and ran her palm across the satin comforter, touched the furniture, and walked to the window. Her mind tried to take in the past with Katie and Anthony and, yes, Henry Chantry, too. Katie had left this very room that night to meet Henry at the stables, to flee to the mission station at Rorke's Drift to find her daughter. It all had ended so tragically. While Evy remembered the history, her heart ached. She looked about her, trying to find Katie, but could not. It was merely a lovely room with ghostly memories. Time had moved on.

What truly matters now is the present. She placed her palm against her womb. *Have I neglected you, my own child? And Rogan—oh, Rogan, my love! Will you ever decide to forgive me? Will this barrier stand between us for the rest of our time together?*

Dear Lord Jesus, she prayed. *Lord forgive me, and help me to trust in You. But now it seems too late for me, heavenly Father. I've set my own course without trusting You or my husband. I desperately need Your guidance, for us—the three of us. And now, for better or for worse, as though my little ship were at sea in the midst of a storm. And will I be pushed onto the rocks, or, by Your grace alone, reach a fair haven? All I can do now is fall upon You, asking that You forgive the path I've willfully taken, and trust that somehow You will be honored. Father, be with me, be with us, all three of us.*

PART THREE

How the gold has become dim!
How changed the fine gold!

LAMENTATIONS 4:1

Chapter Twenty-Two

Bulawayo

Rogan did not recognize Bulawayo from when he'd visited just a few short years ago to accompany Rhodes's delegation to meet Lobengula. Back then this section of land consisted of Lobengula's kraal of beehive-shaped huts and acacia trees. There'd been a *setenghi,* an airy, open-sided hut of white mopane poles and a thatch roof. Lobengula also had a wagon with his throne made of empty canned milk crates. Yet he'd owned bags of diamonds and pieces of gold. Rogan could still envision the giant chieftain standing there with shrewd eyes and a knowing, mocking smile. "You white men have fat smeared on your lips," he'd accused. To this day Rogan thought it a fitting description of a smooth talker! He recalled having to crawl on hands and knees through inches of hot dust to meet with the feared Ndebele chieftain, while flies plastered upon his sweating flesh, biting and stinging him.

Here, Lobengula had held his diabolical ceremonies of "smelling out" his enemies for witchcraft, and executing those he found guilty by hideous means.

"I didn't go on the war hunt," Derwent Brown was telling Rogan. "But I heard about it. Dr. Jameson led the column to strike against Lobengula because the Ndebele were attacking some Shona around Fort Victoria and raiding their cattle. Lobengula's warriors raided some of the pioneers' farms, too, maybe by mistake, but everyone was up in arms.

Dr. Jameson and Sir Julien said we'd never be able to live in peace with them. Now was the time to fight Lobengula once for all. Mr. Parnell went riding through as one of Sir Julien's field officers and had been with Sir Julien to enter the burning kraal after Lobengula fled."

"Yes, the Black Diamond," Rogan stated unpleasantly. "I'd say it was the main reason for Julien's going along. He found out Lobengula had it."

"Aye, not a nice picture, was it, Mr. Rogan? All that bloodshed for gold and diamonds and land."

"We'll make this land into something far better," Rogan commented briskly. "We'll build schools and hospitals. Soon the Ndebele and the Shona, along with new Rhodesians, will have some kind of understanding of peace, so we can all dwell together reasonably."

Derwent shook his head and sighed. "I don't know, Mr. Rogan. You really think that? Dr. Jakob says there's little but suspicion, misunderstanding, and hatred right now."

Rogan's mouth turned as he caught Derwent's sober eye. "Well, if it's up to Rhodes and Jameson and men like them to represent peace and integrity, then everyone is in for more of the same, especially the tribes. Rhodes, Jameson, the others—they're just men who have their own selfish interests at heart."

"Aye, you're right there, for sure. They don't have God's interests at all, but their own worldly kingdom. And the Company would like to stop what they call the missionary lobby from growing in numbers here. Just the way the East India Company put a stop to missionaries entering India. They were set against William Carey, for sure. They're content to let the Africans and East Indians believe in their many gods and idols and don't want missionaries to stir up trouble. For the most part, all the Company wants is rights to the land and rights to the minerals."

"Now you've gone from politics to preaching, Derwent," Rogan said with a smile.

"Guess I have. I've been listening to Dr. Jakob."

"You had a heart for the people long before you listened to Jakob van Buren."

"It's not just Matabeleland and Mashonaland they want for their empire. They want the Boer Transvaal and the Orange Free State, too."

"Of course. Gold was discovered in the Transvaal, Derwent, old friend. Of course they want the Boer holdings. Until gold and diamonds were discovered here in huge quantities, England would have been content to allow the Dutch to have all of South Africa. And that's why there will be a war. They want to get rid of Kruger once for all. And because there're more Uitlanders working the gold fields in the Transvaal than there are Boers, Rhodes thinks they have a right to it."

Derwent looked at him. "How did Bechuanaland escape Rhodes's Company and become a British protectorate, I wonder?"

"Must not be any diamonds or gold there," Rogan joked.

"Now you're pulling my leg, Mr. Rogan."

Rogan reached over and pulled Derwent's hat down. "All right, I'll tell you why. You ought to know the African tribes. They're not a united and peaceful 'brotherhood.' Far from it. The butchery of one tribe against another is fact. They invade another tribe, killing, maiming, taking women and children as slaves, stealing away cattle and goods."

"Aye, it's true enough. Even Dr. Jakob says the Ndebele people raised cattle, but the other half of the time they were out raiding the cattle from the weaker tribes, mostly the Shona."

"So the old Bechuanaland Chief feared the British less than he feared his neighboring Zulus or the Boers. So he signed a concession with Her Majesty's Government. That also keeps Rhodes and others from colonizing the land."

"Seems a good and wise thing to me. Have you seen Sir Julien yet?"

"No. I understand he's hand in hand with Doc Jameson in governing Rhodesia."

"He is. After Chieftain Lobengula's death, Mr. Rhodes appointed Dr. Jameson Custodian of Enemy Property. And Dr. Jameson has been mostly responsible for rounding up the captured herds of Ndebele cattle and redistributing them as booty to his troops, about four hundred soldier police, I'm guessing. They're all volunteers. So they support the cause."

Rogan had heard how Company troops under Jameson, after defeating Lobengula, made huge bonfires of the Ndebele long rawhide shields and hauled away the assegais by the wagonload, disarming the impis and their ruling indunas.

"They took the Martyn-Henry rifles, too," Derwent told him.

Rogan recalled the rifles with which the Company had paid Lobengula for a concession on the mineral wealth.

"I've a feeling that if they hadn't taken them, we wouldn't be able to walk safely down the dirt street in Bulawayo," Rogan commented. But after Anthony's and Major Tom Willet's deaths, he wondered if it was still safe.

Bulawayo was a growing white man's town under British control through the Charter Company of Cecil Rhodes. The indunas had moved farther away into new kraals, living under the rules of the Company. Rules and a lordship that many did not like. Resentment was written on the dignified faces of the warriors of Zanzi blood, royal blood, and hatred seethed in the hearts of the impis, whose assegais had been confiscated and broken, their shields burned, their spears snapped in two. Rogan mentioned to Derwent that he could easily sense the resentment in the sullen Ndebele who worked building roads, mining, and helping to harvest crops.

"Dr. Jakob says the same thing. He's worried about Harry Whipple." The breeze blew Derwent's rusty hair beneath the brim of his Rhodesian style hat. Despite the hot sun of South Africa, his fair skin refused to brown, though the freckles turned a shade darker across his aquiline nose.

"He may have good cause to worry about him. I haven't met him yet, but everything I hear has prepared me to dislike him from the start."

"Don't like him much myself. He takes bribes. And he's too bold with the ladies. I seen him looking at Miss Arcilla in ways he shouldn't. Alice, too. And it's no secret he has a big interest in Miss Darinda. She won't even look his way."

"Smart woman."

Bulawayo was a boom town of sorts, with men of growing wealth, for most of them had ridden here in Rhodes's Pioneer Column and received their grants and gold claims to settle the land. The men, including himself, Parnell, and Derwent Brown, each owned three thousand acres of farmland on the pastured veld.

Most of the men at Bulawayo, himself included, had already nailed their claim pegs into the land and into the reefs in which some gold could be seen in the Rhodesian sunshine.

"I'm thinking, Mr. Rogan, that too many of them reefs are naught but stringers, no gold, or not much in them. And after the bust we had north in the Zambezi, well, I'm not expecting too much."

Rogan walked with Derwent down the dusty road of Bulawayo to the saloon to meet his geologist from the Zambezi mine, Clive Shepherd, who'd arrived that morning.

"We won't give up yet, Derwent. I've been studying Henry's map anew for some time now. I think we were dead wrong in settling on the Zambezi. It may be that Henry discovered an ancient working."

"Instead of a new deposit, you mean?"

"That's what I'm thinking. It makes sense. And we've got to find and peg it before Rhodes's men do."

"Least with Sir Julien all taken up on that diamond in Matopos, he's given us some breathing space," Derwent said.

Rogan had learned from Derwent that there was still discussion about an expedition to the Ndebele sacred hills. "I heard Pritchard stumbled onto a find between the Hwe Hwe and the Tshibgiwe Rivers," Derwent told him with excitement. "He's boasting he's panned some samples at six ounces to the ton."

Yes, thought Rogan with ire, and acting on Cecil Rhodes's instruction, one of the Company men had recently surveyed that same ancient gold reef and estimated that there could be thousands of tons in reserve.

"There's red gold here, Mr. Rogan. Most everybody in town is saying so."

"Maybe...but don't forget the BSA owns half of every ounce of gold discovered and mined here." Rogan's irritation with Uncle Julien and Rhodes came back to haunt him again.

"Seems all the land grants are taken now," Derwent told him. "Good farmland, Mr. Rogan, some of the best if a person knows how to work it right. Now, the Ndebele, they're cattlemen. Rovers, they are. Need lots of land to support their cattle. But farming, there's none that do it better than we colonials. And in the long run, sir, it'll be us who feeds everybody, the Ndebele included."

"I don't doubt it, Derwent. But I'm not a farmer. I'll leave that to the pioneers."

"True enough, Mr. Rogan. Someday I wouldn't mind, but me and Alice haven't fully decided yet if we'll stay in Rhodesia or go back to Grimston Way. They say many of the farms are already being worked plenty good."

"And the mineral rights?"

"Heard there was ten thousand claims registered on the mineral rights. Some of them boast real good crushings."

"That may be, but my mind's set on Henry's map. I've been working on those symbols. They must mean something, though I gave up on that notion when we thought we discovered his deposit in the Zambezi. With it going bust, I'm reconsidering."

Derwent looked at him. "Symbols?"

"I never showed them to you?"

"Don't recall seeing them. Must have been Mr. Mornay who got a gander."

At the mention of Mornay, silence settled over them.

After a moment Derwent said, "Clive Shepherd's arrived. Waiting to meet with you at Ranger's place about the mine at Zambezi."

Rogan strode across the dusty street toward the tavern.

"Sure is a lot going on here now," Derwent said.

There was, but Rogan was not deceived by the boom-town mentality. Bulawayo was alive and growing, and so was danger growing right alongside success, ready to swallow it up.

The tavern was the rallying point for the men of the town. There was a billiard table inside that had been hauled from Kimberly piece by piece. The men came to play and drink Sundowner beer. It had become a tradition in Rhodesia for the men to have a drink at sundown.

"Dr. Jakob preaches against the practice," Derwent was telling Rogan. "He also says that any town built on blood has a foundation of guilt. Someday, unless aggrieved evils are dealt with and God's forgiveness sought, a time of judgment comes to call. No one much listens, though. The gold and diamonds just keep coming, and the folks think they always will."

Inside, the tavern was crowded with men, tobacco smoke, and the smell of stale sweat and alcohol. A small crowd was lined up at the rough wooden counter watching two men playing billiards while the others wagered on the outcome, sipping their beer and smoking cheroots; all the while an old fellow in a dusty black jacket and derby hat played an out-of-tune accordion.

One of the two men at the billiard table was Rogan's brother, Parnell. Parnell had been drinking and was weaving now and then on his feet. Seeing Parnell this way stabbed at Rogan's heart. The sight also angered him. He was throwing his life away. Parnell probably felt self-pity because of failing to win Darinda's heart. In Rogan's mind she was a losing battle. His brother didn't need pity; he needed someone to shake him out of his foolishness.

The second man playing billiards was Harry Whipple, head of Julien's native Company police. Rogan had seen several of the native police sitting outside in the dust waiting, evidently, for their sergeant. Captain Ryan Retford claimed Harry was crooked.

None of this surprised Rogan. Most of Julien's men were bought, except, perhaps, for Peter. Peter had managed to teeter back and forth without completely losing his balance under Julien. Rogan had yet to have the long conversation alone with Peter that he wanted. He would have it tonight, as Arcilla had invited him and Evy to Government House to take dinner with them in their private rooms.

Rogan continued to watch Parnell. He had turned from being the expensively dressed young man about London into a haggard man with a frightened, cynical countenance. Arcilla was right. Parnell was drinking too much.

Harry Whipple was big, but soft and fleshy, with what looked to be a perpetual sunburn. His eyes were a watery blue; his golden hair was sparse. He wore his barber-shop mustache proudly. It was wide and stiff, the tips oiled so that they pointed upward. Suspenders held up his canvas trousers, and the familiar boots that all the men wore were dusty.

Whipple was skilled at billiards. He took careful aim with his stick on the black ball, which knocked two others into pockets. He grinned, then turned to Parnell, chuckling. He slugged him playfully on the shoulder.

"You lose again, Par. C'mon. Let's have another beer."

"He's had enough," Rogan heard himself saying from just inside the door.

Harry Whipple turned his head and looked over at Rogan and Derwent. He recognized Derwent, of course, and gave a brief nod. His eyes came back to Rogan, and he measured him with careful glance, taking in his rugged clothing and the belted gun.

"Yeah? I suppose you want his beer, eh? And who are you?"

Derwent cleared his throat and stepped forward. "Say, Mr. Whipple, you've not met Parnell's brother yet? Rogan here, he's been in Bulawayo a whole week now, staying at Dr. Jakob's."

"Brother?" Whipple looked surprised. "So you're Rogan Chantry, huh? Well, I'm your uncle's head policeman. Harry Whipple. Just call me Harry." He walked over and shoved a big hand toward Rogan.

Rogan took his hand and nodded.

"Parnell," Rogan said, "take a seat over here at the table, and we'll have some coffee."

Parnell walked over a bit unsteadily. Derwent pulled out a barrel seat for him, and Parnell sank onto it. Derwent went to the rough wood counter for mugs of coffee.

Harry Whipple hung around for a minute, sipping his beer and eying Rogan, then drifted outdoors to collect his native police.

The native Company police were a band of Ndebele whom Derwent said were not of Zanzi blood, but despised as dogs by the induna and the impis.

"The police are mostly Ndebele, but there's some Shona, too. Mostly considered low folks by the indunas." Derwent cleared his throat. "The worst of them have been taking their women, even married women. The indunas have complained to Harry Whipple, but he says the indunas are lying."

Rogan thought he could understand what was happening. The ruling class of the Ndebele wouldn't fully cooperate with Julien and his magistrate, Harry Whipple. So Harry had hired the lowest of the low as police. For vengeance he was sending them to patrol those of Zanzi blood. A typical peasant-over-the-lord strategy.

"Why does Julien have a man like Whipple?" he asked Parnell.

Parnell took a drink of his black coffee. He ran his tanned fingers through his chestnut hair and avoided Rogan's eyes. "What do you think? You know Uncle as well as I do. Harry does what he's told and doesn't ask too many embarrassing questions. Why else would he want him? Harry isn't known for his great intellect."

"No, not if he thinks he can deliberately mock the indunas without creating more feelings of hatred. If Julien and the others were smart, they'd listen to Dr. Jakob. Build more medical bungalows, cooperate with the Ndebele culture as far as they can, and use their structure of laws and indunas as steppingstones for working with the Africans. The missionaries can teach the BSA a great deal."

Parnell angrily pushed his coffee away, slopping some over the rim. "Look, Rogan, if you want to lecture, go lecture Dr. Jameson and Uncle Julien, will you? Nobody listens to me."

"Why should they? Look at you," he said brutally. "Arcilla says you're drunk half the time."

"Dashed malarkey. Never mind about me. If anyone's cooperating with Julien, it's Peter. Ask the ol' girl about Peter."

Rogan wondered. "I intend to ask him. Anthony called me to London before he sailed for the Cape. He wanted me to see your letter."

Parnell's gaze shot up. For a moment he looked alarmed, then he scowled and shrugged. "So? It was all true. But don't tell Julien about it."

"I've no intention of telling him."

"I didn't send the letter to you, Rogan, because I didn't want you here stirring up more trouble, for your sake as well as mine. You'll get yourself killed one of these days. Well, you're here now. Look, no matter what Julien says about that attack on Lobengula, what I wrote to Anthony was true. I know. I was there.

"I was there," he repeated. "He lied the other night at supper, telling Darinda and Retford he was a hero when he ransacked Lobengula's hut and wagon. Telling them I was the one that alerted him to fire his pistol at Dumaka. Actually, Julien was down on his knees with diamonds dripping through his fingers when Dumaka showed up. Harry fired at Dumaka, not Julien. Harry knows it, but he's not going to contradict him. I know. I was there."

What was Harry Whipple getting for his cooperation? Money, to be sure. Maybe some promise of a higher position later on. Julien liked to pass out positions. Made even a fool feel important.

"Now, Julien says Harry followed after Dumaka until Harry got him cornered, and a croc finished him off."

"Dumaka?" Rogan was startled. He had always felt there was something between him and Dumaka that would end in a controversy. "Was he shot?"

"Not badly. Harry's a poor aim for being head of the native Company police. He said he cornered Dumaka after he fled. I doubt that, too." Parnell leaned across the table. "There's not a man around who can track a Zulu or outdistance one when he's moving with a purpose. We both know it. But Harry's told Julien he tracked Dumaka to the Shangani, where Dumaka jumped in to swim away, and the crocs got him." He straightened, looking wily. "I say the story's a fake."

Rogan wondered about Dumaka. If he was dead, then Julien had one less enemy to face over the Black Diamond. That left only Heyden van Buren.

A glass of warm beer sat on the table, and Parnell reached for it. Rogan pushed it away. Parnell glared at him, but Rogan did not relent.

"This drinking has got to stop. You're making yourself sick and acting the fool. And I've told you before, you need to forget that woman, Darinda."

"You don't know a thing about her or me."

"I don't need to know everything. It's obvious she doesn't care a whit about you. She's always been for herself. She's Julien's granddaughter and more like him than any male offspring. She's seen you losing your head over her without batting an eye. She wants power. That, and taking over after Julien. And now that Anthony's dead, it looks like she may get her wish after all."

Parnell stood and took a clumsy swing at him, but Rogan pushed him back down. "Sober up, Parnell. You'll get no pity from me, and certainly none from her. The more you carry on like this, the more she thinks you're a fool and a failure. And that's exactly what you are and will stay like unless you stop pitying yourself and act the man."

"I don't want your lectures. I tol' you," he slurred.

"Now that I'm here, that's what you're going to get."

"Say—what d'ye mean?"

"Just this. I'm taking over. It's time you began listening to Dr. Jakob's preaching. In fact, I'm going to have Derwent pack you up and take you out to the mission to stay."

"You can't do that—"

"Just watch me. We're going to make sure you don't get near a jug again."

Parnell glared but apparently realized there was little he could do at the moment. He sank back into the seat and glowered.

"Now," Rogan said comfortably, refilling Parnell's coffee mug, "tell me about Uncle's expedition into the Matopos. What do you know about it?"

He shrugged. "I'll tell you plenty. It will rile the indunas and put us all on the edge, that's what."

"Then he's still going? Nothing has happened since Anthony arrived that altered his plans?"

"Maybe something… He's going, all right, but he's got to bide his time."

Rogan leaned toward him. "What do you mean? I'd think he'd do better to have gone at once. Fact is, I'm plenty surprised he hasn't done it by now."

"Sure, but he *can't*."

Rogan exchanged glances with Derwent.

"Can't? You're not making sense, Parnell."

"Sure I am, little brother. I always make sense." He smiled to himself about something and reached for the leftover glass of warm beer sitting on the table.

Rogan wearily snatched it up and handed it to Derwent. Derwent took it and tossed it out the open window. Somebody bellowed, and Derwent grimaced. "Sorry, mister," he called.

"Better explain yourself, Parnell," Rogan continued.

Parnell smirked. "Am I my brother's keeper, eh?"

"Don't mock. You'll find out at Jakob's. Maybe I'll pack you up and send you back to Aunt Elosia."

"Do that, and it's war!"

"Go on, talk to me about our beloved Uncle Julien."

"What do I get if I do tell you a bit of a secret, eh?"

"Nothing," Rogan said brutally, smiling. "Maybe sugar in your coffee."

"Cruel people. All right." He looked at Derwent as though just now remembering he was there. Parnell pointed a finger at his chest. "And you'd better not say a word of any of this to anyone, Vicar Derwent."

Derwent ran his fingers through his russet hair. "I got no reason to talk, Mr. Parnell."

"Never mind about Derwent," Rogan interrupted shortly. "He's proven himself a friend long ago."

"Better hope so…'cause if word gets around too much about what's planned, there may be more than ol' Cousin Tony dead."

Rogan was ready to pounce on that, and why his brother thought so, but Parnell had to be calmed and steadied. He was darting here and there in his crazed brain.

"What plan, Parnell?" Rogan asked with deliberated patience. "Tell me about the plan, okay?"

"Sure. All you had to do was ask. Julien can't get Doc Jameson to agree about the Matopos expedition. After poor Cousin Anthony's death, Doc Jameson came down as hard on Julien as, well—whatever somebody used on Anthony. 'No Matopos. Understand? No Matopos, Julien!' Doc tells him. And Uncle Julien? He was purple with rage. But he kept quiet. First time I saw Julien take orders."

Rogan stroked his mustache. Important—yes, what he'd just heard was perhaps the most important news so far. He looked at Derwent. Derwent was squinting with intensity.

"So Julien's waiting until Doc leaves Bulawayo. Then he'll make his move."

Derwent changed positions on his barrel and looked at Rogan for a ready response. Rogan weighed his brother's words.

"So that's it. Very significant. So that's why Julien hasn't gone by now. Makes sense. I was worried I wouldn't arrive in time. When is Jameson leaving Bulawayo?"

Parnell looked up and over at the tavern door. "You mean on that… er…secret mission?"

"That's right. The one. When?"

"Haven't the foggiest. Big secret. They're worried about a Boer spy among us. Somebody prepared to send word to Kruger. So Doc and Julien are keeping the day buried."

"Boer spy?" Rogan asked with incredulity. "In the Company?" He laughed. "Surely you jest."

Parnell shook his head. "On the contrary, Julien takes it seriously. That's why if he found out I sent the letter to Anthony, he'd have me for treason or something. He'd think I was the spy." He shook his head suddenly and looked around suspiciously, as though they were being listened to. But the tavern was so noisy no one could have heard.

"I'm not saying any more. I've already said too much." Parnell stood, a bit wobbly on his feet, his hands on the table. "I'm going back to my bungalow—number twelve. Retford has thirteen. Bad luck." He rubbed his forehead and grimaced. "I feel awful…"

Rogan stood, intending to get his brother to the bungalow.

"I'll see he gets home, Mr. Rogan. Look, Clive's just come in to talk about the mine."

At the door Rogan saw the geologist he had hired to work for him at Zambezi. Clive was an older man, tall and gangling, with curly silver hair and a rather rueful smile.

Someone else entered almost at the same moment, and every male eye turned toward the sight. Darinda Bley stood near the door looking toward Rogan's table. She scanned Parnell, and her face hardened.

"Get me out of here, Derwent," Parnell groaned. "She hates seeing me this way."

"Bunge him off to bed," Rogan told Derwent. "I'll be over to the bungalow later. Wait, Parnell—one more thing. Do you know where Anthony's body was found?"

"Sure, on the trail near bungalow number one, where he was staying. Darinda found him—under the wait-a-bit tree. The tree's right there on the trail bank. Can't miss it. Ol' Harry's tagged the tree. 'Bout the only thing he has done so far. Retford says the body was dragged there. Poor ol' Anthony was killed somewhere else. And it all had to happen quickly, too. From the time Darinda first met him on the trail to when she found him dead was, say, somewhere around about thirty or forty minutes."

"Darinda saw him alive on the trail?" She had not mentioned that in her letter to Camilla.

"She met him, all right. Argued with him too." He glanced her way. "She doesn't know it," he slurred, "but Arcilla heard 'em. Real cat and dog fight."

Rogan looked at his brother sharply. "Has Arcilla told anyone else about this?"

Parnell shrugged, quickly appearing to lose interest. "Don't know… She told me. Ask her. Better yet," he said maliciously, smirking toward Darinda, "ask *her*. She's the one who can tell you a thing or two she hasn't told Harry Whipple."

Derwent got Parnell out of the tavern, and Rogan looked across the room at Darinda. She had a bit of spunk coming in here like this. A decent woman wouldn't, but with a grandfather like Julien, she could evidently get by with it, since the men knew who she was. They moved aside as she walked boldly through the center of the room toward Rogan. She stopped, hands on hips.

Rogan glanced toward Clive Shepherd, then lifted his hand. *Later,* he seemed to indicate. He then walked up to the counter to order, carrying his coffee mug with him.

Darinda walked up to the counter. "My grandfather wants to see you."

"Does he? I'll be at Government House tonight to see Peter and Arcilla. I'll look in on him then."

"He wants to see you *now.* I've the trap out front. I'll bring you."

Something about her attitude, or maybe it was just Julien's way of making things urgent when he wanted something his way, provoked him. He picked up his mug and finished the contents, though the coffee was cold.

"I've another matter to attend to right now. I'm meeting someone here."

She lifted her dark, slim brows and scanned him. "Yes, Clive Shepherd. He ran the Zambezi mine after Mornay was killed in the mining accident. The mine's gone broke, hasn't it?"

"Word travels fast, it seems," Rogan said nonchalantly. He knew Darinda was trying to influence him, but it wouldn't work.

"The Company owns half of everything that mine produced. Do you think Rhodes wouldn't know if it had stopped?"

"Forbid. You can include Julien in on that, too. Is that what he wants to see me about, Zambezi?"

"Grandfather has many things on his mind."

"A very industrious man."

"You'll admit, Rogan, you've been in Bulawayo a week, and you haven't called on him yet."

"He's not exactly what I would call *charming* company, Cousin Darinda."

"He expected you would come to him at once."

"No doubt."

"He *is* your uncle," she accused. "And don't forget, he has more to say about your share in the diamonds than anyone else in the family."

He felt an ironic smile tip the corner of his mouth. "And more to say about my bride's? That's it, I suppose. He wants to discuss Evy and her van Buren inheritance. And now that her father's been murdered, she stands to inherit a great deal more from the Brewster side as well. That should be most upsetting for him. And you."

An angry crimson stained her cheeks. Her dove-gray eyes sparked. "What Evy gains by means of her birth, and now the death of Anthony, doesn't interest me."

"No?" He smiled. "Come, now. We're old friends, Cousin. The last time we were together on the Limpopo River and the pioneer trek, you made it excruciatingly clear that you have but one aim in life—to boot Anthony aside and take over the reins of the family business."

"Are you going to come or not?"

"Wait for me at the trap. I'll be there in a few minutes."

She gave a curt nod of her dark head and, turning on her boot, strode from the tavern looking neither right nor left at the men who watched her.

Clive walked over. "Hello, Rogan. 'Bout time you got back."

Rogan smiled and shook hands. "Agreed. Ruddy luck things went to ruin. How's that arm and shoulder doing?"

Clive shook his head sadly. "Not as well as I'd like. Too bad about the mine. It fooled us all, Mornay included. He was depressed toward the end. I couldn't find out what was actually troubling him."

"Troubling him?"

"Rather extraordinary, actually. Couldn't understand why he was so unhappy toward the end. Talked a lot about betrayal. I couldn't tell if he was thinking of himself or someone else."

"He didn't like the BSA." Had Derwent been able to direct his thinking toward eternity?

"No. He didn't respect some of the top BSA men, but he worked for them. Did you get all the papers and reports I sent you on the status of the mine?"

"I got them. Looks to me as though we could mine deeper, but it may be a loss. I'm not sure I care to throw money at it right now."

"I'm still of two minds on the idea myself. You read my report. I think it's time to close down and look elsewhere. Can't see how that particular area could be the golden goose Henry Chantry thought it was."

"I'm convinced it wasn't. I've some ideas we need to discuss in the future. Unfortunately, now isn't the right time for a trek."

"That's right. Derwent said you have your wife here with you now."

Rogan's jaw set. "That's not the reason. She came fully expecting me to go to the Zambezi. Evy's content out at Dr. Jakob's mission station right now. She's discovering her family history."

Evy would undoubtedly talk about the strain in their marriage with Dr. Jakob, but Rogan had no inclination to discuss his personal life with anyone. He wanted to push everything to the back of his mind and forget about it. His wife's lack of trust still angered him.

"With what's happened to Anthony Brewster, I'm reluctant to leave just now," Rogan explained. "On any new expedition I'm likely to follow up on my uncle's old map. Right now, though, I don't want that spread around. We'll keep it between us."

Clive nodded. After a moment he said, "That was an ugly thing about Lord Brewster. I just heard today when I rode in. Whoever did it is still running around loose. Was it a native?"

Rogan had been thinking a lot about that. In fact, he'd done little else on both the train and the stagecoach line between Kimberly and Bulawayo.

"I would have thought so at first because of Major Tom Willet." Rogan briefly explained what he'd learned about the major's death near the Matopos, which was first palmed off as a lion attack, and now thought to be an attack with an assegai.

"Anthony was different. The back of his head was hit badly. My guess is that he knew the murderer. They met on the trail between Government House and the bungalows. Anthony walked away, and then unexpectedly—wham, struck from behind."

"Sounds like there's more than one breed of savages around here," Clive commented, glancing about.

"The civilized ones are most dangerous."

CHAPTER TWENTY-THREE

By the time Rogan reached the dusty street, Darinda was waiting in the horse-drawn trap. On the seat beside her lay a shotgun with its metal glinting in the afternoon sunlight.

"I hope you didn't leave that gun lying there unattended when you were in the tavern," Rogan told her in unabashed correction. "Anyone could have walked by and snatched it."

The breeze ruffled her shiny black hair in contrast with the Victorian white blouse with its lace collar. She wore the blouse stuffed into a pair of pants. He had yet to see the woman wearing a skirt.

"I don't need a man to tell me that," she snapped. "I had it locked in the case in back. You took so long in there I'd almost given up on you. I took it out to keep me company on the way home. There's a lonely stretch of land between here and Government House."

Rogan offered a light bow. "Good to see you've got some sense, Cousin. My apology. Sorry I kept you waiting."

He swung up and settled himself. She flipped the reins and they were off.

"I suppose you're one of those overbearing males who won't allow their wives to breathe without your approval."

Remembering how Evy had taken advantage of him, he found Darinda's charge amusing. A grin tugged at the corners of his mouth as he repressed a chuckle.

Darinda gave him a nasty glance and flicked the reins more urgently.

"Tell me," he said, "if you ever really got angry at a man, would you be heartless enough to whack him when his back was turned?"

She wrenched and jerked the reins, and the horse leaped forward. Rogan grabbed the reins and calmed the excited horse.

"How dare you!" she cried, her cheeks crimson, her eyes flashing. "Accuse *me* of killing Anthony!"

"Then you did not?"

"You beast!" She picked up her horsewhip and started using it on him. Dropping the reins, he caught the whip near the center of the cord so she was unable to swing it again. When she stopped trying, he tossed it in back.

"Then you didn't," he said, satisfied. "I'll take your word for it. What's this about you having met him on the trail and argued with him shortly before he was killed?"

He drove the horse now, and she was breathing hard, looking at him with shock and rage.

"Did Ryan tell you? Why, that traitor. And after he told me to say nothing."

He drove past flat-topped thorn trees. "Ryan? Ah, I see. So it's 'Ryan' now, not Captain Retford, is it? You've got something going with him."

"That is none of your business."

"I'm making it my business. I'm worried about my brother. I think you've run Parnell into the ground long enough. If you've no intention of marriage, then I think it's past time to be fair with him and let him know. If you don't, I will. Is it Parnell or Ryan?"

She glared at him. "It's neither man, if you want to know. I happen to prefer my freedom from men like you."

"Do you mind if I tell Parnell you're being used by Julien to keep him strung up by his thumbs?"

"You may tell Parnell anything you wish. If he hasn't figured out by now that I'm not in love with him, then he's too thickheaded to believe you, either."

"True. He has that tendency," he said dryly. "I told him back on the Limpopo River, but he wouldn't believe it."

"He's not as shrewd as you," she retorted.

He laughed. "I think you have one up on both us poor Chantry men," he goaded. "So now you're baiting poor Captain Retford, are you?"

She folded her arms and stared ahead.

"He's a good man, Darinda. Better than Parnell. I don't like admitting that about my brother, but it's true. Parnell is to blame for the debacle he's in. When he first came to Capetown with the idea to marry Darinda Bley, he had diamonds and power on his mind. Who you were, or what you would become never entered his heart. He's gotten burned. Now in a state of depression, he's surrendered to liquor."

She was quiet and seemed to lose some of her anger. "I didn't want to hurt him deliberately. The romantic game with Parnell was instigated by Grandfather. But I'll admit that I went along with it for my own purposes."

"Are those purposes still the burning ambition of your life, or has Retford pulled you in another direction?"

She sighed. "I haven't decided."

He wondered. Somehow he thought she meant something more than merely trying to decide if she was falling for him or not. "I see."

She looked at him coldly and lapsed into silence.

"So Retford told you not to mention that you'd argued with Anthony on the trail. Did he say why?"

"It wasn't to protect me because I've done something despicable. I wouldn't kill Anthony Brewster, but I did threaten him. It was foolish, I know. I didn't actually mean it. Ryan was afraid Harry would use the incident to his favor in some way." She looked at him. "I was the one who told Ryan about the meeting with Anthony. No one would ever have known about it if I hadn't admitted it."

"I never suspected you of murder, Darinda. But you're wrong about no one knowing that you'd met and threatened him on the trail."

Her eyes were wary.

"Arcilla overheard. Strange how things happen. Just when one thinks they've gotten by with deceit or some other wrong, providence appears to have a final say."

She looked uncomfortable. "Yes... Dr. Jakob said something of that nature. 'Be sure your sin will find you out.' That's stayed in my mind. How did Arcilla overhear?"

"She must have been on her way to Anthony's bungalow when she approached both of you while you were having a heated argument. Knowing my sister, she would have been cautious about getting involved. She stepped aside on the trail until Anthony walked on."

"He was going to meet someone and was in a hurry, I remember that."

"But you've no idea who it was he went to meet?"

"No."

"It was well that you owned up to Retford when you did. It wouldn't look good for you right now had you kept silent only to have Arcilla inform me when I arrived. I'd have wondered if an attractive young heiress might find it in her interest to get rid of a contender."

"If I had wanted to, I'd have used something more feminine," she said maliciously. "Like poison."

She withdrew into silence, but he could see the news had given her plenty to think about.

So Retford didn't trust Harry either. Rogan decided Retford had been prudent when he'd told Darinda to keep her argument with Anthony to herself.

Julien was waiting in his office when Darinda brought Rogan in to see him.

"Thank you, Darinda. Rogan and I will talk privately."

"And if you hear any shots," Rogan commented dryly, "don't call Whipple, call Retford."

"Still the amusing scoundrel," Julien commented. "Sit down, Rogan, sit down, we need to talk. Close the door behind you, Darinda."

Rogan remained standing.

"Smoke?" Julien pushed the ornate cigar box across the desk.

Rogan chose a cheroot and struck a match while Julien poured himself a brandy from the crystal decanter, his back toward him.

"How is Evy taking Anthony's death?"

Rogan's eyes fell upon a gold object sitting on Julien's desk. He stared too long; the match burned his thumb. *The bird on Henry's map.* He wanted to reach for it, then caught himself just in time. *Caution. Show nothing. Nothing.*

"You should not have married her. You got my letter of reprimand, I suppose? Quite a shock to me to have learned of your action after the fact."

Rogan turned a shoulder to the bird to concentrate fully on what Julien was saying.

"I might have invited you to enjoy the wedding," he said flippantly, "but there wasn't enough time to accommodate your voyage."

Julien turned his head and measured him with a thoughtful glance. "Pure rebellion on your part, going against family wishes in this matter, but not surprising."

"When I discovered you'd lied to me that night on the Limpopo about Evy's lineage, I knew any plans for my future must be made apart from your interests. Henry's daughter by Katie van Buren, was she? All along you knew Evy was Anthony's daughter."

"I had hoped to keep you from marrying her. I failed. There's nothing left now but to let the past, with its poor judgments, rush by on the river of life."

"Touching, even a trace of the poetic. You won't mind if I remain cautious?"

"Dr. Jakob informs me you're to be a father. What is there left to us now but acceptance? As I say, I wish to move on, to forget the past, let it lie waste, and build something new—between you and me. I've asked you here to make a bargain."

"Whenever you wish to make a bargain with me, I always get tremors, Uncle Julien. You won't mind if I back off a little to consider?"

Julien's lower lip pulled into a smile. "The cobra pit, eh? No, no, nothing like that. *Gold,* the secret to Henry's map unmasked, and for me, the *Kimberly Black Diamond.*"

Easy, Rogan told himself. He studied Julien, wondering what shrewd scheme he was working on now, hoping to rope him into it. The *secret* of the map? Could he have found out the meaning of the symbols? The gold bird on the desk could imply that, but how? No one else had even known of the symbols, except Derwent and Mornay.

He was strongly tempted to glance toward the gold bird but looked instead at the cheroot, turning his side to the desk. "Gold and diamonds," he commented airily, "what grander topic for greedy mortals?"

Julien chuckled with brazen amusement. "The world, Rogan, is made up of greedy mortals such as you call us."

"Yes, but not all remain such, thankfully. There's Dr. Jakob—and Derwent. Two very different men, yet they have much the same belief in the meaning of life, the same solid character. They seem to be able to look through the fog of ideas and choose what's meaningful."

"Bah. Fools, both. Derwent will never amount to much in this life. If you hadn't taken a liking to the lad, he'd still be stuck in Grimston Way most likely teaching at the rectory in some minor capacity."

Rogan felt the sting. Julien hadn't meant to, but Rogan was aware that by and large he'd been responsible for bringing Derwent to Bulawayo.

"Looking back, I'd do things differently. I wish Derwent were at the vicarage teaching."

"Sentimental tommyrot. I'm ashamed of you, Rogan," he said in mocking amusement. "You're getting a conscience in your old age, or perhaps the idea of becoming a father is turning you into a philosopher."

Rogan sank into a chair, stretching out his legs in front of him, drawing his brows together.

Julien looked down at him speculatively, then he laughed with humor.

"What is it? The married life isn't as blissful as you anticipated?" He laughed again.

Rogan met his gaze evenly, not the least bit amused. "Evy supports Dr. Jakob in his work. She's anxious to use some of her inheritance to expand his medical hut into a hospital."

"And you haven't talked any sense into her?"

"I happen to agree with her on the idea. What we disagree on is her being here at all. I didn't know she was expecting until we were far at sea. Now it's too late. I need to make the best of things."

Julien chuckled. He leaned back against his desk, arms folded, his one good eye glinting with malicious amusement.

"So now your firstborn will be born a Rhodesian. That much is splendid! I'm beginning to like this after all. There may be hope for all I've accomplished and planned for the family in South Africa. I've always said you could be an asset to me, or you could turn out to be as useless as Anthony proved to be. The biggest mistake I made years ago was adopting Anthony and making him a son before it became clear that he never had fire warming his blood."

"Well, he's gone now," Rogan said heartlessly. He had noticed the door move slightly. When Darinda had left the room, Julien had told her to shut the door behind her. It was open a crack. He suspected she was eavesdropping.

To teach her a lesson about trusting Julien, Rogan played along with him. "Maybe you have something there, Uncle. With the inheritance Evy gets from the van Burens, and now from Anthony, along with my inheritance, our children will be strong new blood in the family dynasty."

"I may have found my true heir." He chuckled again and eyed Rogan with alert new interest. "Wisely said. Now you're seeing things as they should be. But don't mention Evy's interest in Jakob's work. That

Boer is more than a thorn in my side. He's an out-and-out sword. Missionaries! They bring nothing but trouble when they arrive. I was against the BSA allowing him to come here and construct that compound out of town. Always harping on native rights and the need to build schools, hospitals, churches—bah! As if the warrior caste will ever want to attend a school!"

It's either churches and schools or assegais and hatred. The colonialists would need to give them something in place of what they were taking from the hills and reefs, but Rogan did not say this aloud.

"Enough of missionaries! I shall be blunt, Rogan. We understand each other. I suppose you think I murdered Anthony?"

"That was the first solution that came to mind."

Julien gave a bitter chuckle.

The door moved silently again and closed.

"One thing about you, you're straightforward. So I, too, will be blunt." He finished his brandy and set the glass down.

That *bird.* Why was it here? Where had Julien gotten it? He wanted to ask, but doing so would give him away. He must move slowly, patiently, to keep Julien in the dark…

"You still intend to search for Lobengula's burial cave, I suppose?" Rogan asked.

"What do you think? Would I allow anything to stop me?"

No, nor would he allow *anyone* to thwart him in his quest.

"The Black belongs to me. It always has. It represents more to me than a mere diamond. It is the start of my kingdom in Kimberly. I've never told you this before, Rogan. I've never talked about my earliest beginnings here in South Africa with anyone. The family believes I always got along with Ebenezer Bley. Nothing could be more ridiculous. I hated him. He tried to control me. He tried to cheat me out of everything I earned in the pit. And in the beginning, it will shock you to know, I played fairly. I worked harder than most, but Ebenezer outsmarted me at every turn. I told him I'd never cooperate with him, but he laughed at me. 'You're like me, Julien,' he'd mock. 'You'll follow in my footsteps.'

"I swore I wouldn't. I partnered with Carl van Buren… We made some crucial finds that allowed us to expand. Then I found the Kimberly Black… It was worth a fortune…"

Rogan was uncomfortable. In listening to Julien's beginnings, he could see himself. Even Julien's dislike for Ebenezer was a parody of how he felt about Julien.

"Wait," Rogan said. "You claim you found it. But I've heard other renditions. I've heard it was Carl, and therefore it's actually Evy's diamond—"

"Bah. That's Heyden's story. That's why he'll kill to get it. He really believes it belongs to the van Burens."

Rogan wasn't sure if he believed Julien. "I've also heard it said that Henry believed my grandfather discovered it."

"So he told me on that day long ago at Cape House. Henry came to get financial backing for an expedition north. The Black was on my desk. He threatened me. He claimed it belonged to the Chantrys."

"And I suppose that's not true?" Rogan asked wryly.

"Naturally not. I discovered it before the day the mine explosion took Carl's life. I tried to save him…"

"Yes, I'd think so."

"But he was too badly injured. So you see the Black represents my beginning, my freedom from everyone and everything that controlled me. Including Ebenezer. That's when I lost my eye…but once I had the Black, I had the key to my future, my kingdom in diamonds. I naturally gravitated toward men like Rhodes and joined De Beers Consolidated Mining Company. Ebenezer became proud of me. He treated me as his heir after that and left me in control. He could see that only I, Julien Bley, had the ability to follow his steps. The Black Diamond represents my purpose in life, yes, my reason to live, my soul. And I will take it back from Lobengula's rotting carcass. It belongs in my showcase at

Cape House. When I need to be reminded of my purpose, I take it out, handle it, look at it, recommit to my goals."

Rogan fought against the rising sensation of disgust. But why should he feel thus? Julien's ambitions were typical of many, though in an exaggerated fashion. While few would go as far as Julien, he had consistently followed his purposes to the fullest extent. Was he not even like him, himself?

"You'll go on the Matopos expedition, as well. So will Retford. You ask why? Because I don't trust some of the men I'll need to bring with me. I'll need protection, and so will the Black until I can return to Capetown."

Rogan was not about to get involved in the Matopos diamond hunt.

"I'll say one thing for you and Retford. I can turn my back to you two."

"That's something Anthony couldn't do to someone he trusted."

"You think it was one of us?"

"Don't you?"

"I'm not convinced. What was there to gain by his death?"

"Maybe it was to cover something up."

Julien's eye twitched. "Such as?"

Rogan stood. If he said anything about the plan to aid the Uitlanders, he might unmask Arcilla's knowledge of what was happening. Parnell, too, might be suspected.

"Just a suggestion. We do know someone did it, and it doesn't appear as an opportune killing by one of the Ndebele." Now was his chance… "So Dumaka is dead, or is he? I've my doubts about that."

"You heard about the tale I told at dinner that night? Yes, Harry got him. Trailed him to the Shangani."

"He trailed a Zulu?" Rogan pointed out doubtfully. "You know the Ndebele as I do. Do you think a man of Harry Whipple's caliber could outrun and outsmart Dumaka? I don't. I'd like to talk to Harry about it."

"Harry has no reason to come up with a story like that. I believe him."

"Because you want to believe Dumaka is dead. As for having no reason, the reason is as clear as you'd want it. For your indebtedness, your favor. And it's worked, too, hasn't it? Why else is Whipple the head of your native Company police? Because of his great ability? It didn't take much to convince me he has little of that. But he's pugnacious and takes orders from you well."

Julien, rather than getting angry, considered. He took a slim Turkish cigarette from his case and lit it.

"I won't deny he's been bought. In some ways I'd trust a spitting cobra before Harry. But in the matter of Dumaka, I do trust him."

"Why, because he says so? Did he bring you any proof?"

Julien paced in front of his desk. Rogan's gaze was lured back to what looked to be a solid gold falcon with wings spread, its head looking to the right. *The exact replica of what Henry had drawn!* Somehow he had yet to bring up the subject. Would Darinda know anything about it? Perhaps—

"I'll call Harry now. Ask him any question you like." Julien walked to the door and threw it open.

"Captain Retford, send for Whipple."

Harry Whipple arrived almost at once, looking curious and pleased with himself until he noticed Rogan. He eyed him warily. Julien motioned for Retford to stay.

"Well, Harry," Julien said in a baiting voice, "you've met Rogan here. He thinks Dumaka is still alive and conniving evil against us. What do you have to say about that?"

Rogan looked at Retford. He seemed alert and interested. Had he doubted the story as well? Rogan credited Retford with having good sense. He was a friend of Derwent, which spoke well for Retford. Darinda had entered the office from another door, and Rogan wondered how much she had heard. He thought she, wily as a little fox, knew just about everything her grandfather was doing in Bulawayo.

Rogan also noticed the enamored glance that passed between her and Captain Retford when they spotted each other.

Darinda walked over to the desk and stood with her back toward them as her grandfather sparred with Harry Whipple.

"Dumaka's dead, all right," Harry stated firmly. "I saw five or six crocs headed straight for him after he jumped in the Shangani."

"But you didn't actually see them attack?" Rogan inquired.

"Now, c'mon, Rogan Chantry, you think you could survive a bunch of hungry crocs?"

"No. But I'm wagering a Zulu warrior could."

"Well, you're wagerin' wrong. There's nobody who could survive that many of 'em."

"But you offer no proof Dumaka is dead. No bit of clothing, his assegai, nothing."

Harry wore a sullen face. "Didn't think I needed any. Saw no reason why I should be doubted, and if I hadn't been sure the savage was killed, I wouldn't have come back saying so. I chased him from Lobengula's hut. Ask Sir Julien. I saved his life that time. Dumaka ran out of the hut, and I was on him like a vulture."

Rogan didn't like the way he averted his eyes when he spoke. He wasn't convinced, but looking over at Julien, he saw satisfaction written on his face. Julien found it easy to believe his enemy was dead.

"There you have it, Rogan," Julien said with the vibrancy of victory in his voice. "Harry is sure the crocodiles in the river finished the job. I for one find his story credible."

Harry cultivated a look of humility. "Thank you, sir. Your trust in me does me honor."

Rogan placed hands on hips and twisted his mouth. Captain Retford smiled.

Darinda turned from the desk, and her face was anything but smiling.

"Grandfather, what if he isn't dead? That may provide a better explanation of what happened here in your office the night Anthony was murdered."

Julien appeared to tense. He turned toward her.

"I don't think we should bring that night up, Miss Bley," Harry said in a baneful voice.

She looked at him. "If you expect to solve a murder, maybe we should."

Rogan tried not to smile, but Harry looked doleful, as though she'd hit him unfairly.

"The spellcasting, the sacrificed animal, the hakata divining bones, I'm inclined to agree with Rogan that it fits Dumaka. For that matter, who's to say he didn't kill Anthony?"

"If he's alive it's possible, but he needs a motive, Miss Bley, if we're to add Dumaka to the list of possible murderers," Captain Retford said.

Darinda looked over at Rogan. "Did Dumaka ever hold anything against Anthony?"

"I think we're jumping all over the place here," Harry complained. "We're assuming too much. I say Dumaka is dead."

"Only indirectly. He may have had a grudge against Anthony," Rogan answered Darinda, ignoring Harry Whipple. "He knew Anthony was in the Cape House stables that night when the Black Diamond was stolen. He must have known Anthony was Uncle Julien's adopted son. He would despise him for that reason alone. And secondly, his sister, Jendaya, converted to Christianity under Dr. Clyde and Junia Varley. Dumaka despised Jendaya for becoming a Christian. In his way of thinking, she'd betrayed the Zulu kingdom and its gods. Jendaya was there at Rorke's Drift when the Zulus attacked. Dumaka was one of those impis. Jendaya managed to escape with Anthony's child. Dumaka could hold that against Anthony. Now, what was that about hakata bones?"

Julien had withdrawn into an uncanny silence.

"The captain can tell you about it," she said.

Rogan stopped him. He already knew all about the nganga and their divining bones. He also remembered that Henry wrote in his journal about Julien having a set, and how when Henry walked in on him once, Julien had been doing something peculiar with them.

"Are you saying Julien's office here was the scene of spellcasting?" Rogan was alarmed. Now he was almost sure Dumaka was alive.

Sir Julien roused himself and took command again. He walked to his desk and snatched another Turkish smoke, lighting it with jerky movements. "Yes. The sign of a black future." He looked at Harry Whipple. "You still stand by your oath that you cornered Dumaka by the Shangani?"

"Yes, he's dead. Whoever did that hokey-pokey will be caught, sir. We're still on it."

Julien looked across the room at Rogan, then back to Harry. "All right, Harry, that's all for now. Keep on it, by Jove. We'll have the fiend who killed Anthony before all this is over. Darinda? You and the captain can go as well. I still have a few things to talk over with Rogan."

They all trooped out, and when the door was shut and they were alone again, Julien turned to look at him. An unpleasant smirk was on his face. Rogan's gaze dropped to what Julien held in his hand.

The gold falcon glittered.

CHAPTER TWENTY-FOUR

Sir Julien chuckled at Rogan. "Did you think you fooled me, my boy? I set it here on my desk to get your reaction. You tried to conceal your excitement, but little escapes me when I'm expecting it. Your reaction proves I was right. Henry drew this bird on his map." Unexpectedly, he handed it to Rogan. "Am I right?" Julien challenged.

Rogan's temper flared. "You'll tell me how you learned it was on the map or—"

"Now, now. You and I are friends at last, remember?"

Rogan laughed. "Like you and Ebenezer, is that it?" He expected his uncle to get angry, but Julien smiled.

"Exactly," he said. "You and I, Rogan. You'll go on the expedition to find the Black Diamond. You and Retford, both. As I've said, I can turn my back to both of you. Harry? He'd steal me blind."

"How did you find out about the drawings on the map?"

"The emblems?" He chuckled. "Giles Mornay."

"Mornay!" Rogan was stunned. He was tempted not to believe him, but how else could he have learned? Julien had never seen Henry's old map. Rogan had made certain of that.

Though Mornay had made a map for Julien that he'd seen hanging in Parnell's office in Kimberly. That only showed the limited information that Mornay could acquire from his father's old records and the memory of past conversations about Henry's trek. But the secret emblems drawn on Henry's map had not been seen by anyone else until Rogan showed them to Mornay and Derwent at the Zambezi gold mine.

"Yes, the *late* Giles Mornay…unfortunate mining accident. A twist of fate. Oh, did I tell you Mornay had a son? No? You do look a bit surprised. He naturally wanted the very best for his son. He's safe in England, attending Cambridge. Took some doing, as the boy wasn't that educated, but with private tutors to help him along, Giles Mornay the second is doing well. In return—yes, he told me what was on the map. Well, actually he was kind enough to draw one from memory. Would you like to see it?"

Rogan was frozen with anger.

Sir Julien removed a sheet from his locked drawer and extended it toward Rogan. "No use being obstinate. Anger and rage will lessen your ability to think clearly."

Rogan walked toward him. Julien spoke cheerfully.

"I have good news for you, Rogan. All the gold on Henry's map is yours. Yes, yours alone. And now that I know where the location of his find is, the Company will let you keep it all. I had to finagle with Rhodes and Jameson to get you this kind of deal. Here, take a look at Mornay's map."

Rogan fought his rising anger. He studied the map, recognizing Mornay's style of drawing. The map was close to the original. The emblems of the bird, the lion, and the baobab tree were correctly displayed.

He might hate Mornay for his betrayal, except that he was dead. And Rogan could also associate with Mornay's wishes to do something for his son. Mornay had never told him about his boy. A pity. He would have done for Mornay's son what Julien had done, without requiring that he sell out his personal integrity. Knowing Mornay, it must have troubled him afterward. His resulting depression was what Derwent had noticed.

Julien chuckled. "The same?"

Rogan met his eye with a hard look that caused Julien to arch his brow.

"Come, come, Rogan. It's not as bad as all that. Had I intended to register the claim for myself, I'd have done so while you were in England. No, you're getting all of Henry's claim, and I'll be content with retrieving the Black Diamond."

"You? Content?" Rogan said with a cool, disbelieving look.

"About the gold on Henry's map? Yes. You may wonder, but yes. I told you one hundred percent, and I meant it. It's yours and Evy's…and your coming child's. Think of the child. You can have it all. Just the way Henry wanted it to be." He poured himself another jigger of liquor. "On one condition."

Rogan smiled wolfishly. "So now we finally get to it. What's the condition?"

"Nothing too difficult. As I've already explained, you'll come with me to the Matopos. Help me retrieve my Black. I don't trust all the men I must take, but you, Retford, and Derwent, I can trust—at least about being shot in the back."

Rogan looked at him. "You think there's someone here who might do so?"

"I don't doubt it for a minute." He took a drag on his tobacco. "You'll be my bodyguard and see that I and the Black are brought back safely and delivered to Kimberly. Do that, and the gold deposit is yours."

Rogan stared at him a long minute without speaking. Was he serious? He could see that he was. The mask was gone from Julien's face, and he appeared almost vulnerable. There was a pitiable look about the haggard face with still a vestige of a handsomeness.

Rogan looked down at the gold falcon in his hand.

"You haven't explained about this. Where did you get it? What has it to do with Henry's deposit?"

"First, you'll need to promise your cooperation on Matopos."

Rogan weighed the falcon in his hand. He was already wealthy without it. With Evy's inheritance they would be doubly wealthy. He also had Rookswood and a chance to make wealth on the three-thousand-acre farm he had here in Rhodesia, thanks to Rhodes's Charter Company and his part in the pioneer trek. No, it wasn't that he wanted Henry's claim to get rich on. It was the need to know the truth after all these years...the need to settle the venture of Henry's map once for all...to fulfill a quest that had nagged at him since childhood. It had caused him years of concern and planning and the investment of his life.

No, it wasn't the gold. It was the adventure of discovery. A *cause* to which he'd given himself since a boy with fanciful dreams, and boasts of finding an answer to Henry Chantry's *secret*.

"I'm waiting," Sir Julien said, breaking the silence. "Well, what do you say, Rogan? Do we have a bargain or not?"

Rogan continued to hold the gold falcon. He'd come too far in his quest to end it now.

"We have a bargain."

"Ah!"

Julien shot down his liquor and banged the glass on the desk. He took the map Mornay had drawn and lit a match to it. As the flames licked and curled the ends of the paper into ash, he spoke casually.

"Ever heard of the ancient ruins of Zimbabwe?"

Rogan looked at him sharply.

"Yes, Zimbabwe. This bird came from there. If you search there you will find the secret of Henry's old map. His gold is an ancient shaft there from yesteryear."

Rogan was elated and furious with himself. He should have guessed Zimbabwe Ruins long ago. Except that Henry had gone to the Zambezi region on his last trek, and it had been his last expedition that they'd all thought held the discovery of gold. The map had intimated Zambezi, not Mashonaland. Had Henry done so deliberately?

"You have a few weeks before anything of importance happens here at Bulawayo. If I were you, I'd go there and satisfy myself that I've directed you properly at last."

Rogan masked his emotions. Evy was with Dr. Jakob. Just where she had wanted to be all along. She would be safe enough. Jakob was a doctor, there was a medical facility right on the station, and Arcilla and

Darinda could visit often. Derwent and Parnell would be at the mission station as well.

"No—keep the bird, my boy, keep it," he said when Rogan began to hand it back. "A token of our bargain," Julien stated with an unpleasant smile. "The thunderbird will make a wondrous souvenir for your son or daughter when they're grown up." He chuckled. "You can tell them all about your Uncle Julien Bley, and what a sinister scoundrel he was in his dark day. They'll most likely be grave and piously utter something typical of a generation or two removed from the time. 'If we had been alive way back then, we wouldn't have been so greedy and *unkind* to the poor natives!'" He laughed coldly, mockingly, as Rogan strode from his office into the common room.

Julien was still laughing when Rogan, frowning to himself, settled his hat on his dark head. It was a Rhodesian style hat, gently curved up on one side and down on the other.

He went out the front door of Government House to where his horse was tied near an acacia tree. Great Zimbabwe.

Rogan stepped into the stirrup and mounted his horse. The gold thunderbird glinted in his hand. He placed it in his jacket and turned the reins to ride toward Parnell's bungalow. He was still frowning as Julien's words echoed in his mind.

The ruins of Zimbabwe were located about twenty-seven kilometers south of Fort Victoria.

Traveling first by C. H. Zeederberg's pioneer stagecoach and mail delivery, then securing horses at Fort Victoria, Rogan, with Parnell, Derwent, and a handful of Basuto, rode to the Valley of Ruins.

Rogan had first returned to Dr. Jakob's Bulawayo Mission to prepare for the trek and to inform Evy in a nonchalant fashion that he would be gone for two weeks. She had surprised him with her cooperation. Then again, two weeks to search out Zimbabwe wasn't a thousand miles north to the Zambezi. He knew that she was also trying to reach out to him to make amends for deceiving him about their coming baby. Rogan remained angry over the deceit. *Stubborn,* she had said, was he?

"Do not let the sun go down on your wrath," Dr. Jakob had confided to him before he rode out of the station. "Unresolved anger leads to a hardness of heart."

He was still in love with her; naturally he would be. When he'd held her in his arms the night before they rode out, she had asked him if he still loved her. What a question! And yet he'd felt angry inside over Julien, over Anthony's death, about Henry's map, about most things, and he had answered her shortly. The fact that he had done so troubled him now, days later as he rode toward Zimbabwe. "Naturally I love you. You're still a beautiful woman, aren't you?" It had been a base thing to say, and if he hadn't been out of sorts with her, with himself, and everything around him, he would have been more reassuring about how he felt about her.

Derwent was singing; Parnell was looking bored, but sober. He hadn't wanted to come, but Rogan had forced the issue.

"For a few weeks you've got a bodyguard," Rogan had said before they left the mission. "Between me and Derwent there'll be no Rhodesian beer. Besides, this way Derwent can preach at you. Maybe you'll learn to stay sober on your own."

Rogan slowed his horse and dropped back beside his brother. "I've traversed these ruins before with Mornay. I don't see how Julien can be right. There's nothing there."

"When did you see the ruins?"

"On Rhodes's pioneer trek."

"I didn't see you go off."

Rogan smiled and shrugged. "You were too occupied trying to please Darinda."

Rogan thought again about his uncle. He felt a rise of frustration. "I should have understood Henry better. He expected me to."

Parnell looked about uneasily. "Not an easy thing to have done. Who knew the thoughts of Henry? He was always secretive. A strange one, I always thought."

Derwent said, "It sure never entered my thinking that the gold on Mr. Henry's old map was here."

Rogan resettled his hat. "Henry used Zambezi on his map for orientation. Just to show where north was. A man as canny as Henry could never have made such a mistake. He was quite the trekker."

Derwent rubbed his nose. "Aye, and maybe he did it to kind of protect his discovery? That way, if the map was stolen from him, then they couldn't find his deposit."

"C'mon, Derwent," Parnell said impatiently, swatting at an insect. "That would be a fool thing for him to do. He left the map to Rogan to find the claim. How can he find it if Henry gives him a misleading map?" He glanced at Rogan. "Unless Uncle Henry was a trifle moldy upstairs."

"Hardly that."

"Well, then—"

"That's not what I mean, Mr. Parnell, about disguising the map. I mean, maybe it was just the *emblems* that were important, that your uncle wanted to impress on Mr. Rogan."

"Perhaps," Rogan muttered. "But I would have needed something else to direct me to Zimbabwe. Otherwise the emblems wouldn't have helped either."

"Sure. And maybe it was the gold thunderbird he used," Derwent said. "Soon as you saw it on Julien's desk, you was alerted to think of Zimbabwe. Most people do. So did Sir Julien. Where did Sir Julien get that gold bird anyway?"

Rogan slowed his horse and came to a stop. Gripping the leather reins he turned the horse to face Derwent, who had also pulled up with Parnell.

Rogan stared at Derwent. Parnell, too, gaped at him.

Derwent flushed and lowered his hat.

"Go on," Rogan said in a low, urgent voice.

"Well—I've been doing some hard thinking ever since we left the mission. Thinking about what Dr. Jakob said about Zimbabwe and how some folks thought it was the land of Ophir in the Bible. Seems to me Henry Chantry would know that kind of talk about South Africa too, and a lot more about ancient history, same as Dr. Jakob. What's to say, Mr. Rogan, that Mr. Henry didn't leave you only the map, but that gold bird? If so, he would have expected you to recognize it as the Zimbabwe bird on the map."

"Well, well," Parnell murmured and looked with enthusiasm at Rogan. "Uncle Julien did come to Rookswood often enough while we were growing up. How many times did you catch him on the third floor in Henry's room sneaking around?"

"Too many times. You're right, Derwent. This bird could very well have been left to me, and Julien found it. Except he obviously didn't connect it with the map until recently because he hadn't seen the map."

"Not until Mornay drew it for him," Parnell said.

"Derwent, old friend," Rogan said, reaching over and swatting his shoulder, "I think you've unveiled it."

Derwent looked embarrassed. Rogan removed the gold bird from his saddlebag and looked at it, holding it to catch the rays of the sun as it shone and glittered in the light.

"This all couldn't be a trap, could it?" Parnell mused. "After Anthony, there's little to surprise me."

"I thought of a trap first thing." Rogan swiveled in his saddle and with narrowed gaze studied the layout of the land. There was open yellowed grassland beneath flat-topped acacia trees along the crest of the ridge.

"Do you see that rocky kopje?"

Parnell and Derwent turned their heads eastward to where Rogan pointed.

"Yes, what about it?" Parnell asked.

"Plenty. Do you know what that distant blue summit is called?"

"The Sentinel," Derwent said.

"Do you notice its shape?"

"A crouching lion," Parnell said with a bit of surprise in his voice.

"It fits the map, too. Henry drew the lion facing Zimbabwe. All right," Rogan said at last. "Let's have a look." He smiled. "Who knows?" He patted his pocket where the gold bird was out of sight again. "This may be the beginning of the end."

CHAPTER TWENTY-FIVE

Rogan sat astride his horse, gazing down from the brow of the hill. The Valley of Ruins was below in the amber-colored brush and grasses. Zimbabwe's past glory was visible beneath the blue sky and hot sun, though no longer as a walled fortress, but as heaps of stone with a mysterious history, reminding him of bleached bones after a massive battle, bones scattered across the valley like some puzzling maze.

Dr. Jakob had identified the one remaining standing structure as a temple. "An elliptical building," he had said. Was he right? And was it shaped this way by these particular ancients to follow the course of the planets?

The Basuto guides found an easier trail down the kopje into the sun-warmed valley, leading the way on foot, leading the mules laden with their supplies. Rogan, Parnell, and Derwent maneuvered their horses down through the dry brush. The sweet, poignant smell of sun-baked brush filled the air. The wind rippled the heads of the ripening grasses, causing a sleepy rustling sound.

Reaching the valley floor, Rogan spurred his horse forward toward the granite walls. But he had not taken lightly what Parnell had said about a trap. With his .45 securely belted, he slowly dismounted, his eyes busy, looking for any sign of danger. He had not yet told his brother or Derwent about Julien's bargain about the Matopos. He thought Julien was clean in his offer about the gold, though Rogan knew he'd been fooled before.

Parnell and Derwent soon joined him, and the Basuto led the horses and mules to a secure spot.

Rogan walked through the tall grasses in the open space, but his boots were calf-length, his breeches stuffed inside, and unless an unwary snake happened to strike at his knee, he was moderately safe.

The sight of the standing walls and broken heaps of smooth stone were enough to spur Rogan's imagination, as it must have Henry's so long ago.

"Aye," said Derwent, pushing his hat back from his eyes and lifting his head to gaze up at the huge stone wall.

"Must be ten meters high in some places, Mr. Rogan."

"All made from smooth stones of uniform size, too, and no mortar," Parnell said.

"The construction is complex," Rogan said with a measuring glance. "There's little proof, if any, that the present tribes produced such a skilled building program as this. If so, why aren't there more ruins like Zimbabwe all over South Africa? The tribes are nomadic. They're not city builders."

"Dr. Jakob says there's a big debate about that," Derwent offered.

"Then who were the men who built Zimbabwe? What happened to them?" Parnell asked in a tone that expected no answer. "These ruins are still a riddle the archaeologists can't answer."

"There's much the archaeologists and scientists don't know," Derwent stated. He ran his fingers through his hair. "Maybe the builders were miners who were sent by the Queen of Sheba—seeing as this area might be the Ophir of the Scriptures."

Rogan had met and spoken with Jakob van Buren at the Bulawayo Mission before leaving there with Parnell and Derwent for Fort Victoria. Jakob had mentioned many ancient artifacts and gold jewelry found here, including giant soapstone eaglelike birds, some carried off to museums, including those in Germany.

Then there were the usual tales of hidden caches of gold and jewels, as well. Rogan was troubled. Could this be what Henry had in mind?

Had it all been some wild figment of his fever-crazed imagination? Had he somehow convinced himself of a gold deposit where there was only mystery?

Yet he could not accept this explanation either. Henry Chantry had not been any more fanciful than Rogan.

Who built Zimbabwe? "No one knows," Dr. Jakob had stated over dinner to Rogan. "Men have always hunted for gold and ivory. Jezebel and Ahab's palace in Samaria was a treasure chest of gold, and it held tremendous amounts of ivory, too. Arabs have also spoken of gold mines in this area of Africa in the eleventh century.

"There have been ancient gold mines here from the times of the African rulers of Monomatapa. Those chieftains, or kings if you prefer, traded with the Portuguese during the sixteenth and seventeenth centuries. Whether an African tribe built these ruins, or the Arab traders, or the ancient Romans, or some other group, it's all uncertain. King Solomon, too, had his miners. Scripture says he had many ships sent out to bring back gold."

And Dr. Jakob had whipped out his battered old Bible and flipped to what he said was Second Chronicles, chapter nine, and read in his gravelly voice with its odd Dutch and South African accent: "For the king's ships went to Tarshish with the servants of Hiram. Once every three years the merchant ships came, bringing gold, silver, ivory, apes, and monkeys. So King Solomon surpassed all the kings of the earth in riches and wisdom."

Apes for King Solomon's zoo sounded to Rogan as if his ships had sailed to Africa.

"Maybe Dr. Jakob was right," Rogan said, feeling the hot sun on his shoulders and back as he gazed at the wall.

"Sure could be, Mr. Rogan. Solomon's miners may have come here for gold and apes. Then forgot the mines when Solomon died and his son Rehoboam took over. As Jakob had said, Israel was divided after Solomon's death with ten tribes in the north, and Judah and Benjamin in the south under King Rehoboam. The mines would have fallen into disuse as wars rolled across Israel until they were taken captive into Babylon."

Rogan passed through a crumbling gap in the massive walls. Stones crunched beneath his boots as he walked up to a conical structure. A temple? "Let's have a look around."

There was a second inner wall about a meter distant that ran parallel. Rogan entered that passage with Derwent and Parnell in single file behind. The passage was narrow and dark, and they sometimes climbed some steps, and sometimes descended. Rogan rounded a curve, and the passage widened into what was probably a religious enclosure of sorts.

"Doesn't look sacred to me," Derwent complained, wiping his brow on the back of his sleeve.

"You have no imagination, Vicar Derwent," Parnell taunted. "You want music, candles, and bells."

"I want truth, Mr. Parnell. I can do without all the religious trappings as long as Dr. Jakob teaches the Scriptures."

"Here, look at that," Rogan said.

In the center of the area there was a cone-shaped obelisk. Rogan guessed it to be nine meters high and maybe five or six at the base. There was also a large, raised flat block of stone to one side of the obelisk.

"What do you think it's for?" Parnell grimaced. He was back to his fastidious ways. He took out a neat white handkerchief and blotted his forehead.

Rogan looked at it questioningly. "Well, Parnell, I'd say it suggests an altar of sorts. Maybe when the stars and planets were in the right positions, the Zimbabweans, like other pagan races, offered sacrifices to their planetary gods. What do you say?"

"Aye, an altar, most likely. The people who lived after Noah built a great ziggurat, and at the top was an altar. They offered human sacrifices to what they thought was the sun god."

"After the Flood? Rather extraordinary! Hadn't they learned their lesson? They couldn't have been dense enough to think the sun god had defeated the flood god." Parnell shook his head. "But why sacrifices, I wonder…"

"It's important that there were true and false sacrifices, Mr. Parnell. After the sin in the Garden of Eden, God told Abel to bring a lamb as a sacrifice for his sin. The lamb was a picture of the Savior who would die on the altar of the cross for the sins of the whole world. When Jesus was pointed out as the Savior, John the Baptist said, 'Behold! The Lamb of God who takes away the sin of the world.'"

Derwent pointed to the flat block at the side of the central cone. "But this was only one of many places where there was a false sacrificial system. The people who lived and spread over the whole earth after the Flood made up their own religions, degrading some of the truths their ancestors knew. They offered sinful sacrifices to the sun, moon, stars, and planets. They turned away from the true and living God to make idols of things in His creation, to nature—the sun, moon, and stars—to gods of spiritual darkness, to demons, and even to Satan himself. All that nagging stuff—the sacrificed chicken and the hakata divining bones— all that comes from the prince of darkness. He has plenty of sway here. And that's why missionaries like Robert Moffat are so greatly needed."

Parnell frowned. "Hakata divining bones—very dark rituals indeed. There's nothing good about that."

"Nothing at all," Rogan said briefly. "But the God who made heaven and earth has both justice and love, justice to require a penalty for evil, and love to be willing to become the innocent suffering sacrifice for the guilty. As Derwent quoted about Jesus, 'Behold the lamb of God which takes away the sin of the world.'"

Parnell rubbed his forehead. "Say, little brother, where'd you learn all this?"

"Vicar Edmund Havering, Rectory of St. Graves Parish, Grimston Way." He smiled. "I listened, old boy."

"Ha! You and those books on South Africa you smuggled in! All right…and that's why we took communion at the chapel, right? The bread and the cup, for His sacrifice on the cross."

Derwent smiled. "You said it right, Mr. Parnell. We do it because Jesus said to, so we would remember His death until He comes again. But you got to have Christ in your heart, or it's just another ritual. Almost like all that hokey-pokey—witchcraft."

Parnell grimaced. "Thanks for the warning, Derwent."

Rogan had walked over to one end where there were several trees growing. He stood, hands on hips, studying them. The trees were rounded, with dense leaves, and offered welcome areas of cooler shadow.

"But it's not a baobab tree."

"And no bird or lion, either," Parnell said wearily. "I'm beginning to think all this is Uncle Julien's folly. Or maybe it's a trap to do us in."

"We could sure use some optimism, Mr. Parnell."

"Yeah. Well, I've reason to be suspicious of Sir Julien Bley."

"To be truthful, I'm a bit uneasy myself about all this. Seems odd to me how Sir Julien just ups and tells Mr. Rogan what he's discovered about the Zimbabwe Ruins."

Rogan as yet had not told either Derwent or Parnell about Julien's bargain to let him have all the gold discovered from Henry's map.

"You two can continue to indulge in your doubts and suspicions all you want, but I'm going to keep looking around."

Outside, standing near the massive wall, Rogan gazed toward the other side of the valley where the hills lifted again toward the brazen blue sky. A few isolated white clouds drifted easily. He studied the second area of Zimbabwe known among archaeologists as the Acropolis. The stone ruins topped a low hill and stared down across the valley as though on guard. *Probably was used as a fortress,* he thought.

Derwent and Parnell walked up.

"There's a path that goes up there," Rogan said. "Let's have a look."

"I'm going to be famished tonight," Parnell complained. "And, Derwent, tell those guards I don't want to eat any more of those mealies!"

The steps, cut out of stone, were exceedingly steep and so narrow that they had to climb single file—no doubt to keep invaders from rushing up by the hundreds to take the fortress. Was it true what Dr. Jakob had told him at the mission? Jakob, who had long been a friend of the tribes and their chieftains, had heard tales in abundance about the ruins of Zimbabwe. Jakob had taken him aside before Rogan left and told him what he'd heard from a deposed induna on the Zambezi years ago. The induna claimed that when he was a boy he'd heard his father say that there was another way out of the fortress of Zimbabwe by way of a tunnel. The tunnel was supposed to have gone through the hill to the other side. Neither the induna's father nor Jakob knew how to find the tunnel if it existed.

Had Henry discovered the tunnel? What had Henry said about fleeing for his life when under attack by Mashona? Was it possible his guide, an old bushman, might have known about the tunnel and led him to safety? Then why hadn't Henry made it clear on the map?

Rogan reached the top of the rocky ascent of the Acropolis, where the end was so low that he had to stoop. He came out high above the Valley of Ruins.

The wind roughed his hair and tried to push him backward. There was an excellent view of the valley, the stone walls, and beyond to the veld and hills.

Rogan took his map and opened it with its rough edges riffling in the breeze. Derwent and Parnell stood on either side of him, bending their heads to see Henry's emblems: the bird, the lion, and the baobab tree.

Rogan looked up and around him.

"I don't see a baobab tree anywhere," Parnell said. "About the birds...I've heard they were large, sinister, eaglelike or falconlike, and carved out of soapstone. They were raised high on tall pillars." He pointed below as though he could see them now. "Strange thing about those birds, Rogan. The Ndebele indunas are talking of the birds... I just now remembered—guess I wasn't all there at the bungalow the night Anthony was found dead."

Rogan looked at him curiously. "The indunas? What do they say?"

"It was something Captain Retford mentioned. He told Peter he expected trouble with the tribal warriors. Retford knows a young Ndebele warrior. His father was one of the indunas that Lobengula had his council smell out for spellcasting against him. The indunas are saying that the bird images flew from the Great Zimbabwe. Now there will be no peace in Matabeleland."

The news was troubling. Especially with Julien's notion of entry into their sacred Matopos to unseal Lobengula's burial cave.

"The indunas say this among themselves?"

"They say the Umlimo is telling the indunas of war and trouble. But it was the birds that I was thinking of just now. Like that golden bird you have. And Uncle Henry's drawing. Do you think the indunas are talking about the same birds?"

"Must be." Rogan took it from his pocket, comparing it again to the one on Henry's drawing. He looked at Parnell. "Looks identical, wouldn't you say?"

Parnell nodded, then looked around them. "So what do the indunas mean when they say the birds have flown from Zimbabwe?"

"Lost power, most likely. What's disturbing is, if they're talking like this, then they have a longing to get their power back. That's normal, but it's bad for the Company pioneers here building farms and stores." He thought of Evy again…and worried. He'd told himself he could go away on a trek and not think about her for a few weeks, but that wasn't proving true. He thought of her constantly. Either the trek had lost its appeal, or he had changed. He felt restless and concerned, not because he wanted to be out on some adventure, but because he wanted to finish the adventure, solve the mystery, and get back to Evy.

"The more I compare Henry's map with this area, the more I'm convinced this is it."

"Sure was a surprise to me." Derwent squinted off toward the hills. "Sure surprised me about Mornay, too. I still can't reconcile his betraying us the way he did. Even if it was to send his son to Cambridge. No wonder he was unhappy toward the end. I think it got to his conscience."

"We can forget all that," Rogan said shortly, still feeling the loss of Mornay. "It's all over. And I hold him no grudge."

"Well, it's all over down here," Derwent said. "But it's just beginning when we step over to the other side of death. I suspect all this gold and diamonds won't mean a thing to us then."

Parnell looked at him crossly. "Can't you stop preaching at us for five minutes?"

"I wasn't preaching at you, but to myself—"

"Well, never mind. Start looking for that baobab tree," Parnell said testily.

Derwent straightened his hat. "I'll start exploring, Mr. Rogan, I think over on that ridge."

"All right, but we stay together, Derwent. We can't be too careful. Keep that Winchester handy."

"I'm a good shot, Mr. Rogan." He started off toward the slope in his ambling stride.

"We should all be back here by the time the sun's shadows are on the wall face," Rogan called after him.

Derwent raised a hand and continued on his way.

Rogan had started to follow Derwent, then turned to look at Parnell. "Let's keep together, Parnell. We'll go inspect Derwent's ridge."

Parnell was sitting on a rock checking his rifle, looking as though he didn't intend to move before sundown. "Gullible, that's what the old bean is."

"Not as much as you think. He's the decent sort."

"I know, I know…" He laid his rifle across his knees. "I'll wait here and have a bit of a nap."

"Get up, you lazy mongrel. You'll need to catch up."

Parnell groaned as he pushed himself up. "All a pot of nonsense, if you ask me. All right, I'm going. Need to keep Derwent from falling into a cockatrice den."

Rogan smiled. He could have mentioned Parnell's failure to shoot the spitting cobra that Darinda had faced a year or so ago.

"If I run into a lion, a bird, or a baobab tree," Parnell said with mild sarcasm, "I'll fire my rifle twice."

Rogan tilted his head and gave him a wry look. He pushed him on the shoulder. "Good man, now get moving."

Parnell took off after Derwent as Rogan stood on the hill with the golden grasses waving hypnotically about his boots.

He looked after them, hand on hip. He sighed and shook his head wearily. *Dear old Henry, why couldn't you have made things clear and simple? What was this with you, a game?* After a moment he turned and strode purposefully after them.

He avoided the wild ebony plants, his boots stirring dust over the dry ground, as he stepped more quickly. Was there a secret tunnel to the other side of the hill? How would he know even if providence would lead him to its entrance?

"Maybe Mr. Henry didn't mean to look for a real image of a bird, a lion, and a certain tree," Derwent said as he walked along with Rogan and Parnell Chantry. They had reached the top of the ridge. Rogan stopped and was glancing about thoughtfully.

"Well, we didn't expect there was going to be a real lion walking down through the yellow grasses," Parnell said with a smirky smile. "Nor a great bird flapping its wings at us."

"I know that, Mr. Parnell. That's not what I mean."

"Well, what do you mean?"

"I'm not sure, but this here whole venture seems—"

A bullet whined past Rogan's ear, striking a rock beside him, spraying chips.

"Hit the ground," he shouted, drawing his .45 and firing two shots toward the brush where he'd heard the shot come from, then rolling away into the cover of a bush.

Bullets thudded, kicked up grit where a moment earlier he'd hit the ground on his belly. Another bullet splintered rock. Rifle shots zinged and ricocheted off the nearby rocks, forcing him to keep his head down.

Where were his brother and Derwent? Were they hit?

CHAPTER TWENTY-SIX

Bulawayo Mission

Evy's first meeting with her mother's blood cousin Dr. Jakob van Buren had been affectionate. They not only had a van Buren connection, but as he'd said right off, "We're eternally united in the family of God."

Jakob did not disappoint her expectations. The big Dutchman had flowing silver hair that made her think of a horse's flying mane when it was running free, enjoying liberty. He wore a typical long beard, Boer style, and he dressed almost always in dusty white, except for his Rhodesian-style hat, this one with a speckled feather stuck in its brim, and rugged Boer leather boots. His eyes, a faded blue, were small and sharp, but kindly eyes that welcomed her with genuine warmth when she'd arrived with Rogan.

Dr. Jakob had been carrying a photograph of Katie in his worn Bible, and he had shown it to her and Rogan at once.

"Well, there you are twenty-some odd years ago. You look just like her. Don't you think so, Rogan?"

Rogan's mouth tipped below his dark ribbon mustache, and his brown eyes glinted. "Not only is Mrs. Chantry the mirror image of Katie in appearance, Doctor, but she's inherited Katie's sprightly spirit."

Evy felt her cheeks warm, but Dr. Jakob couldn't know the content of Rogan's words.

"Well, here she is, Doctor," Rogan said cheerfully. "I've brought her here to you. And we've come by way of storms and swells to get her here too." He looked at her with a disarming smile. "Haven't we, Evy? And we've exciting news, as well. Evy is going to have a baby while she's here."

"A baby?" Dr. Jakob put his arm around her and hugged her with a pat on her head. "Well, bless our God. Isn't that a celebration!"

"And a surprise," Rogan said, folding his arms across his chest and smiling at her. "Nothing like a surprise to add spice to life. My son will be a Rhodesian."

"Son?" chuckled Dr. Jakob. "What if I want a niece?" And he turned to Evy. "Well, I want to be an uncle. 'Uncle Jakob'—that's what you will call me."

In the weeks that followed, Evy had gotten to know Jakob well. She'd had the privilege of aiding him in the medical ward just as she'd hoped and planned. Jakob had told her all about Katie, as much as he knew. "She had a heart as big as life," he said. "Only thing was, she was not submissive to her God. Her strengths became her weaknesses, and her bright spirit and adventurous ways led to calamity. But she loved you, Evy. She fought for you. She would not give you up. And because she had a weak faith in God in a time of crisis, she didn't turn to Him in her dilemma but relied on her own schemes. Not that her desires were wrong, but they needed to be directed by the purposes of God."

Evy had heard a hundred tales about Katie, some humorous and warm, others showing her stubborn willfulness. In the end she knew she was more like her mother than she would have thought.

Perhaps Dr. Jakob had guessed the cracked and hurting relationship between her and Rogan because one Sunday morning his message titled "The Daughters of Sarah" fit her very well.

"Now Abraham failed to trust in the Lord during a famine, and he went down into Egypt. He was afraid of what would happen to him because Sarah was a beautiful woman. So he told his wife to say she was his sister. Now, Sarah could have refused. When the king saw Sarah and took her to add to his harem, she could have taken matters into her own hands, but she depended on the Lord to protect and deliver her, and He did. She called Abram her 'lord' and submitted to him. She submitted because she believed she was submitting to an even higher authority, God. And it was God and her trust in Him that delivered her."

Evy drew her own conclusions as Dr. Jakob's message went on. If she had truly been trusting in the Lord, she would not have needed to deceive Rogan about her pregnancy in order to come to Bulawayo. She would have told him the truth from the very start and depended on the Lord to bring to pass His purpose for her. If He had wanted her here now, He could have worked in Rogan's heart. Instead, she had schemed, taken matters into her own hands, and so she had not only failed to trust God, but betrayed the trust between her and Rogan.

Yet confessing this to Rogan seemed the hardest thing that had ever stared her in the face. Somehow there was always a reason to delay, to try to pretend the anger would just go away and not leave a permanent stain. But the matter did not go away, and the longer it remained, the harder it was to deal with. So that it was easier to pretend all was right between them. And much of the time it appeared so.

Evy found she liked Dr. Jakob for his honesty, his selfless giving to the African tribesmen who came seeking his help. While Rogan was away, which became more frequent, she often talked long into the warm nights with Jakob, so that she felt she knew the van Burens in the Boer state of the Transvaal as well. She worried what would become of them in the war.

It was February, Rhodesia's late summer, and the first bloom of dawn was already hot. A yellow stain bled into the paler blue sky above the sunburnt veld that yawned toward the ominous Matopos Hills.

An eerie silence cloaked Dr. Jakob van Buren's Bulawayo Mission. A crocodile slipped with a whoosh down the bank into the dark waters, and some pelicans broke the stillness by flapping their wings and flying north. A monkey chattered uneasily and left its branches to disappear deeper into the still dark trees.

Evy Chantry awakened in the round, beehive-shaped hut with thick wheat-colored thatch, and for a moment she peered into the first light of dawn, listening. For the last two months she'd lived here with Rogan, though for much of that time he'd been coming and going, sometimes not showing up for several days at a time. Their marriage, thought Evy with grief, was teetering on the brink of disaster. *Oh, Father God, how could something so wonderful have ended like this? Why did it happen?*

Down deep in her heart she knew the answer. She had thought it necessary to deceive him because of her lack of trust in him to make the right decision. Wounded, Rogan could not, *would not,* forgive her. She'd had her reasons to keep the matter of her baby to herself. *Her* baby. Perhaps that idea had been part of the problem? Although she'd never even realized it, her emotions had settled on the idea that this baby was solely *her* responsibility; in keeping it secret, the baby had wrongly become hers, not *ours.*

At the time, her reasons to keep the news from him had made sense to her. If not right, at least she'd felt her reasons were justified. Rogan was controlling. He wouldn't have let her come otherwise. She scowled. She was used to doing as she wanted. But Rogan insisted she had failed to trust in his character and leadership.

She sighed. Could they ever move beyond this? she wondered.

She remained in bed, listening. For what? She didn't know. Everything had grown so still. That was it, so *unusually* still. For the two months she'd been here, each new day came alive with the riot of squawking birds, squealing monkeys, and the trumpeting of a small herd of elephants that came down to the river for their morning wallow. But this morning they'd all quite suddenly become silent.

She continued to listen, scarcely breathing. Her hand reached across the bed, but of course, it was empty. Rogan had left with Parnell and Derwent for the Great Zimbabwe Ruins. He'd said he'd return in two weeks. Three weeks had now come and gone, and there was no word.

Surely he would return soon. She missed him terribly, but a rush of hurtful memories also flooded her heart. The lack of forgiveness between them had become a wall as high and thick as any ancient ruin at Zimbabwe.

The low murmur of the Khami River came in through the bungalow window. She'd resisted open windows in the hut to the bitter end, but there'd been little choice about that, since all of Jakob's bungalows were constructed this way due to the heat. For that matter, if anyone wanted to attack the mission station and burn it to the ground, a windowpane wouldn't stop them. Nothing would, "Except God," Dr. Jakob had interjected when they'd discussed the matter with Rogan. Rogan, too, had frowned about the open window.

"We are all here as secure as the will of our sovereign heavenly Father," Jakob liked to say. Those words fitly spoken like apples of gold in settings of silver usually quieted everyone down, even Arcilla.

True, indeed. Evy quoted Psalm 34:7 aloud: "The angel of the LORD encamps all around those who fear Him, and delivers them." She wasn't thinking of attackers, but nasty bugs. She wasn't as hysterical about them as Arcilla, but neither was she as stalwart as Darinda. The "itchy" insects were a ghastly horror. She frowned, feeling sorry for herself, and scratching her arm. It was time to get up. She wanted her hot sweet tea. Thank God for Mrs. Croft!

She tossed aside the thin coverlet and sat up. The windless morning grew lighter and hotter. Her head ached again. She was listless. She felt as though she weighed a ton. She reached her palms to her swollen belly and prayed for them both. *Both* of them? And her husband and father?

Rogan will return soon. No use being a dullard, Evy Chantry. You're here in this condition, my dear, because it's exactly what you wanted. So get up and be of some use around here.

The sunlight fell across the worn, bare, hand-planed table of heavy mukwa wood, where her hairbrush, hand mirror, and personal items were arranged. Her Bible was there too, still open to where she'd been reading last night through the Old Testament book of Joel: "The field is wasted, the land mourns."

Rhodesia was undergoing a terrible drought, an increase in locusts, and a cattle disease. According to Dr. Jakob the indunas blamed it on the rule of the white man. The spirit gods of the Matopos were not happy.

Evy looked down cautiously before stepping onto the woven mat rug that covered the cow dung floor that had been polished into a smooth, rock hardness.

She walked to the window and looked out.

The clear light told her it must be nearing six o'clock. She breathed in the faint dawn breeze that whispered through the trees and tall grasses growing along the river's bank. The whitewashed walls of the mission reflected the dull yellow glow of the brightening sunrise.

Evy smiled, certain she would never get used to living among lions, elephants, crocodiles, all manner of poisonous snakes and spiders. Rhodesia was a new world, and aside from her personal difficulties, she was quite happy to get to know her mother's cousin, a dear saintly man who bade her call him "Uncle Jakob." She was thrilled to do so, to be here, though she longed for Rogan's return, and sometimes the hardships of the mission station made her sigh for the soft home comforts she'd taken for granted and left in Grimston Way.

Great birds, whose names she had yet to learn, circled and flew in shadows across the mellowing sky. It was the horizon that continued to hold her attention now. There was a dark casting look to it, like a strange cloud moving toward them. According to what Dr. Jakob told her yesterday, the rainy season was not due for some time yet. Could there be grass fires somewhere?

The door to Dr. Jakob's bungalow opened, and he stepped out onto his *stoep* to begin what she knew would be his typical busy day. Evy watched him with a certain family pride. It seemed strange to know she even had a family member.

Jakob carried his scarred leather medical bag in one brown hand, while using the other to place a little pair of glass spectacles on his aristocratic nose. He stepped down to the swept earth to begin his tour of patients before the family-style breakfast in the common room, where they congregated for meals, fellowship, prayer, and Bible study.

Evy leaned out and smiled a welcome.

"Morning, Jakob," she called cheerfully.

"You're just the pretty face I want to see this morning. Mrs. Croft, that dear woman, is feeling her arthritis today. Can you come down to the medical ward and assist me before breakfast? Do you feel well enough?"

She sighed but smiled cheerfully to him. Any idea that she might feel listless would garner too much attention when others needed his time far more than she.

"I'll be right over," she called.

Evy let the reed curtain fall back into place and turned away from the window to hurry and dress.

The fashionable tight-fitting sleek skirts and bodices of London fashion were simply not practical here, not that she could wear them now anyway. She wore a simple light blue cotton top that hung wide and loose over a full skirt that reached just above the ankles. She was far from dressing in fashion, she thought wryly. Out here there were few European women, and they dressed as they pleased. Darinda wore riding habits, and the wives and daughters of the colonial farmers wore a hodge-podge of things they'd brought. Only Arcilla retained high fashion, and much of that was to her personal detriment. She was always tearing her fancy skirts or breaking a heel on her shoes, and then wailing about how long it took to get the new clothes she sent for from Capetown.

Evy found a clean pocketed apron that slipped over her head and tied it in the back. *I almost look like a nurse,* she thought, pleased. She brushed and braided her tawny, thick hair, then pinned the braids out of the way.

Some ten minutes later she came out of the hut to confront the hot morning.

Near the huts, the once eight-foot-tall poinsettia bushes, more like small trees, were dried up and dying. The bougainvillea were stunted and struggling to survive the drought.

Mrs. Croft came from what she called the scullery hut, bearing a mug of black tea. Despite what Jakob had said about her being a bit under the weather, Mrs. Croft looked as robust as always, tall and big-boned, her iron gray hair brushed back from her oblong face into a no-nonsense bun.

"Pah! You'll not be going among the sick and dying without the bracing bit of English tea."

Evy drank the tasty brew and placed the cup back on the small, round tray. "Is Alice up?"

"I'm bringing her some tea now. Alice is to lend me a hand in the garden. That corn's shriveling up like a prune. We need to get it picked this morning. It never did grow well." She shaded her eyes and looked up at the sun. "What we need the Lord to do is bring us some rain."

"Not this time of year," Evy said sadly, looking about at the sparse green. "According to Dr. Jakob there wasn't any rain last year in the rainy season. The river is dangerously low."

"Well, we've got to get down to the garden and start picking that corn before it's so tough we can't eat it. Never thought I'd see the day when Alice would join me in the standing corn! She was always too hoity-toity for muddying her hands. I'll have to admit marriage to Derwent was a good thing for 'em both."

It was true. There was a change in Alice. Evy had noticed it as soon as they met. The silly, mincing girl with her nose in the air of some years back had matured into a woman with three growing children, all of whom, a boy and two freckle-faced girls, were already reading the Bible and saying how "good and kind" Jesus was to them. How time and the challenges of life changed things! Evy thought.

Derwent's influence on Alice and his children was commendable indeed.

"The good Lord knows what He's about," Mrs. Croft nodded again. "All those events we worried ourselves sick about are far behind us now."

Yes, now we have new problems, Evy thought. *Worse problems. Oh, Rogan...*

Evy managed a paper smile. "So you think I did well to marry Rogan Chantry after all?"

Mrs. Croft sniffed. She shook out the dregs from the teacup and watched the dry dust rush to lick it up.

"He's gone off and left you. And you far along too." She eyed Evy's waistline as though weighing and measuring the growing baby.

Evy kept smiling. She knew Mrs. Croft worried about her, and Rogan. Although Mrs. Croft wouldn't admit it, she had a growing affection for Rogan and also worried about how he'd taken Evy's "fib." "I told you and told you, you should have let him know you was going to have a child."

She said to Mrs. Croft, "It can also be said that Derwent has left Alice, too—*and* three children. Rogan's due back any day."

"So you say. He was supposed to be back from those ancient ruins in two weeks."

Evy threw back her shoulders. "I'll come down and help in the garden later too." She turned and walked toward the medical ward, where the convalescents awaited attention.

"You come, but you'll sit in the shade."

Evy walked the path toward the ward, her limp hardly noticeable, but she weighed more now, being pregnant, and her back ached all the more. She sighed. *I feel like I'm a hundred.*

If she were fair with Rogan, she would admit that her success had a great deal to do with his faithfulness to her since their marriage back at Grimston Way. He had stayed beside her for months, working with her on the special exercises to strengthen her back and legs. It hadn't been until he believed she was feeling well that he'd gone to Zimbabwe.

That gold Zimbabwean bird, she thought again. *How intriguing.* If she'd been able, she would have liked to go there herself and see the mysterious ruins. Was Sir Julien right? Was Zimbabwe the secret place that held Henry Chantry's gold deposit? An ancient mine, perhaps?

Evy rubbed the small frown away from between her brows and walked on, determined not to allow Rogan's absence to upset her. She must stay happy and in good health for their baby.

Dr. Jakob's thirty-bed medical ward was ahead, shaded by trees. The patients, mostly Shona, were suffering from malaria. Their families had brought them here and stayed, living on the mission. The families all helped work the big garden and orchard to supply maize and other vegetables for both the mission and the Christian Shona.

The ward, the little chapel with its white cross, and the attendant buildings, all with sturdy thatch roofs, stood some distance from the private huts, while the rust-colored Matopos Hills gazed down sullenly on the compound.

The large vegetable gardens with sections of standing corn stretched down past "Jakob's well" toward the low banks of the shrinking river. The growing but stunted corn stood with stalks and leaves curling in the morning heat.

Already some of the Christian Shona, considered part of "Jakob's family," were headed toward the field with primitive garden tools and buckets for sparse watering.

Below the corn, the red-brown earth was shaded by the dying leaves from pumpkins just beginning to show orange. The pumpkins were small. Nothing like the big round ones they grew in Grimston Way, where water was plentiful in the growing season.

Dr. Jakob had told her it was his godly ambition to make Bulawayo Mission eventually carry on in the same blessed fashion as Kuruman, which had prospered under that great and godly missionary Robert Moffat. "I want the Shona and Ndebele Christians working side by side. There must be plentiful gardens and fruit trees for all, each family working and providing for its own. No laziness, no free food, but godly discipline and thankfulness. We'll feed hundreds of the African natives, we'll teach them Christian hymns, and one day the Scriptures will be in their languages."

Evy entered the medical ward and stopped in the open doorway until her eyes adjusted to the dimness. Dr. Jakob was busy treating the recuperating, but several patients were in a fevered daze.

Evy walked up to where he sat on a hollowed-out log bench. The Shona girl must have been around fifteen, but already she was mature in body. She was naked from the waist up, but Dr. Jakob showed no embarrassment or unease. He seemed used to the women, both Shona and Ndebele, who wore practically no clothes at all. They were all bare-breasted with only loincloths or thigh-length leather skirts, and bangles and beads.

At first she had been embarrassed by the near nakedness, and Mrs. Croft had been quite shocked when they first arrived. After months in Matabeleland and on the outskirts of Bulawayo, they had slowly adjusted to the sight. Nothing could be done about it. Only in the chapel during Bible reading and prayer did Dr. Jakob have her, Alice, and Mrs. Croft hand out "gowns." These were mere square sections of cotton cloth with a hole cut in the center, which the women willingly slipped over their heads. Evidently, they thought it was a ritual of being a "Christian." So far, Dr. Jakob said he had not gotten them far enough along in their knowledge to try to put Victorian fashion on them.

"We must not be so unwise as to make them think they are to become European. I believe that nakedness will fade with their grand-children."

Dr. Jakob was telling Evy, "The young girl from Chaka's kraal has chills. Most likely the fever will peak before sundown."

Evy nodded. The girl's strong young body shook and trembled, and her eyes were rolled back. All Evy could see of them were tiny red veins in the whites of her eyes. Evy wrung a cloth in heated water and gently wiped the girl's flawless ebony face and throat.

There was a new addition built onto the ward. It was called a *godown.* It was open-sided with walls that stood waist high. Upright poles supported a roof of thatch, and in summer, such as it was now, the wind could blow through. When the winter rainy season came, grass mats like rugs were let down to form walls.

The floor consisted of clay and cow dung, and Dr. Jakob made no attempt to separate the healthy members of the family who brought the ill to him. Both the well and sick stayed together in the ward, or camped out nearby.

Dr. Jakob's medical "office" was adobe. Evy wondered that it only had only one small window. He had some shelves built from mopane wood, a table, a workbench, and his life's work of journals and books.

The Shona girl lay sleeping on the mat. Her skin seemed hot, and her lips were cracked and bleeding, so Evy smeared some fat on them, mixed with dried mint or camphor.

"She must be burning up," she commented in pity. "How long can she endure this high a temperature?"

"If it goes above one hundred four for very long, she'll likely die. It's happened before. They go delirious."

Evy watched Dr. Jakob administer the quinine.

"This could help if it isn't too late. The father didn't bring her in until last night. She was already far gone."

From outside there came a babble of excited voices. Evy glanced toward the opening where the sunshine came in.

"Cover her up with the *kaross,* Evy. When she starts to sweat, that will be a good sign."

Jakob stood and walked to look out the opening.

Evy did as Jakob bid her, taking the jackal furs and tucking them around the girl's body.

"A surprising call," Jakob stated. "Trouble, I fear."

Evy looked over her shoulder at him, wondering. The very word *trouble* caused her nerves to tighten. The unusual sights, odors, and customs of Bulawayo at times still left her jumpy and sometimes insecure. Again she wished Rogan were present.

Quarreling voices outside in the yard could be heard.

"What kind of trouble?" she asked quietly.

"We shall see." He slipped into his dusty white jacket, put his hat back on, and turned to go outdoors.

Evy came to him, her hand on his arm, detaining him.

Her eyes searched his for meaning, but he patted her hand calmly, and a brief smile touched the corners of his tan, lined face.

"It is the induna, Shaka. Most likely he's come about the girl from his kraal. They do not all approve of their people coming to me. I shall see what he wants. Most likely he's come to register his complaints to me. They think I can stop the chief native commissioner from his decisions."

Sir Julien was the commissioner.

Evy was not convinced the old induna was harmless. Even before Rogan and Derwent left, Rogan had told her the indunas were against Rhodes and the Charter Company.

Dr. Jakob went out to meet the induna, while Evy remained in the open doorway looking on.

CHAPTER TWENTY-SEVEN

The induna, Shaka, stood back with several warriors. This was the first time Evy had seen a feared induna up close. He was tall and thin, and yet the sinewy muscles of his chest, back, and shoulders left no doubt of the man's strength. There was a pragmatic fierceness about his chiseled face, and his dark eyes glittered like coal heated in a brick oven. He wore the black headring made of gum and clay molded into his hair as a permanent fixture that announced his status.

Evy was startled to see so many battle scars on his body that had healed long ago and were now knotted into hard bumps. Perhaps some were even bullet wounds from the last war at Bulawayo with the British. He stood barefoot in the warm dust, a monkey-skin cloak was thrown over one shoulder, and a buckhorn whistle hung on a leather strap around his thick scarred neck. He would blow a single sharp blast on the whistle if he wished to alert his people.

Evy watched with uneasy silence. Rogan had informed her that the indunas had once been the ruling lords that made up Lobengula's council.

Evy read the distrust in Shaka's demeanor. Treating the sick had gone over well with many, but not with all. Many of the Ndebele knew of missionary Robert Moffat, who had served in Bechuanaland, and the Moffat name was respected as a friend. His son had known Lobengula.

For a moment they stood in silence. Then Dr. Jakob addressed the induna in the Sindebele language. Evy had no notion of what was being discussed, but it seemed a heated debate.

The induna spoke sharply, then turned on his heel and strode away with his men following.

Evy came down to Dr. Jakob. His face was strained.

"What is it? He was angry. About the girl?"

He shook his head. "No. They have grievances with the Company. He insists I speak with the chief native commissioner."

"Julien…"

He nodded. "And Harry Whipple. They accuse Harry of ignoring their laws."

"Is he?"

"I don't think young Harry has any regard for their laws, Evy."

Harry Whipple was apparently disregarding the indunas by using the *amaholi* as his native police. These men were considered lowly and unblooded. Under Whipple they were harassing the *amahoda,* who were the elite young warriors in the kraals, and even insulting the indunas.

"The trouble is the Company police are armed with guns, but neither the indunas nor the impis are allowed weapons for fear of an uprising. The indunas are also angry because Harry is conscripting honored warriors for building roads, when they have a strict caste system. Only the amaholi 'dogs' do the work of slaves. The work forced on them is the work of mere *mujiba,* herdboys, not yet initiated into their fighting regiments."

"Is it true?" she asked uneasily.

"Yes, much of it, sadly, is true. It is also true that the Company *cannot* allow them to own weapons because they may turn against us. Much work needs to be done before there is respect and peace among us. That peace, true peace of brother to brother, can come only through unity in Christ. '"There is no peace," says the LORD, "for the wicked."' And the wicked are white and black, European and African. What we all need is a new heart."

She squeezed his arm. "If only…" She looked at him. "Sometimes there is no true peace even between two Christians…a man and wife."

Jakob looked down at her sadly. "That is often the saddest of all."

There was a moment of silence, then he said, "But between husband and wife, who are Christians, there is the love of God and the power of His indwelling Spirit to heal and mend, to make even stronger, to bless."

Oh, Father, if only this could happen between Rogan and me. May it happen, no matter what.

"Ah! There is a litany of wrongs the induna cry to me about, some fancied, many real, and they want me to do something about them."

She looked at him. "What can you do about it? Julien's in charge, and he's put Harry Whipple at the head of the native Company police."

Dr. Jakob's eyes flashed. "One thing I can do is attend the meeting next week in Bulawayo. Even Dr. Jameson, Mr. Rhodes's chief administrator, will be there. Maybe I can help them understand the unrest."

Evy felt a rush of enthusiasm. "A wise decision, Uncle Jakob. I'd like to go with you." She hastened on when she saw a doubt creep into his eyes. "I'd also like to visit Arcilla and Darinda at Government House."

He agreed, then went on discussing partial reasons for the unrest among the tribe.

"The death of Lobengula simmers in the Ndebele like a boiling cauldron. Now they complain, and rightly so in my mind, of the Company confiscating their cattle. This roughshod treatment of the vanquished can end only in tragedy for us all. Something must be done. It is the Lord's work that suffers. The Africans associate the missionaries with the ambitions of Rhodes, his armed men under Dr. Jameson, and the greedy desires of men like Julien for diamonds and gold."

Evy was inclined to agree. Nor was the British government much help to the missionaries.

Evy knew of the clash of purpose between the British and Boers with the missionary lobby over fair treatment of the tribes. Except for a few outstanding missionaries like Robert Moffat and his wife, Mary, the expansionists saw missionaries as a meddling nuisance, often getting in the way of trade and progress.

The Moffats had developed Kuruman mission station in Bechuanaland, where they had served for more than fifty years before retiring to

England. The great stone church that Moffat had built at Kuruman in 1838 was still standing.

David Livingstone had spent two years training at Kuruman before setting out for Mabosta, two hundred miles north, to establish a second station. Mabosta was not many miles from Rogan's old gold mine on the Zambezi, but Livingstone, more of an explorer and adventurer than a missionary, had never remained in one location like the Moffats. Livingstone had departed for the deeper wilds of Africa, giving up his connection with the missionary society, to accept a commission from the British government that allowed him more funds and equipment for his travels. He had died in 1873 at Ujiji, near Lake Tanganyika.

"Is it true that Robert Moffat was refused permission to print the Bible in the language of the Bechuanans?"

"It is," he said sadly. "The leadership in Capetown did not want rights granted to the tribe. If we printed the Scriptures in their language, you see, then the political authorities believed it would imply that the Africans were on the same level ground as we. That meant future voting rights, and other legal rights as well. Don't be shocked. The East India Company did the same thing to William Carey in India, and in Jamaica in the Caribbean."

"But Robert Moffat did print the Bible in Bechuanaland."

"When God says bring the gospel to every creature under the sun, it's our obligation to do it. Yes, Moffat ended up getting his own printing press to bring the Word of God to the Africans. The Companies, whether in South Africa, India, or elsewhere, are for the most part about commerce and trade, not that there aren't good men involved as well. But from the Christian perspective, Evy, it's more about money and national glory than it is about spreading God's truth. But that's to be expected. Many of these men are very intelligent and talented, but they do not know Jesus Christ. They are not committed to Him. They are committed to themselves."

"Yes...but the Lord has His ways. It's also true that the BSA has made it possible for missionaries to follow in their wake to spread Christianity throughout the British Empire."

"Well spoken, Evy, and may He continue to bless those who bring His truth to all the tribes of the earth."

"But is it a fact that some in the BSA have confiscated the cattle of the vanquished Ndebele farmers for their own livestock?"

"The pioneers heartily deny the injustice and cry foul!" Dr. Jakob said.

Could they be right?

After more work at the medical ward, Evy went back to the bungalows to inform Mrs. Croft she would be going with Jakob to Bulawayo the following week.

Mrs. Croft wasn't at any of the bungalows, and Evy remembered she had gone with Alice to pick the standing corn.

Evy was tired, and the walk to the fields seemed too long on this hot, dusty midmorning. She borrowed Dr. Jakob's horse-drawn trap and drove from the bungalows onto the narrow dirt road to the garden fields belonging to the mission.

Despite the station's being located near the river, the dust was thick, resembling reddish makeup for a powder puff. The South African sky appeared like a sheet of cloudless blue marble. Her skin felt damp and sticky, and the dust settled on her hands and stuck there.

She thought of Rogan, sighed, and flipped the reins. The fields were just ahead. She pulled the trap to the side of the field and stopped the horse.

Her lips turned into a smiling memory that she treasured. It had been wonderful during the first months of their marriage when he had been close by her side.

She climbed down, feeling the heat on her bare ankles with the rise of dust. What was unthinkable in Grimston Way—not wearing stockings—came naturally here at the mission outpost. Out of habit, she gave a quick glance along the edge of the path to make certain no safari ants were on the move, then took the cutoff from the road that led toward the fields.

Odd…she tucked her brows together. The birds were still not singing… For that matter, there weren't any animal sounds at all.

Mrs. Croft was farther ahead, with Alice Tisdale Brown, talking with a Shona woman, whom Evy noticed had come hurrying up from the river, excitedly pointing behind her. Evy paused and looked that way too. She couldn't see much of the river water, as the sloping fields ran down to the banks, where tall grasses and bushes grew.

Alice was standing with a big sunhat on her red-blond hair worn in looped braids across her shoulders. Alice's prissy ways and crisp lace collars had certainly been washed limp by her years in the African velds! Even her pale complexion, with its scattering of freckles, was browned by the scorching summers that were so different from the cool damp ones of Grimston Way. Some distance away, her and Derwent's three children were squealing and playing with a handful of African children of the Christian converts.

Mrs. Croft's cheeks wore two rosy dollops of color from the heat, and her expression was one of fluster and overwork. She stood frowning at the large Shona woman.

"What's that?" Mrs. Croft crowed, showing the language differences irritated her. "Eh? Winged *what*? What'd she say, Alice?" Mrs. Croft put a hand behind an ear and leaned toward Alice.

Evy walked toward them. Alice had picked up some of the Shona language from her years here, but in this situation she appeared dull of senses and merely stood gaping at the African woman, as though Mrs. Croft had not spoken.

Evy laughed at the sight. She couldn't help it. She wished Mrs. Tisdale could see her spoiled Alice now—

Evy paused and frowned. What was that unearthly noise in the distance?

She turned and looked. The sky appeared like the bottom of a sallow pond.

Evy held her canvas hat in place with one hand and shaded her eyes with the other. How very odd indeed! Why, it sounded almost like a coming train, and that was quite impossible.

"Oh noooh," came Alice's whine. Her voice trailed unfinished as she jerked toward her children. "Derry—Katie—Molly, quick, quick, come to Mama—" She hurried to gather them together.

Mrs. Croft was looking all around and up toward the tree tops. "That crazy noise—what on earth—?"

Evy hurried forward. "Sounds like a train, but it couldn't be." Her skin crawled. A lion's roar? No, certainly not. This was different. She turned on the beaten path, looking intently and straining to identify the noise.

"Inside the huts," Alice was shouting toward them. "Hurry, Evy, Mrs. Croft—" She had grabbed her three children's arms and was practically lifting them off the dust and trying to run with them toward the nearest hut.

The Shona woman was shooing the other children toward the huts like a hen with her chicks, kicking up the red dust around them as she did.

The mission station itself was too far to reach for safety, but Evy, confused, wondered what it was they were trying to escape.

So, apparently, was Mrs. Croft, who was still trying to comprehend when Alice screamed, "Locusts!"

Locusts? Evy squinted toward the sky. The horizon was darkening before her eyes. Could there be that many grasshoppers? She stood transfixed, staring.

The sky toward the north looked as if twilight were setting in due to a dark storm, but this seemed to have a bizarre density to it. The size and speed of this dark cloud challenged her courage. For as the dark blotch grew nearer, she could see that the darkness was in the shape of a moving arch, flying as one body.

Her bewilderment turned to dismay as she understood that it was bearing down upon her. The edge of the giant dark blotch seemed to darken the sun with a smoky haze.

Evy saw that Alice and her children were nearing the hut with the Shona. Evy started toward Mrs. Croft, who came toward her, and interlocking their arms, they moved toward the hut where Alice was huddling, beckoning Evy to hurry, but she couldn't run. She felt clumsy with child, and her spine was aching. Her legs wouldn't move smoothly over the uneven rows of corn, and Mrs. Croft refused to leave her.

"Lord Jesus, help us," Evy prayed.

Swiftly the dismal surge of wings canvassed the heavens, and the sun appeared to turn a dull orange, while a massive moving shadow swooped upon the land.

Mrs. Croft was pulling her along with her steady grip. The sound was becoming louder. Looking upward, Evy saw the curtain of flying insects smother the sky, followed by a sound of whirring, tiny wings, millions of them. The brassy sun looked like a misshapen orb.

The sound of wings gathered strength and filled Evy's ears until the horror of the great army of locusts started descending toward her and Mrs. Croft.

The rustling wings turned into an oppressive roar, and then a rush of wind came as the sunlight was shut out. From out of the sickly eclipsed half-light came the twisting columns of locusts.

With the roar of millions of wings descending upon the field where she and Mrs. Croft were seeking refuge, they dropped to the ground on their knees and clung together, heads bent as the locusts struck like grapeshot, smashing into them. Evy felt the stinging impact of each horny-winged body with numbing effect. Evy used her hands to protect her face. She was half-blinded and dazed by the rushing torrent of wings swarming about her head, but when she swatted at the air, they were so thick that she merely caught them in her hands. She could barely see Mrs. Croft, who was covered with them.

Evy looked with horror at a locust in her hand. Its body was twice as thick as one of her fingers, and its wings had bright orange and black designs. The thorax was shielded with a horny armor, and from its helmeted head, multiple bulging yellow eyes looked back. Its long rear legs were fringed with red-tipped barbs that cut her skin. The locust kicked convulsively in her palm, leaving blood droplets. She screamed. Multitudes of them swarmed all around her in a cloud—millions and millions.

She thought of the third plague of Egypt, and the locust army of Revelation, as well as the great destructive army of the Lord in the book of Joel.

She turned her back to the onrushing advance of flying bodies, but it was too late, for they were everywhere—on the ground, in the air, in her hair, on her back, her face, their thorny feet stinging as they vaulted into her. Her mind swam giddily; revulsion choked her.

Mrs. Croft reached for Evy. They held tightly to each other, burrowing their faces into each other's shoulders.

"Lord," she kept praying, "help us, help—"

Then, with an abruptness that was startling, the sunlight broke through, and the air around them was clear.

Evy raised her face and had to shield her eyes from the glare of the noonday sun.

"Th-they're gone—" she rasped, shaking Mrs. Croft's shoulder.

Evy glanced around. "No, they've come down." The locust swarm had landed on the earth, and now the world around them was becoming a skeleton. Evy gasped at the sight. The trees and bushes were moving and squirming with layers of orange and black bodies. The branches trembled under their greedy weight until they snapped every second or two with a repeated hideous sound. The corn stalks they had come to harvest were toppling down to the earth, as though an army of threshing instruments moved forward in unison. The ground seethed with writhing bodies, rustling wings, and the hard click-click of bodies bumping into each other, crawling over each other.

"Oh, dear God," prayed Mrs. Croft in a wail. "It's horrible, horrible—"

Evy laid an arm around her quivering shoulders, an arm scratched in places and speckled with blood. Her face felt sticky and sore.

"What's that?" Evy looked up and around them. Now there came a new sound—excited squawking, chirping, cawing, screeching. Another great army was on the wing. This one of birds, thousands of them gobbling up a great feast of locusts. A myriad of several kinds of birds dived, whirled, and landed with ecstatic glee. Storks were knee-deep in a sea of choice, meaty morsels.

The monstrous devastation from the locusts, followed by a gigantic feast for the birds, lasted less than an hour, and yet to Evy the horrifying experience had seemed unending. In reality, within minutes, the locust swarm, as if on a single cue, arose into the air as one mammoth body. Once more they soared heavenward. Sullen twilight fell across the land again as the sun was turned into a dull orange glow. Then darkness was followed by a burst of dazzling sunlight. The menacing black cloud winged away southward to wreak havoc on new greenery.

Evy and Mrs. Croft managed to get to their feet, holding to each other. They stood in the gaunt, stripped field, two figures huddled with astonishment.

After a minute or two, they were slowly joined by Alice and the Shona woman, all looking weak and small amid the ruined crops.

Evy blinked, dazed. She hardly recognized the area.

The corn fields were gone. Even the corn stalks had been devoured. The meager flowers and vines that had been struggling in the drought for skimpy survival were now no more. There were no feeble flowers with a brave smiling face, no golden grasses waving in the wind, no bush, nothing except some denuded spikes here and there.

The fruit trees Dr. Jakob had planted months ago upon coming here from the Zambezi were all bare sticks. Even the distant trees on the hills and the growth along the banks of the Khami River had been stripped bare by the devouring locusts.

Evy looked near and far to find even one small trace of summer green, and there was none. No leaves or stalks or stems of grass. Nothing was left at all that had not been molested. All that remained was a brown world of death. The locust army had marched through Bulawayo and left it in calamity.

Chapter Twenty-Eight

The locust plague, the cattle disease called rinderpest, and the months of drought had taken a heavy toll on Bulawayo and the surrounding region of Rhodesia. As the cattle were dying by the thousands, a wail went up among the African tribe. "The white chief has brought a great curse!"

The indunas gathered in a secret location and hummed in angry agreement. Cattle were their power and wealth. Who cared for diamonds and gold except the white chief? The white chief had shamed the impis and scattered them like skinny chickens across the veld. No blooded warrior of Zanzi blood knew who could take a wife because the young could not marry until they dipped their assegais into enemy blood. The cattle were cursed, and the sweet grass no longer grew. The rain no longer fell from the sky to quench the parched land.

"The Great One, the Umlimo, says the spirit gods have sent the locusts to punish our weakness. The oracle speaks in many different voices. All the voices coming from her mouth tell us to become strong!" said one induna.

The others hummed. Dumaka looked around at his fellow indunas. He laid aside his leather kilt. He raised his knee and brought his foot down in the dust. "Jee!"

He raised the other knee and brought his foot down. "Jee!"

The humming grew louder and louder. His sleek, muscled body sparkled with sweat. He was joined by the other indunas, who followed him in a circle, swaying and chanting, and the sunlight glinted on the assegai he held.

Evy awoke with a headache and chills. Mrs. Croft came into the hut and looked down at her worriedly. "Cold? On a hot day like this? I don't like that one nasty bit." She placed a palm against Evy's forehead, and her scowl deepened. "You're burning up. I'll call Dr. Jakob."

"No, don't call him. Today's the trip into Bulawayo."

"Posh, the trip's all but an hour. He can be a trifle late to talk to the Company men."

Evy sat up, pushing the coverlet aside. "No, I'm going with him. If you tell him I'm not well, he won't want me to go—" She stopped and bit her lip.

"Aha, so you're about to resort to tricks again to get your way."

Evy tightened her lips and reached for the brush on the table. "No, I am not. I've learned my lesson, I think. It's nothing. Don't worry. Just a bit of fevered chill is all... How is Alice feeling after the locust horror?"

"Fit and dandy, to be sure. That girl surprises me. Dotes on those three honeys of hers. I didn't think she would be the motherly sort. Now she's worried about Derwent." Mrs. Croft cast Evy a side glance as she straightened the coverlet on the bed. "It's been a month now. I'm beginning to wonder what's happened too."

Evy looked at her over the tea mug. Yes, Rogan should have been back by now. What was keeping him? Did he not love her at all any longer?

No, she did not believe that. Their last night together a month ago had convinced her.

"Maybe Arcilla will know something from Peter. I'm going to go see her today. You're coming too, aren't you?"

"No, I promised Alice to help with a dress she's trying to make for

Molly. Gracious, but Alice is all thumbs when it comes to a needle and thread."

Evy tiredly leaned back in the chair. She shivered. She sipped the tea and rubbed her forehead. She did feel quite awful. Maybe she ought to stay here. She rubbed her swollen abdomen. If only Rogan were here to hold her in his arms and tell her he loved her still… Tiredly she brushed her hair.

Mrs. Croft turned and looked at her with unexpected consternation.

"Evy, you've been taking your daily quinine, haven't you?"

Evy grimaced and scratched the mosquito bite on her arm. "I tried, but it wouldn't stay down, so I got tired of it. It's questionable whether that quinine really works. Do you notice how anyone who's been taking it for any length of time looks sallow skinned? Arcilla won't take quinine, either."

"It's that wicked river that's the problem," Mrs. Croft insisted, casting a wary glance out the window in its direction. "Mosquitoes."

"No one knows for certain what causes malaria."

"Well, Dr. Jakob's a knowing man. I'm thinking he knows what he's talking about. And he's certain it's mosquitoes."

"Instead of quinine, ask Dr. Jakob to give me a headache powder, will you, Mrs. Croft?"

Evy forced herself to bathe in the round tub and then dress comfortably to accompany Jakob to Bulawayo. When they arrived at Government House, she was aware of how quiet everything appeared. The once busy common room was nearly deserted.

"For an important meeting with the company administrator and chief native commissioner, it's terribly quiet around here," she told Jakob.

He looked confused. "I'm certain I have my day in order. I'll just ask this young man over here at the desk."

"While you do that, I shall go up and find Arcilla," she told him and walked across the matting to the steps.

Arcilla looked pleased to see her and ushered her into the room with urgent appeal. She appeared frightened as she paced. As usual, she was dressed in a lovely burgundy satin skirt and ivory blouse with a pleated front and puffed sleeves. There were diamonds at her neck and dangling from her wrist.

"If this were London, you'd be robbed," Evy joked. "Really, Arcilla dear, is it necessary to dress as though you're going to a ball?"

Arcilla was lacking her usual flighty mood. She continued to pace while Evy enjoyed holding Baby Charles in her arms and thinking of Rogan and their own little one from God growing in her womb. If a boy, she would call him Rogan, of course, and a girl? *Katie.* Would Rogan approve?

When Arcilla did not laugh as she usually did when Evy made such harmless jokes about her going to a ball, Evy paid closer attention to the strain on her sister-in-law's face.

"What is it, Arcilla? Trouble with Peter?"

She turned toward her quickly and came and sat down, glancing over her shoulder toward the door.

What was she afraid of? The police were doing everything they could to find the person guilty of Anthony's death.

"You know something you're not telling me," Evy said in a low voice, searching Arcilla's wide eyes.

"I know more than it's safe to know. That's what Peter says."

"Peter said that to you?" If he had said that and Arcilla wasn't exaggerating, then something was very wrong indeed.

"What could Peter possibly have meant?"

Arcilla held out her arms. "Here, let me take Charles and put him to nap first. Marjit didn't come today. Detlev has ridden out to look at their farmland again. They may return to farming, so she says."

Arcilla took the baby to the back room and was busy attending him while Evy stood and walked about the room, frowning. Rogan had not yet returned. No one seemed to know what had happened to him, Derwent, and Parnell after they'd ridden from Fort Victoria to the Zimbabwe Ruins. Two weeks had turned into a month. Strange, because Sir Julien was not in Bulawayo, nor was Captain Retford, or Harry

Whipple. And now Arcilla had mentioned the soldier Detlev, who supposedly was away looking over his farmland that he and his wife had abandoned to the brush and wild animals. Evy now wondered if he'd actually gone there or somewhere else.

As she thought through the circumstances of the last week, her fears grew. First, Rogan and those with him had not returned. Now, today, she'd come with Dr. Jakob only to learn that Sir Julien wasn't here. And Dr. Jameson was gone too…

Arcilla returned, quietly drawing the door to the baby's room partially closed.

"We can talk now," she whispered and stood wringing her hands. This nervous manner was so unlike the normally amusing Arcilla.

She studied Evy with a frown between her golden brows. "How are you feeling?"

"You've asked me that twice already. Why do you keep asking? You'll soon have me thinking I'm ill." Evy smiled ruefully. "Do I look that awful?"

"No, no…but you looked flushed, yet you shiver. Oh, preserve us! You're not coming down with malaria, are you?"

"Naturally not, why should I?"

"I should hope and pray not because it's a hideously nasty sort of illness. One of Peter's aides has it and nearly died of fever."

"You're making me feel so much better, Arcilla."

"Sorry…" Arcilla plucked at her diamonds and walked to the window, looked out, then walked back to the chair, sat down, then stood again. "I'm afraid, is all," she stated suddenly.

"About my getting malaria?"

Arcilla shook her head no. "You have Dr. Jakob. At least *he's* still in Bulawayo."

Evy walked up to her and narrowed her eyes. "All right. Out with it. I want to know everything you're not telling me."

She nodded and turned. "I'll make tea first—"

Evy caught her arm. "Forget the tea. No more delays. Sit down. And I'll sit right here—now, what is it, Arcilla, that's troubling you?"

Arcilla opened her mouth, closed it, then began again. She rushed, "Dr. Jameson rode out of Bulawayo late last night. I watched through the window. Peter admitted Jameson took four hundred of the Company police-soldiers and many, many of the pioneers, and two hundred coloreds and loyal Africans. They all had rifles, and the supply wagons were loaded with enough food to last them for two months. The other wagons had Maxim guns and boxes of ammunition. They're going to Johannesburg to aid the Uitlanders in an uprising against Kruger's Boer Government."

Evy caught her breath. So it had happened! "But Rogan went straight to Pall Mall in London when you wired him the secret. That was months ago. Do you mean to tell me the British government hasn't done anything to stop this?"

"They sent—Anthony."

"Yes," Evy said with a wave of her hand, "but my father—" She stopped short, and her eyes searched Arcilla's. The look she read on Arcilla's face alerted her at once. Evy slowly stood, staring down at her.

"You're not saying Anthony was murdered because he'd come to stop the raid into the Transvaal?" she gasped.

Arcilla reached over, grabbed Evy's hand, and pulled her back down to the chair.

"It was part of it, yes, but not all. Peter knows. So does Rogan."

"Rogan? Rogan's told me nothing about it."

"He was afraid to upset you…"

"How do you know Rogan thinks this?"

"He talked with Peter and Captain Retford before he left for Great Zimbabwe."

And she had known almost nothing about this!

Evy listened as Arcilla told her all that had happened, beginning with Anthony's arrival, Julien's disagreement with him over a certain incriminating letter from a George Trotter of Cape Mining Fields, and how within hours of Anthony's death his bungalow had been searched. Evy was speechless when Arcilla whispered of the scrap of paper she'd salvaged from Julien's flame.

"Where is Sir Julien now?"

"He left quietly early this morning. Darinda went along; so did Captain Retford. Even Harry Whipple is riding with Julien. There are only a few of us here," Arcilla said nervously. "Peter and a handful of Company police."

"But where did Julien go, to Johannesburg as well?"

"You mean you don't know?" Arcilla cried. "They're going to the Matopos to search for the Black Diamond. Rogan, Captain Retford, and even Derwent are waiting there to join Julien and his troop. They're going to look for that cursed Black Diamond. Oh! I wish I'd never heard of that thing."

Evy stared at her. So that was why Rogan had not returned. He had told her two weeks at Zimbabwe, then home to Bulawayo, when all along he'd known he would join up with Sir Julien at the base of the Matopos Hills to search for Lobengula's burial cave. So—he, too, knew how to keep a secret from her!

"Dr. Jameson doesn't know what Julien is going to do," Arcilla went on. "He was against the Matopos expedition. Peter says Julien deliberately waited to start his expedition until after Jameson left for Johannesburg."

"Are you telling me all the Company police and soldiers have left Bulawayo?" Evy whispered, trying to keep her heart from pounding.

"Not all. Peter has a few men."

A few.

"What insanity is this?" Evy stood quickly. "After Anthony's been murdered, and that Major Willet brutally attacked near the Matopos—they all rode out and—and left us?"

"Ohhh—" Arcilla placed her palms alongside her temples and bowed her head.

Quickly Evy altered her manner. "Oh, well. Everything will be all right, or they wouldn't have left."

"Peter says not to worry."

"Yes, of course not. And he's perfectly right to tell us that."

"Yes, quite."

Evy sank slowly to the chair and folded her hands tightly. "And of course Rogan knows that Dr. Jameson rode out with all the armed men?"

Arcilla looked up. "No. Peter says he doubts if Julien would mention that."

"No, he wouldn't," Evy said in a cold voice, "because he knows Rogan and Derwent would most likely turn around and come back."

The door opened, and Evy and Arcilla stood at the same time and looked across the room.

Peter entered, looking strained and preoccupied. He shut the door and stood there for a moment, as though he did not even see them. He was staring at the floor, deep in thought.

"Peter? Is...everything all right?" Arcilla asked.

He seemed to pay heed that they were there for the first time. "Dr. Jakob is down in the common room, Evy. There's no one to hold the Company meeting today as planned, so he's ready to return to the mission."

Evy, feeling as though she were in a daze, nodded her understanding and gathered her things slowly. Peter walked swiftly to Arcilla and took her by the arms.

"My dear, I need to be gone for a few days—"

"Peter," she wailed.

"Now, now, it's not what you think," he hastened. "I'm going to try to overtake Julien's column and find Rogan and Captain Retford. When I do, we'll return and join you at Dr. Jakob's. I want you to take Charles and go with Evy."

Evy looked up. She studied Peter's face, and her heart thudded. *He's worried. More worried than I've ever seen him.*

"All right, darling," Arcilla said. "But maybe we should come with you?"

"No," he said quickly. "I'll need to ride fast and alone. And the area I pass through has a bit of trouble right now. You're safer with Dr. Jakob."

"Trouble?" Evy asked from across the room.

Peter looked at her, and she read his effort to conceal his concern. "A few impis have found some of their ritual warrior garb. They've put it on."

"But I thought all that was burned in the fires after the war."

"So we all thought," he said shortly. "Evidently, a few war costumes escaped us."

What else had escaped Harry Whipple? She wanted to ask but thought it wiser not to.

"Can't you send a wire to Fort Victoria or one of the other townships?" she asked.

Peter hesitated before replying, and Evy realized there was more that he was not telling them. "Something seems to have brought down the telegraph poles again. Undoubtedly some hungry wildlife causing us a bit of a scramble. I'll ride. It won't take me long."

"Oh, Peter—" Arcilla threw her arms around him. He held her tightly.

The moment was too deep and profound to be a normal good-bye, and Evy became very frightened. *Peter doesn't know whether he'll make it or not.* Evy's hand went to her mouth, and she turned away. Her eyes shut, and her prayer came urgently.

"Darling Arcilla, I'm sorry I brought you here... I should never have risked you, the baby—"

"Peter! I'm afraid! Come back to me. You've got to come back—"

Evy placed her hands over her ears and closed her eyes and prayed: *Dear Father God, help us. I beseech You for Your mercy and grace. Forgive us our sins through Christ...forgive me, forgive our selfishness, our greed, our lack of wisdom, our wars, our foolishness...*

The Southern Cross glittered in the night sky above the mission station.

Evy awoke feeling more sick than she'd ever felt in her life. She couldn't control her shivering, yet she felt that she was inside an oven slowly baking. Her teeth chattered, and her head ached so dreadfully that when she opened her eyes and tried to focus, all she could see was the bungalow spinning. Her bedclothes were wet. Pain in her womb made her double over. She bit her lip to keep from yelling out.

Rogan, Rogan—where are you my love? I need you and you're not here—

"Lord! Help me!" she choked.

Then, "Arcilla…"

Arcilla groaned and came reluctantly awake, then raised herself to an elbow. She peered at Evy, and her eyes widened.

"Dear God in heaven."

"Arcilla—h-help—don't feel well—baby h-hurts, too—something's wrong."

Arcilla threw the cover aside and sprang from the bed she was sharing with Evy. Her fingers trembled as she struck a match and lit the lantern. She brought it close to Evy and looked at her, touched her burning, flushed skin, then she gasped and stepped back, her hand forming a fist. She pressed the whitened knuckles to her teeth. Blood… blood…on the bed, on Evy, and Evy was convulsing with pain and beginning to vomit…

Arcilla fled from the bungalow barefoot. She ran as fast as she could, stepping on stones, insects, and wet, soggy things as she ran to Dr. Jakob's bungalow. She hammered on the door with both fists until her hands stung.

"Jakob! Hurry! Evy's losing the baby—"

A light flickered, and the door flew open. He looked at her with white disheveled hair. "What did you say?"

Arcilla repeated the words and stood shaking.

"Quickly, go for Mrs. Croft. I'll be right there."

Arcilla found Mrs. Croft grabbing her robe and slipping on her big leather shoes. "Evy? Losing the baby?" she cried, horrified.

Arcilla collapsed into her arms and sobbed. "She's got malaria— that's why—she'll die—"

Mrs. Croft shook her. "Snap out of it, Arcilla. Now is the time for our wits and our prayers! Run, go get me Alice. Dr. Jakob will need us all."

Mrs. Croft flew out the bungalow door, and Arcilla, feeling numb, found her way through the hot, dark night to Alice's bungalow. She staggered up the stoep to the door. Before she did, she looked up at the late night sky at the gleaming Southern Cross and agonized over the prayer that was lodged within her heart.

Jesus, I'm a stranger to You, but I don't want to be a stranger any longer. Lord I need You. We all need You so very much. And, Jesus, if You don't help us, then I don't know what any of us are going to do!

She brushed the tears from her face and lifted her hand to knock on the door. "Alice! Wake up, Alice!"

CHAPTER TWENTY-NINE

Parnell screeched with fear, and jumping up out of the swaying golden-brown grasses, he took off running. Bullets flew around him, splattering rocky soil.

Rogan gritted his teeth, lifted his Winchester, and fired several rounds along the ridge where the first shots had come from, distracting those firing while Parnell escaped.

"Lion!" Derwent shouted from some distance to Rogan's right.

Rogan saw what must have spooked Parnell. A flash of gold fur sped across the far slope of open ground. Rogan swung his rifle up and fired. Another wail came from Parnell. Rogan was up and bounding in his direction, weaving, crouching behind bushes, and darting again as bullets whizzed from behind him on the ridge of the Acropolis. Derwent, too, was running, ducking, running again, coming up from behind.

Once within the thorn trees and scrub bushes, they maneuvered their way on the slope toward some acacia trees.

"Where's Mr. Parnell?" Derwent shouted, breathless from running, and as though in reply, there answered a zing from Parnell's rifle ahead of them in the veld to their right. Rogan ran toward the sound.

"Can you see him?" Rogan called to Derwent.

The bush was a little thicker ahead of them, and the thorn branches whipped at their legs as they passed. Another shot cracked the air, and immediately afterward came the majestic yet bone-chilling roar of a lion. Parnell's shouts of fear drifted to them.

"Aye, he's in bad trouble! Lord have mercy!" Derwent cried as they burst out of the scrub.

Before them lay the veld, with waving, open, yellowed grasses beneath flat-topped acacia trees that dotted the crest of a ridge. Parnell, a hundred meters ahead, appeared to be running for the kopje crest. Rogan could no longer see the lion. But as Parnell came to the ridge, he seemed to simply vanish before their eyes.

"Oh no!" Rogan cried.

A slight vapor of dust remained, followed by Parnell's rifle and hat tumbling down the mound.

Rogan ran ahead and began climbing to the point on the ridge where Parnell had disappeared. He reached the top, out of breath, and looked about him. Derwent clambered up beside him, trying to catch his breath.

"Where is he, Mr. Rogan?"

Rogan stood on the edge of a gully, gazing down into the brush. The silence was more shattering than the commotion that had preceded it. His heart thudded. *Please, God, not Parnell—*

"Parnell!" Rogan shouted down.

There was no answer, no sign of his brother.

Derwent had snatched Parnell's rifle and hat as he'd climbed to the top of the kopje, and he stood now, morosely holding them, looking at them, then down to the copse.

"Parnell's not ready yet, Father… Don't take him yet—"

"Parnell, can you hear me?" Rogan shouted again more desperately. He was just ready to tell Derwent to go for the Basuto, because he was going down, somehow, when his brother's voice sounded, weak and shaking.

"Here, Rogan. I'm down here. I'm all right, I think, no broken bones— Where's that dashed lion? I swear he was chasing *me!* He had it in for me."

"Come out from under the brush," Rogan shouted in relieved frustration. "If that lion had been after you, you'd be dinner by now. This is no time to play hide-and-seek!"

The gully into which Parnell had fallen looked to be six meters deep in places but little more than three meters wide. Brush grew in a tangle of thick creeper so that the trench was barely noticeable. In spite of his dangerous fall, Parnell had escaped broken bones. He had some gashes and bruises, but after lowering a rope that Rogan carried, they hauled him up to safety.

Parnell now sat resting on a rock drinking from his canteen.

"That ruddy lion came out of nowhere," he said with a groan. "Biggest beast I ever laid eyes on. This must be pride territory."

"Never mind the lion," Rogan was saying. "Who was trying to kill us with those rifle shots?"

"I caught a glimpse of two men," Derwent said. "One sure reminded me of your Boer cousin, that Heyden van Buren."

Heyden. Rogan's temperature climbed. Not only had he murdered his favorite uncle and injured his beloved, but now he was trying to kill again! "He must have seen us at Jakob van Buren's mission. I had an uneasy feeling Heyden might be in the shadows keeping watch on all of us, including Julien." He wondered if Julien knew.

"If anyone wants that Black Diamond as much as Julien does, it's Heyden," Rogan continued.

"He's no relation of mine," Parnell growled toward Derwent. "He used to pawn himself off as a cousin when he'd show up as bold as day at Rookswood. Remember that, Rogan? And all the time the Boer was no kin at all."

"Heyden is a killer," Rogan stated coldly. "I've no doubt he'd have killed the three of us if he could. And he won't give up. If he's left for the time being, he'll be back. If not here, then in Bulawayo. But when he does show up again, I'll be waiting for him."

Derwent rubbed his neck, looking unhappy. " 'Course, everything was in a ruinous commotion, and I'd not say on oath that it was Mr. Heyden, you understand. He just had the look about him."

"There were more men besides Heyden," Rogan said. "Did you see anyone else you might recognize?"

"I had a feeling I'd seen the second man before too."

There was a solid chance Heyden and whoever was working with him had been in Bulawayo all along.

"Do you think he killed Anthony?" Parnell asked, licking his lips.

"I wouldn't put anything past him."

"But on what motive?"

"That's the question. I have my ideas, though I'm not ready to say just yet. I want to talk to Retford first. But think about it. Why would anyone want to kill Anthony? There can be only one reason, as I see it. Someone was afraid he had information to ruin either them or their plans. Or they had something to gain. Something that meant a great deal to them."

"The Transvaal is important," Parnell stated woodenly. "If it was Heyden, who sent him here?" he continued, his wary eyes shooting to Rogan. "Who else knew we were coming?"

"No one *had* to send him. He's probably hunting me, but that goes both ways. I confronted him at Grimston Way over Evy. He confessed to killing Henry. I told you about that."

"And Vicar Edmund Havering," Derwent said darkly. "A wicked thing, for sure. A good servant of the Lord."

"It seems bizarre to me that Uncle Julien would send you here to locate the gold, though," Parnell insisted. "All these years he's been trying to jump ahead of you, and now he steps aside. Then Heyden shows up and nearly blows all our heads off."

Rogan tightened his jaw. He saw Derwent watching him with a curious look in his eyes.

"What about the second man?" Rogan asked again roughly.

Derwent shook his head. "Can't be sure. I saw him for just a second or so. Almost thought I was seeing double. They looked alike, or else I imagined it. Then that lion gave me a scare."

"Hah, as it did me," Parnell said and groaned as he moved on the rock. "I think I'm getting stiffer sitting here…" Suddenly he rubbed his eyes and shook his head as though his brains were scrambled.

"Am I seein' things? Over there…"

Rogan turned his head, rifle raised. Some distance away stood an ancient baobab tree, its giant limbs looking like snarled black roots sprawling in all directions, lifting toward the sky. The tree was so old that at least half of the leafless branches were dead with bark falling off.

Rogan whipped out the map and looked at the tree, looked around him, then gazed off toward the Sentinel, the crouching lion.

"The two are lined up with this trench."

Even Parnell scrambled up from the rock and rushed after him.

Rogan strode to the trench and walked along its edge. "There's no disguising it. This is man-made. Take a closer look, both of you. You can see the rock's been broken up here." Rogan stooped down and broke off a bit of rocky earth and crumbled it in his hand. He looked up at them with a ready smile. "I think we're onto something this time… Well, Derwent, do you think the miners who dug through this solid rock could be from the time of the ancient Zimbabweans?"

"Aye, Mr. Rogan, but I wonder how they blasted through the rock?"

"They had their ways. I studied about how they heated the rock with a fire, then splashed it with cold water, causing the rock to split. Then they used plain muscle, mostly slaves and prisoners of the ancient wars. They also had child slave labor, sending small bodies down into mine shafts." He stood and looked up and down the trench. "We need to locate the shafts. This is the place, all right. This is Henry's find."

Derwent and Parnell looked at each other and grinned.

Rogan, with map in hand, once again lined up the ancient tree with the crouching lion. Then he counted off the meters that Uncle Henry had placed at the north end of the map. Thirty meters farther ahead he stopped, coming to a depression in the ground. He stooped, and Parnell and Derwent gathered around.

"The shaft," breathed Derwent, and a wide grin broke. "You did it, Mr. Rogan! You found Henry's prize!"

"No, Derwent, *we* found it. The three of us."

Derwent looked at Parnell, whose hazel eyes glowed with renewed enthusiasm.

The ancient opening of one of several mining shafts on the ridge had been filled in with chunks of rock.

"Henry must have done this," Rogan said. "You can tell it's been opened in the past. He had his natives fill it in again to hide the opening."

Rogan handed his rifle to Derwent, then removed his jacket and rolled up the sleeves of his thin cotton shirt.

"We're going to open it up," he told them. "Parnell, you keep guard."

He and Derwent maneuvered their way into the shallow depression until they stooped over the narrow blocked entrance. Rogan began to clear the rocks, Derwent helping.

They worked for half an hour, then Parnell, who seemed to have forgotten his cuts and bruises, climbed down and began to work while Derwent kept guard.

Rogan used a section of a dry branch to pry loose the boulders, the muscles straining beneath his sweat-soaked shirt. Lifting and rolling the boulders aside, they managed after an hour's work to reveal a square shaft opening.

Rogan looked at the opening with dismay. It was small and narrow, so that he could not carry through his plans to go down a ways with matches to have a look.

"Look, there it is," he called, "Henry Chantry's mark."

Derwent, too, came scrambling down to see.

Rogan knelt and lit a match, holding it there, as he brushed away the dirt. He could read the chiseled words: *H. Chantry, September 13,*

1874. Beneath the date was a crude, hurried drawing resembling the great bird of Zimbabwe.

"So we have it," Rogan said, "Henry's gold reef!" He peered down into the hole. "There's no telling how deep it goes."

"Black as pitch, too," Derwent said warily.

Rogan smelled fungus. Engrossed, he stared into the opening, though he could see nothing.

"If we had a candle…" Parnell said.

Rogan stood. "We need to go back down for our baggage. We'll camp here for the night."

"I'll go back and tell the Basuto," Derwent said.

Rogan stopped him. "We'll all go. I've no confidence Heyden and his friend won't try again. Anyway, we need some things before anyone ventures inside."

"Derwent's smaller than either of us," Parnell said.

"No." Rogan stood and dusted himself off. "One slip and we could lose friend Derwent. We won't risk it till we're ready." He grinned, his face dusty and sweaty. He held out his hand, and the three of them shook hands and laughed in agreement and hearty expectation.

It was toward sunset, and the vast sky was slashed with vibrant colors of burnt orange and scarlet. Rogan walked the narrow passage back to the Valley of Ruins. He took the steep rocky steps downward. Just as he was nearing the bottom of the narrow steps, several riders waited in a half-circle. He lifted his Winchester and motioned behind him to Parnell and Derwent to be ready.

Rogan didn't know who to expect astride the horses after being shot at. He wouldn't have been surprised to see Heyden and some of his Boer zealots. He stopped in his tracks when he spotted the fair face and form of Darinda Bley. Beside her rode Captain Retford, Harry Whipple, and a few other men he had seen around Government House. Julien commanded his attention.

Sir Julien broke rank and rode up. He was dressed in rugged clothing and hat. His black eye patch gave him the appearance of a brigand.

Julien laughed too cheerfully. "Success, Rogan, my boy? Did you taste the sweet cup of success at last? Well, bravo! Henry is dancing a jig." He sobered and waved an arm toward the kopje ridge. "It's yours. A bargain's been made, and we'll keep it."

"What are you doing here?"

"The Matopos expedition. Now is the time. Everything is ready. We've more guards and supplies waiting near the hills. I decided I'd better ride to meet you. Nothing like a safe escort back. I wouldn't want you running into any trouble, or"—his voice changed to a chill warning—"changing your mind."

Rogan had not yet explained things to Derwent. He assumed that Retford had agreed to come…because of Darinda. Had she come only to Zimbabwe, or did she expect to go on the Matopos trek? Rogan was pleased to see Retford. He'd proven a steady, dependable ally on Rhodes's trek to Fort Salisbury. He did not see Peter and was glad of it. He didn't appreciate all the guards being gone from Government House with his sister there.

"We were ambushed up on the ridge. I don't suppose you'd know anything about that?" he asked coolly.

The look of alarm on Julien's face convinced Rogan he'd had nothing to do with it.

Rogan scanned the faces of the other men on horseback. Except for Retford, who was alert and interested, Harry Whipple and the others looked as though they'd been carved from wood.

"Ambushed? By Ndebele?"

Rogan shook his head no. "Winchester repeating rifles. I'm thinking now it was Heyden."

Was he right? Had there been an uneasy movement by one of the

TODAY'S EMBRACE

riders near Julien? Rogan glanced again at the faces, but he must have been wrong. Both Harry Whipple and the others wore angry faces.

"Boers," Whipple said and spat in the dust.

Julien sat tensely. "We can't loiter around here talking much longer," Julien said. "We'll need to get moving."

"I need a few minutes to get organized before I can travel." Rogan went to find Derwent. He knew he had some explaining to do, and he didn't think it would go over well. As for Parnell, he'd already walked up to the side of Darinda's horse.

Derwent had gone to the Basuto and had them gathering up supplies and horses. He was leading Rogan's horse, as well as his own, toward him. Rogan stopped and waited.

Rogan pulled his hat lower and stood as he came up.

"Look, Derwent, I made a bargain with Julien. I can't go back on it now."

"I think you made an error, Mr. Rogan, but I'd sure not be telling you what you can and can't do. Maybe I shouldn't, but I think Sir Julien is a snake in the grass. He'll bite your leg the moment you get too close to what he's about."

"I'm aware of that and have been since a boy. He hasn't deceived me. I'm going to the Matopos to guard him. It's because I want the mystery of Henry's mine solved and put behind us once for all."

"I'm taking you at your word, why shouldn't I? I think I know you through and through. You've been a true friend, and fair with me for sure. I'll be going along, but if anyone needs a bodyguard it's you, Mr. Rogan. Those bullets earlier were for you, not for me or Mr. Parnell. On the Matopos it will be you again that someone's wanting to kill. That's why I'm going."

"Heyden," Rogan repeated. "It has to be. He's heard of the diamond, knows the story about Lobengula, and he'll kill anyone who stands in his way of getting it."

"Seems like Sir Julien and Mr. Heyden are cut from the same piece

357

of cloth. There's going to be more trouble than we can shoo away if they both reach for it at the same time."

"If I had my way, that diamond would be better off if no one had it."

"You mean leave it with King Lobengula?"

"Suits me. From the time I was a child, all I heard about at Rookswood was that diamond."

"I wonder where it first came from."

Rogan turned and looked after Julien, who was waiting a good distance ahead.

"Julien claims he found it when mining with Carl van Buren. I'm not convinced. Dumaka brought that diamond to Zululand and King Cetshwayo before the Zulu war. Then he carried it to Lobengula. I think there's more to how Julien got hold of it than he's telling."

Derwent nodded. He shook out his hat and put it back on. "I just wish there was a way to let Alice know why I won't be coming back when I said I would."

Rogan avoided his eyes. He reached over and took the reins of his horse and shoved his Winchester in the rifle boot. He had promised Evy he'd return in two weeks. At least she was safe with Jakob and Mrs. Croft. At any rate, he'd be back in plenty of time for the birth of their baby.

"We'll be at Fort Victoria soon. You can send a wire for both of us to Peter. He and Arcilla can ride out to the mission and tell Evy and Alice where we are and not to worry."

"Good idea, Mr. Rogan. I'll do that."

Rogan mounted and was going to ride over to Retford. He passed Parnell on his way and leaned from the saddle.

"What are your plans, Parnell?"

He looked grumpy. "I'm trying to talk sense into Darinda. I want her to come back to Bulawayo with me. Is that woman wild or not? She insists on going to hunt for Lobengula's cave." He shook his head, his chestnut hair ruffling in the breeze. "Why can't she be content like Alice and raise children, sew, and things like that?"

Rogan smirked. "You know what I think about it, Parnell. You should forget her. Can't you see she's fallen for Retford?"

Parnell looked over at her and the captain. They were riding side by side. "She might have other reasons for playing her hand for Retford."

Rogan wondered what he meant, but whatever it was, it sounded like something he didn't like. Retford was a gentleman. If Darinda was with him for some ulterior motive, Rogan had a notion to derail her.

"What do you know, Parnell?" he asked evenly.

Parnell met his gaze thoughtfully. For a moment Rogan didn't think he would answer. Then he surprised him.

"Julien thinks Retford is a Boer spy," Parnell said quietly. "He's had Darinda trying to find out who it is in the Company that has contact with Kruger."

So Julien had talked her into another messy arrangement. "What's she getting out of it?"

"What do you think? Anthony's vacant position."

Rogan was angry.

"Don't tell her I told you," Parnell said.

"What are you going to do now?" Rogan asked.

"I wouldn't set foot in those cursed Matopos for all the diamonds sprinkled over Lobengula's bones."

Rogan smiled. "Good. Go to the mission station and stay out of trouble, will you? And do me a favor?"

Parnell looked surprised that he would ask him for something. He looked almost eager to please him.

"Watch over Evy while I'm away," Rogan said roughly. "And, should anything go wrong and Heyden happen to be waiting with a bullet around some rock, see that she and my child are taken care of. I'd like her to return to Rookswood, or at least to Capetown."

Parnell scowled. "What ruddy thing is this? Of course nothing is going to happen to you. Be careful," he said. "And watch Julien. He's a serpent, that one."

"That's two warnings I've heard about the serpent Julien Bley."

"Then I'll add something else." Parnell's hazel eyes were wary. "Julien killed Anthony. I'm almost sure of it."

They looked at each other soberly, then without another word, Parnell walked to get his horse.

Rogan sat there a moment, digesting his brother's shocking words. Then he rode and caught up with Captain Retford and Darinda.

"Did you find Henry's gold deposit?" she asked almost carelessly.

"Yes. Do you mind if I talk alone with the captain?"

She raised her dark brows, and glancing toward Retford, she flipped the reins and rode ahead.

Rogan fell in beside Retford. "Slow down a minute, will you? We need to talk."

Retford smiled, but there was a tension and a wariness in his eyes. What would Retford think about Julien being Anthony's murderer? Rogan intended to find out.

CHAPTER THIRTY

Rogan settled his hat and looked directly at Captain Retford. "What are your conclusions about Anthony's death? Was he killed by one of us, or an irate African tribesman?"

Captain Retford appeared taken off guard by the blunt approach, but he recovered.

"You want it straight? All right. Sir Julien Bley."

Rogan looked at him intensely. "Any evidence, or is this a guess because you don't like him?"

"I don't care much for him, you're right. I wouldn't trust him in a tight spot. Nor do I approve of the way he's raised his granddaughter. He's taught Miss Bley to scratch her way to the top. Get what you want in any way you can. But she is learning, I think. Learning it doesn't always work. And when it does, it doesn't bring satisfaction."

"Is that why you told Darinda to keep quiet about meeting Anthony on the path that afternoon?"

Retford's head turned sharply. His blue eyes searched Rogan's face.

"Darinda had a rough disagreement with Anthony about her place in the diamond business, didn't she?" Rogan continued mildly.

Retford showed no unease. "I did advise her to keep silent. I don't trust Harry Whipple. He's no policeman. He's a thug."

Rogan agreed. "Why not Harry, then? On orders from Sir Julien?"

"Is that what you think?"

Rogan was silent a moment. "Maybe. Why not Darinda? She's got nerves like an impi, is strong enough, the least likely to be suspected, and has the most to gain."

Captain Retford appeared to remain calm. He rubbed his chin. "First, I don't think she could do it. And secondly, if she had, she would never have wanted to tell me that she'd argued with Anthony just before he was killed."

Rogan gave a half smile. Retford had looked at the situation honestly.

"I checked Lord Brewster's injury carefully. The women, I think, are out of the game. His body was also dragged to the tree. He was too heavy for her to do that."

"A man would have carried him to the tree."

"You would. I would. We're strong enough," Retford said. "But there are men among us who wouldn't have had the strength to carry him. Lord Brewster was a large man. Whipple, for instance. He couldn't have carried him."

"So Whipple might have done it, then, and dragged the body to the tree. But why drag the body to the tree? Why not leave it where it was? I've been thinking about that tree," Rogan said thoughtfully. "Darinda's idea about the wait-a-bit—"

"So she told you?" Retford looked curious.

"No. Peter mentioned it. She brought it up to him. I think she could be right. The tree is symbolic. Add that to the spellcasting rot done in Julien's office the same night, and you come up with a man who either believes in African symbols and spellcasting or wanted to make it look like that. No one else even considered the symbol of the tree. So that wasn't much of a message to most of us. But it must have been to whoever did it."

Captain Retford looked at him intently. Again he rubbed his chin. Rogan waited for his insight. Retford knew a good deal about tribal customs and superstitions.

"That makes more sense than anything I'd thought of so far… Then it just may be that it was neither Sir Julien nor Harry Whipple. That complicates things, Rogan. Don't you think so?"

"No. There's one man who hates Julien enough to try to terrorize him with the notion a nganga put a curse on him, who knows this land and the Ndebele customs well enough to try to blame it on an irate impi or induna, and that's Heyden van Buren."

"But no one's seen Heyden. I talked to Dr. Jakob first thing after Lord Brewster's death. He hasn't seen him either."

"Derwent saw him," Rogan said coldly, thinking about the rifle shots.

"Those rifle shots you mentioned today?"

"And Derwent says someone was with him. Someone who looked like Heyden. Although Derwent didn't say so, I think he meant the second man looked Dutch. Have you seen Detlev around?"

"Detlev?" Retford looked shocked. "Detlev wouldn't—"

"Sure of that? He's a Boer. What do you know about his loyalties to the Company at Bulawayo? For that matter, to England?"

Retford frowned. "I don't, actually. None of us do. He was a farmer, he and his wife Marjit, but they walked away from it. Your sister, Mrs. Bartley, and Peter hired her to help out. Detlev became an aide." He frowned again. "He's back at Bulawayo now."

"Maybe he's there. We've no way of knowing."

"You could be right about Detlev. Though he appears to be a nice chap, I've noticed he's made comments about the Transvaal once or twice that put Kruger in the right. I let it go. A slip of the tongue, I thought. After all, he's bound to have strong feelings about his ancestry. The man is of Boer descent."

"He could be working with Heyden."

Retford nodded slowly. "The more I think this over, the more concerned I'm becoming. It could very well be Heyden and Detlev."

"Either of them could have killed Anthony for the same reason Julien is suspected."

"The letter from Capetown?"

"The letter. It incriminated Julien and Doc Jameson for planning a Johannesburg foray to support the Uitlanders' uprising against Kruger. Heyden, too, wanted that letter."

Retford scowled doubtfully.

"Think about it," Rogan pursued. "If Heyden had the letter, he could threaten to go with it to newspapers in London. Pacifism runs deep in London these days. The British people don't see a need for involvement in Africa. They won't want to send sons and husbands off to war to fight the Boers. We think colonization of Africa is important for the British Empire, but ask the English shopkeeper, the flower girl on the corner, or the fisherman what he thinks. They don't want war with the Transvaal. Heyden could've stopped Jameson from going through with his plans if he'd been able to get that letter from Anthony."

"Yes…you're quite right, Chantry. I didn't see it that way before, but it could be, except for one thing." He looked at Rogan. "Sir Julien had the letter in his possession. He was burning it when Mrs. Bartley entered his office."

"That," Rogan admitted, "sends my little scenario into a spin. How did he get it from Heyden or from Detlev?"

Retford shook his head. They lapsed into thoughtful silence. Then Rogan sighed. He might as well get it over with.

"There's something I need to warn you about, but you're not going to appreciate it."

"I'm listening."

"You said Harry Whipple can be bought. Julien has gone through life buying people. He's using his granddaughter now. She's spying for him. She's trying to find out if you're a Boer spy, and who it is in the Company you're working for."

"I'm aware. Peter told me. He also said I could trust you, though I already knew that. I'm no spy, Chantry. I'm a soldier, nothing more. Sir Julien has it wrong. How he came to single me out is a mystery. There's nothing in my record that suggests I've ever worked as a spy."

"Maybe Detlev is our Boer spy."

"Possible. It would fit."

And it would fit Rogan's belief that he and Heyden were working hand in hand.

A few days later Rogan's and Julien's small expedition was camped below the southern end of the Matopos Hills when the sun broke through the dawn, turning the rock into a dusky pink glow.

"If I was superstitious, I'd say the Matopos look menacing," Harry Whipple commented over his tin mug of morning coffee.

He looked grumpy and tense, Rogan thought. He had seen him with Julien last night, when they'd walked away from the camp and stood talking. Julien's voice had risen in anger. Rogan had tried to catch what was being said, but Julien had then walked away from Harry in an angry mood.

"Does Julien have any idea where Lobengula's buried?" Rogan inquired. "We could spend months searching if he hasn't a clue."

Derwent, who was cooking their breakfast of mealies over the campfire, added, "Must be more caves than anyone's ever counted up there."

Harry Whipple grinned. "You don't need to worry. Julien has his collection of secrets. He'll surprise us all this morning." He gulped his coffee and looked around the bush country, then toward the Matopos.

Rogan always suspected that Julien knew more about that burial cave than he'd explained.

What did Harry have on his mind as he looked toward the foothills that way?

Darinda had come up so silently no one noticed her until her voice startled them. "Grandfather does *not* know where the burial cave is located, but he knows someone who will show him. That's where he went"—she gestured to the lower rocks and boulders—"to bring the guide."

"Who would know except a Ndebele?" Rogan asked.

Darinda shrugged. "He hasn't explained to me either. But he was in a good mood this morning. Oh! Good morning, Captain. Coffee?" She smiled as she poured Retford a mug and brought it to him.

Derwent dished out the mealies. "Here you are, Mr. Whipple."

Harry took a double portion.

Rogan grimaced as Derwent scooped some of the cereal into his cup. "I know this is your favorite breakfast food, Mr. Rogan." He grinned as he handed it to him.

Harry Whipple settled himself on his haunches a few feet away. "Ever hear the story of the witch we got when we fought Lobengula?" He dug into his food with relish.

"Didn't know there was more than one Umlimo," Rogan admitted, interested at once. He walked over to where Harry squatted and sat down on a boulder. Maybe he could get him to boast and tell more than he intended.

"There are a succession of 'em," Harry said. "They get a little girl and train her in the cave to take over when one of 'em dies. Nasty business, if you ask me. The whole lot of 'em ought to be cleaned out— same as you clean out a rat's hole. Burn 'em out maybe."

Darinda looked over at him. "I'm sure it wouldn't trouble you to do so at all."

"You bet it wouldn't, Miss Bley. Sooner all that is ended, the safer we'll all be."

She turned her back on him and drank her coffee.

Rogan didn't want to discuss evangelism right now. "I suppose you know more about these hills than any of us," he offered humbly. He saw Derwent's glance.

The compliment went over as Rogan had expected. Harry Whipple pulled his shoulders back and readjusted his position. "I've seen my share of things, that's for sure. I've been around plenty."

"I'm sure you have."

Even Darinda turned her head and looked at Rogan. Her lips curved. Captain Retford smiled into his cup.

"Take my father, for instance," Harry said. "He was killed, but not before he got himself many of the Zulus, I'll tell you that. He was there with the British troops when they took Zululand. Ol' Cetshwayo took off for the bush, but they caught him in time. Should have killed him, but they didn't. They sent him off somewhere in exile."

"Your father must have been a brave man."

"Oh yeah, he was, all right. That's where I first heard about Dumaka. My father met his father in a battle before the Zulu War of 1879."

Rogan was careful not to react. This opening was one he'd been hoping for. He even took a bite of the mealies and swallowed it. "Oh? Dumaka's father? Interesting. I've met Dumaka myself."

Harry looked up at him, leaning against the sienna-colored boulder. He measured him. "When did you meet Dumaka?"

"On Rhodes's pioneer trek to Fort Salisbury. When did your father meet Dumaka's?"

"The Zulus made a raid on Natal. Troops were sent in to quash the rebellion. Julien was there too. And Carl van Buren. They captured Dumaka's father. He was an induna. He had all kinds of costume. War rattles, feathers, spears, even some dia—jewels."

"Is that when they found the Black Diamond?"

His question was so casually put that Harry stopped chewing and looked at him surprised. "Then you know about it?"

Darinda whirled, and Rogan could feel her steely gaze on them both. He thought she would say something and ruin his opportunity, but she stood in frozen silence.

So that's the way it was with the Black Diamond, was it? Just as Rogan and Derwent had thought some years ago.

"Who told you about it? Dumaka?" Harry asked, shoveling in another mouthful of mealies.

Rogan took a bite to cover up his silence.

Harry wasn't the sort who liked silence. He said with malice, "Dumaka always claimed it belonged to the witch. He wanted to return it—I was going to tell you that story about the one in power when we went to war with Lobengula. Julien had some soldiers, and they hunted her down up there and destroyed her at the beginning of the war. That made Dumaka furious. Well, they've another witch now. Naked as a beanpole. Speaks in several voices. Possessed by spirits. They train girls, nothing but children in the beginning, and they grow up there in the cave. Major Willet was killed near here. No one's convincing me it wasn't an impi, maybe an induna who got him…" He paused, looking uneasy, and his Adam's apple bobbed up and down as he swallowed, glancing around them.

Derwent stood, wiping his hands. "Then the infamous Black Diamond isn't the *Kimberly* Diamond at all, is it?"

Harry shrugged.

"You've talked too much, Harry," Darinda said in a chilled voice. "Even I never knew any of this till now."

Harry looked sullen. "Julien took it from Dumaka's father."

Darinda's mouth tightened, and she looked ashen—stunned but also angry. She started to walk toward Harry, but Captain Retford took hold of her arm and turned her toward him. He said something quietly, and she listened. After a moment they walked away together to a rock and sat down with their coffee.

"What about Carl van Buren?" Rogan asked.

Harry glowered after Darinda. "That woman is as mean as her grandfather." He looked at Rogan, shrugged, and stood, stretching. He rubbed a palm over his belly, satisfied. "The Boer, Carl? I guess he didn't like what Julien did. Was afraid they'd be hunted by the Zulus to get the diamond back. I guess he caused Julien no end of headaches about it. Then the accident came at the mine. I never met Carl."

"Ever meet Heyden van Buren?"

"No. Heard of him, though. A murderer, isn't he? Well, I'll get him someday," he boasted and tossed his dirty bowl to Derwent. He strode off into the bush.

Rogan had watched his face carefully when he'd asked him about Heyden. There'd been no response. For Harry that was unusual. He tended to show what he was thinking.

Then Harry wasn't working with Heyden. Rogan didn't think he'd done Julien's bidding in killing Anthony, either. The answer lay elsewhere.

Derwent looked after him. "So that's the root of it all, Mr. Rogan. Now we know about the diamond. But looks to me like Mr. Whipple is just boasting about catching Heyden. He's not trying very hard."

Rogan was looking toward the rocks and boulders nearby. Julien came riding toward them. With him were two of his men and an African woman. From the looks of her, she was Zulu.

The Umlimo?

Julien was laughing as he rode up. He dismounted and entered the camp. Darinda and Retford walked over. Darinda looked at the woman curiously.

"Who is she, Grandfather?"

Julien held up a hand to shush her. His eye was on Rogan. "Well, Rogan, you look inquisitive. Derwent, get me some coffee."

Rogan studied the woman. Her eyes came to his as though she knew who he was and wished to communicate.

"You have the Umlimo?" Rogan asked.

Julien laughed. He turned to the woman. "He insults you, Jendaya. Are you demon possessed or a devoted Christian?"

Jendaya! Rogan stared at her.

"Jendaya?" Darinda breathed. "How did you find her?"

"We found her months ago sneaking about Jakob's mission."

"I was not sneaking, but trying to find him. You were wrong to hold me prisoner."

Darinda looked at her grandfather in distaste. "You held her a prisoner all this time? Where?"

"Never mind, Darinda—"

Jendaya pointed toward the boulders. "There. Locked up in a hut."

Rogan said sharply to Julien, "Major Tom Willet was killed near here. Was he a guard?"

Julien waved a hand. "You're both making too much of this. She was taken care of and treated well. Do you see any marks on her? Is she underfed? Yes, he was a guard. And some Ndebele found him and chopped him up. Savages!"

"They were looking for me," Jendaya said. "I have said I will help you find Lobengula's burial cave. Let me speak to this man alone first." She nodded her gray head toward Rogan.

Rogan stepped toward her, but Julien came between. His mouth twitched. "No." He turned to Jendaya. "So you can pass secret messages to him? Sit down." He drew his gun on Jendaya. "What you say, Jendaya, you will say before me."

Rogan turned on him angrily. "Put that away. You think she's a fool? You need her to bring you to the cave. You don't frighten her. You don't frighten any of us. You lied to me. The Black Diamond was not discovered in the Kimberly mine as you've attested all these years, but stolen from Dumaka's father, a Zulu induna. Is that right, Jendaya?"

She nodded. "This man killed our father and took the diamond."

Darinda's hands clenched.

"Our father was coming here to bring the diamond as a gift to the Umlimo. That was before I believed in the true God. Katie's father, Carl van Buren, was against taking the diamond. It was black. It was for the Umlimo. Carl would not do as Julien said—"

"Your mouth, Jendaya, speaks too long," Julien interrupted icily.

"Julien killed Katie's father in the mine. Dumaka knew it. He was spying on them."

Julien stepped toward Jendaya.

"Later, Dumaka, my brother, worked as an amaholi at Julien's house. Julien did not know who he was. Dumaka was not seen by him and Carl when they had my father."

Julien stepped closer and backhanded her across the face.

Darinda's breath sucked in.

Jendaya remained standing, only her head turned from the force. Her eyes came back to meet Julien's one eye.

"You are full of serpent juice. You have no hope without Jesus the true One."

Rogan took hold of Julien and pulled him away.

Julien's one cold eye spat venom at him. "That diamond's mine, and I'm going to get it. No one's stopping me. Not you, not anyone."

"Then you do your treasure hunting on your own. I'm through," Rogan gritted.

"You can't walk away. We made a bargain."

"You will all die if you do not listen to me," Jendaya spoke. "Dumaka is not dead. That man"—she pointed at Harry Whipple—"did not kill my brother as he boasts. Dumaka is alive. He leads the impis against all who are in Bulawayo."

Julien whirled to face Harry. "Does she speak the truth, Harry? Come! Out with it."

Harry wiped the sweat from his face. He nodded. "He...he got away. I was afraid to tell you."

"You blundering fool. You should have told me." Fright danced crazily in Julien's eye. He turned to Jendaya. "Where is he? Where is Dumaka?"

She pointed. "Bulawayo. They did not turn in all weapons to this man's police. They have kept the assegais here—with the Umlimo." She pointed up at the Matopos and looked at Rogan. "Katie's daughter is with Jakob." She shook her head. "I cannot save them. I tried. Dumaka will not listen. By sundown none will be alive anywhere. Not even babies. You waste time."

Rogan stared at her; a cold panic gripped him.

Derwent dropped his pans with a clatter.

Captain Retford lifted his rifle. "What?"

"Jameson has over four hundred troopers," Rogan stated sharply. He was trying to talk reason to his own leaping fears.

Jendaya shook her head, then Julien said, "No, Doc Jim has left Bulawayo."

Rogan grabbed him roughly. "Gone?"

"They left for Johannesburg days ago. I left immediately afterward to head to Zimbabwe."

Harry Whipple's voice was hoarse with fear: "Then no one's there except Peter and a skeleton crew at Government House."

Rogan ran for his horse. Captain Retford touched Darinda's shoulder, and their eyes clung a moment, then he joined Derwent in running for their horses.

"Come back!" Julien shouted angrily, starting after them on foot. He walked into the rugged bush and flung his arms up. "Do you hear me? Come back here!"

Darinda sank to a rock and dropped her face into her palms.

Rogan dug his heels into the sides of the horse and galloped at a dead run for Bulawayo. *Dear God, what a blundering fool I've been. I never should have left her, never.*

Derwent was low in the saddle, using his small whip on one side of the horse. Captain Retford eased up beside Rogan and shouted, "I know a shortcut to the mission station. Follow me!" He turned the reins and rode north toward Shiloh.

CHAPTER THIRTY-ONE

Jendaya led Sir Julien, Harry Whipple, and three other men up a steep, rocky path to the mouth of a cavern. The cavern was wide, but the rock ceiling was hardly high enough to clear her head. Once, long before her time, this opening had been fortified with blocks of stone, but now there were gaps.

She followed the twisting pathway through the cavern, which narrowed. Here, in the stone walls on either end, were catacombs.

Jendaya paused and pointed ahead. "There."

Darinda hung back, for her courage had melted. The smell was nauseating. She held a water-soaked cloth to her nose and mouth and glanced at her grandfather, but he seemed too excited to notice anything. Harry Whipple looked pale and frightened and gripped his rifle.

Darinda looked ahead but saw nothing in the darkness until Julien had the men light the oil lamps they'd brought for just this purpose.

When Lobengula drank poison and died, his slaves laid the body out and walled up the entrance of the cave. It had since been opened. By whom, Darinda did not know. Nor did she care now. If only she had listened to Ryan and left Bulawayo weeks ago, taking Arcilla and the baby with her. Were they all dead? She swallowed, her throat dry, her heart beating fast.

The dim yellow lights from the small lamps flared, illuminating the tomb.

Jendaya pointed inside again. "The king is dead. Only one true King rose from the dead after they laid him in a tomb. Jesus."

"Keep quiet!" Julien told her. "Move out of the way."

He pushed past her, and Harry and the others followed him inside. Darinda hung back, although she could see.

The corpse was laid out with all manner of objects deemed important for a proper burial of a Ndebele king. Rats and other bugs ran from the light. She saw his earthly possessions all around him: a stool, a head pillow carved out of what looked to be ivory. The sleeping mat might have been fur, like his kaross. There were beer pots and meat bowls, guns, and his huge war shield—he had been a big man. Leaning against the cave wall were a battle-ax and the feared stabbing spear, the assegai. This one looked silver. There were small pots of clay, and Harry Whipple accidentally kicked one over in his clumsy fashion. Out spilled white diamonds that mingled with rotting flesh.

"A man takes nothing with him when he dies," Jendaya warned. She stood, looking unafraid of them, her arms folded like a queen. "White man, black man, it matters not. All die, all turn to corruption, all have no hope without the Great Savior Jesus."

They were not even listening. Julien was laughing. It was a harsh, almost hysterical sound that turned Darinda's heart sad and cold. Harry Whipple was down on all fours scooping diamonds toward him. He scooped them up in his palms and tried to dump them inside his pockets. His shirt pockets swelled in front.

The other three men were sorting hastily through diamonds and objects. One had the fur kaross over his shoulder, his face damp with sweat. Another had the assegai, running his fingers over the jewels that were encrusted along its shaft.

Darinda turned away. *Air—I must have fresh air—* She started back through the narrow passage toward the opening, wanting to gag.

Jendaya was right behind her. "Hurry," she whispered. "Hurry."

They ran together out through the cave into the hot sunshine. The glare was so bright that at first Darinda did not see *them*.

Jendaya spoke first, and from somewhere ahead a male voice spoke Sindebele.

Darinda backed up against a boulder. There, coming up the steep path, were a dozen elite fighting impis led by a tall induna of regal bearing. He wore a kilt and cloak of tanned leather, Zulu feathers, war rattles, and regimentals of fur and plumes of marabou stork upon his head.

Her heart trembled like a reed in the wind. She had no strength to even reach for her gun. It would have done her no good.

Jendaya stepped between her and Dumaka, her younger brother. She spoke in low words, some of which Darinda could understand.

"Mission station? Good Jakob? The little girl of Katie?"

Dumaka snarled his words, his eyes angry and fierce as he pointed to the burial cave.

Jendaya made a hopeless gesture.

Dumaka turned and faced his warriors. He beckoned sharply for them to follow.

Darinda cringed as they neared her, but they trotted by on bare feet, looking neither right nor left. When the last had entered the cave, Jendaya grabbed her arm and they ran. Darinda stumbled down the steep path.

Inside the burial cave Julien was holding the Black Diamond on his sweating, dirty palm. He saw not what the others were doing, for he did not care. He had his treasure, which he had been seeking all these years. Heyden van Buren had wanted it too. Heyden, who had also wanted the incriminating letter sent from Capetown...

As Julien stared at the large diamond, his mind stepped back to when he'd come secretly along the path from Government House to the bungalows, coming the back way so as to avoid meeting Arcilla and Darinda on the front trail.

Julien came to keep his secret meeting with Heyden van Buren. Heyden, the wretched Boer who had threatened him, who had been a curse for years. *Heyden,* who knew too many of Julien's secrets: about the Black Diamond, about where he'd first gotten it, about Carl and the mine explosion. Too many secrets that could incriminate Julien.

Heyden had appeared from the dappled shadows of the trees. He'd just left Anthony, he'd said, and now possessed the incriminating letter from Capetown. "Ha ha! The big diamond magnate will go to prison. You'll hobnob with petty thieves."

Heyden had walked right up to him *laughing.* Nobody dared laugh at Sir Julien Bley. So Julien drew his .38 and squeezed the trigger. The bullet went straight through Heyden's heart. It was well enough. Heyden was a murderer anyway.

Julien stooped and searched for the letter, but it wasn't on him! Had he lied?

Anthony appeared. He came running toward him. Shocked, dismayed, he'd looked from Heyden to Julien. "You killed him!"

Julien panicked. He grabbed him, appealed to him, begged for the Capetown letter. Anthony was his adopted son. Had he not given him everything? Anthony was indebted to him. "Give me the letter from Trotter!"

But Anthony shook him away in disgust. "You've stepped over the line this time, Julien. I can't hide murder or condone what you've done."

"Heyden tried to kill me."

"He has no weapon on him."

Anthony was walking away…

Julien took a few steps after him, pleading. Anthony kept walking away… He dared not use his gun again. He'd already made one mistake in firing it. Someone might hear.

A huge hunk of wood lay on the ground just off the path. He stooped and picked it up quietly, then hurried up behind Anthony and—

Julien searched Anthony for the letter. What had he done with it? He must have brought it to his bungalow. He had to find it; he would need to search his things.

But what to do with his body? With Heyden's?

Everything was crumbling beneath him. Someone would be coming soon; someone would have heard that shot.

That was when Detlev appeared.

"Get rid of them, Detlev. If you do, I can make you rich. Wouldn't you and Marjit like to be rich? I can give you anything you want, Detlev, *anything!* I am a very wealthy man. You know how *rich* I am. You can have anything you want, go anywhere you want, even return to Holland a rich and powerful man."

Detlev licked his lips. He'd shifted from one booted foot to the other. "I'll do it."

"Make it appear the impis killed Anthony Brewster."

"I know their customs, Sir Julien."

So Detlev, self-serving man that he was, had taken care of the body of Heyden and kept his mouth shut. Then Detlev had dragged Anthony to the wait-a-bit tree.

But…Rogan. Rogan was always trouble. Julien had seen through him. Rogan had been suspicious about Anthony. So what to do? Julien had made plans. Henry's gold—yes, he would give it all to Rogan along with the Zimbabwe thunderbird. Yes, that was it—make friends with Rogan.

Afterward, he would lure Rogan to the Matopos, pretending he needed him as a bodyguard. Once the Black Diamond was his again, he would bribe Harry Whipple to arrange an accident for Rogan on the way back to Bulawayo. A fall down the rocks, perhaps.

Captain Retford. Julien's remembrance was still racing through his mind, and he wiped the sweat from his face. Another dangerous man to have snooping around. Better not take chances. Harry could arrange something for both men on the Matopos.

Until then, Rogan must be led to think Heyden was alive and trying to kill him. That would keep him from concentrating too much on Anthony. What to do—

Detlev. He would have Detlev follow Rogan to the Zimbabwe Ruins and fire his rifle. Detlev even looked like Heyden.

Yes, he thought then and now, everything was going to work out after all.

Inside the cave where Lobengula's body was laid, Julien gripped the Black Diamond. His, again, at last. He smiled.

Suddenly a throaty gasp of terror came from Harry Whipple. A rifle shot exploded, and some pieces of gritty dirt fell on top of Julien's head. More rifle shots. Then—

Julien turned and looked up toward the cave mouth.

"Dumaka—" Julien's voice cracked.

"You are cursed."

The spellcaster! "You! My office—the hakata bones—"

Dumaka raised a fist. "Jee!" came the deep, drawn-out war chant of the fighting impis.

"Bayete!" The impis shouted the royal salute from behind him toward their dead king.

Julien caught a last horrifying glimpse of the shiny assegai blades pummeling down upon him—

Dumaka drew a rasping breath. He wrenched the diamond from the white chief's bloody hand and wiped it clean on a piece of the dead man's soaked shirt. *Dog.*

A few minutes later, the impis threw the dead bodies of the invaders into a ravine and shut the royal cave with heavy boulders.

The sun was moving across the brittle sky above Matabeleland, heading toward the eastern mountains. Dumaka and his impis trotted silently along the twisting path up to the cave of the Umlimo.

She appeared with a talisman hanging around her throat between her naked breasts. Dumaka and the impis groveled and laid the Black Diamond at her feet. Her eyes rolled back into her skull. Saliva drooled from her mouth.

"Victory will come," came the high-pitched, rasping voice, a voice not hers. "The white chief and his dogs will fail. Kill them. All must die. The land must be purged. The oracle has spoken."

Down the crooked, serpentine path, Dumaka and his loyal warriors trotted, hearts beating with warlike ecstasy. Down the ascent of the great rocky hill of the sacred Matopos they went toward Bulawayo.

Chapter Thirty-Two

LORD…in wrath remember mercy.
HABAKKUK 3:2

Bulawayo lay in the grip of silence and death. In Government House a trail of bodies led to the upper rooms, where Marjit was found with five women and children. Sir Julien Bley's bedroom was overturned, everything in disorder. The dead marked the trail to the bungalows, to the police station, to the farms.

The hot wind scuffed up drought-stricken dust into little eddies. The thorn trees rustled with dead leaves, insects buzzed, vultures sat hunched on the bare branches of trees, too full of food to fly.

Rogan rode into Bulawayo Mission at a full gallop, reined his foaming horse to a halt, and was down from the saddle in an instant, his boots kicking up a cloud of dust. All was still except for the wind moaning through the stripped acacia tree branches.

Derwent and Captain Retford dismounted, rifles in hand. Rogan gestured, and they spread out toward the bungalows and the medical ward.

Rogan circled his and Evy's bungalow. All was silent. He came up the stoep and opened the door. Empty—the bedding was gone and the garments were tossed about. His gaze fell on Evy's dressing gown. He snatched it up. It was saturated with dried blood. Devastated, he stood there staring. In a moment she passed sweetly before him from their youth in Grimston Way to his last cruel words to her when he'd ridden out to chase after Henry's gold. He groaned and leaned against the wall still holding the garment, his head bent, heart throbbing with the pain of loss and regret.

Fool. You had what you wanted. Yet you gambled it away on folly, on pride, on the stubborn refusal to forgive.

There were footsteps outside. He gripped his gun. Blinking hard against the tears, he straightened from the wall and threw the door open. It crashed into the wall and then swung a moment on a broken hinge.

Derwent stood there. He looked up at Rogan with the question of why in his eyes.

"Dead," Derwent choked. "All of 'em. And I'm afraid to look in my bungalow…"

Rogan went to him and threw his strong arms around him.

Captain Retford walked up. His soul was desolate. He had found the patients in the ward, all dead.

Though the fig tree may not blossom, nor fruit be on the vines; though the labor of the olive may fail, and the fields yield no food; though the flock may be cut off from the fold, and there be no herd in the stalls—Yet I will rejoice in the LORD, I will joy in the God of my salvation. The LORD God is my strength; He will make my feet like deer's feet, and He will make me walk on my high hills.

Derwent looked up suddenly at Retford. Rogan noted the spark that showed in his eyes. "Deer's feet," Derwent breathed, turning. "Deer can run fast," he said. "Deer can climb steep places to get away from wolves. God will make our feet like deer's feet." And he walked quickly from the bungalow to the front of the mission.

Rogan thought Derwent had lost his senses, but he followed him.

They were in the front of the mission. It was then that Rogan saw a new cross near the church, miraculously left untouched by the impis. He ran there and knelt. The grave was very *small*. On a piece of wood was freshly carved: *Rogan Anthony Chantry*.

He stared, and scooping up a fistful of soil, he let it seep through his strong, tanned fingers.

"Evy—Evy—I wasn't here—I failed you."

He was still kneeling there after an indeterminate amount of time when he heard muffled voices behind him. The impis. He felt nothing but grief. He had no desire to pick up his rifle. Without Evy there was nothing left. The Lord had given her to him, and the Lord had taken her away. The Lord had taken their baby in a miscarriage. He had no desire except to be alone, to go away, far away. He stood and turned.

It was Dr. Jakob running toward him, and with him came Arcilla and Peter! Alice and Derwent with their children. Derwent was smiling again. Then he saw Parnell behind them, Parnell and—Evy.

Evy, thin, pale and drawn, but it was his *beloved*, smiling at him as tears coursed down her cheeks. This was his beloved.

Rogan ran to her, and she took weak steps to meet him, her arms open.

They met in an embrace and held to each other tightly. He wept into her hair, and her voice kept repeating, "I love you, Rogan, I'm sorry, so sorry…"

"I'm at fault," he whispered into her hair. "This is my fault. Can you forgive me? Can we start over?"

"Oh, Rogan, yes, yes… We can start over, we *will* start over."

Later, Dr. Jakob told him what had happened.

"Induna Shaka trusted me because he knew the God we served had an interest in helping him regain his cattle. He came to warn me late in the night before the attack. Evy was very ill, but Peter arrived, and so did Parnell—thank God! We were able to make a stretcher and carry her into the higher hills, where the induna led us. He hid us there during the attack."

Peter then told them his story. "When I couldn't locate Julien, or you, Rogan, at Zimbabwe, I went on to Fort Victoria. I wired Salisbury, and Rhodes himself led a relief column to rescue Bulawayo. The fighting even now is continuing, and the Ndebele under Dumaka are being pushed back into the hills."

Arcilla held Baby Charles in her arms while Peter held her, as though afraid she might disappear. Peter had already told her that when feasible, he would tell Rogan it was time to take his family back to England.

Derwent and Alice were thanking God for sparing them and their three children. Alice, too, told Arcilla that she wanted to go home to Grimston Way to visit her parents, Dr. and Mrs. Tisdale.

Dr. Jakob, Rogan, and the other men buried the dead, taking time for Scripture reading and prayer. Evy was mourning the loss of their baby with sorrow, but she took comfort in knowing he was with the Lord.

"Heaven is a little more precious to us now," Rogan told her gently. "We have our firstborn there waiting for us. Someday we'll join him."

Evy smiled through her tears and hugged Rogan.

"We sorrow not as those who have no hope," Mrs. Croft said, dabbing at her eyes.

It was two days later when Darinda arrived with Jendaya. Darinda was pale and grief stricken. Retford went to her, and she ran to meet him, weeping in his arms.

Parnell sighed and looked at Rogan. "Looks like I lost out."

"Cheer up. Grimston Way still has enough pretty girls to ease the ache of a young man's heart," Rogan told him and smiled as he put an arm around his brother's shoulders.

"I'm taking Evy back to Rookswood for a time. Why don't you come with us? You haven't seen Father in a few years."

Parnell looked pleased that Rogan had suggested he come with them. "I will," he said simply.

Evy at last met Jendaya and gave her the heart-shaped necklace that had been Katie's. "Thank you, Jendaya, for all you've done to help me. You saved my life at Rorke's Drift. Can I do anything for you?"

Jendaya looked at her long and solemnly. "Yes, there is something. I want to stay here with Dr. Jakob. I want to help look after the sick. You ask him for me?"

Evy laughed and took both her hands. "He will be delighted, I know."

The news of what had happened on the Matopos was delivered through Captain Retford. Darinda had told him all she had seen. Later, the remains of the corpses were discovered on the rocks of Matopos, devoured by animals.

"Guess we'd never know who killed Mr. Anthony," Derwent said to Rogan, "if it hadn't been for Detlev."

The troopers had found Detlev hiding in the Matopos, frightened out of his wits. When Rogan was able to meet with him, Detlev admitted everything, including firing the rifle out near the ruins. The news about Julien came as a surprise. Detlev confessed that it was Julien who killed both Heyden and Anthony.

"After all this, Mr. Rogan, Grimston Way is going to look fair indeed."

Rogan touched him on the shoulder. "One of the first things we're going to do, friend Derwent, is go riding in Grimston Woods again. Then, I'm going to make sure you and Alice and the children have a big farm."

Derwent laughed. "Sounds good to me. Alice will be happy about that. And who knows? Maybe someday we'll all come back to Rhodesia. This land kinda grows on you."

"It does, Derwent. Once you have Africa in your blood, it's nearly impossible to say good-bye forever. Besides, Henry's gold belongs to us now. You, Parnell, and myself. One day we'll reopen that ancient mine."

Rogan walked with Evy in the late afternoon when the sun colored the Rhodesian sky a burnt crimson and gold. They stood there looking out at the veld, hearing the distant roar of a lion.

He looked down at her and ran his fingers through her tawny hair. "I confess I still love this land."

She put her arms around him. "So do I, darling. More so because of those buried here. Maybe someday when the harsh memories have healed, we'll come back?"

"Someday. But first you and I will learn to forgive each other and begin anew, building our marriage on the one solid foundation of truth and trust."

She sighed. "Rogan, that's what I've been asking of our heavenly Father, our forgiveness and a new beginning."

He kissed her fervently and held her tightly against him. "The baby, Evy— I'm sorry—"

She placed her fingers against his lips, and her eyes told him she loved him. "God has forgiven us. We have forgiven each other."

"Love is forever, Evy, my beloved. There will be new babies too," he said. "If God wills."

She nestled her head against his chest, content and at peace at last. *Yes…God is good.* She knew that. He had delivered them and brought them back together. Their love, their marriage, was stronger now than ever. Surely He had plans for them in the future. He would answer their prayer for a child of their own in His time.

Together they stood looking out in the bush, holding each other, watching a lioness leading her two cubs across the barren fields touched with the crimson glow of the setting sun.

Then you will lay your gold in the dust,
And the gold of Ophir among the stones of the brooks.
Yes, the Almighty will be your gold
And your precious silver;

For then you will have your delight in the Almighty,
And lift up your face to God.
You will make your prayer to Him,
He will hear you,
And you will pay your vows.

JOB 22:24-27

About the Author

Linda Lee Chaikin has written nineteen books for the Christian market. *For Whom the Stars Shine* was a finalist for the prestigious Christy Award, and several of her novels have been awarded the Silver Angel for excellence. Many of Linda's books have been included on the bestseller list.

Behind the Stories, a book about writers of inspirational novels, offers Linda's personal biography. She is a graduate of Multnomah Bible Seminary and taught neighborhood Bible classes for a number of years before turning to writing. She and her husband presently make their home in California.